SONS OF MAFIA

To my new "Wonderful"
friend Sara.
"Enjoy" the Novel

Warm Regards
and "Best Wishes"!

Ed Frederico

SONS OF MAFIA

Inspired by True Events

Ed Frederico

Hierarchy Productions
3565 Las Vegas Boulevard South, Suite 120,
Las Vegas NV 89109
(702)808-4509
efrederico@hotmail.com

Library of Congress Control Number: 2010906887
ISBN: Hardcover   978-1-4500-9643-0
                 Softcover   978-1-4500-9642-3
                 Ebook   978-1-4500-9644-7

This book was printed in the United States of America.

To order additional copies of this book, contact:
Xlibris Corporation
1-888-795-4274
www.Xlibris.com
Orders@Xlibris.com
78801

Heavenly Dedication

I dedicate this novel to God for blessing a person like me, who has only read one novel in my life; the idea, desire, genre, and ability to write a novel like *Sons of Mafia*.

A Peek Inside
By Judith Johnson

When I first met Ed and became aware that he was writing his story, I could not wait to read it. Ed's goal was to surpass the great Mario Puzo's novel, *The Godfather*. This very much intrigued me because of the monumental challenge. Therefore, Ed was willing to allow me to read his chapters as he wrote them.

I was blown away! Ed has an extraordinary gift, both in story telling and beauty of prose—and language, which I found enormously compelling, especially due to the subject matter.

This is not just another mob story. There is romance, humor, strong women, and funny stories that are true, along with characters you will come to love and hate.

There are eleven twists and turns that will surprise you as you journey through this amazing story of both truth and fiction. This book is like nothing I have read before. *It is magical*!

Mr. Ed Frederico will mesmerize you with his authorship. *Sons of Mafia* is a must read. It is thrilling from the first page to the very last.

Yes, Ed. You have surpassed your goal and taken story telling to the next level.

Sincerely,
Judith Johnson

Meet some of the characters. Most of them you will love and others you will hate.

MEN:

Eddie D'amico
Sally Barratino
Don Francisco Barratino
Dominic D'amico
Lorenzo LaRocca
Joey Cariola
Allan D'amico
Nick the Greek
Chicky Blandino
Bee Stinger
Jimmy the Brute
Turk Scotto
Vinnie Barratino
One Eyed Jack Shepard
Duke Donnelly
Judge Carmen Carlivatti
Frederico Fellini

WOMEN:

Danni D'amico
Megan Schimmel
Cat Ladd
Carmela Barratino
Nicoletta Barratino
Senora Marisa Danielli
Rose Carlivatti
Connie Barratino

Author's Notes

Dear reader, I truly hope you enjoy my story. It is a real story of the secret world of the Mafia. A world of crime, drugs, power, money, and death.

It is a real-life drama full of suspense, humor, romance, and sex; and it is full of surprises.

All about a life I *knew* a long time ago.

I would love to hear your comments. To make it easy for you to contact me with your thoughts and comments, I have placed a prepaid postcard in the back of the book for you to use.

Wishing you and your loved ones God's best.

Ed Frederico

Earthly Dedication

To my dear friend and confidant, Judith Johnson.
Without her encouragement, assistance, and editing, this book would never have been completed.

Introduction

Dear Reader,

It's a strange and bizarre story. Listen to me, and I will tell you. Stay with me now—I am anxious, very anxious, to tell you my tale.

For my story, timing was all-important, all-governing. Timing became the master of my desire to tell. Timing became the lord of my pen. I have been patient, indeed. Waiting and watching myself grow older. My once-very-dark hair has become spun with thin slivers of gray. Day by day, and year by year, I waited, not patiently, for each moment to elude me, to escape me, to be forever gone from my grasp, but waiting for the safe haven of a felicitous time.

Death came stalking a time or two. I saw his black image, his frozen and frightening face. With crooked finger, Death beckoned to me, tried to rob me of my right to tell my tale. But I stood fast in my resolve. Begone, Death! I have a story to tell before I heed your eerie call.

Finally, we are here together. Our moment has arrived. Here, take my hand. Listen to me now. I have waited over two decades to tell you my story.

Trust me. Take a leap of faith and accompany me on a journey through the pages of time past. Together we will plunge as if winged angels into the dark abyss of my memories and my creations.

Along our path, we will find good and evil, love and hate, as well as life and death. We will observe, and we must take heed. We will be entering a dangerous and deadly world—the world of the Mafia, a world I knew of a long time ago.

You will share with me the influence of my knowledge and the power of my pen. Together we will share the beginning, the middle, and the end. The almightiness of my pen will allow us the privileges reserved only for the gods. For, alas, my story is inspired by true life. For you alone, I will expose the secrets, removing their covers like peeling the skin off a grape. The bombastic puissance of historical events has long since been decided by the true ruler of the universe. You see, for some, the decision has already been made as to who shall live and who shall die. The fates of others lie waiting before us.

Hush now. We must walk softly and be unobtrusive. We must hope that the passage of time has healed old wounds and made old wars become forgotten. We would be in great danger if our presence was viewed as an intrusion by those who still live.

Hang in. Don't run. You will see my story through my eyes. You will know the secrets I know. Go with me as I brush away the haunting cobwebs and blow away the dust of time that has covered my tale for so many years.

Even though there is danger, I will not lie to you. I will not deceive you. But I must use caution. We will rely on the magic of my pen used to obscure and mask the identities of real people. You and I must be careful not to let them know we are intruding in their lives. The legerdemain of my pen has transformed the true locations and embellished certain fictionalized events. If my pen and I have told the story well, you will not be able to discern where we have crossed that mystical line—where truth ends and mendacity begins.

Come now, dear reader. Let us embark on our perilous journey. We must cross the violent and venturesome river that moves with swift and deadly current in my mind. Let us tread its waters to the other side, where I will introduce you to the Sons of Mafia.

You will meet Eddie D'Amico. He is a charming, handsome womanizer. A cunning conniver, an opportunist who uses his clever mind to satisfy his penchant for power and greed. But do not judge him too quickly. Eddie has some redeeming values. He has a heart and a conscience, which creates a constant struggle in his life as he walks the line between good and evil.

Eddie D'Amico is a Mafia son, but certainly through no fault, if you will, of his own. For I ask you, are we not all prisoners of our own personal fate? Like us, he is innocent in that regard and should not be held responsible for his lot in life. For his birth cast him into a family ruled by the Mafia. Fate stripped him of any choice as to who his parents would be. So in a sense, he is a victim, an unwitting pawn, locked in the prison of his upbringing, moving along his own personal path to meet his date with destiny.

At a very early age, he learned how to be a survivor. He was an only child; his mother died shortly after his birth, leaving him to suffer the unconventional rearing of a Mafia-ruled father.

As he grew older, he drew on the natural instinct of the cunning and clever mind with which he had been blessed. And so, by choice, he became an enigma. He learned well the ways of the Mafia. He chose to live his life recklessly, balancing himself on the precarious edge of an abyss between two very different worlds. He teetered between the common and respectable world that so many of us live in and can relate to and the other world—the kind of place most of us only read about or hear about, a world of fierce power, corruption, and evil. And yes, even death. The world of the Mafia.

So it was. Each day of his life, Eddie D'Amico stepped, with the skill of a circus tightrope walker, along the dangerously thin line between his two worlds. Over the years, he had tried, really tried, to make the right choice—to play it straight, to get off the edge. At forty, he hadn't fallen yet. Still, he lived in fear that someday he would make a mistake.

Eddie tried to shun his father's world, but his attempts to escape it were to no avail. His human frailty and his greed compelled him to keep playing the game. He continued, willingly, to take the risks, playing both ends against the middle. With each decision he made, he always used his typical Italian justification that it wasn't his fault that he was born into a world of crime and violence. Destiny had picked Dominic D'Amico to be his father. Even before Eddie was born, Dominic was a high-ranking member of the rich and powerful Barratino crime family. Through no conscious choice of his own, Eddie was wrapped in the mantle and the power of the Mafia and his godfather, Don Francisco Barratino, the man who had baptized him.

Time and time again, Eddie resigned himself to his dilemma. He played the hand that was dealt him and sought his own solutions. His cleverness enabled him to figure it all out. How to have it all.

He took full advantage of the power and the money that was offered by his connection to the world of the Mafia. Yet he also walked in the cloak of respectability that felt somehow equally important to him. Through his shrewd and wily ways, he had managed to have the best of both worlds.

Dear reader, on our journey, we will find answers to questions of Eddie D'Amico's destiny. Will he continue to make it all work, or will he become entangled in the complexity of his web? Will he finally outsmart himself and get caught up in his own dangerous trap?

There is another Mafia son I want you to meet. His name is Salvatore "Sally" Barratino. He is the adopted son of the powerful Don Francisco Barratino, ruler of the Barratino crime family.

Unlike Eddie, Sally doesn't worry about making choices. He made his choice at a very young age. Sally's one and only driving ambition in life was to follow in his father's footsteps. He had made up his mind that one day he would take over as head of the Barratino crime family. He would become the don. It was his right. He was his father's only son. In his mind, he was a Mafia prince.

From early childhood, Sally often and openly displayed his quick temper and mean spirit. His selfishness and heartless attitude were nourished by his lack of conscience. He ignored his mother's efforts to train him in the Catholic religion. He didn't have time for religion. A parsimonious loner, he could never even get along with any of his five sisters. He became an egotistical sycophant, well suited for the world of power, violence, treachery, and death.

Since his youth, Sally had waged his own war in his head. It was fueled by raging jealousy. He was determined to win the war at all costs, for he knew that his victory would give him the greatest trophy of all—his father's love and respect.

In unrecognized self-denial, Sally never admitted the shortcomings in his character that turned his father away from him. All of his life, he had watched his father turn his attention and affection toward his godson, Eddie D'Amico. Sally blamed and hated Eddie for coming between him and his father.

Now, at age thirty-seven, he was more determined than ever to have his way. To have the revenge he swore against Eddie.

So, my friend, will Sally's promise come to pass? Will he be able to outsmart and outmaneuver the clever and cunning Eddie D'Amico? Come, dear reader, we are on our way to the answers.

Opening

Christina Carlivatti stood motionless, peering through the ice-frosted window of her second-story bedroom. Large heavy snowflakes slowly drifted downward and were beginning to obscure the barren branches of the stately old oak tree that stood like a silent sentinel outside her window. Her thoughts raced back to her younger days when she would climb that tree and hide from the world in the comfort of its strong and lofty arms.

Huge tears welled up in her eyes and spilled out, running down her tear-chafed cheeks with a fiery vengeance. "You can't protect me now," she barely whispered to the unhearing tree. "Nobody can help me anymore."

Her body jerked from a sudden, loud knocking, startling her from her reverie.

"Christina?" her mother called out. "Do you hear me? Hurry, honey, or you'll be late for school." Rosie Carlivatti's voice trailed away.

Quickly wiping her tears on the sleeves of her blue flannel nightgown, Christina hurried to her small white desk. She pulled a notepad from underneath a disarray of birthday cards she had received on her fourteenth birthday the day before. Her trembling fingers found a pen in the cluttered desk drawer. Unable to fight back her freely flowing tears, she began to write.

Dear Mommy and Daddy,

Please forgive me. I can't take it anymore. I can't live another day with the bad memories. I really and truly tried, but this is the only way I can get over it. Please understand. I'm so sorry. I love you both very, very, very much.

Christina

She rose from her desk and walked with deliberate steps to her bed. From underneath, she pulled out a bright orange jump rope. Then picking up the desk chair, she placed it in the center of her room. Christina stepped up onto the chair and began tossing the jump rope up toward the ceiling fan. After several attempts, the rope found its target. Christina gave a couple of tugs until she knew the rope was securely anchored around the motor.

Jumping from the chair to her unmade bed, she rummaged through her sleep-rumpled sheets until she felt the well-worn, soft fur of her cherished pink teddy bear. "Oh, Pinky, come here," she pleaded, hugging the bear tightly as she climbed back onto the waiting chair. Holding the bear by one paw between her teeth, Christina reached for the loosely hanging orange rope and began wrapping and tying the ends around her neck. When she finished, she clutched the bear tightly to her chest and whispered softly, "Pinky, I'll miss you."

Then without hesitation, Christina put her right foot on the back of the chair, pushing it over and out from under her body. The fastening devices of the fan gave a crack and a groaning sound under the newfound weight but held fast to its mountings. Pinky slipped from Christina's grasp, landing faceup below her. Through unseeing bright-colored plastic eyes, Pinky seemingly watched as the life ebbed from Christina's young body as it swayed back and forth and then jerked convulsively before going limp.

Across town, Eddie D'Amico was walking across the snow-covered parking lot toward his car. The frigid early-morning air knifed through his cashmere topcoat, causing him to shiver uncontrollably. Pulling up his collar, he quickened his pace, noting that his black Cadillac was nearly hidden beneath the new-fallen snow. Reaching the car, he fumbled with the frozen lock for a moment before he was able to turn the key. He gave the door handle a forceful pull, but the door would not open. It was frozen shut. "Come on, you son of a bitch! Open," he muttered as he pounded on the outer edge of the stubborn door with his gloved hand. Grabbing the handle again, he yanked with a herculean effort. The door flew open with such ease it nearly caused him to lose his balance and fall. A broad smile crossed his face; he was happy with his victory over the challenging door. As he slid into the ice-cold car and turned the key in the ignition, he groped for the heater and defroster controls, making sure they were in the High position. Then he reached under the seat and pulled out a snowbrush, pausing a moment before opening the door to once more brave the bitter cold. Upon exiting the car, he caught the sudden sound of tires screeching and spinning wildly on the frozen pavement. The squealing tires telegraphed an instant message that Eddie clearly understood.

"My god, no!" he muttered as he watched the large black sedan bearing down on him and careening wildly from side to side with the ominous silhouette of gun barrels protruding from the front and rear windows.

Instinctively, Eddie dove, headfirst, into the hardpack, trying desperately to roll underneath the protective cover of his big car's underbelly. Too late. The would-be assassins had already begun firing. *Rat-a-tat-tat*, their weapons shouted out in unison as they began delivering their deadly message.

Instantly, Eddie was covered with a shower of broken glass from the exploding car windows as the murderous missiles struck. He could hear dull thuds as the bullets embedded themselves in the door panels only inches away from his body.

*Who the fuck is doing this to me? It could only be—*His thoughts were interrupted as two of the projectiles entered his body. The pain was immediate and unbearable. *Please, God, don't let me die*, he thought as the sweet peace of unconsciousness engulfed him.

A stocky gray-haired nurse took note of the nun who had arrived shortly after the young Christina Carlivatti had been brought into the emergency room. The sister stood at the foot of Christina's bed as the doctor pronounced the young girl's death.

Not long after, the nun, who was still present and praying over Christina's body, quickened when she heard the sound of the emergency room's automatic doors slide open. A loud voice shouted, "We've got a shooting victim here!" From her line of vision, she caught sight of two nurses bolting from their chairs and running toward the fast-rolling stretcher flanked by the racing paramedics. As they wheeled quickly past her, she was horrified at discovering the identity of the person on the stretcher.

The nun unconsciously began scurrying after the stretcher being rolled toward two large gray metal doors. As the doors were swung open, the nun was startled by a sudden grasp on her arm from behind.

"Excuse me, Sister, but we can't allow you to go in there." The nun turned to look through her large watery eyes at the short, somewhat-overweight nurse with closely cropped gray hair. In a panicky voice, the nun blurted, "I'm sorry, but . . . but . . . that's Eddie D'Amico! Oh my god, this can't be true! Is he going to die?"

"Sister, the doctors will do everything they can to help him. Come with me. Let's go to the chapel."

With rosary beads in her hand, kneeling before the altar, she prayed fervently, but the humanness of her worrying about whether Eddie would live or die was distracting and made the hours pass ever so slowly. At last, the chapel door opened, and she heard the now-familiar voice of the gray-haired nurse.

"Excuse me, Sister, I don't mean to interrupt you, but Mr. D'Amico is in his room, and you may see him now."

The nun's knees refused to straighten as she tried to quickly stand after the many hours of constant kneeling. Hurriedly, the nurse came to steady her. She gladly accepted the white-uniformed arm waiting to escort her to Eddie's room.

"How is he? Is he going to be all right?"

"Well, Sister, it's not my place to say. I'm sure the doctor will be down shortly, and he can answer all of your questions," the nurse answered as she opened the door to Eddie's room.

As the nun approached Eddie's bedside, she stared at his motionless body and immediately noticed that his usually well-tanned face was ashen white. She took his hand in hers, softly calling out his name. Still heavily sedated, he did not respond. Turning, the nun walked to the corner of the room and sank into a well-padded chair. She closed her eyes and reflected back on the horrible events that had taken place that day. *My god, how can it be that little Christina is dead? And Eddie is shot on the very same day? There's been so much killing . . . so much sorrow . . . Why, Father, why? . . . When is it all going to end?* She drifted off into sleep, awakening with a start at the sound of footsteps. A nurse had come in to check Eddie's vital signs. Glancing down at her wristwatch, she realized that over an hour had passed since she had entered the room.

After the nurse left, the nun walked back over to the bed. She began gently stroking Eddie's forehead as she whispered his name. After a moment, his eyelids began to flicker. She watched as he struggled to regain consciousness. She reached for his hand and continued to softly say his name. Slowly, his eyes opened a bit, straining to focus, trying to recognize the face bending over him. She kept repeating his name. Finally, a faint smile crossed his lips. The vision of the face belonging to that sweet and familiar voice crept into his mind's eye as he realized that the figure above him was that of his lifetime friend, Sister Carmella Barratino.

"Carm," he croaked weakly through parched lips, "they tried to kill me."

"I know, Eddie, I know. You've been playing with fire all these years. I told you, sooner or later, it would come to this, but you wouldn't listen," she said sadly.

With a barely discernable movement of his head, he nodded affirmation to his friend's remarks and closed his eyes. *She's right*, he thought. He struggled to flash back into time, to remember when it all began. Slowly, ever so slowly, he managed to recall. *Yes . . . yes, that's it, I remember now. It was the morning of my godfather's seventieth birthday. He called and ordered me to come to his home. That one phone call changed my whole fucking life.*

Exhausted, he fell asleep.

And so, dear reader, our story begins . . .

Chapter 1

E ddie D'Amico was just about to enter the partially open door of his white Ford station wagon when he paused for a moment to stare at the sky. Closing the car door, he folded both arms on the roof of the vehicle and stood motionless, gazing in silent appreciation at the early-morning sunrise.

God, what a magnificent sight, Eddie thought as he marveled at the way the sun had painted fiery crimson red streaks across the horizon, setting it ablaze with flaming color for as far as the eye could see.

The sound of a horn blowing brought him back to reality and out of his nature appreciation respite. Suddenly a gruff voice called out from a blue pickup truck.

"Hey, buddy! What are ya doin'? Going out or in?" asked the driver, who was looking for a place to park.

"Out!" yelled Eddie in response as he quickly jumped into the station wagon and started the engine.

The beat-up old truck moved out of his way, and Eddie backed his car out of the parking space, fumbling with the car radio at the same time. He was trying to find his favorite station that played soft, easy-listening elevator music. Suddenly, the clear, pleasing, melodic voice of Frank Sinatra filled the station wagon. *Ah, perfect!* Eddie thought. He began singing along with Frank as he drove, and he was wishing he could sing like his cousin Allan.

Eddie was feeling relaxed and in a good mood. But he always felt that way after spending Saturday morning at the public market. He loved the hustle and bustle of the throngs of people that created a carnival-like atmosphere at the market each Saturday, but Eddie's main reason for going to the market was Jimmy's Restaurant. It was a place like no other in the city. The eatery had become an institution, and for over fifty years, the powerful and the humble, the rich and the poor would stop at Jimmy's for a cup of coffee or a bite to eat. But mostly, people came to enjoy the give-and-take of the fast-paced conversation that was sure to be taking place over the white porcelain-topped tables. Usually, Eddie would spend an hour or two talking politics and bullshitting with his friends and cronies, who, like him, also had become addicted to the camaraderie always found at Jimmy's and that made the restaurant their Saturday morning stomping ground.

Eddie sang along with Frank as he carefully maneuvered the station wagon through the heavy vehicular and pedestrian traffic, which was a daily occurrence at the market.

Yep, it's a great day!" Eddie thought to himself. He reached into his left shirt pocket and pulled out an expensive panatela cigar. As he lit the cigar, his car phone rang. He lowered the volume of the radio and picked up the receiver.

"Hello."

"Hi, Eddie," said the sweet-sounding female voice.

"Hi, Cat. What's up?" asked Eddie. It was the voice of Catherine Ladd, one of his high school sweethearts and a long-time friend.

"Eddie, I'm in sort of a jam. I've had some plumbing problems in one of the apartments, and I gave the plumber a hot check. I need five hundred till my rent checks come in." Her voice was pleading.

"Hell, Cat, what difference would the rent checks make? You never pay me back anyway," he said, kidding on the level.

"Well, maybe that's true, but you know you have good collateral. You're always welcome to take it out in trade," she replied with a purr in her voice.

Eddie knew that wasn't a bad deal either. That was usually the only way he ever got paid back by Cat. He was sure of one thing. Having slept with a lot of women, Cat Ladd was the best sex he'd ever had.

"OK, Cat. I'll stop over tomorrow."

"Oh, Eddie, can't you stop by now? I need to drop it in the night deposit, and besides, I want to go out tonight, and I'm dead broke. Pleeeease?" Cat begged, her voice sweeter than a spoonful of honey.

"All right, all right. I'm about fifteen minutes away," said Eddie.

"Gee, thanks, hon. Use your key. I may be in the shower," she purred again and then hung up.

Her voice was gone, but thoughts of Cat were racing around in Eddie's head. Memories of her made him forget about the slow-moving traffic. In Eddie's world, Cat was considered a knock-around broad.

She was street-smart and knew all the angles, using her charm and good looks like a weapon to get what she wanted.

Over the years, Eddie had screwed Cat Ladd more times than he could begin to count or even remember. But putting their lustful physical attraction for one another aside, Eddie thought of her as attractive, smart, and one of his best and most trusted friends. *She is a stand-up broad who could be trusted to keep her mouth shut*, he thought.

He turned the station wagon down a wide tree-lined street in one of the better sections of town. Eddie slowed the vehicle, signaled a left turn, and pulled into a wide driveway. He drove past a sign with a large picture of a red cupid painted against a white background. On the sign were the words "Cupid Apartments," and at the bottom, just above the "No Vacancy" sign, appeared the words "Catherine Ladd, Owner."

Cat had chosen the name for these apartments because she knew that it was only her romantic involvement with Eddie D'Amico that had made it possible for her to purchase the fifteen-unit apartment complex she called home.

Eight years earlier, Eddie had heard that the units were in a bank foreclosure. Cat was then going through her second divorce, and she was in a deep depression. Trying to help her, he put the real estate deal together in such a way that it became possible for Cat to purchase the apartments; but all of the money for the down payment was Eddie's.

He drove to the rear of the complex and pulled into the carport of the detached manager's quarters where Cat resided. He cursed as he fumbled around in his glove box, looking for the key to Cat's door. He knew the key was in there somewhere, but it had been several months now since he had used it last.

Eddie finally found the key and walked briskly to the door of Cat's apartment and let himself in. The exotic scent of her cologne filled the air in the well-kept apartment. She had it very femininely furnished, and in keeping with her name, the theme of her decor was cats. Pictures of cats were hung on all the walls; stuffed cats were placed all around the room, and cat figurines were neatly arranged on the coffee and end tables.

"Cat!" Eddie called out.

She didn't respond, but he could hear the sound of running water coming from the direction of the open bathroom door through the master bedroom. He walked toward the sound and entered the steam-filled room. The silhouette of Cat's magnificent body was framed like a portrait behind the opaque glass of the shower door.

Eddie slid the shower door open, and she jumped, startled for a moment. When she saw Eddie, an inviting smile crossed her face.

"Hi, handsome! Would you like to wash my back?" she asked in her usual sexy voice as she offered the bar of soap to Eddie.

"No, thanks," he replied with a smile on his face.

Cat was in a playful mood.

"Not interested in my back, huh? Would you like to wash some other part of me?"

She began rubbing the soap seductively over each of her firm breasts. Eddie watched in silence as she moved the soap around each breast and then slowly back and forth over the tip of each nipple until they became hard and firm. She watched his face as she ran her tongue around her full, lush lips, licking the water droplets.

Eddie continued to watch as she moved the soap slowly down below her breasts in a circular motion and then tantalizingly slid it between her beautiful long legs.

"How about here? Would you like to wash me here?" she asked in a taunting voice, her eyes smoldering.

Her eyes were half closed as she moved the soap sensuously back and forth between her wide-spread legs. Her body began to move and undulate with each stroke of her hand as the soap passed back and forth over her temple of love. The electrical energy that always seemed to be present between Eddie and Cat made him tingle inside. She was beginning to turn him on. He felt a hardness and swelling rise up between his legs.

The urge building inside him made him want to rip off his clothes and satisfy his desires, but his head reminded him he had promised his wife, Danni, that he would be home early, so this was not the time to indulge his pleasures. At least for the moment, Eddie's head won the battle between desire and practicality. His body remained frozen, hypnotized by the beautiful wet body moving and swaying in front of him.

"Talk to me, Eddie. Talk to me," she whispered in a husky, pleading tone.

In trying to turn Eddie on, she had gotten herself excited. Her body was filled with lustful desire, and the aching between her legs was crying to be satisfied. Now thinking only of herself, she wanted to have the relief and pleasure she knew an orgasm would give her, even if she had to satisfy the burning craving between her legs by herself.

"Talk to me!" she pleaded, arching her body up and down with the rhythm of the moving soap.

"Do it, baby. Do it for me, and let me watch you make it," he whispered.

"Yes, yes, oh yes! Watch me, Eddie! Watch me!" she delighted.

With abysmal desire, she continued on, passionately caressing herself to the rhythm of her body motion. Her eyes were closed, and her head was thrown back. She had forgotten all about Eddie and was oblivious to his presence. For the moment, it was her alone in the world enjoying her fantasy and the pleasures of her own body.

"Oh yes! Oh now! Now!" she moaned as she compulsively pinched and rubbed her nipples with her free hand. She began to tremble and weaken under the power of her orgasm.

Drained from the physical and emotional sensation, she reached out and turned off the shower, holding on to the valve to steady herself. She turned and looked into Eddie's smiling face.

"How did you like the show?" she asked sheepishly. Now that the passion of the moment had passed, she appeared to be embarrassed.

"It was great! We both enjoyed it," he quipped, pointing to the bulge in his pants.

He wrapped a towel around her shoulders as she stepped away from the shower. Eddie knew that Cat always had a strong craving for a cigarette after sex, but as usual, he was craving food.

"Cat, do you have anything to make a sandwich with? I'm starved! You know, I always get hungry after sex," he kidded.

"Shit! I'm glad I only crave cigarettes after sex. God! If I craved food like you do, I'd hate to think how much I'd weigh!

"So does that mean I have to have a cigarette sandwich, or do you have any food in the house?"

She let out a raucous laugh at his comeback.

"You know I always keep some of that Genoa salami you like in the fridge," she answered, still panting as she dried her long blonde hair.

"Perfect," he said as he gave her an affectionate pat on her bare behind.

Eddie was at the kitchen table finishing the last bite of his salami sandwich when Cat walked into the room.

"I drank the last of your milk," he said, nodding at the empty milk carton sitting on the table.

"That's OK. Nobody around here drinks it anyway," Cat replied as she lit a long filter-tipped cigarette. She walked over to the kitchen sink and picked up a clean ashtray. She could sense that Eddie was watching her every move. As she turned around, their eyes met, and she smiled. Leaning back against the counter, she kept her eyes on his face as she took a long drag from her cigarette, tipping her head back to direct the smoke toward the ceiling.

Eddie could see that all she had on was a short powder blue satin wrap. The nipples of her breasts were titillated by the touch of the smooth, soft fabric against them. They were hard and firm, protruding out under the covering that was holding them prisoner. Her long blonde hair, still damp, was cascading wildly and naturally over the tops of her shoulders.

She's still a gorgeous-looking broad! Eddie thought to himself as he stared into her sultry green eyes. He knew he needed to hurry and get out of there when he began to feel the throbbing and swelling between his legs again.

Eddie hurriedly stood up and pulled money from his pocket. He quickly snapped off the rubber band and counted out five one-hundred-dollar bills and laid them on the kitchen table. As an afterthought, he took out a five-dollar bill and laid it alongside the empty milk carton.

"There's five bucks. Buy yourself some milk."

Cat suddenly sensed Eddie's urgency to leave, and she began walking toward him, opening the belt on her wrap at the same time. Still standing by his chair, he watched as she let her wrap slip to the floor just as she reached him.

"Come on, Eddie. Loosen up. You've got time. Let me make you happy."

She couldn't resist throwing in a little humor. "Come on, baby, let me make you come before you go," she whispered in his ear.

Her soft full lips and tongue were warm and wet as she kissed and licked Eddie's face. She reached down between his legs and began to stroke him, thrusting her tongue in and out of his mouth at the same time. She could tell by the throbbing in her hand that Eddie wouldn't be leaving right away. They kissed passionately, and she pressed her body tightly to his.

Knowing exactly what he liked, she gently pushed his body back into his chair and opened his zipper. She unbuttoned his shirt and slowly ran her tongue around his nipples and down to his stomach. He was becoming increasingly excited.

"Slow down, big boy. We need to do this together," she whispered as she rose to her feet and straddled him, purring and running her tongue around his ear at the same time. "I want to feel the warmth and the strength of you inside of me," she said, breathing heavily between sighs.

She lowered herself gently onto Eddie and began moving her body ever so slowly in a circular motion. Eddie and Cat looked into each other's eyes, smiling at each other as they shared their secret moment of pleasure and ecstasy.

Gradually, she increased her gyrations to better enjoy the full pleasure of him. "Oh God, Eddie, it feels so good," she moaned as she moved more quickly and forcefully, slamming her body into his.

"Oh yes, Eddie, yes!" She continued to move for a moment; then she slumped exhaustedly on top of him, her body involuntarily quivering all over. They remained locked together in their position of passion for several minutes. Finally, the power of Cat's craving for a cigarette prevailed. She rose to her feet, picked up her wrap from the floor, and slipped it on. She lit a cigarette and took a deep drag to satisfy her urge.

"Well, hon, I've got my cigarette. Do you want me to make you another salami sandwich?"

"No, thanks. Now I'm running late. I've gotta go," he said, knowing full well that Danni would be watching the clock, waiting for him at home.

"All right, then. Thanks for the loan, Eddie. I'll call you when I get my rent checks."

He affectionately patted her behind a couple of times and walked out the open door. She called after him, "You know it's true what they say about you dagos—you really do always pat women on the ass!"

He turned his head around as he continued to walk, smiling a silent answer to her comment. She felt a pounding in her heart as she looked at Eddie's handsome face. Cat knew that she had always been in love with him. They had been lovers since they started high school—that is, until he met Megan.

Cat had been with a lot of men in her life, but for her, Eddie D'Amico had more class, style, and charm in his little finger than all of the rest of them put together.

Overcome with emotion, she yelled, "Hey, Eddie! Don't be such a stranger!" He waved and got into his car.

Chapter 2

E ddie was feeling calm and relaxed, taking pleasure from the lingering thoughts of his love tryst with Cat as he nosed the station wagon through the driveway. He had no sooner pulled into the street to head home than his car phone rang. *Damn*, he thought. *It's probably Danni wanting to know what time I'll be home.*

"Hello." A loud crackling noise was coming from the other end. Eddie could hear someone talking, but he could only make out a single word—*buddy*—coming through the static. That single word was enough to let Eddie know that it was Don Francisco Barratino, his own godfather as well as the Godfather of the crime family that bore his name. *Buddy* was a pet name given to Eddie by Don Francisco when Eddie was just a young kid growing up in the predominantly Italian neighborhood where they both once lived.

"Don Francisco, you're breaking up. Can you hear me?" Eddie asked.

"Yes, yes, I can hear you, Eddie. Undo sta ti mo?" responded the Don in Italian.

"I'm just leaving the public market," he lied in reply to the Don's question.

"I want to talk to you as soon as possible. It's very important," said the Don with an unmistakable sense of urgency in his voice.

"Well, you know I'm planning to be at the farm at five o'clock for your birthday party. Did you forget you're seventy years old today?" asked Eddie with a joking tone in his voice.

"Fuck my birthday party. There's some serious business and important matters that you and I need to discuss as soon as possible."

"How 'bout if I come over an hour before the party?" Eddie asked.

"Eddie, tu monga capire? Get your fucking ass over here *subito!*" ordered the Don, and the line went dead.

Eddie stared at the silent receiver in disbelief. Don Francisco had never talked to him like that before. He placed the handset back in the cradle and turned the car to head in the direction of the farm. The good feeling he had been enjoying moments before was suddenly gone. He couldn't understand why the Don would talk to him that way. He was deeply concerned over the Don's menacing attitude. Eddie began racking his brain, trying to recall if there might have been something he did to offend his godfather. But to no avail; he wasn't able to think of anything he might have said or done that would have put Don Francisco in such a foul mood.

Ever since he was a young boy, Eddie had always enjoyed a close, personal relationship with the Don, but he knew better than to be misled by the kind way the Don had always treated him. Eddie had seen the Don's dark side. He was aware that behind the kind and gentle facade was a man who possessed a violent, evil temper. Connected Mafia people who knew the Don well clearly understood the rules: fucking with him or pissing him off could have very serious consequences. Eddie knew that for some, it had even meant death.

The Godfather's anger on the phone caused Eddie's mind to flash back to a night many years ago. It was on that summer night that he first became aware of the violent and dangerous side of Don Francisco's nature. That night, Eddie and the Don's oldest daughter, Flora, were sitting on the Barratinos' back porch swapping spits. While they were making out, Don Francisco had been talking for quite a long time to some unknown stranger in the kitchen. Neither Don Francisco nor the stranger was aware of Eddie and Flora's presence on the back porch just outside the open kitchen window.

Suddenly they were both startled by the sound of Don Francisco's voice roaring in anger and cursing in Italian as it came gushing out of the open window.

"Luigi, sono disgracciata figu da butana! A mo, la conzona sono finito!" the Don yelled. He paused for a moment to catch his breath and then continued in English, "It's time for him to visit the junk man! Tu capire?" the Don asked the stranger in a loud, stern voice.

"Si, Don Francisco. Io capire," replied the stranger.

"Bono, allore sono finito."

The Don, obviously pleased with the stranger's response, was now speaking in a quieter, subdued tone.

Eddie remembered wondering on his way home that night if the Don had been talking about his own uncle, Luigi Cappobianco, who had been his business partner ever since they arrived in America from Sicily many years ago. Eddie recalled being puzzled that night when Don Francisco told the stranger it was time for Luigi to see the junk man. And he remembered wondering what that could possibly mean. Several days later, after Luigi's mysterious disappearance became known, everyone was told that he had gotten homesick and returned to Italy.

Years later, Eddie learned that when Don Francisco used the term "seeing the junk man," it was his way of putting out a contract on someone he wanted permanently out of the way. He also later learned that the term originated with a longtime family member, Stefano Carlucci. He was the family hit man, who owned a large junkyard where cars were dismantled and wrecked. He had devised his own special simple and effective method of getting rid of bodies. It also guaranteed that bodies would never be found. At the junkyard, old cars to be destroyed were first dismantled and then put into a giant hydraulic press that would crush the cars into rectangular-shaped bales that were then stacked and readied for shipment to the smelter.

Mafia people understood that anyone who lost favor with Don Francisco Barratino would soon end up with a contract on their head. Once they were killed, the body would be brought to Carlucci's junkyard. The unlucky victim would be crushed into the metal that became part of the bale that would be sent to the smelter and melted down. They would disappear forever in the fiery, red-hot crucibles. That was referred to as the victim's last ride.

Eddie glanced down at the dashboard clock—it was 8:10 a.m. He was still fifteen minutes away from the four-hundred-acre estate that Don Francisco called home. A thought crossed his mind. He reached down, picked up the telephone, and dialed a number.

"Hi, it's me," he said when a man's voice answered. "Did I wake you up?"

"Yeah, you did. What's up," the voice growled back.

"I'm on my way to the farm," Eddie said with apology in his voice.

"So fuckin' what! You woke me up to tell me that?" the voice asked with obvious irritation.

"No. I'm calling you because the old man just called me and told me to get my ass down there right away! Is there anything I've done to piss him off that I should know about?"

"Nuthin' that he told me," said the voice on the other end.

Eddie breathed a sigh of relief. He knew that the person on the other end of the line would have been the first to know if something was wrong.

The voice continued, "Don Francisco's been really upset over something for the past week. Whatever it is, he hasn't even discussed it with me." The voice paused for a moment and then continued, "But yesterday he did call a special meeting of the family council for eleven o'clock this morning."

"Doesn't it seem a little strange to you that he'd do that on such short notice?" questioned Eddie.

"Yeah, it's strange, but all he said to anyone is that he's made some important decisions that deal with family business. Look, I gotta take a piss so fuckin' bad I can taste it. I'll see you there," the voice concluded.

"Yeah, OK," said Eddie as he finished the conversation with his father, Dominic D'Amico.

After talking with his father, Eddie relaxed a bit, knowing that his father was the Don's consigliere. As a high-ranking advisor, Dominic should be privy to any problems that might have existed between Eddie and the Don.

Mafia kids are not always told the truth by their parents. Eddie recalled that as a young boy, he had been told that his father was a truck driver for Don Francisco's wholesale liquor business. Later, when he was in his early teens, he figured out, from overheard bits and pieces of conversations, that all of the time spent at the Barratino family home was actually a result of the fact that his father was a high-ranking member of the mob. It was during those years of Eddie's youth that the Don developed a real affection for the smart, good-looking young boy, and he treated him just like a son. This created a problem for the Don's adopted son, Sally, just three years younger than Eddie. At a very young age, Sally developed a strong dislike for Eddie and sorely resented the way his father ignored him and doted on his godson.

The station wagon was now cresting the steep hill on which the farm was located. Eddie instinctively backed off the accelerator pedal and gazed out the window at the magnificent view. Even with the other things on his mind, he could not help but notice the beauty of the landscape stretching out for miles before him. The bright morning sun seemed to give the green fields and stately large trees a vivid life of their own as they basked in the warmth of its rays. Off to his right, about a mile away, Eddie could see "the farm." His eyes came to rest on the stark white eight-foot-high concrete walls that created Don Francisco's ominous, fortress-like compound and etched themselves dramatically against the dark green background of the surrounding pastures. He knew that behind those walls stood a magnificent barn and the large house that Don Francisco Barratino called home.

Feeling a sense of foreboding, Eddie turned into the driveway and brought the station wagon to a halt opposite the stainless steel call pedestal. He rolled down the driver's window and entered his secret code number. The large white iron gates, with an ornately designed letter *B* mounted in the middle, began to swing open.

Since Eddie was not a "made" member of the family, he knew that some members of the mob were highly resentful of him having his own secret entry code. They knew better, though, than to bitch about it to anyone. They accepted it in silence. For them, it was just one more example of the station of privilege Eddie enjoyed because of his close, personal relationship with their boss.

He drove through the gates and continued down the long, curving driveway. Having spent a good deal of time at the compound, he knew the inside of it like the back of his hand. To the left of the driveway stood the Don's beautiful white Victorian home in all its restored splendor. Eddie did not stop his car in front of the house but continued on down the long driveway. Knowing Don Francisco's habits, he assumed that at this time of day, he would be in either his garden or his greenhouse. Both were located behind the large white barn near the rear of the compound. As he slowly drove past the house, Eddie glanced over to the pool and tennis court area. He could see people standing on ladders, putting up decorations for the Don's birthday party to be held later that day.

The driveway was now curving to the right around the beautiful park-like greenbelt area that was located in the center of the compound. It had mature trees and well-manicured lawns. In the middle of the lawn area was a large fountain surrounded by a dazzling array of colorful summer flowers. As he passed, he could smell their heady, pungent odor that filled the air.

Reaching his destination, Eddie pulled the station wagon into the graveled parking area that was located between the barn and horse stables. He stepped out of the car and paused for a moment to stretch and try to decide whether to first look for Don Francisco in the garden or the greenhouse. Since it was a beautiful summer morning, and knowing how much the Don enjoyed the outdoors, Eddie chose to look in the garden first and turned to walk down a flagstone path. He was hatless, and the morning sun gave a bright sheen to Eddie's full head of wavy black hair. He wore his hair a trifle too long, but well groomed. The way it was styled complemented his full face and high cheekbones, which were accentuated by his expressive large dark brown eyes. Eddie's smooth, well-tanned skin revealed that he was a person who spent a lot of time outdoors.

He walked briskly down the pathway with a strong, athletic gait. The flagstone pathway ended abruptly, and he stepped into the Don's secluded, fence-enclosed garden. Eddie looked around the garden and then walked over to search behind the heavy foliage of the grape arbors. He called out Don Francisco's name, but he could not find the Don anywhere. Remembering that the Don had just purchased a new stallion, he decided to try the stables. Eddie retraced his steps and was soon inside the large well-kept horse area. Suddenly, he heard the sound of Don Francisco's voice echoing through the cavernlike expanse of the building.

"Whoa! Whoa! Take it easy, boy, eeeasy. Attaboy. Eeeasy."

Eddie walked to the far end of the building, which opened out to the corral. He watched as the Godfather tugged on a rope, attempting to unfasten it from a training harness worn by a magnificent black stallion. The powerful muscles of the huge animal quivered as his wild, penetrating brown eyes watched the Don suspiciously. Don Francisco gently stroked the white blaze between the horse's eyes and spoke to him in soft, soothing tones to quiet him down. When the Don finally unfastened the training rope, the noble animal sensed his freedom. With nostrils flaring, he snorted and reared high on his hind quarters, flailing in the air with his front legs, causing Don Francisco to beat a hasty retreat.

Bucking and kicking, the stallion let out a loud whinny and began galloping and prancing proudly around the corral. His jet-black coat glistened like polished onyx in the early-morning sun. The Don paused to admire the superb animal and then turned to leave the corral.

Eddie called out to the Don as he waved his arrival.

"Boun giorno, Godfather!"

The Don hailed back, "Hey, buddy, you made good time! Well, what do you think of him? Did you ever see such a fine-looking animal in your life?"

"No, never! He's really incredible! But he sure looks like he's got a fucking mind of his own!"

"Yeah. Just like his owner, huh, Eddie?" the Don joked.

With one hand, the Don removed the battered straw hat he was wearing, revealing a head of full-bodied silver-gray hair. With his other hand, he whipped out a red bandanna from the right rear pocket of his coveralls and began wiping the perspiration that was running down his fully tanned face.

Placing one hand on his hip and stretching backward, the Don tried to limber his back as he said, "Aaah, la vicuia a caronia, Eddie."

"Yeah, I know, but we all have to get old someday," Eddie said in reply to the Don's comment.

As he approached, Eddie studied the Don's well-chiseled features in an effort to see if he could read what he was thinking behind his piercing dark eyes. The Don reached out gently and took him by the elbow.

"Let's go inside so we can sit down and talk."

They began walking side by side through the stable and down to the wide path leading to the Don's office in the rear of the barn. Eddie's nerves were frazzled from the war he had allowed to rage in his head ever since the Don had called him on his car phone. Eddie was a man of little patience, even on a good day, and he was anxious to get some answers. He could not stand the suspense a moment longer, but he knew that Don Francisco had a short fuse. He must be careful not to piss off or offend the old man by acting too pushy or by coming across as being disrespectful in any way.

Eddie chose his words carefully.

"Don Francisco, with all due respect, I have been very upset over your call to me this morning. When you hung up the phone on me, and after the way you talked, I became very concerned. I've been worried that perhaps I had done something to bring you displeasure or in some way show you disrespect."

Eddie sighed heavily after getting that off his chest. It was not his usual style to mince words or walk on eggs.

Don Francisco now stopped walking and turned to face Eddie, putting one hand on each of his broad, muscular shoulders. The Don stood there, in silence, for a long moment, staring into Eddie's face. Then he began to speak.

"Early this morning, I received information that, for me, was probably the most disturbing and terrible news I can remember receiving since, bon arme, the death of my mother. The information I got required me to make some important decisions and take some immediate precautions. These things must be done with someone I trust beyond a shadow of a doubt. Knowing me, you can understand that I gave this matter a lot of thought. Many names crossed my mind, but each time, your name rose to the top of my list."

The Don paused to watch his godson's reaction. Eddie's eyes were now riveted on Don Francisco's face.

"Listen, buddy, when I called you this morning, I was frustrated and very angry—not with you but with my situation. I realized after I hung up on you it was not the right thing to do. I knew you probably felt I was angry with you, but that's not the case. So now, my young friend, your godfather offers you his sincerest apology."

The Don's words were good news. Eddie was thankful that he had been worrying his ass off over nothing. He felt as if a great weight had been lifted from him, and a sigh of relief escaped his lips. He gave serious thought to what he was going to say before speaking, making sure he said all of the right things. Cleverly, he followed the Don's lead.

"And, Don Francisco, I apologize to you for doubting the depth and power of our relationship," replied Eddie, full of emotion, partly from relief after finding out the Don was not angry with him and partly in sympathy for Don Francisco's plight.

Eddie knew that the Don must have a terrible problem. It was difficult for him to understand how this man of power and strength could be sounding as if he was in such a vulnerable position. Before he realized what he was doing, Eddie put his arms around Don Francisco, and with strong emotion in his voice, said, "I love you, Godfather. You know you can count on me to do anything I can to help you."

The Don responded, "And I you, buddy. But come, enough of this sentimental crap. Let's go inside. We have much to talk about."

They entered the Don's office through the rear door that was directly off the gravel parking lot. The window coverings were drawn, and the room was dark. Eddie was having a difficult time adjusting his eyes after walking in from the bright, summer sun. Slowly, his eyes began to focus and roam around the large room. His eyes stopped at the wall behind the Don's massive hand-carved desk. The wall was covered with shelving that contained a large collection of law books. Very few people knew that as a young man, Don Francisco had studied law in Milan before coming to America.

Eddie turned and watched as Don Francisco went over to the radio. He moved the dial until it came to rest on the Saturday-morning Italian music program. "O Sole Mio," a man's voice was singing. The Don turned the volume down. The man's voice continued, "Stan fran ta te." Don Francisco flipped a switch, and the soft music began to flow out of the many speakers located around the room. The music was relaxing. Eddie felt a smile begin to form on his face as he watched the Don. He knew exactly what motivated him to turn on the radio, and it wasn't any compelling desire to hear the music.

Old habits never die, Eddie thought. *Mafia men always turn on a radio or a television when they are talking in a room.* In the ways of their world, it was their belief that in the event a room was bugged, the background noise of a radio or television would scramble the sound of their voices, making it difficult for anyone that might be eavesdropping to hear what was being said.

"I've gotta take a piss and get out of these coveralls. There's some fresh espresso behind the bar. And don't forget my twist of lemon," said the Don.

Obediently, Eddie walked over to the black slate-topped bar and poured two cups of espresso, putting a twist of lemon in each. He then walked over to a small love seat that was part of a conversation area in front of a huge fireplace. He set both cups on the coffee table between matching burgundy love seats.

I wonder what the fuck this is all about, Eddie wondered. Filled with overwhelming curiosity, he tried to remain calm, sitting down and taking a sip of his espresso. *Hmm, he thought of a lot of people, but my name rose to the top of the list.* With rabid eagerness, he anxiously awaited what Don Francisco was about to tell him. "This must be something that nobody else knows. Why me?" his mind questioned. He didn't know whether to be proud or worried.

His mind continued to race. *Holy fuck! Maybe I don't want to know! I'm not a made member of this family. I've spent my whole life trying to keep my distance from all their illegal activities and bullshit. And now he's gonna tell me something nobody else knows! Shit! It might even be something that could get me killed! I've got to play this very carefully*, Eddie thought.

The Don's voice startled Eddie out of his daydreaming. "Ahh, you got the espresso. Good!" he said as he sat down on the love seat opposite Eddie. He took a sip from his cup and said, "Then let us begin".

"Look, Don Francisco, before you start . . . You know I've never had any official role in your family. We both know it's been *my* choice to keep my nose out of your family business. I'm very grateful to you for honoring my decision, but I'm really worried now that what you're about to tell me is private information that maybe I really shouldn't know anything about."

"Relax, Eddie, relax. It's nothing like that. The things I am going to discuss with you are matters of a personal nature. What I'm about to share with you will not put you in danger."

Don Francisco settled back in the love seat opposite Eddie, and propping both feet up on the white marble coffee table between them, began speaking.

"My story has two parts. The first deals with a serious problem for me within the family. That part is dangerous and is a matter that I, alone, will have to deal with. But because of this problem, I have decided there are some immediate precautions I must take that are strictly of a personal nature. This is where I am going to need your help," said the Don.

Me, help him! Eddie thought. He couldn't help feeling flattered by the Don's statement. Don Francisco had never asked him for his help before.

"But before I begin my story, I must have your solemn oath of secrecy. You must pledge to me that you will carry to your grave the things that I am about to share with you. You must never divulge my secrets to anyone. When you hear what I am about to say, you will understand the importance of my request," said the Don, speaking in a low, confidential voice.

The Don's piercing eyes were focused on Eddie's face, causing him to shift uneasily in his seat. He knew then that the Don was expecting him to speak. For want of something better to do, Eddie picked up his espresso and nervously took a sip.

Both men sat for a moment in silence. The Don's eyes were trying to read Eddie's mind through his facial expression. Eddie was attempting to collect his thoughts and choose the right words to say before answering the Godfather.

It was Don Francisco who broke the silence first.

"Well, Eddie, do I continue? Or do we end this conversation here and now?"

Eddie was sensing the Don's attitude, and it made him nervous. He knew this man of cunningness and power was backing him into a corner. The Don already knew what Eddie's answer would have to be. Wanting to make sure he said the right thing, Eddie rose from his seat and began to nervously pace the floor, stalling for time. He knew he was screwed, and he knew, because of past favors, there could only be one answer. He was in no position to refuse Don Francisco anything.

This crap about me having a choice in the matter is only bullshit, Eddie thought, and they both knew it.

The silence between the two men was becoming unbearable for Eddie. He went back to his seat, hoping if he sat down, he could relax a little, and that by some mystical force, the right words would come to him.

Eddie leaned forward, placing his empty cup on the marble coffee table; and looking the Don squarely in the eyes, he began to speak.

"Don Francisco, you have just hit me cold with a request for my oath of secrecy." Eddie paused, still trying to choose his every word carefully. "Ever since I was a young boy, you know you have had my love and my loyalty. In my opinion, along with loyalty go honor and respect. To me that also means if I knew something that could ultimately be harmful to you, then, of course, I know I must keep it my secret." Eddie continued slowly, "Now you are asking me to reaffirm my loyalty by taking an oath of secrecy about things which you haven't even disclosed to me. Godfather, I am worried that they are things I want to know nothing about."

Eddie paused, taking a deep breath before he went on.

"With all due respect, Don Francisco, I believe you already know there is nothing that I would not do for you, providing it's not illegal or criminal in any way."

Don Francisco continued to sit and listen without expression, so Eddie continued. "But if what you are going to request of me has to do with you personally, or if it's some kind of legitimate matter, then of course, you have my word that whatever you reveal to me will be our secret alone forever."

Don Francisco leaned across the coffee table and smiled, pleased with Eddie's answer. He patted the top of Eddie's hand as he spoke.

"Good, my boy. Good," said the Don, rising to his feet and heading to the bar for another cup of espresso.

Eddie felt some relief come over him, but he hoped he wasn't feeling comfortable too soon.

As the Don was pouring more espresso, he looked over at Eddie from across the room and said, "You know, Eddie, I find it interesting that you expound all this pious morality bullshit to me about not becoming involved in the ways of my world. Yet on the other hand, you take and enjoy all of the privileges that my world gives to you. I find that irritating and hypocritical."

The Don's remark clearly revealed that he was agitated.

"What do you mean?" asked Eddie with a puzzled look on his face.

He was attempting to play dumb, but he knew exactly what the Godfather meant; Don Francisco was referring to Eddie's game of straddling the line between the two different worlds of crime and legitimacy. He also knew that the Don was aware of his selfishness in wanting the best of both worlds and his cunning attempts at trying to have it all.

"What I mean, my young friend, is that you try to convey the impression that you are so sanctimonious and too *good* to be involved in the ways of my world. But I know that time and time again, you have used our relationship for your own personal gain. You've benefited by receiving many favors from the unions, my bank, and also many others in the business world. You were given those favors and special considerations, not because you are the fucking virtuous Eddie D'Amico, but because you walked in *my* shadow and because you have been wrapped in the power of *my* world and the power of *my* name! Do you think I am stupid or that people don't come back and tell me of the things you do in *my name?* I want you to understand that I've known about this all along. I allowed you to take these liberties because of my fondness for you and because your actions did not harm me in any way. I only bring this up now because I want you to know that I know what you have done and that you haven't been fooling me all these years!"

The Don was speaking in a reprimanding manner with a deep frown on his face.

Eddie was blindsided and caught completely off guard by the Don's remarks. He was embarrassed and could feel his face turning red. He knew that the Don's words were very true. The name *Barratino* was a formidable weapon to have in one's arsenal in the wars of the business world.

The Don's words had made Eddie feel like a kid who just got caught with his hand in the cookie jar. Since he had no justifiable excuse, he was searching his mind for something nice to say to his godfather to redeem himself. Suddenly, an idea came to him.

"Godfather, what you have just said is all true. It is embarrassing that you waited until now to say something to me about your feelings. When I took favors in your name, I never thought I was imposing on our relationship in any way. But with hindsight, maybe I did take a few things for granted. But I too have had thoughts that I've never shared with you. Since it appears that today is going to be our day of confession, then I feel compelled to tell you something I've kept a secret about our relationship."

Although anxious to hear what his godson was about to confess, the Don kept a poker face, calmly returning to his seat and leisurely sipping his espresso, but very eager for Eddie to get to the point.

"Your presence has been in my life since I was a young boy because of my father's involvement with you and the family. You always made me feel that you really cared about me. You always treated me with kindness and generosity, and I have never forgotten that. It was you who first taught me how to hunt and fish. It was always you I came to for advice. My own father never cared as much. In fact, he never seemed to give a damn about me! And I remember when I was older and started working in construction for my uncle it was you who I came to with my dream of wanting to go into business for myself. You understood, and you told me 'it is good for a man to follow his dreams.' Everyone else laughed at me and said I was too young. You were the only one that ever gave me any encouragement, not only with words but by loaning me the money to make it happen. You have always been there for me in more ways than I can remember. I'm not stupid. I know, even if I live to be a hundred, I would never be able to repay you for all you have done for me," Eddie said, his words coming straight from his heart.

Don Francisco was listening intently to Eddie with a smile on his face, obviously pleased at what his godson was saying.

"Look, Godfather, what I'm trying to say is that ever since I was a kid, I felt that you have been more of a father to me than my own father!" he blurted.

"Your words have made your godfather feel good, Eddie."

Don Francisco looked at his watch.

"We're running out of time. Let's get back to business and the problems at hand. But first, I'm going to ask you one small favor before I continue. As you know, we Sicilians are rooted deep into our culture and our traditions . . ." The Don paused for a moment. "Back in the old country, pacts such as you and I will be making this morning are always sealed in blood," the Don continued.

Oh no! I hope this doesn't mean what I'm thinking, Eddie thought, feeling the nervousness creep back over him.

As the Don began speaking again, he produced a small red pen knife from his left shirt pocket. Looking into Eddie's eyes, he smiled evilly.

"I hope you don't mind allowing an old man his indulgence by sealing this pact in the tradition of my world," he said as he opened the razor-sharp blade on the knife, not waiting for Eddie to respond.

With a quick, deft movement, Don Francisco ran the blade across the palm of his right hand. Blood appeared and began to run slowly from the small incision. Eddie looked on in stunned, squeamish silence. He shuddered in fearful anticipation. His turn was coming next.

Without another word, the Don took Eddie's limp right hand into his. Eddie felt a sense of evil emanating from Don Francisco as the Mafia ruler side of the Don's persona began to take complete charge and control over what was now happening. With the knife in his bleeding right hand, the Don turned Eddie's right palm faceup and made a swipe across it with the blade of the knife. As Eddie's palm began to bleed, Don Francisco pressed their two hands together and held them locked in a powerful viselike grip. Eddie watched silently as the Don's face became like a twisted, wicked mask as he uttered in Italian, "La sanga tu, a la sanga io, mo sona uno."

Eddie was disturbed at what was taking place. He unconsciously translated the Don's words: "Your blood and my blood are now one."

The baneful ritual over, Don Francisco let go of his hand, and Eddie lay back in his seat, feeling emotionally drained. What took place next made him suddenly realize that Don Francisco had taken a lot for granted. The Don picked up two small white hand towels that he had neatly folded and placed on the edge of the coffee table where they had sat unnoticed until now.

Son of a bitch! He orchestrated the whole fucking thing! Eddie thought to himself, realizing now why the towels were placed there.

Don Francisco kept a towel for himself and threw the other one across the table to Eddie.

This is too fucking much, Eddie thought. "You had this all planned, didn't you?" he asked out loud.

"Remember this, Eddie. It is important to plan well for everything you do in life," the Don replied without giving a direct answer to Eddie's question. "Planning is the reason you are here today. Together we are going to make a plan that we have just sealed with our blood," said the Don, his voice very serious and businesslike. "Eddie, my problem began ten days ago when I received a call from my cousin Carmine Catalano. You know the name."

"Sure," replied Eddie. "He's the godfather of one of the large New York families."

"Si," said the Don. "My cousin called to tell me that a trusted member of his family had heard a rumor through the grapevine that there was a serious problem within my family. He went on to say that he believed my life might even be in danger. Naturally, I was very shocked and concerned to hear this news. My cousin told me he would be doing some more checking and call me back when he has some more . . ."

Eddie interrupted. "Come on, Don Francisco. That shit can't be true! If you had that kind of serious dissension in the family, certainly you would know it, or at least sense it, wouldn't you?"

The Don nodded with a sly grin on his face, admiring Eddie's perceptiveness, and answered, "You are exactly right, my friend, but therein lies the problem. I have suspected for some time now that there are members within the family's inner circle who are dissatisfied and pissed off about some things they want me to change, but it is apparent from my cousin's call that I could be making a deadly mistake by underestimating the seriousness of the situation."

Eddie was leaning forward on the edge of his seat, intrigued with Don Francisco's story and hanging on every word.

The Don continued, "This morning I received the call I was waiting for from Carmine. It came just a few minutes before I called you on your car phone. That's why I was so upset. He told me he had done more checking and that his information came from some very reliable sources. The news was worse than I expected. I tell you, never in a million years would I have believed that members of my own family would be conspiring to kill me! For me, it was unthinkable! Almost impossible to believe!" he said in stunned disbelief.

"According to Carmine's sources, the word on the street is that I have grown old and soft. They say I have lost my balls. That I do not have the courage to expand the family or to move into new territories. I know what they want, but I also know that what they want me to do is very risky. It will surely put our family in a major fucking war."

Eddie listened intently as the Don continued.

"It's fucking ironic that I should get this news on the very day that I have called a special meeting to discuss these very matters. Those fucking degenerate bastards do not even know my final decision! Yet they secretly talk among themselves, conspiring and plotting their treachery against me! Well, fuck them! Today they will get my answer! And they will not like what they hear! I will not let anyone fucking force me into anything I do not believe is right for my family!"

"But won't you be putting yourself in more danger if you do that?"

"Danger? Danger is nothing new to me. In my world, we live by the sword, and we die by the sword. It is the risk we all take and must live with each day of our lives. At least now, thanks to my cousin, I am forewarned. As soon as I am sure which of them are involved in this conspiracy against me, I will make my move. When I am finished with them, they will find it would have been better for them to burn in hell forever than to fuck with Don Francisco Barratino!"

"But, Godfather, you have me confused. I hear what you're saying, but I'm lost in your story. What is my place in all of this?" Eddie asked nervously, believing he really didn't want to know.

"Buddy, I told you I need someone I can trust completely. If these bastards have even an inkling that I suspect them of anything, it may force them to move more quickly against me. I need to stall them for at least a day or two so I can check things out and make sure who is involved in this plot before I act."

"I understand all that, Godfather," Eddie responded, struggling to keep his emotions hidden.

Eddie didn't like what he was being forced to hear. *What have I gotten myself into?* he pondered. *He's matter-of-factly telling me he plans to kill several people! I can't believe this is happening! I'm just sitting here like a real fuckin' idiot listening to him confide these secrets to me! He's making me part of a conspiracy to commit murder!*

Eddie wished he could just stand up and leave the room. *Oh my god! I've gotten in way over my fuckin' head! Now I know too much! I'm fucking sucked in—trapped with no way to back out!* he thought to himself.

The Don was reclined with his head resting on the back of the seat. With unseeing eyes, he stared into space toward the ceiling and appeared to be deep in thought. Without taking his eyes from the ceiling, he began to speak again, this time more to himself than to Eddie.

"Maybe those dirty cocksuckers are right. I am getting old and soft. I've grown to be happy and content with my life just as it is. But now those degenerate pricks are trying to back me into a corner. Now I have no choice! It will have to be either me or them," the Don muttered. Then, sitting upright and looking straight at Eddie, he spoke through clenched teeth. "I promise you, Eddie, it won't be me."

"But, Don Francisco, is there no other way for you to resolve this problem?"

"No, Eddie. There is no other way," replied the Don matter-of-factly. "Once you become a Don, the road that we must travel is full of danger, deceit, and risk. You understand these risks. It is a choice we all make. Unfortunately, I have reached the age where I have had my fill of fighting wars with other families. But one thing is for sure! I will not let these motherfuckers force me into starting a war when we have been at peace for so many years."

The Don now had a reminiscent look on his face.

"It was different when I was a young don. I was like a lion. I had balls bigger than a fucking elephant. I took anything I wanted, and anyone who challenged me or stood in my way would wind up swimming with the fishes. But quite frankly, Eddie, they are right. I do not have the stomach or the desire to continue with this kind of life anymore . . ."

He let the sentence die off, collected his thoughts, and then went on.

"You will soon see that over the years, I have saved enough money to last me a hundred lifetimes. Now all I want to do is spend time enjoying my grandchildren, working in my garden, and living out whatever time I have left in peace."

Eddie, spellbound with the Don's story, was now on the edge of his seat. He was waiting in eager anticipation to hear more about the money that Don Francisco said was enough to last a hundred lifetimes. Money was a subject that always piqued Eddie's interest.

As if he was reading Eddie's mind, the Don said, "Money. My problems are all about fucking money. It's money that's causing members of my own family to betray me. I have taken care of those ungrateful bastards all these years. Now those stupid sons of bitches are just like fucking animals, biting the hand that feeds them! Threatening my life because they want more money! Shit! Because of me, most of them have made more money than most people make in a lifetime! I made it too fucking easy for them! But most of them pissed their money away as fast as they made it. They blew it on gambling and women, big cars and diamonds. They saved nothing, only caring to indulge themselves in every kind of vice and luxury imaginable. But they are stupid! The dumb fucking idiots never stop to realize that those things only serve their pleasure for a short time. Now because of their costly indulgences, the fucking assholes want me to break the peace and start wars to expand our business so they'll have even *more money* to fuck away on foolishness!"

Eddie's curiosity and impatience was beginning to get the better of him.

"So what's it all about, Don Francisco? You still haven't told me what my part is in all of this."

Don Francisco looked at his watch again. "I still have many more important things to tell you, but we're out of time for now. You will hear all the rest soon enough at the meeting."

"At the business meeting? I'm not going to the meeting!" Eddie thought.

He wanted to remind the Don that according to his own rules, only "made" members of the family were allowed to sit in on family meetings. Since Eddie had no "official" status in the family, he knew that there would be no way he would be attending such a meeting. But he knew it would be better for him now to keep his mouth shut and just continue to listen.

Don Francisco puffed deeply on his cigar, his eyes focused on Eddie's face.

"And now, Eddie, the part of all this that will directly affect you."

Finally! he thought. *He just dragged me into a fucking murder conspiracy! The rest of this better be good!*

"I personally have no fear of death. The thought of it is something a don lives with all of his life, and you simply learn to come to terms with it. But it would be very foolish for me to take lightly my cousin's warning about a plot to have me killed. If it is true, and now I must assume it is, then I must face the reality that they could succeed before I have a chance to stop them. The main reason I wanted you here as soon as possible this morning was to talk to you, but more importantly, to give you some documents that I took the liberty of drawing up. In the event my death does occur, I am deeply concerned about making sure that my wife and children are well provided for and—"

"Excuse me, Godfather, but shouldn't you be telling this to your attorney?"

"No, Eddie. I thought everything out carefully. My situation is unique. You see, because of the fact that I cannot let all of my assets be shown in a traceable will, I must make separate arrangements with these matters, and this is where I need your help," said the Don as he reached underneath a magazine on the coffee table and pulled out two white envelopes.

Eddie could see that both envelopes were sealed. He continued to watch with excited new interest as the Don squeezed each envelope with his fingers as if by doing so he could tell the contents with his touch. Finding the one he was looking for, he stretched his arm across the table and handed the envelope to Eddie.

"This is an original copy of my will that I had drawn up sometime ago. It's pretty standard and relatively clear and simple. You will notice that the original executor was my attorney, Anthony Banducci, but your name now appears in that position. What this will contains is only a small part of my estate. It deals with the ordinary kinds of things such as houses, cars, real estate, and my other declared holdings. You can read it later when you have time." Don Francisco paused a moment to check the expression on Eddie's face.

Eddie's ears had perked up at one of the Don's words. He had immediately picked up on the word *declared*. That one word sent a signal to Eddie that there was going to be more to come—much more. He could hardly wait to hear the rest.

Eddie looked on as Don Francisco glanced at his watch again. It was apparent that the Don was feeling the pressure of time. He couldn't move fast enough now to satisfy the overanxious Eddie D'Amico.

With a sense of theatrics in his voice, the Don continued.

"And now, my young friend, this is what Don Francisco Barratino's life has been all about."

He waved the second envelope in front of Eddie.

Eddie's eyes were glued to the innocent-looking envelope, wondering what the hell one envelope could possibly contain that would sum up Don Francisco's entire life. He would soon find out, he thought, as the Don threw the envelope on the table with a dramatic flick of his wrist.

With his eyes on Eddie's face, the Don said, "Open it and see what's inside." His words were in the form of an order, but there was a tone of expectation in his voice.

Trying hard not to appear overly eager, Eddie picked up the envelope and tore it open. Exposing the contents, Eddie pulled out two old, well-worn dark blue bankbooks. He studied the covers of the books for a moment. The gold printing was almost completely worn off, but still visible enough for him to see that they were both from the same bank in Switzerland.

Opening the first book and knowing exactly what he was looking for, Eddie went immediately to the last page, searching for the last entry that would show the total amount of money that the worn, old book contained. Finally finding the figure he was looking for, he began shaking his head in utter amazement and disbelief. He unconsciously leaned back in his seat, flabbergasted at what the little blue book had silently revealed.

Don Francisco watched the expression on Eddie's face with a sense of pleasure. He knew that his surprise had just blown Eddie's mind. A broad smile of pride grew across his face. He was thoroughly enjoying his godson's reaction.

"Oh my god, Don Francisco! This is absolutely unbelievable! Abso-fucking-lutely unbelievable!" Eddie exclaimed, tossing the first book down on the table in front of him and picking up the second book, all in one motion. He was now anxiously trying to find the last page in the second book.

When he finally found the last entry, the old book screamed out its numbers with such deafening force it caused Eddie's jaw to drop, and he helplessly gasped.

"Holy shit!" Eddie exclaimed, looking up from the little blue book that had just grown to the size of a giant in his mind. "This fucking book has even more money than the first one!"

Never in his wildest dreams would he ever have guessed Don Francisco could be so rich! The shock of his discovery put Eddie off-balance and at a loss for words. He fell back in the love seat, not knowing what to do or say next. Don Francisco sipped his anisette silently through the proud smile still etched on his face.

The Don was relishing this moment. He was beginning to solve part of his problem and had shared with Eddie a secret that he had kept to himself for over thirty-five years. It had given him great pleasure to finally share the secrets of his treasure with someone else. But there was still more to come.

Don Francisco knew that his story had not yet reached its conclusion. He knew that Eddie D'Amico still had another, even bigger, surprise in store for him. The Don felt the warm glow of the smile on his face now spread deep inside him in expectation of Eddie's reaction to the rest of his story.

Eddie was slowly recovering from the shock he had received from the little blue books.

"Millions! Fucking millions of dollars are in these accounts!" exclaimed Eddie, holding up the two books. "How did you do it? How in the world were you able to amass such a fucking fortune without anyone knowing?"

"Brains, buddy. Brains and planning. My years in college were not wasted. It was my training in legal matters that gave me the ideas. My legal background has served me well over the years. That, along with discipline and a commitment I made to myself to provide well for my family and their future. I made many profitable investments in the stock market using assumed names and identities. I also made a great deal of money in real estate investments in foreign countries using untraceable shell corporations," Don Francisco explained. "But the bulk of the cash came from skim money from my silent interest in the Vegas casinos."

Silent is right! Eddie thought. Never once had he ever heard even a rumor about the Don having any interest in Las Vegas casinos. He would bet there wasn't a single member of the family that knew it either.

"Godfather, I am honored and flattered beyond words that you have shown your faith and trust in me by sharing such incredible and private information," Eddie said humbly. "But I am still at a loss to see the connection of what any of this has to do with me. Why have you decided to tell *me* your most personal and private secrets?"

The Don rose from his seat and headed for his desk, talking to Eddie over his shoulder as he walked.

"Just be patient, my young friend. You will soon have all of your questions answered." Don Francisco took a folded document from the desk drawer. "Everything you are wondering about is all in here. You will soon see that you play a key role in the rest of my story."

I need a fucking drink! Eddie thought. *What bombshell will he drop on me next?* he wondered as Don Francisco unfolded the document and handed it to him.

As Eddie began to read the document, he kept lifting his eyes from the paper to glance at the Don. Eddie's face was registering a shocked expression of disbelief. Don Francisco did not wait for him to finish reading before he began speaking again.

"Well, buddy, as you can see, the document in your hand is a power of attorney, along with all of my secret code identifications. I have written it to instruct the bank that in the event of my death, you will have irrevocable and unrestricted control over all of the funds that I have deposited in both of those accounts," explained the Don calmly.

There didn't seem to be an end to the Don's surprises. Eddie was in shock, struggling to digest the total significance of what Don Francisco had just revealed to him.

Ignoring Eddie's apparent bewilderment, the Don continued, "I have set things up so that all you will have to do to activate the terms and conditions I have outlined in the document is to supply the bank with proof of my death. That proof must be in the form of a duly executed original death certificate."

As the Don spoke, Eddie couldn't help but marvel at the matter-of-fact manner in which he talked of his own death.

"Again, I remind you of our pact of secrecy, which we have sealed in blood. I want you to clearly understand that even after my death, you still are not to tell anyone the size of my fortune, nor that I have turned control of it over to you. If the time comes that you are asked anything about any of this by my wife or children, be vague and tell them you and I had some joint venture investments that you had sheltered from the IRS for us. And because there is still the matter of your own personal privacy, you tell them you can say no more than that," the Don said, finishing his directions to Eddie.

"But why go through all this cloak-and-dagger shit? Wouldn't it make more sense to let your own son, Sally, handle these matters?"

Eddie knew that Sally couldn't be trusted and was incapable of handling this type of business, but he felt he had to ask the question out of respect.

"It grieves me to say this, but I think you probably already know that Salvatore has been a great disappointment to me. Over the years, he has given me many reasons to doubt and distrust him. I know that based on his past behavior, he cannot be trusted with anything. You know him as well as anyone. I am sure that you are aware of his shortcomings. I know you have seen his evil and violent temper. It clouds his judgment and continually gets him into trouble. Sometimes I wonder if he even has an ounce of sense in his head or a heart that beats inside of him," the Don said with disappointment in his voice. "I know that he has always wanted to take my place when I retire, but deep in my heart, I know I could never give him my blessing."

Eddie was surprised at the Don's comments about his son. All this time, Eddie had thought that Sally had his father completely fooled. He was amazed to find out that Sally had not bullshitted his father one bit. Don Francisco had just described Sally to a tee.

"Now that you know my thoughts and the choices that were available to me, I'm sure you can understand my decision. Because of my trust in you and your knowledge of business and tax matters, you became the most logical choice, even over your father and the other family members. Now that you know the seriousness of the problem that I have within my own family, I'm sure you can see why I wanted to get this pact between us completed as soon as possible. My instincts tell me that when I make my final decisions known at that meeting, the shit will hit the fan. If my cousin Carmine's information is true, then it is very possible that my life will be at risk from that moment on," Don Francisco finished with a deep sigh.

Eddie had already come to his own conclusions regarding the danger that Don Francisco was in. He could also see, now that he had all the facts, why Don Francisco was anxious to immediately take the necessary precautions to protect his fortune before anything happened to him.

Fuck yes! Eddie thought. He could definitely see the urgency of Don Francisco's situation. *If something did happen to the Don and nobody was to find where he had hidden the two blue bankbooks, all those millions of dollars would be lost forever! My god! What a horrible fucking thought!*

Never in his wildest dreams could he ever have imagined the turn of events that had taken place in his life this morning. But now, the overwhelming magnitude and significance of what had just transpired began to sink in. He wasn't dreaming. It was true. Someday, all the money reflected in those books would be under his control. It still seemed almost impossible to believe. He realized his life would never be the same. His business sense told him, even before their meeting ended, that the Don would be giving him the two bankbooks along with the power of attorney. He was sure that the Don would want to have those documents completely out of his possession right away, or at least until he felt that he was safe and could take them back again.

The sound of Don Francisco's voice brought Eddie from his thoughts with a start.

"Hey, Eddie! Are you in a fucking daze or something?" asked the Don, who was pacing the floor and looking down at his watch.

"I'm sorry, Don Francisco. But your story has given me so much to think about. My mind must have wandered," apologized Eddie.

"We still have a couple more things to iron out," said the Don as he returned to his seat across the marble table from Eddie. There are a few conditions you will have to agree to before we can consider that you and I have a done deal."

Here it comes, Eddie thought to himself. *I wonder if he's gonna tell me I have to kill someone first?*

He was feeling that the Don was about to burst his bubble with some kind of request that he wouldn't be able to agree to.

"Please listen very carefully, and remember: I have spent my whole life planning all this out. I always intended that my fortune would be used to provide for my family's future. I know from some of our dealings that you have been very clever in finding ways to legitimately fuck the IRS. I want you to use your knowledge of business to set up lifetime trusts for all of the members of my family, including my grandchildren.

See that they all receive adequate monthly incomes for the rest of their lives. I will leave it to your best judgment to determine what will be suitable amounts. Those amounts will change in the framework of the time that you will need to make those decisions. You also must be very careful with what you do. You will need to find ways to launder the money. It won't be easy because of the large amounts. But remember, Eddie, I'm counting on you to figure out ways to fuck the IRS as much as you can. Why the fuck should they get any of my hard-earned money? The dumb bastards running the government only piss it fucking away on bullshit anyway!" said the Don.

Eddie couldn't help but smile to himself at the Don's referral to his hard-earned money. *Shit! The way he made it sound, you'd think he had a real paying job digging ditches or something,* Eddie thought, chuckling to himself.

"Secondly, Eddie, and this is very important to me. When any of my children or grandchildren get married, you are to make sure they have the finest of weddings. I want them to have weddings like no others. Give them a wedding worthy of a member of Don Francisco Barratino's family. When that time comes, you will tell them that I had made the arrangements and reached my hand from out of my grave to give them such a wonderful wedding."

The Don's request sounded too easy. Eddie was wondering if there was another surprise coming.

"One last thing, buddy. From time to time, I am sure my family will have some special needs. As these kinds of things arise, you are to take care of them as you see fit. Buddy, I know you realize that I am entrusting you with a great deal of money and an even greater amount of responsibility. I know that you have the balls and the mental capability to do all of the things I ask. As long as you see that my family is well provided for, as I have requested, then you are free to do as you choose with the balance of the money. My fortune will make you a very rich man, and with that kind of money will go a tremendous amount of power. Use your power wisely! Remember the ways of your godfather, who, with all his money and power, never forgot to take care of the meek, the poor, and the humble! Always remember the widows and those less fortunate than you. Help them when they are in need. And never overlook the most loyal to you. Make sure they are well rewarded."

Eddie could not believe his ears! He had been expecting some kind of request from the Don that he either couldn't, or wouldn't, fulfill. But the Don had just made things incredibly easy for him!

He could tell their conversation was coming to an end when the Don picked up the power of attorney and the two blue bankbooks and handed them to him. He said, "Here, my young son. I'm giving you these now to take care of for me. I want you to keep these in a safe place and guard them with your life until I ask that they be returned."

Eddie took the documents. "You can trust me, Godfather."

Don Francisco stood up and leaned over the table, placing both his hands on each of Eddie's shoulders. He was relieved to have this matter off his mind. He knew he could depend on his godson. Even with all the money that was involved, he was sure he had made the right choice. Still holding Eddie's shoulders and looking deep into his eyes, he counseled, "I want you to know I have complete faith and trust in you. I know that when the money becomes your responsibility, you will not squander it but invest it wisely. You have never failed me in the past. I know that I can count on you to see that your godfather's wishes will all be carried out. You said I have been like a father to you, and now I'm sure you realize that I have given you all that I have to give. I could do no more even for my own son."

Eddie felt emotionally spent. By accepting the responsibility of Don Francisco's vast fortune, this Mafia son was now pulled closer to the world he had tried so hard to evade. He stood up slowly, aware that Don Francisco had finished his story and his instructions for the conditions.

Don Francisco could see that he had shaken Eddie up, and that he was trying to hold back tears of emotion that were ready to trickle down his face. The Don reached out for him, and the two men gave each other a long, fond embrace.

As they embraced, Eddie reached down and lifted the Don's left hand up toward his face. He tightly squeezed his hand and kissed the large gold ring on his finger.

"Godfather, I wish you a hundred more years. My wish for these papers is that they are something I will never have to use," said Eddie, holding up the documents.

"I am humbled with the trust and the generosity which you have just bestowed upon me. I want you to rest assured that I will be worthy of that trust. I reaffirm my pledge to you that all you have asked of me will be done."

They heard the sounds of voices and car doors slamming and knew that the others were arriving for the meeting. Eddie headed to the private bathroom in the Don's office, and Don Francisco headed to his chair behind his massive desk. It was time for him to hear the weekly requests.

Chapter 3

It was a long-standing tradition. Every Saturday morning was known as the Day of Requests. It wasn't unusual for the Don to schedule other meetings on this day, but his rule had faithfully remained written in rock. The requests always came before any other business.

Seated at his desk, Don Francisco once again checked the time on his watch. It was 10:50 a.m. *Ah shit!* he thought to himself. His meeting with Eddie had taken much longer than he expected, but his cousin Carmine's call had mandated its inevitability and timing. Now he was seriously overscheduled with appointments to hear requests for favors, hold the family council meeting, and then be ready for his birthday party scheduled to begin at five o'clock.

What a fucking day this is going to be, he thought to himself.

His thoughts were interrupted by a knock on the door that led from his office to a large great room.

"Enter," he called out.

The doorknob jiggled, but it was still locked from his private meeting with Eddie. The Don rose to unlock the door. He twisted the lock but did not open the door.

"Come in. It's open now," he said as he returned to his desk.

"Excuse me, Don Francisco. Three people are waiting to see you about their requests." Dominic D'Amico announced. Eddie's father held a prominent position in the family as not only the Don's consigliere but also as his chief advisor. Because he had been Don Francisco's counselor for so many years, he knew the Don's habits and ways better than anyone. He already knew the answer to the question he was getting ready to ask, but for him to make the decision, without the Don's input, would be considered by his boss a serious breach of respect.

Completely wise in the ways of the Mafia, Dominic knew that the powerful men who had already arrived to attend the family meeting would be very angry if they knew they were being kept waiting while the Don listened to a couple of old widows.

"I just figured, with the party today and the family meeting, you might have wanted me to cancel the requests for today," said Dominic. "How do you want me to handle this? It's almost time for the meeting."

"You go tell the boys to shoot pool or play cards or something until I'm ready. They know it is my custom to handle the requests first! I'm not going to change that for them or anyone else!"

"OK, but you know how they are. They're gonna ask me how long they have to wait," said Dominic.

"Listen to me, Dominic! You tell the big shots out there that they know Saturday is the day my home is open for the people with problems to come and see their Don for solutions! So if you're asked, you tell them they will fucking wait, and I will be there as soon as I am finished!" snapped the Don.

"Done," replied Dominic, but he knew full well he wasn't going to say anything like that to the boys.

Just then, Eddie emerged from the bathroom.

"Hi, Dad."

"Hey, Eddie, are you stickin' around? I wanna talk to you after the meeting."

"No. I'm just on my way out. I have some business to take care of before the party, so I gotta get moving."

"Oh no, Eddie, you're not going anywhere. We're not done. Just sit down and relax!" ordered the Don. "Dominic, tell Cappy to bring in Senora Arcarrissi and her son. And as soon as you're done talking to the boys, I want you back in here too.

As Dominic left the Don's office, he recalled Eddie's phone call to him earlier that morning. He wondered what the hell Don Francisco could have been discussing with his son that was so secret that he had locked the office doors. He had always resented the relationship between the Don and his son.

As the door slammed behind Dominic, Don Francisco turned his attention to Eddie.

"Buddy, I want you to attend the family council meeting with me today. I have something I want you to do for me in there."

"B-b-but . . . ," Eddie stuttered.

The Don interrupted, "No fucking *buts*. I know what you're going to say. Remember, I am the fucking boss. I make the rules, and I can break the rules. I don't want you or the others out there in that fucking room to ever forget that!" growled the Don with fire burning in his eyes.

Eddie sat quietly, submissively listening. He knew better than to question Don Francisco when he was in one of his moods.

"What I need you to do in the meeting is to be another pair of eyes for me. I want you to watch for any body language or eye contact between the boys. If you notice anything suspicious, make a mental note. I'm pretty sure I know who is behind this fucking conspiracy against me. If it's who I think, they are stupid, ignorant assholes! I believe, because of their stupidity, they will tip their hand in the meeting when they hear my final decision. But you must be careful not to be obvious, or they will know that I suspect something. It is important for me to know if you see what I see. Do you understand?"

Eddie felt a little irritated that he was talking to him like he was a young kid. Of course he understood.

"Yes, Godfather. I understand," he responded respectfully.

"Good. Now wait in here, but go sit in the back of the room. Just relax while I attend to these requests."

Eddie got up to change seats, just as the silence in the room was broken by a knock on the door.

"Come in," Don Francisco called out from behind his desk.

Eddie watched as the door opened and a young man about twenty years old entered, followed by a woman who Eddie assumed was his mother. Behind her walked Carlo "Cappy" Capparella with pad and pencil in hand.

Don Francisco, with a smile on his face, rose from his chair and walked across the room to greet his guests. He went first to the woman and gave her a warm, affectionate embrace.

"Senora Arcarrissi, como se va?" the Don asked.

"Buono, grazia," the woman replied.

Pointing to her son, she introduced him to Don Francisco. "E son a filia, Giuseppe," she said, continuing to speak in her native tongue.

"Hello, Joseph," said the Don, shaking hands with the young man.

"Hello, Godfather," Joseph replied with an obvious tone of respect in his voice.

Eddie watched as Cappy Capparella silently walked away and melted into the background. He nodded an acknowledgment to Eddie as he took a seat at the rear of the room.

Don Francisco took the woman's hand as he placed his right arm gently around the widow's shoulders. He escorted her to one of the chairs in front of his desk. Seating the woman, the Don motioned to Joseph to sit down in the chair next to his mother and went around to sit in the large leather chair behind his desk.

Leaning back in his chair, Don Francisco began to speak softly, addressing his comments to the widow, who was a longtime acquaintance from the old Italian neighborhood.

"Well, Teresa, how can I help you today?" the Don asked in a kind and gentle manner.

"It'sa my son. He'sa need a job. It'sa harda for me to paya da bills. I no make enougha money witha my little sewing beezinus," she answered in choppy English with a heavy Italian accent.

Don Francisco turned his attention to her son, Joseph.

"Have you really been looking for work, or are you just bullshitting your mother?" the Don asked the boy in a stern manner.

"No, sir. I really been trying. I been trying to get a job wid da County Parks Department as a laborer. Dey're supposed to have some openings, but I go dere every day, and for some reason or udder, I can't get hired. Finally, the udder day, one of da guys working dere told me you have to know somebody to get a job. When I went home and told my mudder, she said we will go see da Godfather. He will take care of dis for us, and here we are," the young man concluded.

He was obviously intimidated by the powerful figure seated in front of him and relieved that he was finished with his answer. Proud of the fact that he had said it just as his mother had coached him earlier.

Don Francisco raised his eyes and looked toward the sound of his office door closing as Dominic quietly entered the room and sat down next to Cappy.

"Senora, is that all you request?" the Don asked the woman.

"Si, Godfather, that'sa all. The money and-a the docators inasurance woulda be a nice-a blessing."

The Don smiled.

"Then, Senora, today is the day for you to consider yourself blessed. What you ask for today will be done," said the Don as he turned his attention to Cappy.

"Do we have Carmen Corelli's home telephone number?" the Don asked.

"Yes, sir."

"Good. Call him and tell him I'm sending someone to see him on Monday. It would please me if he did the best he could for this young man," said Don Francisco as he took a Barratino Farms business card from the holder on his desk. Turning the card over, he wrote the name *Carmen Corelli* and handed it to Joseph.

"First thing Monday morning, you go to the county personnel office and ask for the name on the back of this card. Give the card to no one but him. I repeat, no one but him. Do you understand?"

Joseph nodded.

"Tuesday morning you will begin work. I am doing this for you, but you'd better make sure you help your mother with the money you earn. If I find out you don't, then you will be answering to me. Capire?" asked the Don in a threatening tone as he rose to shake Joseph's hand.

"Ya sure, Godfather, I understand. Don't you worry. I won't let you down. Tank you, sir! Tank you!" exclaimed Joseph, happily pumping the Don's hand.

Still standing, Don Francisco opened the top right drawer of his desk. He pulled out a well-worn metal box. Opening the box, he reached in and brought out a large stack of bills. He counted out ten one-hundred-dollar bills and laid them on top of his desk. He returned the balance of the money to the box and placed it back in the drawer.

The young man and his mother watched the Don in awe, their eyes wide open in amazement. They had never seen that much money before in their lives. Don Francisco picked up the bills and walked around the desk to the woman. Taking her hand, he placed the money in her palm and cupped her small hand in both of his. The woman stared at him in disbelief.

"You know, for you, Teresa, my door is always open," he said to her in a tender voice.

Small tears were running down her cheeks as she replied, "Grazia. Grazia, Godfather." Now completely choked with emotion, she could say no more.

Don Francisco nodded to Cappy, who came over and escorted the mother and her son from the room. The Don sat on the edge of his desk and lit up his cigar while he waited for his next appointment.

Eddie had watched with great interest how the Don had treated his two visitors. He was impressed with the way Don Francisco had made them feel completely at ease, and at the way he had handled the situation.

Taking advantage of the break in activity, Eddie quickly moved to a chair beside his father. Leaning over, he whispered in his ear, "Those fucking guys out there must be furious by now at being kept waiting."

"They are!" Dominic whispered back.

Cappy entered the room again, this time accompanied by another widow and her tall handsome son. Eddie watched as Don Francisco repeated the very same routine in greeting them as he had with the first mother and son. It appeared to Eddie that everything had been rehearsed.

"Well, Senora Vernacottala, how can I help you today?" Don Francisco asked with a disarming smile on his face.

"Godfather, my boy, Anthony, he'sa very smart. He'sa wanna go to the navy college. But his-a teachers say he'sa gotta have a sponsero from-a Washingatona. Ahh, but Godfather, I no even-a vote! I don't even-a know anyone!" she said.

"Ah, but Senora, you are wrong. Are you not here in my home today? Do you not know me?" Don Francisco asked, continuing to smile at her.

"Well-a, yes-a. I'm-a sorry, Godfather. I meana, I knowa no one besides-a you," she answered, appearing to be embarrassed by the Don's questions.

"Ah, but Senora, you will see that knowing me is enough."

He then turned his attention to talk to her son, Anthony.

"Anthony, you have set very high sights for yourself. Do you have the proper grades to meet the academic requirements for the naval academy?"

"Yes, sir! My advisors have told me that my grades more than meet the entry requirements for the academic scholarships that are available. But the problem is, I need to be sponsored by a U.S. senator or congressman," said Anthony.

Don Francisco nodded his head knowingly. He leaned back in his chair, looked toward the back of the room, and spoke out in a raised voice.

"Dominic, you handle this. Call Senator Casey and Congressman Paglia. Tell them I would greatly appreciate their help in this matter. I don't know how we cut through the bureaucratic red tape. Let them decide between themselves the best way this should be handled," said the Don as he rose from his seat to reach out and shake the young man's hand.

"Well, Anthony, if your grades are as you say they are, then we will soon have a fine navy cadet among us. Congratulations and best of luck! I am sure you will make your mother very proud of you. If for some reason you have any problems with your appointment, call this number immediately and ask for Dominic," said Don Francisco, handing the young man a Barratino Farms business card.

The Don walked around his desk and took the woman's hand into his own. With a kind smile on his face, he said, "You have a good son. He will make a fine officer. I know he will make all of us proud of him. You may rest assured, Senora, that what you have asked of me today will be done." He continued to smile patronizingly at the woman as he placed his hand on her shoulder.

"Thank you, Godfather! I don'ta know howa to paya you back!" the woman said, her voice filled with emotion.

"Ah, but Senora, you already have—with your respect and loyalty."

Cappy, sensing the meeting was over, moved forward to escort the mother and son from the room. Eddie watched as Don Francisco glanced down at his wristwatch. He could tell that the Don was feeling pressed for time.

"Dominic, are LaRocca and the Turk here with the Kid?" asked the Don.

"Yeah. They've been waiting outside in the car."

"OK. Go and tell them to bring him in. When Cappy comes back, you and him go out to the meeting room and start rounding up the others. Get them seated and tell them I'll be finished in a few more minutes, and we can begin our meeting.

Dominic walked out of the door leading to the parking lot and immediately returned with the three men. The first through the door was Lorenzo "the Enforcer" LaRocca, a frightening-looking tall man. He had big protruding serpentlike eyes that looked like they belonged more on a reptile than on a man. LaRocca exuded a sense of anger and evil from his very being. It was said that he made even the bravest of men quiver in his presence.

Don Francisco treated LaRocca with a great deal of respect. He knew that LaRocca was his most powerful weapon when problems arose. It was always the Enforcer the Don called on first to use his special talents to resolve any problems. LaRocca was feared by everyone. In the world of the Mafia, he had a reputation of being completely fearless. Because of his furious nature and unquestioning loyalty to Don Francisco, he was considered by everyone a very dangerous enemy to have.

Following LaRocca into the room was a guy Eddie recognized as Mickey Siciliano, better known around town by his boxing nickname, Kid Sicily. He walked with his head down and his eyes toward the floor. Eddie had seen him fight once or twice, and he recalled that the Kid, at one time, had been a ranking heavyweight contender. The story on the street was that too much booze, gambling, and too many women had put an abrupt end to Kid Sicily's promising career. Now he was nothing more than a barroom drunk.

Eddie stared at the Kid's face. He must have sensed Eddie's gaze and raised his head. Their eyes met for only a moment, but it was long enough for Eddie to see the fear and anxiety in the Kid's face. He wondered why the Don's musclemen had brought the Kid here today.

Behind the Kid walked Anthony "Tony the Turk" Scotto—short, squat, and well built with coarse features and long apelike arms. The Turk had a big square head and enormous powerful shoulders. His lifeless gray eyes were sunk deep in his skull. His facial features and the grayish color of his skin made him look like a walking dead man. He had a large flat nose that was pressed so far into his face it caused him to make a constant wheezing noise as he breathed. Together, the Turk and LaRocca created a dangerous and deadly enforcement team against the enemies of Don Francisco. Both men had a reputation for killing at the Don's command, without question or reason.

Dominic, as the Don had ordered, was leaving the room. "Lock the door behind you!" the Don called out.

Looking at LaRocca, he ordered, "Put the Kid in the middle of the room." Don Francisco pulled away one of the chairs from in front of his desk and slid it over to LaRocca.

There was a knock on the door just as LaRocca pushed the Kid down into the chair. Don Francisco nodded to the Turk, who walked over and opened the door. Through the door came a small bent-over old man with silver-gray hair. He was dressed in a shiny well-worn dark blue gabardine suit with frayed cuffs. Around his neck, he wore a stained floral tie over a shirt that was more gray than white. He walked slowly toward Don Francisco, who had motioned him to come and sit in the chair next to his desk.

Eddie was watching the Kid's face as the old man entered the room. He noticed Kid Sicily's eyes begin to blink nervously while his jaw dropped and his face turned ghostly white. Up until now, the Kid must have been at a loss as to why he was picked up by the Don's men, but when he saw the old man, the look on his face reflected his sudden realization of why he had been brought to the farm. He knew now that he was in big fucking trouble.

The Don was sitting on the edge of his desk next to the old man, who was staring at the Kid and shaking his head from side to side.

Eddie watched as LaRocca and the Turk, moving in unison like they had practiced some kind of marching maneuver, both took up positions behind the chair in which the Kid was seated. After the Turk and LaRocca took their places, it became obvious to Eddie what was going to happen next. All that remained unanswered now was *why*. Eddie knew that question would soon be answered when the old man began telling his story.

"Do you know this man?" the Don asked, gesturing to the old man.

"Yes," muttered the Kid.

"I can't fucking hear you!" the Don growled.

"Yes. I know him," the Kid replied in a much more audible tone.

"What's his name? Tell me his name!" ordered the Don.

Eddie could see the sweat beginning to run down Kid Sicily's face as he began to crumble under Don Francisco's questioning.

"What's his fucking name?" LaRocca wheezed as he reached forward and slapped the Kid hard across the face with his bearlike hand.

"Pietro! Pietro Provanzano," the kid answered, a small stream of blood running from the side of his mouth.

The old man was obviously becoming very uncomfortable with this situation and stood up to address the Don.

"With all due respect, Godfather, like I told you on the telephone, all I wanted you to do for me was get him to stay out of my bar. Please, just tell him to do his drinking somewhere else!" the old man pleaded for Kid Sicily.

The Don stared at the old man with ice-cold, unseeing eyes. "Sit down," he ordered. "When you called me for help, this became my problem, and I will handle my problems my way."

Frightened by Don Francisco's words, the old man meekly sat back down and placed his head between his hands, staring silently at the floor. Don Francisco, with his eyes now riveted on the Kid, reached into the desk drawer. A smile began to form on his face as he took out a pair of black leather gloves.

Kid Sicily watched fearfully as Don Francisco began to slowly and deliberately put on the tight-fitting gloves. While doing so, the Don continued to stare fiercely into the Kid's eyes.

Eddie quietly moved around to position himself in a better vantage point where he could clearly see the expression on everyone's face. He had never seen anything like this before and was fascinated by the melodrama taking place before his very eyes.

Eddie's gaze went back and forth to the faces of LaRocca and the Turk. To his surprise, both men were smiling broadly, like it was some kind of a show and they were enjoying the way Don Francisco was playing this scene with the Kid. Eddie turned his attention to the old man's face. It was drawn tight in stunned disbelief. He could see by his actions and the look on his face that the old man had no idea, when he called Don Francisco for his help, the kind of serious and deadly trouble he would be causing for Kid Sicily.

The Don looked vicious and evil as he slowly approached the Kid.

"So you think you're a fucking wolf! A real tough guy! Now let's see how fucking tough you really are!" roared Don Francisco as he smashed the Kid squarely in the face with a powerful roundhouse punch.

The force of the impact tipped the Kid's chair backward into the waiting arms of the Turk and LaRocca, who immediately pushed it back into an upright position.

My god! Eddie thought to himself. *I can't believe it! Don Francisco can be a fucking Jekyll and Hyde at will!*

Eddie looked over at the Turk and LaRocca and could see that they were still smiling broadly, loving every minute of the drama that was taking place.

The Kid's nose and mouth had begun to bleed profusely from Don Francisco's blow. Seeing the blood, Don Francisco walked over to the coffee table, where the towels that he and Eddie had used earlier still lay. He picked one up and threw it to the Kid as he walked back toward him. Eddie realized that the gesture was not motivated by any compassionate act of kindness, but was only done as a practical matter by the Don to keep the Kid's blood from messing up his expensive Oriental carpet.

"So, Mr. Tough Guy, Mr. Provanzano tells me you go into his bar and get so drunk that you start fights with all of his customers. In fact, it has gotten so fucking out of hand people are afraid to go in his joint. You, personally, are responsible for ruining his business!" said the Don between clenched teeth. "Is that true?" he barked at the Kid.

"Yeah, I guess it's true," said the Kid, removing the blood-soaked towel from his mouth so he could speak.

"Then why don't you go into an Irish joint, or a Polack joint, or some other joint and bust them up?" questioned the Don.

The Kid, being a survivor, instinctively knew that in his predicament, it was better to keep his mouth shut if possible. He simply shrugged his shoulders to indicate to Don Francisco he had no answer to the question.

"Then let me give you the answer, you fucking asshole! You only go into the Italian joints and play Mr. Tough Guy because you know they won't call the fucking cops on you! You know that if you pull your tough-guy shit somewhere else, the joint owners would have your ass in jail so fucking fast it would make your stupid head swim!" snapped the Don, ending his sentence with two more powerful punches to Kid Sicily's face.

Mr. Provanzano—a kindly, meek man—had no idea that Don Francisco would resolve his problem in such a frightening and violent manner. He never would have thought he could feel sorry for his tormentor, but after watching what the Don did to Kid Sicily, the old man knew he couldn't take much more and hoped that it would all be over soon. He let out a sigh of relief when he noticed that Don Francisco was taking off the leather gloves.

As he removed the gloves from his hands, Don Francisco began speaking to the Kid, who was still wiping blood from his face.

"Listen to me good now, you motherfucker! If I ever hear that you have fucked with Mr. Provanzano again or, for that matter, any other Italian businessman, I am going to send you swimming with the fish! Do you understand me, Mr. Tough Guy?" asked the Don viciously, staring into Kid Sicily's eyes.

Too frightened to answer, Kid Sicily could only nod his head in the affirmative. He knew that Don Francisco wasn't just making idle threats. The Kid knew that if he caused one more problem for Mr. Provanzano, he would die.

Looking toward the Turk and LaRocca, the Don said, "Get this fucking piece of shit out of here! Have one of the boys take him where he wants to go, but I want both of you guys to stay here for the meeting."

The Turk and LaRocca picked up Kid Sicily from his chair and took him out the back door.

Mr. Provanzano had risen from his chair and was trembling over the scene he had just witnessed. Without a word, he took Don Francisco's hand into his small quivering hands and bent over to kiss the big gold ring on the Don's finger. He was relieved and full of gratitude toward Don Francisco for fixing a problem that, in his mind, had appeared to be impossible to fix.

"Don Francisco, I had no idea when I asked for your help that this kind of thing would take place," said Mr. Provanzano apologetically.

The Don, in a regal manner, like a king talking to one of his subjects, placed one hand on the old man's shoulder, giving him a warm, comforting smile.

"Don't you worry, my old friend. People like him are nothing more than wild animals. The only way to control a wild animal is through force and fear. He won't be bothering you again."

Mr. Provanzano, feeling a rush of relief flow over him, began to weep. Suddenly he felt secure and comfortable being under the protection and control of such a wonderful and powerful man.

"How can I repay you, Godfather?" humbly asked the old man.

Without hesitation, Don Francisco replied, "With your loyalty and respect. Who knows? There may even be a time when I may call on you for a favor in return." The Don put his arm around the old man's shoulders and escorted him to the door that led to the parking lot.

Everyone was gone from the room now except for Eddie, who was sitting quietly in his chair. He was reflecting on the events he had just watched take place. The Don's voice broke the silence.

"I've gotta take a piss," said the Don, looking at his watch as he walked briskly toward the bathroom. When he emerged from the bathroom, Eddie noticed that he had freshened up and combed his long silver-gray hair. He watched with interest as Don Francisco psyched himself up for the next big ordeal that was awaiting him in the next room. Don Francisco stopped just outside the door leading into the great room. He straightened up to his full six-foot height and at the same time, took a deep breath and pulled in his stomach.

At seventy years old, Don Francisco is still a fine figure of a man, Eddie thought as he got up to go with the Don into the meeting.

"Don't forget, Eddie, you are coming only to observe. Watch the faces, but mostly the eyes. The eyes tell everything. Always remember that the eyes are the windows to the soul. But I must caution you to be very careful not to be obvious or to tip our hand," said the Don in a soft, secretive voice.

Then placing his hand gently in the middle of Eddie's back, he pushed him forward so that when he opened the door, Eddie would be the first one entering the next room.

Chapter 4

It was an hour beyond the appointed time of the family council meeting. As Eddie and the Don entered the great room, a hush began to fall across the cavernous space, gradually drowning out the noisy clamor of male voices and laughter.

"Well, it's about time!" Eddie clearly heard the snide remark but could not distinguish the voice behind it. Nor could he discern from which part of the room it came.

All eyes began to focus on the Don as he walked toward a folding table that had been set up on the large raised hearth of the imposing fieldstone fireplace.

Eddie drifted as inconspicuously as possible to one of the rough-hewn planked staircases winding upward along each side of the room. He chose to sit on the third step, feeling he would be able to see the faces of everyone in the room from this vantage point.

By raising his hand, the Don brought all of the men to silence.

"I am pleased to see that you all made it to this meeting since I gave you such short notice." He paused and then continued, "And I apologize for making you wait, but I had some important matters that needed my immediate attention."

"It's OK, boss!" yelled a voice. "I won eight hundred smackers playing cards!" It was Jimmy "the Brute" Testa, laughing as he spoke.

The sound of laughter filled the room. But behind the smiles and beyond the din, Don Francisco could sense that some of his family members were boiling inside from having to sit around and wait for the meeting to begin. Deciding to take advantage of the Brute's remark and lighten up the atmosphere, the Don, known for his quick wit, fired off a reply that embodied the kind of humor that appealed to these men.

"OK, then, Jimmy! Get your ass up here and pay me my usual 10 percent vigorish!"

Laughter burst out around the room. Several of the boys began poking each other and pointing fingers at the Brute.

They knew that making his wisecrack was actually going to cost Jimmy "the Brute" 10 percent of his winnings. But eighty dollars was an amount he would gladly pay in return for the attention he was getting from the Boys. Everyone's eyes were on Jimmy's short, round figure as he proudly strutted across the room toward the Don. Stepping onto the hearth, he handed the Don a hundred-dollar bill and held out his hand.

"What are you waiting for, Jimmy?" the Don asked, smiling broadly and playing to his crowd.

"My fucking change!" he said, with a wide grin across his chubby face. "Ten percent of eight hundred dollars is eighty bucks! That makes your vig eighty bucks. You owe me twenty smackers!" His expression boasted self-pride in his mathematical skills.

Jimmy kept his hand outstretched toward the Don as he turned to smile at all of the laughing faces.

"Tell you what, Jimmy, let's just call the twenty a tip," said the Don, flashing his white teeth in a broad smile. It was obvious that he was also enjoying the humor of the moment, and realizing he was on a roll, he continued.

"As a matter of fact, tell you what I'll do, Jimmy. Tomorrow I'll put the twenty bucks in the collection basket at church and ask Father Azzi to say a prayer for you that the prick fairy will come to visit your house one night and make your prick grow as big as a chicken's!"

At that, he pushed Jimmy off the hearth with a friendly shove. The men roared with laughter. Above the loud clapping, they jeered him and playfully grabbed at his crotch as he made his way past them.

Don Francisco was a master at manipulating people and situations. With the skill of a professional performer, he had instinctively played Jimmy's chance remark to his benefit. He waited patiently for the laughter to subside before speaking.

"OK, OK. Now that we've had our fun, it's time to do business. Anyone here who is not a member of the family council now needs to leave the room."

Eddie heard the sound of chairs scraping across the floor. Several men rose and filed out the door. He assumed that all of these men were either drivers, bodyguards, or stooges of the family hierarchy.

While Don Francisco waited for the men to leave, he called out to his nephew Vincenzo "Blackie" Barratino. Blackie had the reputation of being a small-time hood with big-time ideas. Eddie knew that the Don was not very fond of his nephew and thought of him as a two-bit punk.

"Blackie, get some music on!"

"No problem," Blackie replied as he immediately rose and went to the sound equipment.

"That's OK, just a little louder. Yeah, right there. Perfect."

Blackie nodded an acknowledgment and returned to his seat.

Don Francisco looked around the room to make sure he had everyone's attention and then officially began the meeting.

"I have called . . ."

"Excuse me, Don Francisco! With all due respect . . ."

The Don cut off Sam Lacavoli, who had risen to his feet and interrupted him in midsentence.

"What's your fucking problem, Sam?" the Don snapped.

"It's Eddie D'Amico. Did you know he's still in the room? He has no business being here. He's not a made member of the family! He has no sponsor, and he's never taken the test of fire!"

The test of fire that Lacavoli referred to was a ritual of the family whereby a tightly balled-up piece of paper would be placed into the hand of a person being initiated into the family. The paper would then be set on fire, and as it burned, searing the flesh of the person's palm, they were expected to withstand the pain and, at the same time, take an oath of secrecy and make a pledge of undying loyalty to the Don and the family. Anyone being initiated into the family clearly understood the rules: any betrayal of the oath would carry with it an immediate penalty of death.

Don Francisco angrily rose to his feet to deal with Sam Lacavoli. What Lacavoli didn't know was that the Don was aware of the conspiracy against him and that he suspected Sam as the ringleader of the treacherous plot.

Don Francisco pounded his fist on the table.

"Do you think I am stupid and don't know who is in this fucking room?" he yelled. "Eddie D'Amico has a sponsor! I, Don Francisco Barratino, sponsor him!"

Daring and unintimidated by the Don's anger, Lacavoli undauntedly, continued to bore in.

"Then what about the test of fire?" he demanded. "He hasn't taken the test of fire! Rules are fuckin' rules! That means he has no fucking business in this room!"

The other men looked around at each other in complete shock at Lacavoli's challenge and disrespect of the Don's authority. Eddie began to feel uncomfortable and embarrassed by the attention and the friction his presence was causing. He started to rise from the step.

Seeing Eddie's movement, the Don yelled at him.

"Just stay right the fuck where you are!" he ordered, knowing full well there was no way he was going to cave in to his antagonistic challenger.

He glared at Lacavoli as he spoke, his eyes ablaze with fury.

"As the ruler of this family, I waive the test of fire! I have known Eddie D'Amico for over thirty-five years. He has already proven his loyalty to me and to our family. Thirty-five years is a long time. For that matter, it is a lot fucking longer than you have been in this family, Mr. Lacavoli! More importantly, Eddie D'Amico has proven his loyalty by passing a more difficult test. The test of time! This issue is settled!" he yelled, slamming his hand on the table. The Don continued to glare through evil eyes at Sam Lacavoli until Lacavoli finally lowered his head and sat back down.

Before the Don seated himself again, he angrily looked around the room.

"Now! Does anyone else have a problem with my decision?" he challenged.

He slowly and deliberately scanned all of the faces of the men seated before him. There was the silence of death as every head in the room shook from side to side.

Eddie gazed around the room and noticed that LaRocca and the Turk had positioned themselves in the rear of the room. They were standing with feet spread apart and hands inside their jackets.

Holy shit! Could this challenge of authority result in the Don ordering Sam Lacavoli being blown away right here in front of everyone? Eddie wondered.

The incident regarding Eddie's presence was obviously settled, but Don Francisco turned his head to glare again at Lacavoli.

"Now that the bullshit is out of the way, let me tell you the reason for the meeting today."

Faithful to the Don's instructions, Eddie began to closely watch the faces of the family members present. As he scanned the faces of the men in the room, he felt a sense of naivety come over him. After all these years of closeness to the Don and the family, he thought he had known who most of the family members were. Today he was surprised to see faces of men he never would have guessed had anything to do with the mob.

Present in the room were some of the major players in the Italian business community. Freddie "Flowers" Sortino, a florist shop owner. Enrico Cappiano, a wealthy member of the local social set, was a shoe manufacturer. His picture was always in the paper for donating to charitable causes. Sitting with Enrico was the owner of the city's largest lumber yard, Luigi Lanza. His name was plastered all over the outfield walls at the baseball stadium.

There were others. A popular, well-known wrecking contractor, Rocky Nucci, then Mr. Terranova, the meek-looking old guy who owned a large music store. Sitting next to him was Romy Marchetti, a wealthy commission house owner, whose business was selling wholesale fruits and vegetables to the local supermarkets. Marchetti had also become politically powerful. He was well known throughout the city for his reputation as being one of the largest contributors to political campaigns. Because of his donations, Romy had many politicians in his back pocket.

Eddie wasn't surprised, however, to see the junk man, Stefano "Lucky" Carlucci, who killed people and made dead bodies disappear in his junkyard for the Don.

Eddie suddenly realized he had allowed his thoughts to wander away from the meeting and hastily returned his attention to what the Don was saying.

"And so I have given the matter much thought and have come to these decisions. With regard to expanding our territories across the river into East St. Louis, my answer is no. That decision is final and not open for any further discussion."

The Don paused and watched the men as they absorbed his words, checking faces for any sign of a negative reaction.

Eddie noticed Sam Lacavoli catch the attention of his brother, Nick, seated at the next table. Nick, ever so slightly, raised his eyes to look at the ceiling. Eddie had no doubt that there was some kind of silent communication taking place between the brothers when he saw Sam acknowledge Nick's gesture with a barely discernible nod of his head.

"And we have lived in peace with our black friends across the river for almost twenty years. What they have done on their side of the river has been their business. What our family does on our side has been our business. One-Eyed Jack has been a man of honor and respect. Over the years, he has proven to me to be a man of great courage. He also has balls. Big balls. We have managed to live together in peace.

I have no quarrel with him. He has lived up to our agreement, but I have no doubt if we fuck with him and his people and try to invade his numbers and drug business, it will most certainly bring about a bloody war. A war in which many on both sides will die. A war that, even if we win, will turn the taste of victory to bitter ashes in our mouths because of the price we will have to pay with the lives of many of our family members."

Eddie knew that the Don was referring to Jack "One-Eyed Jack" Shepard, ruler of the black mafia of East St. Louis.

At this point, Eddie noticed that most of the men were nodding their heads in agreement. He knew, as well as the rest of them, that war would certainly mean giving up the peace and freedom they had become accustomed to and enjoyed for so long.

"Some months ago, some of you discussed that we also consider expanding our operations into the drug trade. Since then, we have had no further discussions about it at our meetings. I know there are some of you that still have the interest and believe it is the right thing for us to do. As I promised, I have given the idea some serious consideration. I realize that the drug business offers the opportunity to make large profits, but after I weighed everything up very carefully, I have come to the decision that we do not need the troubles that the drug business would bring to our family . . ."

Again, Eddie caught sight of the Lacavoli brothers exchanging eye contact and sharing what they thought were their own secret little smiles. They seemed oblivious to the fact that he was now watching their every move.

"And that the profit from drugs is not worth the risk," continued the Don in a serious and somber tone. "But nevertheless, my final decision is to stay as far away from the drug business as possible. Believe me, it is a filthy, dirty business that destroys people's lives. That kind of business has no place in our family. We will leave it to those who have no soul or conscience. To those who answer to and only live for their own greed."

A few of the mobsters began whispering to one another. As Eddie perused the faces of the powerful and wealthy men assembled in the room, a light suddenly went on in his head. He flashed back to something he had overheard his father discussing with the Don over the telephone many years ago. His father talked about loaning people money, taking back 50 percent interest and still having the loan paid back. Eddie was only a kid then. He had forgotten all about it. None of it had really made much sense until just now. All of the businessmen in that room today were obligated to Don Francisco in a very big way.

My God! Eddie thought to himself. *What a fucking score! These guys are here because the Don is a silent 50 percent partner and owns a piece of every business represented in this room! No wonder he's been able to accumulate such a fortune!*

Eddie realized that he had allowed his mind to wander away from the meeting again. He was irritated with himself and hoped he had not missed something crucial in the Don's words or the faces of the men he was supposed to be watching.

"And drugs are a rotten business that sooner or later will wind up in the hands of children." The Don's voice softened as he continued, "We call our business our familia. We pride ourselves in protecting the widows and caring for anyone who falls under the umbrella of our family and is in need of our help."

Don Francisco rose from his chair and began talking like a father to the men in the room.

"Are we, then, for a few fucking dollars, going to turn ourselves into animals, greedy pigs, and destroy the very heart of what we and our familia is all about? No! We are men of honor and respect, and we will remain true to our principles! My friends, there will be no drugs in our family! We will start no wars with our black friends across the river by invading their territories! My decisions are final!" His closed fist pounded the table after his last word.

Freddie Flowers jumped to his feet and began clapping enthusiastically at the Don's conclusion. "Bravo, Don Francisco! So be it! It is done!" Freddie called out.

Don Francisco's son, Sally, along with Jimmy "the Brute" and Cappy were the next to stand and clap. All of the other men in the room quickly joined them in the applause. Even the Lacavoli brothers appeared to willingly join the applause.

Eddie rose to his feet to get a better view, still trying to take careful note of the reactions on the faces of all the men in the room.

Don Francisco, with a broad smile on his face, had his hand raised, gesturing for silence.

"Listen," the Don called out, "our business is over, but don't forget, the party starts at five o'clock. I'm looking forward to seeing all of you there."

Don Francisco began working his way across the room to where his son, Sally, was talking to Tough Tony Battista, Billy "B" Bellini, and Nappy Napolitano.

Tough Tony was a captain in the family as well as an enforcer. His job was to control the family loan-sharking business. Quite adept at making collections on late payments, he wouldn't hesitate to break an arm or a leg or anything else he deemed required.

Billy "B" Bellini's assignment was acting as liaison between the labor unions and the Barratino family.

Nappy Napolitano, who had more talent than brains, possessed a special forte when it came to cracking safes or any other kind of lock.

As the Don neared his son and the three men, Tough Tony spoke up. "Hey, boss, you're right! We're doin' OK the way we are. We got enough ways to make money without fuckin' up the kids and startin' wars." Billy B, nodding in agreement, added, "Hey, boss, if dese fuckin' guys want more money, let dem go blow a box like I do or pull a job or somedin'. Tell dem to get off der ass and go do a honest day's work for a change. Dis is da land o' opportunity, right? Der's plenty a ways to make a buck without fuckin' wid da kids," said Nappy.

"Yeah, thanks, fellas. And don't forget, I'm expecting to see you all at the party later," said Don Francisco as he put his arm around Sally's shoulder, steering his son away from the group toward a private corner.

"What's up, Pop?"

"Sally, I'm really going to need your help tonight at the party. There will be many important people here. Some I haven't seen in years. Everyone will be wanting to spend time with me. I want you to take some of that heat off me by mingling more with the guests. Tu capire?"

"Yeah, Pa. Sure. No problem."

"I mean it, Sally. Don't be late. I want you here at five o'clock when people start arriving."

"Hey, don't worry about it, birthday boy. I'll be a perfect host," Sally said, smiling.

"Make sure of it," his father warned as he caught Eddie's eye across the room.

Don Francisco gave a slight nod toward his office. The exchange of glances between his father and Eddie did not go unnoticed by Sally. He angrily wondered what was going on now that he was excluded from once again. His jealousy and hatred for Eddie grew more intense with each passing day.

Eddie was already seated in one of the big comfortable chairs when the Don entered, closing and locking the door behind him.

"Well, what did you see, buddy?" the Don asked as he sat in the chair opposite Eddie.

"You were right about the eyes. There's definitely something going on with the Lacavoli brothers!"

"Yes. The looks they gave each other didn't escape me either. I purposely didn't tell you any names before the meeting because I didn't want to influence your observations in any way. I'm glad you were perceptive. I've been suspicious of those two for a while now. By this time tomorrow, I'll have them singing like canaries," said the Don with a great deal of self-assurance.

"But can you wait till then? Isn't that too risky?" asked Eddie with sincere concern.

"Those idiots have no idea I suspect them. I'm not worried. Tomorrow after church will be soon enough. Those two jack-offs don't have the balls to act against me on their own, and from the way the meeting ended, I'd say they have no support within the family," the Don comfortably replied.

"Godfather, with all due respect, I think maybe you should confront them now."

"Well, buddy, I think maybe you should get going so you'll be dressed better for my party! It's only a few hours from now, you know."

Chapter 5

T he blaring car horn from behind jolted Eddie from his absorption, and his car tires squealed as he stepped on the gas, finally seeing the green light. Blindly, he reached to the passenger seat, picked up the nondescript manila envelope, and fondled it as he drove. A swift chill ran up his spine. *My god, I'm holding Don Francisco's whole life in my hand!*

Nearing his home, he traveled down the long wide boulevard lined with stately mature oak trees. The scenic beauty distracted him from the envelope. His mind shifted to the huge old homes that in their day had been considered mansions. He admired their expansive front yards resplendent with gigantic well-manicured trees rising from the lush green lawns. He turned into the long driveway of his English Tudor home and parked opposite the side door and then climbed the three steps and opened the heavy, solid wood door that led into the kitchen.

Danni had the telephone to her ear but quickly hung up the receiver when she heard him come in. She was a tall, willowy woman with a fine, curvaceous body and full, round breasts. Her jet-black hair was fashioned in a short pageboy style, and her flashing dark brown eyes gave a hint of her full-blooded Italian ancestry.

"Hi," he said nonchalantly.

She placed both hands squarely on her hips. "I was just trying to call you on your car phone. As usual, you screwed me over again! You promised me you'd be home right after the market. You couldn't have been at the market all this time! Where the hell have you been?"

Cat's face and her wild blonde hair flashed in his mind. "Hey! Settle down. I've been at the farm all day," he lied, feeling his usual sense of momentary guilt.

"Don Francisco needed to see me on some business matters. We just finished up."

"Liar," she spewed under her breath.

Wanting to change the subject, he asked, "Are you coming with me to his birthday party?" But he already knew what her answer would be.

"Hell, no! They're your friends, not mine! Not one of them is worth the powder it would take to blow them all to hell! They're nothing more than a bunch of criminals and hoodlums!"

"I guess that means you've made up your mind," he cracked.

"It's not funny, Eddie. You go ahead and keep kissing their ass. Someday you're going to pay, and pay plenty. When that day comes, you'll wish you had listened to me," she ended.

"It's getting late. I've gotta shower," he said, recognizing the futility of their conversation. He bounded up the stairs.

His pursuit of success in close association with members of the mob had strained their marriage to the point of total destruction. He had been raised to believe that only money and power were the true yardsticks in measuring a man's success. This philosophy had caused him to be so driven by those goals; he had neglected his marriage, spending very little personal time with his wife.

In return, she sought vengeance and began using deprivation of sex as her tool of punishment, but her contrivance only drove him from her bed into the beds of copious other faceless women. Danni lived with her own guilt, having come to realize that her self-righteous and judgmental attitudes, as well as her piercing tongue, had only helped to drive a wedge between them. Overtime, she could no longer compel herself to stroke his big ego with the praise and recognition he constantly craved and considered his due merit for all of his efforts to succeed at all costs.

Danni knew that she had made a serious mistake and wanted him back desperately, but too much had passed between them, and she knew that she would never have the patience to compete with his goals, which ceaselessly took priority over her.

And so they remained living together. Bound devoutly to her Catholicism, Danni refused to even speak of divorce. As time went on, he continued to provide very well for her and their teenage daughter, Ashley, never denying any monetary thing they asked for. But only when they were together in public did he make a special point of showing his wife a great deal of respect so that no one would ever suspect that their marriage had been over for years.

In Eddie's world, cheating men were envied and held in high regard by their peers, proudly referred to as "cocksmen" among themselves. On the other hand, if the wives cheated on their husbands, the women were ostracized and looked down upon with disdain. They were considered *butanas*—whores—typifying the double set of standards by which Eddie and other Italian men lived.

As he showered, he reflected on his marriage.

What a mess! Eddie thought to himself, feeling as if he was in a prison that he had built for himself and from which there was no escape.

Danni stuck her head into the bathroom and called out loud enough for him to hear over the running water.

"Eddie, it's Carmen. He needs to talk to you. Says it's very important." She handed him the portable phone as he stepped out from the shower.

"Hi, Carm."

"I'm sorry to bother you in the shower, but I wanted to catch you before you left the house."

"Well, you got me. Stark ass fucking naked, to boot", Eddie wisecracked.

"You're going to the Don's party, aren't you?" Carmen asked.

"Are you kidding? How could I not go?" responded Eddie.

"Would you mind picking up me and Joey? You know the police and the FBI will be out there taking pictures and license plate numbers, and I'd rather they didn't get mine."

"Why, Carm? No balls?" he quipped.

"My balls are just big enough to go there, but I don't need to see a picture of my license plate on the front page of the fucking morning paper!"

"I was just fucking kidding, Carm. Don't come unglued! The ride's no problem, but I'm gonna be leaving pretty soon. I told Don Francisco I'd be there on time."

"Shit, Eddie. I didn't plan on being there this early."

Judge Carmen J. Carlivatti, one of his closest friends, lived just a few houses down the street from him.

"Look, I'm standing here soaking wet. What's your pleasure?" Eddie asked.

"OK, OK. Come over when you're ready. I'll have Joey drive to my house now. We'll both be ready when you get here. Thanks, Eddie," said the judge.

"You got it, Carm. See ya in about half an hour."

He had blown dry his long black hair so that it was fluffed full and wavy. His tanned face was accented by the whiteness of his teeth and his high cheekbones.

Eddie's vanity guided him in selecting a white suit with matching white shirt, socks, and shoes, knowing it would admirably accentuate his deep tan and dark hair. He wanted to look his best, knowing there would be a lot of important people at the party.

Danni walked back into the room just as her husband was placing a powder blue silk hanky into his jacket pocket. *His favorite color*, she thought. Sitting on the edge of the bed, she silently watched him finish dressing.

He's still a good-looking son of a bitch, she thought to herself admiringly.

She couldn't help but notice how dashingly handsome her husband looked.

What really bothered her was knowing that other women would be thinking the same thing.

I wonder who he'll be fucking tonight, she brooded to herself.

He walked over to the bed and kissed her on the cheek. He knelt down on one knee in front of her so he could look her squarely in the eye.

"Danni, I wish you were coming with me," he said sincerely.

Danni knew he meant what he said and sadly closed her eyes to hold back the tears she felt coming.

Down the street at the judge's home, Rose Carlivatti walked into the bedroom just as her husband was putting the finishing touches to his tie.

"You know, you're making a big mistake by going there," she said. "You don't have to kiss anyone's ass anymore. Remember, you're a judge now. But you'll never get to be a Supreme Court judge if you keep screwing around with those people."

"Look, Rose, you don't understand. That has nothing to do with it. Don Francisco was like a father to all of us when we were growing up in the neighborhood," answered the judge.

"Oh, give me a break! For crying out loud, Carm! The police and the FBI will be there taking pictures! You don't need those kinds of problems! Because of your so-called friendship with them, your image has been tainted since you first became a judge. Isn't enough enough?" Rose pleaded.

"Look, honey, after all this time, you still don't understand Italians. It has to do with honor and respect. Respect must be paid back with respect. Maybe paybacks are a bitch, but in the Italian world, they must be paid back nonetheless," the judge philosophized.

"Carmen, what the hell are you trying to tell me? That putting your career at risk is some kind of Italian thing?" she asked in disbelief.

"Look, honey, in the first place, I don't believe I'm putting my career on the line. Secondly, Don Francisco has been good to a lot of us guys who struggled to get out of the old neighborhood and make something of ourselves. Shit, Rose, he loaned Eddie D'Amico the money to go into business. He also loaned me and Ricky Riccio the money to go to college. That's just to name a few off the top of my head. And have you forgotten that when we tried to pay him back he wouldn't accept our money? Now that we've become successful, thanks to his help, it wouldn't be right if we treated him like some kind of leper. He's deserving of our respect, and if Eddie and I, and guys like us, have to take some heat by doing the right thing, then that's the way it will have to be!" said Judge Carlivatti, trying to prove to his wife that his reputation as a principled, stand-up guy was well earned.

The sound of a horn ended their discussion.

"That's Eddie. Will you run down and tell Joey to go out and tell him I'll be right there?"

Feeling thwarted again in this recurring controversy, Rosie flung both arms up in the air as an I-just-give-up attitude.

Joey Cariola also grew up in the old neighborhood. As a child, he had never been allowed to hang out at the Don's house with the rest of the kids. But because he was now the judge's bailiff, the Don had requested that the judge bring him to the party. Don Francisco never missed taking advantage of anyone who could potentially be of any service to him.

The white Fleetwood Cadillac sped west down the deserted country road. Eddie glanced at the dashboard clock. It was 5:05 p.m. He pushed down harder on the accelerator. The needle moved effortlessly to eighty-five miles per hour. From his position in the front seat, the judge leaned over to look at the speedometer.

"Hey, cowboy, you're going to get yourself a ticket. They have speed traps through this corridor," the judge said knowingly.

"Shit, Carm, you need to take a Dale Carnegie course and get a better sense of your own importance," joked Eddie. "What cop is gonna give me a fuckin' speeding ticket with you sitting at my side?"

Joey piped up from the backseat.

"Don't worry, Eddie. If you get a ticket, just give it to me. I'll take care of it. Everything passes across my desk anyway," chortled Joey, referring to the fact that as the judge's bailiff, he was responsible for setting the judge's calendar. The three friends chuckled at his remark.

"Joey, have you ever been out to the farm?" the judge asked.

"Yeah. Once, a few years ago, I attended a political barbecue the Don was hosting for one of the county supervisors. But I didn't get to see much. It was held outside by the pool. Hey, but tell me something, Eddie. I heard a rumor sometime ago that you did all of the remodeling and construction work on the farm for the Don—is that true?"

"Yeah, Joey. It's no rumor. It's a fact. I did the new buildings, all of the remodeling and grading—the whole nine yards."

"Geez, from what I saw out there, that must have been some big job! I heard the Don's got the big bucks. Did you take him for a bundle?" Joey asked.

Eddie laughed, looking at his friend in the rearview mirror.

"I wish, Joey, I wish." Eddie turned toward the judge and smiled. "Tell him, Carm. Tell him the way things work when you do business with Don Francisco."

Carmen turned halfway around in his seat to face Joey.

"Joey, when people do work for the Don, there's one unspoken rule that everyone understands going in. Nobody but nobody makes money on the Don for anything. In fact, you consider yourself lucky if you get your cost back and he lets you keep your balls!"

"Get outta here! Is that what happened to you, Eddie?" Joey asked. "You had to do all that fucking work for no profit?"

"Yep. He treated me just like everybody else. But it wasn't such a bad deal. Ya see, he likes me, so he let me keep my balls.

They all laughed.

"There it is!" Eddie exclaimed as they came over the top of the hill.

"Yeah, and there's the cops babysitting outside the front gate," said the judge, sliding down as far as possible in his seat.

As they drove closer, Eddie could make out two panel trucks and several unmarked cars that he assumed belonged to the FBI and the local law enforcement agencies. As they neared the entry to the compound, Eddie and his passengers watched with silent interest the scene going on outside the gates of the Don's estate.

Upon pulling into the driveway, they passed several men standing against the hood of a car parked near the driveway entrance. They were busy writing down the license plate numbers of all the cars entering the compound. As he drove by, Eddie recognized that part of the group taking down the numbers was Lou "Bee" Stinger, an undercover vice cop and a very close friend. When Lou saw Eddie, he dropped his eyes to the ground as the white Cadillac passed.

Allowing his attention to become distracted by the group of cops taking plate numbers caused Eddie to almost rear-end the big black Lincoln in front of him. The Lincoln was stopped alongside a rent-a-cop security officer who was stationed at the gate collecting invitations. Eddie noticed an official brass city emblem attached to the rear of the Lincoln above the license plate frame. Just as the gate began to swing open for the Lincoln to pass through, its driver turned around to speak to one of his passengers. Eddie recognized the driver as city councilman Elwood Doyle, a corrupt politician who had been in Don Francisco's back pocket for years.

When the judge saw the councilman hand his invitation to the security guard at the gate, he was prompted to ask, "Eddie, did you remember to bring your invitation?"

"No. I left it home."

The judge looked upset at Eddie's answer.

"Shit! I didn't bring mine either. I thought for sure you'd have yours," said the judge with concern in his voice.

Eddie turned and gave the judge a smug smile.

"Just cool your fucking jets, Carm. I'll handle it," boasted Eddie.

The rent-a-cop motioned Eddie to pull forward. Ignoring the officer's signal to stop, Eddie tried to drive right by him so he could get to the call pedestal and enter his code that would open the gate. His plan, however, was disrupted by one of the other security officers who jumped in front of the moving Cadillac. Eddie had to slam on the brakes to keep from striking him.

The security officer who was in charge of taking invitations stormed over to the open driver's window of the Cadillac. It was instantly obvious from his demeanor and red face that he was in a controlled rage.

Glaring at Eddie, he put on an act of civility.

"Afternoon, sir," he said in a surly tone through clenched teeth. "May I have your invitation?"

Eddie glanced in his rearview mirror and saw that the cars behind him in the driveway were backed up almost out to the highway.

"I left my invitation at home, but if you let me get to the pedestal, you'll see that I don't need one," Eddie said in a polite and friendly tone.

The rent-a-cop didn't like Eddie's attempt to usurp his authority and drive past him as if he didn't exist. He decided to teach this wise guy a lesson.

Snidely, the guard announced, "I'm sorry, sir. That's going to present a problem. My instructions are very clear. No invitation, no admittance. So I guess that means you'll just have to go home and get it."

The guard smiled and was obviously enjoying sticking it to Eddie. Without waiting for a response, he began signaling the cars behind Eddie to back up so the Cadillac could turn around.

Now totally embarrassed by the scene he was causing, Eddie's temper suddenly flared.

"Hey, Officer! Come back here!" Eddie yelled. "Tell your man to get out of my fucking way so I can drive to the call pedestal, and this whole problem will disappear!"

The guard ignored Eddie's request and continued to motion the whole line of traffic to move back toward the highway.

Eddie was now furious at the guard's stupidity. He began moving the Cadillac slowly forward, pushing the bumper against the body of the guard who was still standing in front of the car. The guard refused to move and placed his hands on the hood of the car. But when Eddie continued to inch the Cadillac forward, the guard began backpedaling as quickly as he could. The other guard took notice of what was happening and came running back over to the open window of the Cadillac. Now only a few feet from the pedestal, Eddie ignored the guards until one of them, now fuming in anger, placed his hands menacingly on his service revolver.

"Stop this car right now!" he ordered.

"And I'm telling you, you dumb motherfucking asshole, let me get to that pedestal, and you'll see the only problem we have here is in your stupid fucking head!" shouted Eddie loud enough to wake the dead.

Suddenly, the ominous figure of LaRocca appeared from out of nowhere. Standing just to the other side of the gate, he yelled over to the guard. "Hey, dickhead! You heard him—get the fuck outta the man's way!" LaRocca ordered in his usual menacing manner. Both guards shriveled up at LaRocca's frightening presence and immediately moved out of the way of the Cadillac.

The judge could tell that Eddie was embarrassed by the incident and decided to rub it in a little.

"Just cool your jets, Carm," mimicked the judge laughing.

"Yeah, Eddie. You were one slick motherfucker! You almost got us shot just getting through the gate!" Joey joked.

"Fuck you, guys!" he laughed.

He punched his code number in at the pedestal, and the gate swung open. As the Cadillac passed through the gate, Eddie thought he could discern a slight smile on LaRocca's terrifying face.

"My god, Eddie, who's that fucking monster?" asked the judge, turning in his seat and continuing to stare back at the massive lurking figure. "Is that LaRocca?"

"Yep, Lorenzo LaRocca, in person," Eddie replied. No further explanation was needed.

"So you have your own security code to this place. Don't you think you're getting yourself a little too involved?" the judge asked.

"It's no big deal, Carm. I was given the code when I had men working here every day. I had to be able to come and go at will. When the work was done, the Don just never took my code out. That's what you call trust!" said Eddie, winking at the judge.

"Yeah, I got your trust right here!" replied the judge, grabbing his crotch.

"Whoa! Look at all the cars! It's early, and there are already loads of people here," noted Joey.

Eddie was having difficulty finding a place to park. The early arrivals had already parked bumper to bumper on both sides of the wide driveway all the way down to the barn. He knew that there would be plenty of parking on the large gravel lot behind the barn, but he didn't feel like walking that far. He cruised around again and spotted a small opening between the bumpers of two parked cars. He squeezed the Cadillac between them and parked on the lawn under a large oak tree.

"You're parking on the grass!" Joey warned.

"No shit. Do you think the Don will have me shot?"

Laughing, they got out of the car and followed several groups of people heading toward the canvas-covered tennis courts. The canvas was a festive pink-and-white-striped pattern. Eddie admired someone's clever idea to completely cover the top and all sides of the tennis court's chain-link fence, converting the entire area into a huge colorful tent.

As the men were walking, Joey and the judge were looking off to the side, admiring a sumptuous brunette, when suddenly Eddie stopped in his tracks, causing the other men to bump into him.

"Hey! What the fuck's the matter?" Joey asked.

"Listen!" The light wind was carrying the sounds from the speakers inside the tent in their direction. "When the moon hits your eye like a big pizza pie . . . ," the words of the song drifted. "Do you hear it?" asked Eddie.

"What? The music? You'd have to be deaf not to hear it! So what?" asked the judge. "Hey, wait a minute! You aren't thinking what I think you are, are you? You don't think they brought in Dean Martin?"

"Fuck no, Carm. Can't you hear? It's Allan! I had no idea he was going to be here," said Eddie.

The judge and Joey knew that Allan was Eddie's younger cousin, who made his living as a nightclub entertainer.

As they neared the tent, the large crowd made it difficult for the three men to remain together. They each spotted friends and drifted apart. Eddie made his way over to the entrance of the tent, where he spotted Chicky Blandino, one of his oldest and closest friends.

Chicky was not a made member of the mob, but he was, in Mafia parlance, "connected." To be connected, you had to have the reputation of being a stand-up guy with big balls, as well as close friendship ties with some of the made Mafia members.

"Hi, Cumba! Did you just get here?" asked Chicky, blowing a puff of smoke from his ever-present cigarette.

"Yeah. I came with Carm and Joey Cariola."

"Nicky the Greek called me at the last minute and needed a ride, so we rode out together," said Chicky.

Nicky the Greek was another longtime friend of Eddie's. A product of the old neighborhood. Over the years, Nicky had become a powerful and dominating figure in local city politics.

"Where's the Greek now?" asked Eddie.

"The last time I saw him, he was at the bar talking to Senator Casey and Congressman Paglia."

"No shit! I'm impressed! I wouldn't have believed they would have the balls to show their faces here!" said Eddie.

"I know. I couldn't believe it myself when I saw them," agreed Chicky.

"Well, it proves one thing for sure—they've got balls. And I'm sure that their showing up here today will translate into big fuckin' bucks for them from the Don at election time."

Chicky had had enough of the small talk. He was anxious to find some action and engage in his favorite pastime: watching the broads.

"Eddie, let's go down to the barn and check things out. The boys are planning a crap game," said Chicky.

"Nah, I'll catch you later. I wanna go inside and show my face."

In keeping with their normal custom, the two men gave each other a quick embrace and then headed off in opposite directions.

Along the far end of the tent, two bandstands had been set up: one for a group of musicians who played contemporary music and backup for Allan, and the other was for neighborhood musicians who were old-time Italians, all friends of Don Francisco's. They played nothing but old Italian favorites.

Allan D'Amico had just finished singing, and a crowd had gathered in front of him, applauding enthusiastically. He jumped off the stage to greet them and shake hands. He was smiling and enjoying his admirers' attention when he spotted Eddie walking toward him.

Allan and Eddie had always been very close since their childhood, growing up together more like brothers than cousins. Eddie loved his cousin, and he watched with pride as the strikingly handsome Allan worked the crowd with his boyish charm and disarming smile. *He looks great*, Eddie thought.

Allan was dressed in all white, with his usual thick lock of curly jet-black hair cascading down the middle of his forehead. He was extraordinarily handsome with brilliant hazel-green eyes that were always enticing.

"Hey, cuz, what's up?" Allan asked as he fondly embraced his cousin.

"Nothin' new, but I was pleasantly surprised to see you here."

Allan gave his cousin an affectionate pat on the cheek.

"It wasn't planned, you know. It just happened on the spur of the moment. I was scheduled to open a four-week gig in Miami tonight, but the Godfather called and asked me to come and sing for him. Of course, he never talked about money, but I knew I was going to get paid off in uppercuts anyway. I figured, what the hell, the old man had been really good to all of us in the old days, and I thought I owed him my respect. So here I am in all my magnificent splendor!" said Allan, arms outstretched, flashing his dazzling white capped teeth in a broad smile.

"How long will you be in town?"

"Just tonight. I leave for Miami tomorrow on the afternoon flight."

"So where are you staying?"

Allan lowered his eyes and shuffled one foot, pretending to be embarrassed.

"Well, to tell you the truth, cuz, I was gonna ask you if it was OK for me to flop at your little hideaway at the 111 tonight," replied Allan, eyes twinkling.

Allan was referring to Eddie's penthouse suite in the prestigious 111 Park Avenue Hotel. Eddie used the suite as a tool to gain political favors, by making it available to prominent politicians and other influential friends for them to use when they carried on their illicit love affairs.

"The place is yours. You know you didn't have to ask," said Eddie as he put his arm around his cousin's shoulder. "But what if *I* get lucky tonight? Then where do I go?"

"Hey, what are cousins for? Bring her over, and I'll give her a jump. Then we'll let her decide who's a better lay," joked the silly-natured Allan.

Eddie laughed and grabbed at his cousin's crotch.

"Where're you heading now?"

Allan looked at his watch.

"Nowhere really. I've got about a half hour before I have to go up again. But now that I have a nice place to stay tonight, maybe I'll mingle around a little and see if I can get lucky." He gave Eddie another soft, affectionate pat on the cheek.

"I've got a better idea. Have you seen the Godfather yet?"

"No, not yet. I started singing the minute I got here."

Then let's go find him together. I think he'd like that," said Eddie.

Allan nodded in agreement, and the two cousins started looking for the head table. The music was playing loudly, and a large crowd was gathering on the dance floor. The spectators were hollering and whistling as the musicians played a rollicking version of the popular Italian dance number the tarantella.

By the time Eddie and Allan reached the outer fringes of the crowd, the people standing in the front rows around the dance floor were clapping in time to the music and laughing and joking as they watched the dancers on the floor.

After much effort, they finally reached the perimeter of the dance floor and found themselves standing next to Don Francisco's son, Sally, and a good friend of theirs from the old neighborhood, Richie Riccio. They could now see that to everyone's delight, the special attraction on the dance floor were Don Francisco and his wife, Nicoletta, who, with hands on their hips, were twirling and kicking to the fast-paced tarantella as the crowd cheered them on. Eddie couldn't help but notice that in sharp contrast to his wife's appearance, Don Francisco looked extremely fit and considerably less than his seventy years of age. Nicoletta, on the other hand, was overweight and looked tired and dowdy in comparison to her husband's vibrant, tanned good looks.

Checking out the onlookers, Eddie spotted the Don's five daughters clapping their hands and laughing with delight at their parents' performance. An idea came quickly to his mind.

"Come on, you guys," said Eddie to Sally and Richie. "Let's give them a surprise." He nodded toward the Don and his wife. "Follow me, Allan."

They headed in the direction of the five Barratino sisters. On the way, Eddie spotted Nicky the Greek and pulled him out of the crowd onto the dance floor.

"Nicky, grab one of the daughters and dance," ordered Eddie.

"OK, let's dance!" laughed the Greek, full of good humor. He began twirling and snapping his fingers as he moved in the direction of the five sisters.

Sally, in a good mood for a change, had wasted no time and was already dancing up a storm with his sister Angie. Laughing and cutting up, Allan had grabbed the hand of Margie, and Richie Riccio was attempting to pull the bashful Flora onto the dance floor.

"Nicky, grab Julia!" said Eddie to the Greek, who was still showing off dancing alone to the cheers of the crowd.

Things worked out perfectly for Eddie, who wanted to save Carmella for himself. She was dressed in her nun's street wear and stood out in the crowd. She was so completely engrossed in watching the fun her parents were having on the dance floor she didn't see Eddie coming up beside her. Her eyes lit up when she saw his face.

"Well, hello, stranger," she said.

"Hello yourself. Come on, Sister, are you ready to trip the light fantastic?"

Carmella nodded and took his outstretched hand. The two old friends began dancing their way to the center of the dance floor to join the others. When the happy crowd saw Sister Carmella dancing, they began to applaud and cheer her on wildly. Eddie noticed that several dancers were beginning to tire, particularly the overweight Nicoletta. As he grew more concerned about her overdoing it, he caught the bandleader's eye and gestured the sliding of a finger across his throat. The bandleader acknowledged with a nod of his head and quickly brought the music to an end. The crowd roared and clapped their approval of the dancers' performance.

The moment the music ended, well-wishers ran over to join Don Francisco and Nicoletta on the dance floor. Eddie took Carmella by the hand and led her through the crowd that was now surrounding her parents. The people in the crowd respectfully stepped aside to allow

Sister Carmella to pass. As she hugged her father, Eddie gave Nicoletta an affectionate hug. Then he embraced the Don.

"Happy birthday, Godfather. I wish you a hundred more," Eddie whispered in his ear.

"Thanks, buddy."

As more well-wishers were waiting, Eddie felt pressured to make room for them. When he began to move away, he was surprised when the Don held him tightly by the arm with a viselike grip. Don Francisco whispered a message: "Go over to my table. You and I are going to take a walk. I have some important people I want you to meet."

Eddie nodded his head, put his arm around Carmella, and walked her over to a quiet corner.

"You look great!" He stepped back to admire her.

"You look pretty wonderful yourself," she said as she straightened his tie.

"How long are you going to be in town?"

"Till next Sunday. Then I leave for a world tour of the church's missions."

"Sounds pretty exciting," Eddie responded with fake enthusiasm.

Carmella was perceptive and sensed the false tone in his remark.

"Well, for me, it is, Eddie," Carmella said softly, but emphatically.

"Tell me, Carmella, are you happy? I mean, really happy? Did you make the right decision?"

She looked a bit irritated with his question.

"Yes, Eddie. I'm really happy. Why is it you ask the same question every time I see you? You seem to find it so hard to understand. I was never cut out for all of this," she said, letting her eyes roam around the room to make her point. "I love my father, but I can't accept nor condone the path he has chosen. I'm not stupid—I know what his position means and the things it represents. I can only imagine the terrible things he must have done in his life. Someday he will have to answer for all of them when he stands before God in judgment. You see, Eddie, for me, I have found peace and happiness in the church with my god. So yes, Eddie, I am happy. Very happy."

Eddie wanted to remind her of all the good things her father had done to help so many people, but when he started to speak, Carmella interrupted him.

"And for your information, it might please you to know that I still keep you in my prayers every day. God only knows from the reports I hear about you, you need them," Carmella scolded.

He wondered how much she really knew about his life and who she was getting her reports from.

"Thanks, Carm. And you're right! I do need them. I am really happy for you. I'm glad you've found happiness and peace. I only wish I could say the same."

"It's really very simple, Eddie. You make the right choices, and the peace and joy will follow."

He gave her a brotherly hug and a tender kiss on each cheek; then he led her toward the family's table.

"Oh, Carm, before I forget . . . how about dinner some night before you leave? I'll take you to some posh restaurant where the food is rich and decadent. It'll give you something to remember when you're in the jungle swatting flies and eating coconuts at one of your missions," he joked as he pulled her chair out to seat her at the table.

"Sure, Eddie, I'd like that. Oh, any night but Wednesday—I'll be in church."

Eddie remained standing as the Don and Nicoletta were approaching the table. Don Francisco seated his wife, kissed her on the cheek, and motioned for Eddie to follow him. Carmella looked over her shoulder and spoke an affectionate reminder to Eddie: "Remember, Eddie, the right choices!"

Eddie wasn't big on patience. It seemed to take forever to cover the short distance between the tent and the house, but the Don was obliged to stop every few feet and shake hands and exchange pleasantries with scores of well-wishers who crossed their path. They finally entered through the kitchen door, and the large country kitchen was a virtual beehive of activity. Caterers and servers were everywhere, scurrying back and forth carrying trays of food.

Don Francisco and Eddie made their way through the confusion and went directly to the large seldom-used formal living room located in the front of the house. A strong, pungent odor of cigars and smoke filled the room. Don Francisco put his arm around Eddie's shoulders and led him over to where three gray-haired men were playing cards and drinking the Don's homemade red wine.

Knowing the ways of the Godfather, he understood that the Don's arm around his shoulders was a contrived gesture of affection for the benefit of the strangers seated at the table.

"Gentlemen, I would like you to meet my godson, Eddie D'Amico. I bring him to meet you so that if ever he ever comes to any of you in need of anything, you understand that what you do for him, you do for me."

A thin old man with piercing dark eyes peering from his leathered once-handsome face rose and smiled at Eddie. His smile revealed small worn teeth that were permanently stained yellow from so many years of smoking the strong rope cigars.

"So be it, my friend Francisco. It is done," said the old man, reaching for Eddie's hand.

Don Francisco was proud that the three men had graced his party with their presence. In his world, it was a great honor. For him, it was like having royalty in his home.

"Eddie, you are shaking the hand of a man who has become a legend among the people of my world. This is the Capo de Capos, Patrino Marco Milano."

Eddie was impressed. *capo de capos*, in Mafia parlance, meant "head of all heads." This man whose hand he was shaking was the notable ruler of the entire national crime syndicate.

"It is an honor, Patrino," said Eddie with utmost respect.

Speaking perfect English, the Patrino answered, "You must be a fine young man for your godfather to open the doors to our friendship so wide for you. But I caution you to always remember that we are all men of honor and respect. If ever it is known that you dishonor those principles, the door that Don Francisco has opened for you today will close forever. Capire?"

Out of the corner of his eye, Eddie noticed the other two men nod their heads in agreement with the Patrino's words of caution.

"Yes, Patrino. I understand well the ways of your world. You can be assured I will never let my godfather down."

The other two strangers remained seated with slight smiles of approval on their faces. They were pleased with Eddie's response.

"Good. Then let me introduce you to my friends."

"This gentleman who is winning all of the money is Guido D'Augustino, known to his friends and family as Don Cheech," said the Patrino.

Don Cheech was a short, chubby man with a pleasant round face, who remained seated as Eddie shook his hand. He gave him a warm, friendly smile and said, "Mio piacere, Eddie."

The other man also remained seated. He had friendly large eyes, and he stretched out his hand to shake Eddie's before the Patrino made his introduction.

"This is Don Pasquale DePrima."

The presence of these three men in the room made Eddie suddenly realize that Don Francisco carried a lot more respect and a higher standing in the structure of the national crime syndicate than he had suspected. He had seen and heard the names of these men many times before, in newspapers and on television. They were three of the most powerful crime lords in the country, especially the Patrino, Capo de Capos.

Eddie wanted to make Don Francisco look good in front of his friends, and he also wanted to cash in on the opportunity to make some points with these powerful men, in case someday he ever would need a favor from them. Knowing the way to an Italian man's heart is either through his stomach or his dick, he walked over to his godfather's side and began to put a plan into action.

"I want to thank you, Godfather, for giving me the honor and privilege of meeting such powerful and influential men. It would give me great pleasure to take our friends to dinner and have a fine feast prepared in their honor. After dinner, we can go to my penthouse for dessert and some cards. If our friends choose, I can make arrangements to have some beautiful *comares* come and join us for dessert."

Don Cheech immediately rose from his chair.

"You have a fine godson, Don Francisco! You should be proud. My friends and I, we always enjoy fine food and good wine. Shall we accept our young friend's offer?" Don Cheech asked, looking at his companions.

The three men smiled their approval at his suggestion.

"Then it is done," said the Patrino, smiling slyly.

"Good. So be it," said Don Francisco. "But, Eddie, you realize they are leaving town on Monday, so the dinner must be done tomorrow night. Who knows? The right dessert may help us remember what it is like to be young again!"

They all laughed and nodded to each other in agreement.

"I must return to my other guests now."

As they made their way back to the tent, Eddie asked, "Are the Lacavolis here? I haven't seen them tonight."

"Don't concern yourself. Tonight we celebrate my birthday. Tomorrow I will celebrate my plan for those bastards. Right after church."

Chapter 6

S am Lacavoli was standing outside a telephone booth staring at his wristwatch. His brother, Nick, waited behind the wheel of a late-model black Cadillac parked along the curb. Time seemed to be standing still, and Sam was growing impatient as he waited for the precise time to place his call.

In Chicago, Vincent Cavelli, the Don of one of the less powerful Chicago crime families, was waiting in a phone booth for Sam's call. At precisely 7:00 p.m., Sam Lacavoli dialed the number. After two rings, a voice answered.

"Yeah."

"It's me," said Lacavoli.

"Well, was the meeting held?" asked Cavelli.

"Yeah, this morning, but the cocksucker was an hour late and made everyone wait," Lacavoli answered as he nervously looked around to see if anyone was watching him.

Lacavoli listened to Cavelli and then responded, "There was no change. It was just as we suspected it would be."

Sam listened longer this time. When Cavelli stopped talking, Sam responded, "OK, I understand. Consider it done." He hung up the phone and jumped into the waiting car.

"Hurry, Nick, get to the party before we're missed. Everything's gotta look normal," said Sam.

"Well, are you gonna fuckin' tell me? What the hell did he say?"

"We go with the plan immediately. But Cavelli said something strange. We're not in this fuckin' thing alone. There's somebody else he called Mr. X. He said we'd know after the job was done."

"Who the fuck can it be?" asked Nick, a puzzled look on his pockmarked face.

"I don't fuckin' know, but I guess we'll find out soon enough."

Nick grunted in agreement as he steered the car onto the highway heading toward the farm.

Across town, the judge's wife, Rose Carlivatti, was on the phone talking to Eddie's wife, Danni.

"I called because I was just curious to see if you had gone to the party."

"Are you kidding?! You know how I feel about those people, Rosie. They're despicable. I wouldn't be caught dead at that party! But, Rosie, what about you? Are you OK? You're slurring your words—it sounds like you're in your cups."

"Yeah, but so what? It makes me feel better. At least the booze deadens the pain and gives me a sense of worth," Rose lamented.

"My god, Rosie, you shouldn't talk like that. You should count your blessings. You have a lot to be thankful for. Just look what you and Carmen have managed to accomplish. You should be proud of what you both have done together," Danni returned sympathetically.

"Yeah, well, he's proud, but I can't sit around waiting anymore while he's out trying to save the world. So I just sit at home and find my fun and self-esteem in the next shot of vodka."

"Oh my god, Rosie! I'm really worried about you. Are you going to be all right? Do you want me to come stay with you until Carmen comes home?" Danni asked, full of concern for her friend.

"No, I'm OK. The girls are home with me. I'll just do what I always do when I'm bored—jump into the rest of my bottle and pull the cork over my head."

The line went dead. Danni stared at the phone in her hand.

Eddie's right, she thought, *Rosie Carlivatti's drinking is getting way out of hand.*

At the party, Eddie D'Amico was looking for Chicky Blandino and Nicky the Greek. As he walked across the driveway toward the barn, he came face-to-face with Freddie "the Fuck" Bentivegna, who had two gorgeous hookers hanging on each arm. Freddie was a soldier in the Barratino Family. He also ran Don Francisco's very successful restaurant, the Black Orchid, most favored hangout for the city's mobsters.

"Hi, Freddie. Do you have one more of them that's just as pretty?"

Freddie just laughed and beamed proudly. The hookers flashed flirtatious eyes at Eddie, looking him up and down.

"By the way, I'm glad I ran into you. I have some friends in town who need three comares tomorrow night."

All the guys knew that Freddie had a bevy of hookers at his beck and call and that most of them hung out at the Black Orchid.

"You have only to ask, and you will receive," responded the dramatic Freddie. "That is, for the appropriate fee, of course," he added.

As the two men spoke, the exotic black-haired Oriental-looking hooker pulled away from Freddie and moved closer to Eddie. Taking his hand, she said, "Look, honey, if you want to party, we can start right now. And since it's my day off, it's on the house." She placed Eddie's hand on her full breast and gave him a suggestive smile. Eddie withdrew his hand and looked into her fascinating dark eyes.

"What's your name, honey?"

"Lori."

"Lori, let me do you a favor. There's somebody I'd like you to meet. He's singing in the tent. You might recognize him from some of the movies he's made," lied Eddie. "If you like what you see, and I'm sure you will, just go up to him and make your own arrangements—he's only in town for the night. His name is Allan. Tell him his cousin Eddie sent you to see him. You got all that?"

"Sure, I got all that. What do ya think, I'm brain dead?" Lori responded with an irritated look.

Realizing she felt he had insulted her, he tried to redeem himself.

"Hey, honey, I'm sorry, but it's really hard for me to concentrate when I'm looking at someone as beautiful as you," Eddie said.

His buttering-up worked. Lori was satisfied with Eddie's comeback and smiled at him apologetically.

"Hey, handsome, what am I? Chopped liver standing here?" asked the other very attractive hooker. "Do you have a movie star friend for me, or do Lori and I have to share this guy?"

"I just hope this Allan guy looks as good as you," Lori interjected.

"Thanks for the compliment, but next to him, I look like the Hunchback of Notre Dame," Eddie said with a laugh.

The hookers glanced at each other and smiled.

"Hey, if you guys are setting up an orgy, count me in," called out Chicky Blandino as he neared the group. He immediately recognized by the way the two women were dressed that they were hookers; besides, they were with Freddie "the Fuck."

"Hey, Freddie Fuck, how you doin'? Long time, no see," said Chicky, exhaling a cloud of smoke in Freddie's face.

"Hi, Chicky. How's tricks?"

"You tell me, Freddie. Looks like you're the one with all the tricks," Chicky quipped, eyeballing the hookers.

Chicky honed in on Lori's friend and asked, "What's your name, baby?"

"I'm Starr," she replied. "And thanks for asking since nobody else did." She gave Eddie a sideways glance to see if he caught the dig she had given him.

"Well, hello, Starr! My name's Chicky, and now that we've got the small talk out of the way, do you want to fuck?"

Starr liked Chicky's humor and thought he was cute. She grabbed him by the arm with her one hand and by the crotch with her other, saying, "Oooh, I love that kinda talk! How can I resist your offer, you smooth-talking motherfucker?" She squeezed his balls on the hard side, making him jump.

"OK, OK, enough o' this foreplay," said Freddie. "This bullshit's been nice, but we've gotta get going. Eddie, call me tomorrow about the broads. If I'm not at the restaurant, you have my home number."

"Thanks, Freddie. Nice meeting you, ladies," Eddie said, using the term loosely. "It's been a pleasure. Maybe I'll see you tonight," he said, winking at Lori knowingly.

Chicky couldn't stand being excluded from anything. As Freddie and the hookers walked away toward the tent, he asked, "What's this shit about tonight?"

"Allan's staying at 111 tonight, and Lori's a dynamite-looking broad, so I sent her over to see him—maybe he can get lucky."

"I just left the barn. It's dead as a fucking doornail," said Chicky, "The action won't really start until some of the high rollers show up. I could use some luck! Let's go in the tent and find those broads again. I'd really like to nail that Starr!" proclaimed Chicky. He always purported a perpetual hard-on. Chicky loved carousing and chasing women.

"OK, I wanna see the look on Allan's face when Lori goes over to talk to him," snickered Eddie.

Just before they reached the entrance, a voice called out, "Hey, Eddie! Wait up!" It was Dominic.

"Hey, I can't hang around while you talk to your father. I'm on a mission! See ya later," Chicky said as he acknowledged Dominic with a wave and went inside the tent.

"So, Eddie, tell me something. What was the big fuckin' meeting about this morning between you and the Don?" Dominic asked, looking intently into his son's eyes.

"Fuck, Dad, you're one of his most trusted confidants, don't ask me. Go see him. Why are you putting me on the spot like this?"

"Remember me? I'm your fucking father."

"Yeah, I remember, but you're the one who taught me all my life that men of honor always obey the code of silence. You know I can't talk about what the Don discussed with me unless he chooses to tell you himself."

Eddie was trying to appease his father, but his answer only served to piss Dominic off.

"I'm your fucking father, asshole! Show me some respect! You know you can trust me to keep my mouth shut. I'm the one who taught you everything! Remember?"

"So what? So you're my father. Big deal! You want respect? You have to earn it!"

Eddie's flip reply was off the wall and made Dominic go ballistic. He glared into his son's eyes, clenched his fists, and then spun around and stormed away in a rage.

Fuck him! Eddie thought. *He always talks about respect, but he never gave me anything to respect him for.*

This wasn't the first time he and his father had this kind of disagreement, and he knew it wouldn't be the last. He was Dominic's only son, but Eddie had never had any real bond with him. Their relationship had always been strained. Dominic had always been envious and resentful of his son's special friendship with the Don. Most of the time, they, at least, tried to be civil to each other, but it was an arduous exertion on both their parts.

As he entered the crowded tent, Eddie heard the sound of Allan's melodic voice crooning the heart-wrenching Italian ballad "Mama." Not seeing him on the stage, Eddie figured he must be singing with a portable mic somewhere in the thick mix of people down on the floor. Eddie followed the eyes and attention of the crowd to the Don's table. Making his way over, he at last spotted Allan serenading Nicoletta on bended knee. Don Francisco looked on, beaming with approval.

Eddie stood motionless, enjoying his cousin's voice.

That son of a bitch can really *sing*, he thought to himself.

When the song ended, the throng clapped, cheered, and whistled their overwhelming approval. Allan rose from his knee and kissed Nicoletta on the cheek. In a show of appreciation, the Don got up and gave Allan a long, affectionate hug.

Eddie's thoughts returned to Dominic. He needed a drink. He made his way to the bar.

"Vodka rocks," he ordered, placing a generous tip into the jar.

"Thank you, sir!" the bartender exclaimed, acknowledging Eddie's noble tip. "Twist or olive, Mr. D'Amico?"

"Twist."

Eddie gulped the vodka and held up his glass to get the bartender's attention.

"I'll have another."

He looked around the tent and spotted Senator Casey and Congressman Paglia talking with Councilman Doyle. Eddie picked up his drink and walked over to the three men.

"Hello, gentlemen," he said, respectfully shaking each man's hand.

"Nice to see you, Eddie," said Senator Casey.

"Thanks. You're looking well, Senator. I was surprised to see both of you in town at the same time," said Eddie, addressing the congressman as well.

"We were just talking about that very thing with Councilman Doyle. We both came in for the dedication of the new federal courthouse, and the timing was perfect for us to have the opportunity to come by and pay our respects to Frank on his birthday," said Congressman Paglia.

Sure, Eddie thought to himself. *"Opportunity to come by" my ass.*

He was sure they had received personal invitations from the Don. Nevertheless, he felt a newfound respect for the two men who proved they were real stand-up guys just by their presence, knowing the potential backlash they could inherit.

"Well, that's great it worked out so well. I'm sure Frank feels honored that you stopped by." And in a complimentary tone, Eddie added, "Especially since he knows there are people out front taking license numbers and pictures and you came anyway."

Eddie immediately turned the conversation to Councilman Doyle.

"So, Elwood, what's new and exciting down at City Hall?"

"Shit, Eddie, you know as much as I do. You and that Greek friend of yours are up to your asses in city politics."

Eddie heard Allan just finishing a number and looked over to see him motion to him.

"Well, gentlemen, it's been a pleasure," he said, shaking hands before taking his leave.

Allan gave a thumbs-up sign to the other waiting musicians to start playing before he jumped off the stage and landed beside his cousin. He threw his arm around Eddie, his face beaming with delight.

"Where the fuck did you ever find that broad?" Allan asked excitedly.

"Why? She's no good?" Eddie asked jokingly.

Allan could hardly contain himself.

"*Mengya!* Are you fucking kidding? She's a knockout!"

"Allan, you do know she's a hooker, don't you?" Eddie teased.

"Well, no shit. You'd have to be blind in one eye and can't see out of the other to not know that! But what the fuck kinda story did you tell her? She wanted to know if the movies I made were dramas or musicals," Allan said, laughing almost uncontrollably.

"More importantly, what did *you* tell her?" asked Eddie, laughing heartily, caught up in the humor of his lie.

"I told her I did both!" Allan blurted, now laughing so hard tears were streaming down his face.

When it came to humor and laughter, Allan owned his cousin. With an ever fun-loving demeanor and silliness since they were both young kids, Allan could literally make him laugh at will over things that no one else would even find humorous. This was now the case. Watching Allan break up in laughter was contagious to Eddie, and he lost it too, wiping tears of laughter from his eyes.

"But get this! She said if I pick up the tab for the drinks, she'll pick up the tab for the sex," giggled Allan.

"So you get a free lay and a free place to stay, all for the price of a few drinks?" kidded Eddie.

"Yeah, but so you get your money's worth for the suite, why don't you drop by and we can both nail her?" Allan suggested.

"Are you fucking kidding? I couldn't do that to you! If I fucked her, she'd throw you out of the room!"

"Fuck you!" Allan replied, smiling.

Feeling hunger pangs, Eddie suggested they check out the spread. They nudged their way over to the long line of food tables along one wall, where every imaginable Italian succulent was beautifully displayed and accented with a wide array of dramatic floral arrangements.

"*Mengya!* Look at all this fuckin' food!" exclaimed Allan. "Suddenly I'm starving!"

The pastaholic cousins headed straight for the table that held all the different types of pasta and began filling their plates.

"You know, I hate these damned buffets," lamented Eddie. "Everything looks so good I can never make up my mind. I want it all!"

"Yeah, I know what ya mean," said Allan. "They really should put sideboards on these plates."

Suddenly, Eddie felt a soft touch on his elbow and turned to see who it was.

"Look who's here, Eddie!" said Carmella.

Eddie's heart instantly began beating wildly inside his chest. Standing at Carmella's side was his former fiancee, Megan Schimmel. It had been nearly fifteen years since he had last seen her—the girl that he had been so madly in love with and had almost made his wife.

"Hello, Eddie," said Megan. "It's been a long time." She paused for Eddie's response, but he was speechless. She added, "You look great."

He finally managed words.

"Thanks, Megan. You look pretty terrific yourself—as beautiful as ever," he said sincerely. He allowed his eyes to boldly roam her up and down, taking in the classic, sensual beauty of her face and body. Her golden-colored straight hair was long, much longer than he remembered. Her slender, beautifully shaped body with small well-rounded breasts made him recall the times they were his for the taking. But her large almond-shaped eyes seemed somehow different. They were bluer than he remembered them to be.

God, he thought to himself, *all this time has passed, and she really hasn't changed one bit! She's a dynamite-looking broad!*

Megan was feeling uncomfortable under Eddie's close scrutiny and felt a flashback of butterflies in her stomach, reminiscing on the intensity of their youthful love. In an attempt to quash her embarrassment, she forced herself to turn her attention away from him.

"Hello, Allan. It's nice to see you again. I must say, your voice is better than ever," she said, holding out her hand to him.

"Thanks, Meg. You're still a better-than-ever knockout!"

Allan gently took her hand and gallantly kissed it.

Carmella touched Megan's arm, saying, "I'm going back to my family's table. I'm sure you and Eddie have a lot to catch up on."

"OK, Carmella. Thanks for helping me find him. Then, smiling coyly, "I know I'll be in good hands with Mr. D'Amico!"

Before leaving, Carmella leaned over and whispered in Eddie's ear, "Remember, Eddie—the *right* choices." Then she turned and walked away.

Eddie reached out and took Megan's hand and placed her arm through his. Glancing back at Allan and offering up a guileful wink, he said as he led Megan away, "Well, cuz, I'll see ya around sometime."

"See how you are!" Allan shouted after him. "A beautiful girl comes along, and you dump me like a piece of shit!" he joked. Allan smiled and nodded to Megan as she waved a good-bye to him over her shoulder.

Chapter 7

Eddie escorted Megan from the tent. The two former lovers walked leisurely, hand in hand, down the winding path that led to a small guest cottage located at the rear of the compound.

"So tell me, Megan, are you still married to that Kraut you dumped me for?"

"Actually, no, I'm not. But that's not fair, Eddie. You know I loved you, but I was forced into that marriage by my father."

"Come on, Megan. I know your father was tough, but you were an adult. You could have made your own choices."

She had crushed his ego when she returned the engagement ring he had given her, and he couldn't help still feeling resentful.

"Maybe you're right. I know I made an awful mistake, but I was young and naive and deathly afraid of my father. You know that!"

Eddie knew it was the truth. She had suffered through a terrible and difficult childhood at the hands of her domineering, Hitler-loving father. Her mother was a poor, meek soul, afraid to protect her daughter for fear of receiving a beating for her efforts. It still torqued Eddie and made his blood boil every time he thought of it.

"So anyway, tell me. You divorced him?"

"No. I had the marriage annulled."

"Annulled! When?"

"It's been years, Eddie."

"Years? Then why didn't you look me up?"

"I did, but it was too late. I heard you were engaged to Danni, and I didn't want to screw up your plans the same way my father screwed up ours."

Eddie stopped and turned to face her.

"Megan, what about now? Are you married now?" Eddie asked, hoping in his heart that her answer would be no.

"I did remarry . . ." She paused, and Eddie felt a sickness in the pit of his stomach. "But I've been divorced from him for three years now. He became a terrible alcoholic, and it was another disastrous marriage that I don't even want to think about. I just couldn't take any more. I guess you can see that men and marriage haven't been one of my strong suits," Megan said wistfully.

They walked on to the cottage. Eddie tried the door. It was locked.

Shit, he thought.

Suddenly he remembered that when he built the cottage, he kept a key hidden in the electrical box around back. It had been placed there for his subcontractors to use. He hoped it was still there.

"I'll be right back!"

He ran around to the rear of the cottage, opened the box, and reached into a small open seam and found the key. He ran back to Megan at the front door, and they entered the small comfortably furnished quarters. Eddie pushed the door closed behind them. The slamming of the door had the same effect on them as a starter's pistol would have on a runner ready to race.

Now alone, they both began to feel the fire of desire that had been smoldering within each of them for so long. As they touched each other, they felt it ignite and burst into hot, passionate flames.

Eddie's entire body was filled with the urge to pull her into his arms and crush her to him. But he remembered Megan's soft, sensitive nature. She preferred being made love to gently and tenderly. He decided to move slowly, entirely unprepared for what happened next.

Acting completely out of character for the Megan he remembered, she threw her arms tightly around his neck and began kissing him passionately. Her full, lush lips were pressed hard against his, and she thrust her searching tongue into his mouth, driving herself into a sexual frenzy. As she kissed him, she stood on her toes, pressing her petite firm body into his, as if by her actions, she could make them one person. Her body moved passionately, grinding against him as she hooked one leg around his to draw him even tighter to her.

Suddenly she realized he wasn't responding to her advances. She immediately backed away, visibly embarrassed. Lowering her eyes to the floor, she timidly asked, "Is something wrong?"

Eddie stepped over to her and lifted her face in his hands.

"Nothing. Nothing's wrong, Megan. You just took me a little by surprise. I enjoyed it, but it was slightly out of character for the Megan I remember."

He tenderly kissed her forehead and said, "I had it in my mind to do it more like this."

He pulled her gently into his arms. His lips touching her skin with a feathery touch, he tenderly kissed her eyes, her nose, and then her waiting lips. He continued, placing gentle kisses down her neck, and he felt her body quiver under his touch. Then his tongue delicately moved up her neck until their lips met in a passionate kiss, and his tongue searched for hers. She willingly obliged as he enveloped her tighter with his strong, muscular arms. Wanting more and more of him, she moved into him as if trying to pass through the barrier of his flesh. It was as if their bodies were made for each other, coming together as a perfect meld.

Gently touching her breast, he ached for more. He wanted desperately to feel her bare flesh. He unbuttoned the front of her dress, fully exposing her braless breasts. They were firm and round, and once again, his for the taking. Megan's dress fell to the floor. With polished skill, he picked her up effortlessly and carried her to the sofa, where he delicately laid her down. Dropping to his knees, he slowly moved his tongue around her breasts, teasing and tantalizing her hard pink nipples.

Megan was pulling him to her, craving the hardness she felt between his legs. She wanted him, all of him, deep inside her. She moaned in pleasure. He sensed that she was ready to follow him down any carnal path his desire could conjure.

He continued to toy with her sensitively, and her body began to shiver. Eddie decided he would wait to satisfy his own desires. This moment would be all Megan's. He wanted to let her soar to the heavens and ride on the wind of her own passion. He wanted her to enjoy the pleasures of her intimacy and her own sexuality alone.

He kissed her lips tenderly, slowly moving his tongue in and out of her mouth. Then he slowly began rubbing the tip of his tongue against the roof of her mouth as she shivered in delight.

Eddie reached down with his hand and felt the softness of the flesh of her thigh. Megan sensed a touch of magic as his hand moved up her leg. She dropped one leg to the floor, opening herself to him as far as her position on the sofa would allow. Removing her panties, he touched her gently and felt the soft wetness of her in his hand.

Oh yes! Yes, Eddie! Touch me! Hurry and touch me more! Touch me inside! her mind screamed out.

Ever so slowly, he fondled the depths of her. Sensing the peak of her passion, he began to move his hand with a steady, rhythmic motion, each time driving his hand harder against her yielding body. Her body undulated in passionate fury to the rhythm of the relentless, satisfying pounding of his hand. Megan's body began to quiver uncontrollably. She cried out as she felt the ecstasy and excitement of her orgasm. Eddie withdrew his hand and buried his mouth between her legs until he knew she had enjoyed the full measure of her release. Then he began kissing away the tears of pleasure from her face.

He then slowly rose to his feet to remove his jacket. Knowing his intentions, Megan suddenly sat upright and tried to cover her nakedness with her hands and arms. Seeing her reaction, he covered her with his jacket.

"Please, Eddie! No, not now! Not here like this!" she pleaded. "I know you must think I'm terrible, getting you all worked up and asking you to stop after I've had my pleasure. But I just couldn't help myself."

Megan's voice was tearful.

"I can't tell you how many times over the years I've fantasized to be with you like this. I used to close my eyes and dream of us—only, I was always disappointed. Every time I had an orgasm, it wasn't your hand bringing me pleasure, but my own," she said, turning red with embarrassment. "The minute you began to touch me there, I lost it. All my desires and fantasies were suddenly coming true in one big rush. When you touched me, it was more than I could bear," she confessed sheepishly.

Eddie knelt down in front of her and continued to listen carefully as she shared her thoughts and feelings with him.

"When Carmella asked me to come to the party and spend the week with her, I only accepted when I knew for sure you would be here."

He moved to sit down next to her. Eddie found himself enjoying Megan's confession of her private thoughts.

"Carmella thinks it's shameful that I don't care that you're married, but she told me herself that you and Danni are having serious problems. I know I'm being selfish, but I never stopped loving you. I've only been with three men in my life. You were the first, and then the two men I married. And it's been years since a man has even touched me!"

Megan turned to look at him. She couldn't believe this handsome face that had filled her fantasies over the years was finally in front of her. Her dreams had finally come true. She had to reveal it all to him now in case she never got another chance. He had to know how she had felt all these years. And she had to know more about him, whatever the outcome would be.

Eddie took her hand and looked lovingly into her eyes.

"Go on, Megan. I think you feel there's more you need to say."

"Well, when Carmella called, I decided then and there that if I was ever going to sleep with anyone again, it was going to be you. I didn't care about the consequences as long as I knew you still wanted me. This is really embarrassing for me to say, Eddie, but I came here with the express purpose of wanting you to make love to me. But now I realize that I've waited so long. I want things to be right. Not like this. Not here. I want us to make love to each other—not just fuck."

Megan was crying uncontrollably now. Eddie held her tightly and whispered in her ear, "It's all right, baby."

She buried her head in his shoulder.

"Megan, listen to me. I understand, and it's all right. I've thought a lot about you too, wondering what things would have been like if we had gotten married. I can't believe you're here with me. But I know one thing for sure, I'm not gonna let you walk out of my life again."

His words were reassuring. She felt better after getting her feelings out in the open, and what he said to her made the hurt she had felt for so many years begin to disappear.

She sat up, and he wiped the remaining tears from her eyes.

"Megan, why don't you get dressed and we'll make a pot of coffee and talk things out."

"I'd like that, Eddie."

They stayed in the cottage, bringing each other up-to-date with their respective life stories. Eddie and Megan listened to each other with great interest and fascination as they shared their innermost secrets. So intrigued with each other time had escaped them. Eddie suddenly looked at his watch.

"Holy shit, Megan! It's late! We have to get back to the party!"

They left the cottage holding hands, running toward the sound of the music.

Chapter 8

Still holding hands, Megan and Eddie entered the tent just as Allan was leading the two bands and the crowd in a rousing version of the birthday song.

Thank God! The timing couldn't have been better! thought Eddie.

Allan grabbed a portable mic and jumped off the stage. He headed to the Don's table, singing and leading the crowd with his free hand. The birthday song was the prearranged signal for the caterers to roll in the huge red, white, and green three-tiered cake boasting seventy blazing candles. People moved out of the way to clear a path for the parade of ten men and women dressed in white chef's garb rolling a large cake cart over to the Don's table. Complying with the caterer's instructions, the Barratino family members all stood around Don Francisco as the enormous cake was brought to a halt in front of him. The seventy candles were blazing merrily, illuminating the smiling faces of the Barratino clan with a soft, warm glow.

Don Francisco looked fit and handsome in his teal green shirt and white slacks. He was smiling from ear to ear, enjoying the moment and all of the attention he was receiving.

When the singing ended, Allan had trouble bringing the jazzed-up crowd back to order. After several attempts, he finally silenced the charged-up group. Allan gave Don Francisco a birthday hug and handed him the microphone.

Don Francisco rose to the occasion. With his usual quick wit, he shouted into the microphone, "Hey, will somebody out there please bring me a fire extinguisher!"

The crowd roared. Don Francisco motioned to his family members, who were gathered around him.

"Come on, everyone! Help me!"

He counted to three, and together, all the Barratinos blew out the candles. The crowd cheered and clapped. Allan immediately broke into "For He's a Jolly Good Fellow," and all of the well-wishers joined in the singing.

At the end of the song, a hush fell through the tent. Everyone's attention was on the Don. Not one guest dared to disrespect him by engaging in any side conversation.

"Thanks to all of you, this is a day I'll remember for the rest of my life. And at seventy, I'll probably be lucky to have fifty more good years left!"

Don Francisco waited for the laughter to subside.

"Now I must be serious and honest with you. When my wonderful wife, Nicoletta, first told me she wanted to have this party, I objected."

The crowd was silent as they watched the Don put his arm around his wife and pull her close to him.

"I said, 'No way, Nicoletta! Parties are for kids,' I told her. And you know, I still think I'm right! Parties are for kids! Parties make kids feel happy and full of joy. Parties also make kids feel important in the eyes of the guests who come to the party to help the guest of honor celebrate. Most importantly, parties make kids feel the love and affection that their guests bring with them. But I just found out today that parties are for kids of all ages—even an old seventy-year-old kid like me! So I want to thank all of you for today, for making me feel important by your presence, but most of all for allowing me to feel the sense of love and affection that each of you has brought me as your gift. Yes, my friends, because of all of you, this old man feels like a kid today!"

The Don paused a moment, appearing to choke up with emotion. The crowd whistled and cheered. He composed himself and quieted the crowd.

"Listen, everyone! The party is not over. You are all welcome to stay and enjoy yourselves! There's still plenty of food. In fact, you're welcome to take some home if you wish. Again, thank you for coming. God bless you all!"

Overcome with emotion, Don Francisco was no longer able to speak. He handed the microphone to Allan. Caught up in his emotion, the Don sat down and wiped tears from his eyes as the crowd continued to cheer and applaud.

Allan signaled the band to start playing. The room became quiet as he started singing "My Way." The words seemed to be an appropriate tribute to Don Francisco's life.

Dabbing a tear from her eye, Megan said to Eddie, "I'm going back to my table. I really can't take much more of this. Please take me out of here as soon as you can."

"Give me about an hour—and don't eat. We'll have a late dinner, listen to some nice, soft music, and then . . ."

With a sexy smile, he let his voice trail off, leaving the rest to her imagination.

"Sounds wonderful! Please don't be late. I'll be with Carmella—so find her, and you've found me."

She smiled and blew him a kiss as she walked away.

Eddie looked for Allan and spotted him talking to a crowd of people. As he walked over, Allan excused himself from his admirers.

"Have you seen Chicky? I need to see if he'll take the judge and Joey home."

"Now that you mention it, I haven't seen him since we talked to Freddie. He seems to have disappeared," said Allan.

"Well, if you see the judge, tell him I'm at the crap game in the barn and I need to see him. And by the way, you did a great job today. Your voice is better than ever!"

Allan giggled.

"It must be the music lessons I'm taking for the movies I'm doing," he joked.

"Hey, Eddie, *aspeta*!" It was Don Francisco. "Are you going without saying good-bye?"

"No, Godfather, I was just heading down to the barn. I'm sure the crap game is going strong by now. Oh, and I made arrangements for tomorrow night, including the dessert . . ."

The Don interrupted him.

"We'll see, we'll see. Let's talk about that tomorrow. It's been a long fucking day, and I'm tired. I don't want to think of anything right now but my bed."

Eddie gave his godfather a long, affectionate hug.

"Allora buono sera, Godfather. Be careful, huh?"

"Don't worry. I told you—tomorrow after church, my problems will all be over," said Don Francisco with a knowing smile on his face.

"Francisco! Camina!"

It was Nicoletta—she was ready to go.

Across the room at the family table, the Don's son, Sally, had taken it all in. He had watched as his father suddenly rose from his seat and walked briskly away. Curious to see what had prompted his father to move so fast, Sally stood up on his chair to look over the crowd. He became furious when he saw his father and Eddie together again. He seethingly watched the long embrace between them at the end of their conversation.

So angered at the scene, Sally fell heavily back into his chair and pounded a fist on the table. His wife, Connie, who was seated next to him, had to grab her wineglass to keep it from tipping over.

"What the hell's wrong with you?" she asked, startled by his actions.

"Did you see that fucking old man of mine go running out of here?" Connie was puzzled at his reply.

"Yeah, so what?"

"I'll tell you so what!"

The volume of Sally's voice was quickly escalating.

"He nearly broke his fuckin' neck gettin' out of his chair to run over and talk to his kiss-ass godson!"

"I'll say it again—so what? It has nothing to do with you. Why are you so upset?"

"That's just the fucking point, Connie! It has nothing to do with *me*! My father and D'Amico have all these cozy little fuckin' secrets going on between them. *I'm* shut out of everything! Shit! My father wouldn't run after me even if I was on fire and he had to take a piss!"

Connie couldn't believe her husband was carrying on this way. Embarrassed by his outburst, she tried to calm him down.

"Come on, Sally, aren't you acting just a little melodramatic?"

Her question only angered him more.

"Why don't you fucking get it, Connie? Are you stupid or something? Ever since we were kids, that fucking Eddie has been a thorn in my side, always pushing his way between me and my father! Are you blind? Can't you see my father treats him more like a son than he does me! I hate that dirty son of a bitch!"

"Oh, drop it, Sally! You're getting yourself all worked up over nothing."

"Drop shit! D'Amico's given me nothing but hurt and pain. I'm tired of dropping it. Someday I'll make him pay, and pay big! Someday I'll teach Mr. Big Shot Cocksucker, Eddie D'Amico, what real pain is!"

Connie figured it must be the booze talking.

"For crying out loud, Sally. Quit it now—you're talking crazy."

Chapter 9

Walking alone toward the barn, Eddie's thoughts were of Megan. It was like they had been locked in a time capsule. All the years they had been apart seemed to never have existed. He knew, in his heart, he loved her, but his mind still didn't want to admit it was possible.

How could someone simply walk back into your life after all those years and, in just a few fleeting hours, cause you to feel love like this again? he wondered.

This whole thing with Megan somehow didn't make sense to him at all, yet he couldn't deny the feelings he felt inside when he was with her. Now that she was back in his life, he had some difficult decisions to make. There was Danni, and Ashley. Thinking about his marriage made him feel like he was sinking in quicksand. Megan seemed like the rope he needed to pull himself out of that mire. Thinking of it all was giving him a headache.

What a fucking predicament I'm in, he thought to himself.

As he neared the barn, he could hear the sounds of loud voices coming through the open windows. When he entered the brightly lit building, the bustling activity of all the people gambling brought to his mind the atmosphere of the Las Vegas casinos. People were packed elbow to elbow around a crap table. They were all laughing and yelling as they placed their bets. The players and their fortunes were being controlled, moment by moment, by the awesome silent power of two little red cubes that bounced and rolled across the dark green felt.

In a far corner of the room, Eddie saw several well-dressed women slamming coins into the bank of Don Francisco's illegal slot machines as fast as their hands could move. He knew that Don Francisco had those machines rigged tighter than Kelsey's balls.

Those women might just as well be throwing their money over their shoulders, he thought to himself.

Eddie felt like playing poker. He walked over to the card tables and circled them, looking for an open seat, but to no avail. As he walked past the pool table, he noticed that it had been pressed into service as a second crap table, and a high-stakes, rough-and-tumble game was taking place on its smooth green surface. He couldn't get near either of the packed crap tables, so he headed for the bar.

Yes, sir! What can I do for you?" the bartender asked.

"Vodka rocks—with a twist."

Unconsciously, Eddie set a bill on the bar. The bartender delivered his drink and pushed his money back toward him.

"Oh no, sir, you're Don Francisco's guest today. Everything is on the house!"

"Hey, bartender! Make mine a beer," said Joey Cariola from behind Eddie.

"Where the hell have you been? Joey and I've been looking all over for you," said Carmen Carlivatti.

"I've been looking for you too. I'm glad you guys found me. I was gonna tell you ya need to find a ride home. I'm gonna be tied up."

"Tied up, my ass! You got lucky, didn't you?" asked the judge.

"I'll never tell," Eddie smirked.

"Come on, Carm. Forget him. We'd better go find a ride. That bastard's gonna go get a strange piece of ass tonight, and you and I have to go home to the same ol' stuff," said Joey jokingly.

"What's the matter, Joey? Is the same ol' stuff all that bad?" teased Eddie.

"Well, no, I'm not saying it's all that bad, Eddie, but last night I wanted to ask her if she'd reached an orgasm yet, but I didn't want to wake her up!"

Joey broke up at his own joke.

"You fuckin' asshole, go find a ride," said Eddie, still chuckling.

"On that note, we'll go find a ride. Here's to good fucking, Eddie. Call me next week, you lucky bastard. We'll have lunch," the judge said as he pulled Joey away from the bar.

Just then, their attention was drawn to the sound of loud, angry cursing coming from one of the card tables.

"Hey, come on! Let's go see what's going on!" said Joey.

The three friends rushed over to the commotion.

"What happened?" Joey asked a bystander.

The man cupped his hand alongside his mouth to mask his voice and semi-whispered, "See that fucking gorilla over there?" He pointed with his eyes.

Joey interrupted, "Look, Carm! It's the monster we saw at the gate coming in!"

"Well, anyway, the gorilla just lost a big fucking pot—I'd say it must've been over a grand—to that little guy with the gray hair and glasses," said the bystander, pointing to the man Eddie knew as Mario Terranova.

Mr. Terranova appeared to be a quiet, nice old man. But Eddie knew he was a high-ranking member of Don Francisco's family and that he wasn't as quiet and meek as he appeared. To have achieved the position of power and respect that he held in the Barratino crime family, Mr. Terranova had to have big balls, and somewhere along the way, he had to have "made his bones."

"Watch that gorilla drink!" whispered the bystander, "He's gulping scotch right out of the bottle! He's gotta be drunk as a fuckin' skunk by now!"

Eddie stood alongside the blow-by-blow spectator, and they continued to watch as LaRocca lost hand after hand. The more he lost, the more he drank, taking huge gulps from a bottle of Chivas Regal. Because LaRocca was losing so badly, Eddie became very curious to see how he was playing his down cards. As inconspicuously as possible, he moved over behind him to watch how he played his poker hands and to peek at his hole cards.

The game was seven-card stud with the first two cards down, four up, and the last one down. This deal, LaRocca had two aces wired in the hole with an ace and a king showing. LaRocca was pushing all the bets; he kept raising and bumping.

No wonder he's losing! He's playing like a fucking idiot! Eddie thought to himself. *He's driving the bets so hard he's forcing everyone out of the fuckin' game.*

That is, everyone except the meek-looking Mr. Terranova.

The last card was dealt, down and dirty. Eddie lowered his head to peek as LaRocca picked up the corner of his card. It was a king. He was sitting with a full boat, aces over kings.

Eddie leaned over to check out Mr. Terranova's cards. He had a ten, a seven, and a pair of deuces up. His deuces were high. He bet $500.

The two men battled it out, bumping and raising three times, which was the game limit. LaRocca was obviously feeling no pain, and when the betting came to an end, he played out of turn, proudly flipping over his full house. He immediately began reaching for the pot as he said laughing, "Read 'em an weep!"

Eddie figured the pot must have contained at least five thousand dollars.

The meek-looking but big-balled Mr. Terranova calmly rose from his chair with a slight smile on his face.

"Hey, Lorenzo. Not so fuckin' fast. I've got two pair. Deuces over deuces."

Suddenly realizing that Mr. Terranova's four deuces had beaten him out of the enormous pot, LaRocca went berserk. Letting out a loud roar of anger, he jumped out of his chair, pummeling a tirade of obscenities at Mr. Terranova; and with one mighty thrust of his powerful hands, he jolted the table, sending the cards and all the cash flying high into the air. Money and people began to scatter everywhere in the aftermath of LaRocca's violent temper tantrum. He stood and looked at his handiwork for a moment and then turned and staggered toward the restroom.

After helping Mr. Terranova gather his winnings from the floor, Eddie noticed some space at one of the crap tables. He hurried over to take a little action. The stickman was Vinnie Sortino, a soldier in the family. The Don's son, Sally, had just arrived and was handling the cash for the house, raking off the Don's percentage of each pot. No chips were ever used in the games at the farm, only cash money.

Eddie's luck was poor, and it didn't take long for the galloping red dice to cost him several hundred dollars. Sally showed obvious pleasure at Eddie's losing streak by smiling and glaring at him every time he lost a bet. Sally was irritating him. He decided it was time to leave and go find Megan, just as the ominous figure of LaRocca pushed through the crowd and staggered up to the crap table.

"Gimme a grand till tomorrow," he wheezed at Sally.

Without a word or any hesitation, Sally counted out the money and made him sign a marker. Breaking the rules, LaRocca pushed his way in front of Nick Lacavoli, who was waiting his turn to be the next shooter.

"I roll next! Any fucking problem wid dat?" LaRocca shouted defiantly, glaring at Nick Lacavoli.

Nick had a big set of balls, but he knew that arguing with the drunken LaRocca would be foolish and a waste of time. He shook his head.

LaRocca lost bet after bet. Nick decided to get even and shake LaRocca up by breaking his balls. He bet against him on every roll and was cleaning up.

"Stop looking at me, you asshole!" LaRocca ordered. "You're bringin' me bad fuckin' luck!"

Nick was enjoying playing with LaRocca's drunken mind and wanted to see how far he could push him.

Unintimidated, he answered, "Fuck you! I'm watchin' my money!"

No matter how LaRocca would bet, Nick Lacavoli would bet opposite and win.

"Listen, you cocksucker, I said stop looking at me! You're giving me the *mal-occhio!*" LaRocca screamed.

From inside his shirt, he pulled out a large gold Italian horn charm hanging on his neck chain. He held it up and pointed it at Lacavoli, believing in the legend that the horn had the power to ward off the "evil eye."

LaRocca bet and lost again. Nick Lacavoli was sadistically loving the head game he was playing and kept staring and smiling at LaRocca.

"That's it, you fucking asshole! I'm tellin' you for the last fuckin' time, STOP GIVING ME THE EVIL EYE, or I'll throw ya through da fuckin' window!"

"Aw, come on, Lorenzo. You wouldn't do that, would you?" Nick taunted as he pulled back his sports coat to reveal the gun in his shoulder holster.

"OK, guys! Enough is fuckin' enough!" barked Sally.

Several other people saw Nick flash his gun and immediately left the barn. Eddie decided to hang around and see what was going to happen next. He was amazed at the size of Nick Lacavoli's balls. He could think of no one else he knew that would fuck with the monster this way.

Suddenly, without warning, but with the quickness of a striking cobra, LaRocca lunged at Nick, reached into his jacket, and stripped him of his gun, which he threw to the floor. Then in one swift motion, LaRocca lifted the stocky, well-built Lacavoli off the floor like he was a feather. He crushed him to his body and held him in a powerful bear hug.

"LaRocca! Put 'im down!" ordered Sally.

All the other players had fled the table.

"Fuck you, Sally! This degenerate motherfucker won't stop giving me the evil eye, so he's gotta pay! You heard me, I warned him!"

LaRocca promptly carried Nick over to the window and, as he had threatened, threw him through it. Fortunately for Lacavoli, the windows were all open, so he only went through the screen that covered the opening.

LaRocca stormed back over to the crap table and ordered, "Hey, don't anybody fuckin' leave! I'll be right back!"

He staggered over to the door that led into the kitchen area of the barn. LaRocca reappeared almost immediately with a rope of garlic hung around his neck.

"I can't fucking believe this!" Eddie whispered to Vinnie.

They were all fighting back the urge to burst out laughing. Sally understood the serious consequences that their laughter would bring.

"Hey, D'Amico, don't be an asshole. If you laugh, we'll have a real donnybrook in here," warned Sally. "Vinnie, this guy's an accident waiting to happen. You know what to do."

Vinnie nodded, and Eddie wondered what their plan was. Only the strong-hearted players had returned and taken their places around the table. They too were fighting back the urge to laugh, but since all of them were Italian, they understood the superstition and the significance of LaRocca's garlic necklace: If all else failed, the superstitious believed that garlic around one's neck was a powerful medicine that would ward off the evil eye and evil spirits.

"All right, I'm ready for all you pricks now," said LaRocca, placing his bet on the table.

The mood around the table was lightened by LaRocca's garlic necklace. The magic power he believed it possessed seemed to be working. He suddenly began to win with each toss of the dice.

"Are you doing what I think you are?" Eddie whispered to Vinnie the stickman. Vinnie winked at Eddie and smiled at his perceptiveness.

"It was better than having someone get killed at the Don's party," Vinnie whispered back. "They stay in until he's even."

Vinnie is slicker than shit, Eddie thought to himself.

Although he was watching carefully and knew it was happening, he could not see Vinnie make the switch of the loaded dice every time LaRocca rolled.

He'd finally seen enough. Eddie had been in the barn over an hour.

"I've gotta get going. Megan must be wondering where the hell I am."

He found Megan and Carmella alone in the front parlor. As he entered the room, their conversation ended abruptly. He had heard just enough to let him know they had been talking about him.

"I'm ready any time you are," he said.

"I'm ready too. I'll just go get my things."

He sat down next to Carmella while he waited for Megan to return.

"You're having a problem with all this, aren't you? You don't approve."

"Those kinds of judgments I leave to God, but you are still a married man. I'm just afraid you're going to hurt her. She's sensitive and vulnerable. Her life has been very difficult, and I can see her going from the frying pan into the fire. I think Megan sees you as an opportunity to escape the tragic memories of her past."

"You're wrong, Carmella. It's different with her," Eddie argued.

"Come on, Eddie, let's be honest with each other. We're old friends. You can't fool me. Let's face it, she's just another conquest for you. What's so different? You're just another married man out screwing around on his wife."

"Carmella, I wish you could understand. My marriage with Danni has been over for years. She—"

"Eddie," Carmella interrupted, "I understand perfectly. If something in your relationship with Danni is broken, fix it—one way or another. It's never too late if you really want to try. Don't you think it's time you did something right in your marriage?"

Feeling uncomfortable with her comments, he wanted to end the conversation. He knew she was right. He had a lot to think about.

"Thanks, Mother Superior, I'll think about everything you just said."

"Don't just think about it, Eddie. Do it!" she answered, giving his hand a sisterly squeeze.

Their conversation ceased when Megan returned carrying her purse and a small overnight bag.

Chapter 10

Eddie tuned the radio to soft mood music and lowered the windows to allow the balmy night air to carry the pleasant odor of freshly cut hay into the car. They rode along without speaking for some time. When she could stand it no longer, Megan broke the silence.

"Eddie, what did you and Carmella talk about before we left?"

"Come on. That's a no-brainer. I'm sure you know, Megan. She's worried about you, about us, about me hurting you. It bothers her that I'm married. My god, Megan, don't you see what a mess it could be if we start getting serious with each other again?"

"What do you mean 'again'? It's not again for me. I made the mistake with us a long time ago, but I never stopped loving you. This isn't again for me, Eddie—it's still!" she responded emphatically, obviously hurt by his remark.

"Look, Megan, you dumped me for whatever reasons, and I was devastated. It hurt for a long time, but I had to get on with my life. I loved Danni when I married her, but I can honestly tell you that I never loved anyone else the way I loved you."

"Then how could things possibly be any more of a mess for me than my life has already been? The only other thing in my life that hurt nearly as bad was when I finally got pregnant and my husband beat me when he was in one of his drunken rages and I had a miscarriage. I can't tell you how much I wanted that baby!"

Remembering the horrible incident, she began to sob.

"You told me at the cottage that you really haven't had a marriage with Danni for a long time. I'm sure you've been unfaithful to her, and I'm sure she's not stupid. No doubt she knows it too. You say your marriage is over. Can't you just end it so we can be together? Let's do what's right for us for a change," she pleaded tearfully.

Eddie felt stuck for an answer. All at once, Carmella's voice was ringing in his ears—"Make the right choices."

Eddie kept glancing from the road to Megan's face. She looked beautiful as the reflection from the streetlights danced in and out of her liquid blue eyes. He felt overcome by a desire to touch her. He reached out and took her hand.

"Megan, you need to know that as soon as I saw you today, something came alive inside of me—something that's been dead for a long time. I don't know how to explain it, but it felt good, and being with you again feels right."

Now her eyes brimmed forth with tears of joy. These were the kinds of words she had hoped to hear from him.

As if they were two young lovers, she snuggled up to him and relaxed back into the comfortable seats of the big car. She closed her eyes and enjoyed the moment, the music, and the wind in her face.

"You know, Eddie, you really had me upset and worried when we left the party. You aren't going to change your mind about us, are you?"

Still apprehensive over the problems that would confront him, he admitted, "Shit, Megan! I hope you know what this means I'll have to face! You know, before we left the party, Carmella said something to me that really struck home. She told me to do something right for a change with my marriage. You know, she was absolutely right. I think I should finally take her advice."

"What do you mean?" she asked nervously.

"I mean . . . I just want everything to be right for a change. We can't do this the wrong way. I can't do it to Danni, or to you . . . or even myself, for that matter. I'm tired of playing games. I want you to be my wife, not my broad."

Megan was not at all prepared for what he had just said. It was much more than she had expected, but all that she had hoped for.

"Oh my god, Eddie! I've waited so long to hear you say that. This time, I'll do whatever you say. I swear, I don't want us to blow it again! All I want is to be with you for the rest of my life!"

"Then there's some things you need to understand. First, I'm going to have to sit down and get things squared away with Danni. I'm tired of all the lies and the guilt I feel every time I go home and have to look at her face after I've been out screwing around with other women."

Megan put her arms around his neck and kissed him on the cheek. She'd never felt happier in her life.

"Eddie, I'm not hungry anymore. It's already so late. Can we just go somewhere and spend the rest of tonight together?

As his answer, he pressed the accelerator to the floor as she reached out and placed her hand between his legs, devouring him with her eyes.

Eddie ushered Megan into the elegantly furnished lobby of the 111 Park Avenue Hotel.

"Eddie, this place is gorgeous!"

Thinking he would check in at the desk, he instead escorted her directly to the elevator doors. When he pushed the button for the top floor, Megan incredulously whispered, "Don't tell me this is where you live?"

"No, this is where I play," he answered honestly.

Alone in the elevator, they kissed passionately until the doors opened. Hand in hand, they walked down the wide hallway on thick, plush carpeting. Eddie unlocked and pushed open the set of grand double-entry doors, revealing a beautifully appointed three-bedroom suite. Megan gasped at the splendor of the furnishings and the extensive use of white marble throughout the decor.

"My god! Is this yours? It's so beautiful!" she exclaimed as she danced across the room and ran her hand along the mantel of the superb marble fireplace.

"Eddie, can we light a fire?"

"Baby, we can do anything you want. But it'll get hot as hell in here."

"Then we can open the windows and doors!"

Acting like a kid who had just received a new coveted toy, she ran to the double french doors, opening them fully, and stepped out onto the balcony.

"Oh my! This view is magnificent! You can see the lights of the whole city from here!"

He followed her out and wrapped his arms around her waist.

"Do you really like it?" he asked.

"You must be joking! What's not to like? It's fabulous!" she exclaimed, taking in a deep breath of fresh night air.

Standing there holding Megan in his arms confirmed for him a need to make an honest attempt at changing his style of living. For years, his sole purpose in keeping this apartment was for nothing more than entertaining women, mostly strippers, for his and his friends' illicit love affairs. He decided that with Megan in his life, he would no longer have a need to use the apartment as a whorehouse.

Megan turned and reached up, trying to kiss him. He pulled his head back and looked seriously into her eyes.

"Megan, tell me something. Would you like to live here?"

"Come on, Eddie, don't tease me," she responded with wide-eyed wonder.

"No, baby, I'm serious. I wouldn't kid about something like this. I just know that when I leave Danni, I'll give her the house. For her and Ashley, it's only fair. So it seems logical that you and I can live here if you'll be happy with that."

"Oh, Eddie. What am I supposed to say?"

"Well . . . let me think . . . how about something simple, like 'yes'?"

"Yes, Eddie, yes! Yes! Yes! Yes! Is that enough?"

She kissed him fervently and then snuggled her head into his shoulder. Overwhelmed by it all, a thought crossed her mind.

"Tell me something, Eddie. Are you rich?" she asked innocently.

Her question immediately made him think of Don Francisco's bankbooks.

"I get by," he answered.

"You call all of this getting by?" she asked in amazement.

Suddenly another thought occurred to her.

"Tell me the truth, Eddie, I have to know . . . you're not one of them, are you? I mean, like Carmella's father?"

"No, Megan. I'm not one of them."

He pulled her gently to him and kissed her softly on the lips. Taking her hand in his, he led her inside to the fireplace and lit the gas log.

"I need to grab a quick shower. There's some Asti Spumante in the fridge—why don't you get us some while I change?"

Eddie had just finished drying off and slipping into a white silk robe when Megan entered the master bedroom carrying the bottle of champagne and two glasses.

"Eddie, I can't believe this place! The kitchen is incredible—it has everything! Do you cook here a lot?"

"Sometimes. Cooking's a hobby of mine."

"Well, that's good. So at least one of us can," she quipped. "Eddie, tell me again. Are we really going to live here? I'm afraid if I pinch myself, I'll wake up, and this will all be just a dream."

"Yes, Megan. Someday. Someday soon. You and I will live here."

They clicked their glasses and sipped the champagne, toasting their newfound union.

"Now why don't you get more comfortable. There's another robe in the closet."

As Megan headed toward the closet, Eddie took his glass and the bottle of champagne to the sofa in the living room. While he sipped the Asti, he lay back, and his mind started spinning as he reflected on the life-altering events that had taken place that day. His meeting with the Don and the millions of dollars in those little blue bankbooks. His first Mafia council meeting, the Don's birthday party, and, on top of it all—*Megan!* She walked into his life from out of the blue, just like a ghost from his past. And he realized that she was the peace he'd been in search of for a long time. He dozed off to sleep.

"Eddie, Eddie . . . wake up."

She was standing over him in a white silk robe that was much too large for her. The smooth silk fabric clung to her breasts, revealing firm, erect nipples. Megan felt a fiery passion of desire burning inside her. She lowered herself to her knees and opened his robe, focusing her gaze on his face. Eddie reached out for her, but she pushed his hands away. She had waited a long time for this moment. She wanted to control everything that was about to happen just as she had fantasized so many times before.

Megan began tenderly kissing his body. Her searching lips and tongue tasted him unyieldingly, touching him everywhere and stopping nowhere. She loved the touch and the taste of his body as her tongue moved gently down his one leg and then back up the other. She paused only long enough to tenderly massage his erect manhood with the softness of her cheek and lips.

Together they were feeling the ecstasy of her artful oral manipulation. She was driving him deeper and deeper into pleasure, arousing in herself an overwhelming desire to drink him up and devour him. Great waves of sexual excitement coursed through his body.

Megan reached for his champagne glass and slowly trickled the sparkling liquid over his erection. She placed her face between his legs and began licking the sweet-tasting liquid from his flesh.

Again, he reached for her; but once again, she brushed his hands away. Finally, she wasn't fantasizing or dreaming. She had the reality of her desires—his body alone with her.

With a moan of pleasure, she took him passionately and deeply into her mouth. Tasting the very essence of him made her lose herself in the ecstasy of the moment.

Eddie stroked her hair and gently held her head in his hands. A strong, animal-like instinct made him want to thrust himself deeper into her mouth, but his love for her made him remember how long they had both waited for this moment. He didn't want to end it in such a singular manner.

"Wait, Megan," he breathlessly whispered. "Not me alone."

Her oral foreplay had served to fuel the passion of his compelling desire to taste the sweetness of her in his mouth. She didn't try to stop him as he rose from the sofa. He picked her up and carried her like a child in his arms to the white bearskin rug in front of the fireplace. When he gently laid her down, she watched him passively, with half-closed, love-filled eyes as he removed the silk robe from her body.

Eddie noted the reflection of the flames from the fire dance in her eyes as he lowered himself down beside her. He kissed her ever so gently—once, twice, and then again. His hand moved caressingly over her breasts and down her body. He softly stroked her between her legs, and she spread them wide apart, inviting him to have his way with her.

Megan felt the warmth and wetness of his tongue on her nipples while his fingers moved deeply into her, exploring her most intimate and secret places. He raised himself up on one arm and positioned himself on top of her. Lowering his body, he kissed the softness of her flesh, moving downward until his tongue met with his treasure between her legs. The taste of her intoxicating sweetness in his mouth drove him almost to his crest. Her body responsively quivered as she felt her climax drawing near.

"Now! Please, Eddie, now . . . take me now . . ." Her voice trailed off.

Adeptly, he shifted his body over hers. Then he tenderly and gently penetrated the wet softness of her. He slowly entered and withdrew from her several times and then remained motionless.

"No," she whispered breathlessly, "don't tease me . . . Please, Eddie . . . Please put it in!"

Her words excited him, and he drove himself into her, deep and hard. With eyes closed, she moved her body in time to his rhythm.

"Do you love me?" he panted. "Tell me, tell me, Megan."

"Yes, yes. I love you, Eddie."

"Together, Megan, both of us together."

"Wait, Eddie, wait! Not yet!" she pleaded as she began thrusting her body into his with heedless abandon.

"Yes! Yes! Now, Eddie, now!"

She felt the hot force of him explode inside her as her own orgasm released intense and unrestrained excitement throughout her being.

Exhausted from spent emotions, they lay locked in the communion of their naked bodies. Gradually, their passion subsided. Only the truth of their renewed love remained.

"Oh, baby, you are flesh of my flesh and heart of my heart. Our two bodies are now one," he whispered.

"Yes! I love you, Eddie, and I've never felt happier in my life! Do you know it's been over five years since I've been with a man?"

"What!" he exclaimed. "I thought you said it's been three years since your divorce."

"It has been three years, but we stopped sleeping together two years before that. Besides, most of the time during our marriage, he was so drunk he couldn't even get his eyelids up," she quipped.

He laughed. "Hey, that was pretty cute. Did you think of it yourself?"

"Yeah, I'm a quick study. I'm already learning to be a smart-ass like you. I thought it would sound like something you might say," she teased.

He whisked her up in his arms to carry her to the bed. "Well then, come on, my little smart-ass. Let's try to get some sleep. Do you realize what time it is? The sun will be up long before we are."

Overwhelmed by all that had transpired that day, Megan couldn't help but wonder what kind of surprises were still in store for her. She would soon find out.

The sound of voices coming from the next room awoke Eddie with a start. His movements getting out of bed woke Megan.

"Who's out there?" she asked, sleepily rubbing her eyes.

"I'm sure it's Allan," he answered as he put on his robe and headed for the door.

As he walked down the hall, he could hear a woman's voice coming from inside one of the guest bedrooms.

"Go, baby, go! Oh yes!"

As Eddie opened the door, he heard the bed slamming against the wall and the bedsprings screaming out and groaning in protest. He saw Lori, the exotic-looking hooker, as naked as a jaybird. She was straddling Allan and riding him with the fury and determination of a cowboy riding a bull in a rodeo.

As tired as he was, Eddie couldn't help but chuckle at the sight of his cousin's head bouncing against the pillow each time the bed hit the wall. Lori was giving Allan the ride of his life, and he was enjoying every minute of it.

All of a sudden, Allan noticed Eddie standing in the doorway.

"Hi, cuz! W-w-what're you d-d-doin' here?" Allan stuttered between the bounces of his head against the pillow.

"This is my apartment, remember?"

Without missing a beat of her rhythm, she turned her head to look at Eddie.

"Hi, baby. Are you waiting on deck?"

Her words were slurred. It was apparent that she had consumed too much alcohol.

Without waiting for a reply, Lori turned her attention back to Allan and her mission at hand. She seemed hell-bent on bringing herself to another orgasm, at the expense of Allan's already-worn-out pecker.

"What's going on in here?" Megan's voice asked from behind Eddie as she peeked over his shoulder.

Allan gave them one of his silly, boyish smiles and at the same time rolled his eyes in pleasure. He shrugged his shoulders and closed his eyes as the dauntless Lori rode on.

"Let's go," Eddie said as he turned and took Megan by the arm.

"Eddie, what are *they* doing here?"

"Well, shit, Megan. I thought it was pretty damn obvious what they're doing."

"For crying out loud, Eddie, you know what I mean."

"I told Allan he could stay here tonight. He brought some broad here with him to get laid. Geez, Megan, now I'm wide awake, and my stomach's growling."

"Oh God, Eddie, I'm not hungry. It's too late for me to eat."

"Yeah, but I'm Italian, remember? We can eat anytime. Come on, let's go to the kitchen and see what we can find."

"You're not serious, are you?" she asked.

"Of course. Coming with me, or are you going back to bed?"

In answer to his question, she wrapped her hands around his arm and smiled at him lovingly as she teased, "You know I'll follow you anywhere! Even to the kitchen in the middle of the night."

"OK, then. Come on. I could really go for a nice dish of pasta."

"Pasta! At two o'clock in the morning? You gotta be kidding!"

Megan suddenly realized she had a lot to learn about Italian men and their lifestyle. She watched him with admiration as he moved around the kitchen with the skill of a chef.

"Hey, babe, there's a square plastic container of sauce in the freezer. Can you please get it for me?"

Eddie put the large container of sauce in the microwave and set the controls on high. He had already put a large pot of water on the stove over a high flame. While Megan looked on, he continued to remain busy, preparing a platter of his favorite Italian cold cuts.

The pungent odor of the thawing sauce began to fill the kitchen, and the tantalizing smell began to drift throughout the apartment. Allan suddenly appeared in the doorway of the kitchen. He was dressed in a white silk robe, identical to Eddie's. His bedroom gymnastics had gotten his wavy black hair all mussed. Several curls falling down his forehead made him look like a young boy.

"Tell me I'm not dreaming, cuz. Am I really smelling sauce?" he asked.

"You're not dreaming, Allan. Mr. Chef over there got a yen for pasta," Megan told Allan with a smile on her face.

He picked up a piece of salami and walked over to Eddie's side.

"Boy, that Lori is one great piece of ass! She nearly killed me!"

"How the hell would you know? From what I saw, she was doin' all the work! Last I saw, she was riding you like a Brahma bull!" Eddie teased.

"That's no shit!" Allan chuckled. "She nearly took my cowboy on his last ride," he giggled, pointing between his legs.

As Lori neared the kitchen, she heard them talking about her. She paused for a moment to listen to most of the cousins' conversation. When she finally entered the kitchen, she too was wearing a white silk robe.

Lori was quick-witted and full of fun. She decided to play along with Allan's cowboy analogy, which he didn't know she had overheard.

"Well, how 'bout yoo, buckaroo? Yoo wanna take a ride through these here mountains?" she asked, placing her hands under her enormous breasts and pushing them up.

Her robe draped open, leaving her standing there with a smile on her face and her bare tits in her hands. Megan had never been in the presence of women like this before. She was embarrassed by Lori's crudeness. Sensing Megan's uneasiness, Lori quickly covered herself up and smiled an apology to her.

"Hey! What the fuck's going on here?" shouted a voice from down the hall.

It was Chicky Blandino. He knew Chicky like a book. He was sure he wouldn't be alone. When Eddie heard his voice, he shook his head from side to side.

"Is he going to be in for a surprise!" Eddie chuckled to himself.

Because Chicky was such a close friend of his, he had given him his own key to the apartment. He often picked up broads and brought them there to get laid.

Megan was watching the expression on Eddie's face and wondering what he was finding so amusing. She soon found out, when Chicky appeared in the kitchen doorway, dragging Lori's friend Starr behind him.

Chicky and his hooker were a sight. Their clothes were all disheveled, and he had red lipstick smudged all over his face. Eddie could immediately tell that Chicky was wasted.

"You f-f-fucker," Chicky stuttered. "You're havin' a party and didn' invite me, your best friend," he slurred with a scowl on his face and an unlit cigarette hanging from his lips.

"What the fuck you talkin' about, Chicky? You're the one who did the vanishing act at the party!"

"Yep," he burped. "I'm jus like Houdini! Tha's me—Chicky Houdini!" he giggled drunkenly.

"Hey, how come I'm the only girl here with clothes on? You got any more of those robes?" Starr asked.

"Just go look in a closet, honey. This place has everything," Lori volunteered.

Eddie was glad that the water on the stove had not yet come to a boil. With two more guests, he would need to cook more pasta.

"Megan, could you look in the cupboard over there and find me another box of rigatoni?"

"This place is a zoo!" she whispered as she handed him the pasta. "Is it *always* like this?"

"No. Not always. Sometimes it's much worse," he joked.

"OK, smart-ass," she said as she playfully poked him in the side.

Eddie was just about to dump the two pounds of rigatoni into the boiling water when the telephone rang. He looked at Megan and saw the question on her face. He knew what she was thinking. He looked at the clock on the kitchen wall. It was three o'clock in the morning. He just laughed and shrugged his shoulders as he answered the phone.

"Hello."

"Eddie, it's me," whispered a male voice.

He motioned to Megan to listen as he held the receiver away from his ear so they both could hear.

"Me? Who's me?" asked Eddie, not recognizing the caller's voice.

"For crying out loud, Eddie, it's me! Carm!"

"Oh, Judge, it's you! Why the fuck are you whispering? You in trouble or something?"

"I'm on the fucking house phone downstairs. I'm in the lobby, and I don't want them to hear me!" the judge whispered.

"Who's them?" asked Eddie.

He was feeling as if he and Carmen were doing their own version of "Who's on first and what's on second?" comedy routine.

"OK, listen. Frankie Diamond offered to give Joey and me a ride home from the party, but on the way home, he stopped at the Ecstasy Club. He wanted to have a couple of nightcaps and watch the strippers . . ."

"Carm, are you going to get to the fucking point?"

"I'm trying, I'm trying! Listen. Frankie introduced Joey and me to these two great-looking strippers, and they took a liking to us! They came and sat with us between their acts! Well, anyway, one thing led to another, and we started playing a little kissy-face and touchy-poo in the joint, and the next thing we know, they're hot to trot! Joey and I didn't want to pass up the chance to get a strange piece of ass for once in our lives, so I thought of your place, and here we are! Can we come up? I gotta get outa this lobby before somebody sees me with them!"

Megan was staring at Eddie in disbelief. He just shrugged his shoulders at her again. Their chance for a quiet night alone was already screwed up. Then suddenly, Eddie got a devilish idea. He decided to pull a gag on the unsuspecting Carmen.

"Look, Carm. Give me about ten or fifteen minutes to dress and get out of here. I'll leave the door unlocked for you."

"Great, Eddie!" the judge whispered. "Oh, by the way, is there any food or booze up there?"

"Don't worry, Carm. You'll find more here than you would expect."

Megan realized from the innocent-sounding semantics of Eddie's clever comment that he was going to play a practical joke on his friend.

"You're a devilish rogue!" Megan commented, laughing as she began to sense the humor of his plan.

"Come on, baby! We've gotta move fast!

He grabbed Megan's hand and ran through the apartment calling out to the others. Chicky and Starr emerged from one of the bedrooms asking what was wrong.

"Nothing's wrong—just hurry and come to the living room so I can explain," Eddie answered.

All of the white-robed guests gathered in the living room, and Eddie hurriedly divulged his plan to them. They were all giggling as they headed for their hiding place behind the double doors of the master bedroom. Eddie pulled Megan behind him to the kitchen, where he quickly threw the pasta into the boiling water.

"I'm going to eat tonight if it kills me!" he said.

"It might at the rate you're going," she quipped. "Come on, pasta boy! We've gotta hide!" she said, pulling him toward the master bedroom.

All of the others were huddled inside the bedroom door, laughing and talking.

"Quiet!" Eddie ordered. "They should be here any second!"

They all fell silent just in time to hear the sound of the entry door opening.

"Wait till you see this place—you won't believe it!" said the judge. "It belongs to a friend of mine."

"Wow, honey! This is some place!" said one of the strippers in a strong Southern accent.

All at once, the double doors to the master bedroom flew open, and the six white-robed figures ran out yelling "Surprise!" It startled the judge and his friends, leaving them dumbfounded, wide eyed, and open mouthed.

The stripper with the Southern accent regained her composure first.

"Hey, judgie boy, you didn't tell us we were goin' to a party!"

Looking at the six people dressed in white robes, the other stripper chimed in, "This looks like my kind of party! You got any more of those robes?"

"You fucking Eddie, you'll never change," said Joey laughingly.

The judge was still in shock from Eddie's surprise, but suddenly the humor of his friend's practical joke began to sink in. At first he started to chuckle; then he began laughing so hard tears were streaming down his face.

"What the hell's going on here? You all look like fugitives from a gospel choir practice," he joked.

"Sorry, Judge, you missed the choir practice, but you got here in time for the pasta-eating practice!" said Eddie, still laughing. "Hey, while I finish cooking, make yourselves at home. The bar's over there," said Eddie, pointing. "Allan, why don't you and Lori make everyone comfortable. Turn on some music, sing or do something."

"No problem, cuz," answered Allan.

Chicky and Starr strolled back to their bedroom. Eddie took Megan's hand, and they went to the kitchen to check the pasta.

"Megan, there's too many of us to eat in the kitchen. Will you please move everything out to the dining room table?"

He opened two bottles of Chianti to give them time to breathe. Just as Megan finished setting the table in the dining room, the two strippers, Dixie and Blaze, appeared wrapped in towels. The towels were arranged on their bodies leaving very little to one's imagination. Megan was amazed that they were coming to the table with only towels wrapped around them.

Everyone had taken their seats at the table. They drank the Chianti and munched on the cold cuts as they told jokes while they waited for their dinner to be served. When Eddie emerged from the kitchen carrying a huge platter of steaming rigatoni, Allan rose to his feet, lifted his wineglass, and started singing "O Sole Mio." The other men also stood up, raising their wineglasses in a toast to the arriving food, and joined Allan in song.

My god! Are all Italian men like this? Megan wondered. "Addicted to food, fun, wine, and women—not necessarily in that order?"

With just this small glimpse of Eddie's lifestyle, Megan was beginning to understand what Carmella meant when she said he lived his life in the fast lane. As they all sat around the table enjoying the food and company, Megan found herself enjoying the camaraderie of her strange new acquaintances.

The conversation around the table was light and fast-paced. As Megan watched Eddie, she marveled at how relaxed he was, taking note of his enjoyment and feeling right at home in this type of environment. She had to admit to herself that she was having a great time too.

She found these Italian men fascinating. Their penchant and passion for life was contagious. Megan found herself being swept up in the current of their fun and pleasure. She realized that she was enjoying herself as much as anyone seated at the table.

Suddenly a sobering and chilling thought crossed her mind. With the exception of Allan, every man at the table was married and cheating on his wife. She sensed the anger and hurt their wives would feel if they could see their husbands frolicking around with these hookers and strippers.

Eddie was pouring after-dinner liqueur. As Megan was having her first taste of sambuca, the judge and Dixie excused themselves. Joey and Blaze followed. They disappeared down the hall toward the guest bedrooms to fulfill their fantasies. The two men were getting their wish for a strange piece of ass, and with two gorgeous strippers, to boot. Not bad for their maiden voyage.

Everyone else continued to enjoy the conversation at the table. They were bonded together by the common denominator of their passion. For some of them, it was a natural happening. For the rest of them, it was a wonderful but strange experience. But for all of them, the evening turned out better than anything they could have planned.

With Lori at his side, Allan went over to the white baby grand piano. He began to play softly and sing in whispered tones some old-time favorite songs. Moved by the music, the others joined in, accompanying him in song.

After a while, the judge and Joey returned from their fantasies. Their respite was over. Now it was time for some in this group to leave and face reality. For the judge, Joey, and Chicky, it was time to begin thinking about what lies they would tell their wives.

When they had said their goodbyes, Eddie and Megan crawled exhaustedly into bed. She snuggled close to him and put her arm around him. For her, it was the perfect ending to a perfect day. They said goodnight for second time.

Chapter 11

T hin golden rays of early-morning sun were streaming through the bedroom window. Don Francisco was luxuriating in its soothing warmth as he lay in bed when that inner voice arose, tormenting him, playing tug-of-war with his mind, forcing him to think the thoughts that he had been trying to forget.

What a fucked-up day I've got ahead of me. I have to deal with those animals, the Lacavoli brothers! I have to order them killed to save my own ass! In "my" world, it never ends. The killings used to come easy. Now they're the hard part. When it's over, I have to look into the faces of my wife and children. Now even my grandchildren. Hoping they won't see the death blood on my hands and in my eyes. It used to be so easy. Ah, so what happened? Did I develop a conscience all of a sudden? It never bothered me in the old days. Then I had the balls. I guess I have to face it. I have grown old and soft. Time is the only enemy I can't defeat.

Come on. Why don't I admit it? I've been fed up with my lifestyle for years. I want out of this thing I call my world. Oh sure, I loved it when I was a young stud. All that fucking power! The fast and easy money. And what about all those trashy women I liked so much? Ah, I was a great one with the women. I never could keep my prick in my pants. I even screwed my best friends' wives. But I was lucky my indiscretions were never discovered.

But it's too late. Much too late. There's no going back. I can't retrace my path. I burned my footprints in the pages of time. I made my choices. I fucked up. All the things I used to laugh at—they're not funny anymore. Those things used to sound so ordinary and dull. Now they're important. Enjoying my garden, working with my horses, playing with my grandchildren. Peace of mind. Just a little peace to enjoy for the rest of the time I have left. But enough of this. I have business to attend to. At least I'll have peace of mind today after I kill those traitorous Lacavolis.

He glanced at the luminous red figures on the clock. It was 6:00 a.m. "Shit, I wanted to sleep in for a fucking change," Don Francisco groaned as he slowly got out of his bed. His disturbing introspection had depressed him.

He showered hastily and donned a comfortable robe before descending the stairs. The aroma of freshly brewed coffee met him midway down the steps. When he entered the comfortable country kitchen, Carmella was sitting at the long wooden table reading her Bible. Sensing his presence, she looked up and smiled brightly. "Good morning, Papa."

He managed to convey a forced smile.

"Morning, honey. What got you up so early?"

"I just thought it would be nice if we had breakfast together before church."

"Yeah, breakfast sounds good. I'm famished. I was so busy last night I hardly ate. But I don't know about church. We may not go today."

"Oh? How come, Papa?"

"Ahhh, your mother, Carmella. She really knocked herself out at the party. She overdid the dancing and twisted her ankle. She was in a lot of pain before we went to bed last night."

"Oh, poor Mama. You know, Papa, you need to talk to her. She really needs to lose some weight."

"You don't have to tell me. I've told her a hundred times. But what the hell else can I do? Put a muzzle on her face? She loves to eat."

Don Francisco shook his head and took a sip of his coffee.

"Carmella, were you planning on going to church with us?"

"Well, I was. You see, my car was making some strange noises on the way over here, so I thought I'd ride with you and Mama. But I need to be at the hospital right after Mass for prayer rounds. Papa, would it be all right if I used one of your cars?"

Her question further irritated his already-foul mood.

"My god, Carmella! Why do you even ask?" he snapped, "You may live in a convent now, but remember, you're still my daughter!" he scolded.

"I'm sorry, Papa, but living in the convent, you get used to asking permission for everything."

"Well, damn it, you're not in the convent today. You're at home now," he answered flatly.

"You're right, Papa," she responded meekly. Wanting to change the subject, she asked, "What would you like for breakfast?"

"I don't care, Carmella. You know me. I'm easy. Why don't you surprise me."

Don Francisco got up and headed for the door.

"I'll be back in a few minutes. Yesterday I noticed some of my flowers in the front yard are dying. I want to check the watering system."

Before he could leave, Nicoletta called out from upstairs.

"Francisco! Come help me down."

"All right, Nicoletta. I'm coming, I'm coming."

When they appeared in the kitchen, Nicoletta was hanging on to her husband's arm with one hand and leaning on a cane with the other. Carmella noticed that her mother was dressed up, obviously planning on going to church.

"Ma, how's your ankle? Does it hurt?"

"Ah, whya sure ita hurt. Cornea look, Carmella. It'sa big as a balloon."

Don Francisco shook his head as he helped her sit down at the table.

"If it hurts you so bad, why don't we stay home today? I have some important business to take care of anyway."

"Beeziness, beeziness. Alaways beeziness. Today isa Sunday, Francisco. Today we takea care ofa God'sa beeziness."

"Nicoletta, why are you so damned stubborn? Why don't you listen to me? It makes no sense for you to walk on that ankle any more than you have to. Let's stay home today. It won't kill us to miss church one week."

"Papa, if she feels up to it, take her. You'll make Mama and God both happy."

"Ah, you women! I can never win in this house," he relented.

Don Francisco approached the intercom on the wall and dialed the number to the loft apartment over the barn. The loft had been well planned and designed. It contained several bedrooms and a kitchen, as well as a large comfortably furnished family room. Any of the boys who were assigned to duties at the compound used the loft as living quarters while on duty. But under Don Francisco's order, either LaRocca or the Turk were to be at the compound full-time whenever he was home. This morning, it was the Turk who answered.

"Ya, boss," he answered sleepily.

"How's your head this morning?"

"I'm fine, boss. But ya got da wrong guy. Lorenzo's da one who got fuckin' wasted last night. In fact, I hadda drag his big ass up da stairs and put 'im ta bed."

"Well, is he up yet?" the Don asked.

"Ya, he's in da john takin' a steam. He's tryin' ta sweat da booze outa his system," he half laughed.

"OK, good, because I want both of you to drive us to church. You and Lorenzo are going to have to take care of some business for me right after Mass."

"OK, boss. Whatever you say."

"Turk, bring the limo around front at eight thirty."

"Eight thirty it is, boss, wit bells on."

Carmella had taken in her father's conversation.

"See, Papa. Don't you feel better now?"

"I don't know, Carmella. Something tells me it would be better if we stay home today and I take care of my business."

"I tolda you, nevera mind the beeziness! Go, Francisco, go now. Geta dressed. You'lla feela better aftera you go to church," Nicoletta said petulantly.

LaRocca skillfully eased the big black limousine to a halt alongside the curb in front of St. Francis Catholic Church. Other arriving churchgoers paused as they walked past the limo, trying to peer inside through the black-tinted windows, most of them knowing its passengers were the notorious Barratinos.

The Turk jumped out and opened the door to for Nicoletta. As she tried to move, she experienced a sharp pain in her ankle. Even with the Turk's assistance, she was having trouble getting out of the car. Watching her futile efforts became irritating to Don Francisco. He was fast growing impatient, and his anger was mounting.

Her ankle is only part of the trouble. She's getting too damned fat! he thought to himself.

His bad mood flared, and he threw open the other door, jumping out of the car.

"What a hardhead she is," he muttered to himself. "I knew we should have stayed home today."

Realizing his boss was upset and unguarded, LaRocca sprang from his seat and ran around to assist the Turk with the disabled Nicoletta. Passersby couldn't help but stare as the two frightening-looking men were trying to extricate the overweight old woman dressed in black from the vehicle. Don Francisco was growing even more annoyed and frustrated with each passing moment.

"At the rate we're going here, we'll be lucky to get to church in time for Christmas Mass! Turk! Go inside and get a wheelchair! There's usually one in the entry somewhere," the Don ordered.

The Turk stepped away from the limo and cautiously looked around. Don Francisco went around the vehicle and took his wife by the arm.

"You know, Nicoletta, why is it you never listen to me? I told you this was not a good idea!"

She dropped her eyes to the ground.

He'sa right, she thought. *Now my whole leg isa killing me.*

Not wanting to anger him any more than she already had, she remained silent, leaning on her cane. She was glad to see the Turk running down the sidewalk with a wheelchair. She could no longer stand the pain and was anxious to sit down.

In his usual custom, LaRocca walked in a guarded manner behind the Don as the Turk pushed Nicoletta in the wheelchair up the slight grade into the church foyer.

"Do you want us to come in, boss?"

"No, Turk, thanks. I can handle it now. We'll sit in the last row, and I'll park the wheelchair in the aisle. Just make sure you and LaRocca are here in an hour. No more than an hour, you got that?"

"Got it, boss!"

"In the name of the Father, the Son and the Holy . . ."

Don Francisco couldn't keep his mind on what the priest was saying. He drifted back to his sentiments earlier that morning. The thoughts were haunting him. *I've wanted to retire for a long time. Money is certainly no problem. I have all I'll ever need. Power—no problem. I've been one of the most powerful dons in the country. Yes, in my world, I managed to have it all. There's nothing more I need. Except peace. Peace of mind. Just peace of mind . . .*

"And that is the word according to St. John . . ."

The thought of handing down his power was beginning to put him in a good mood and excite him.

Maybe I could return to Sicily and buy a farm.

With each moment that passed, he became more firmly entrenched and pleased with the idea of retirement. There was not one thing he could think of that could justify his continuing on any longer.

A few unfinished business matters can be handled by Dominic. Yes, in fact, Dominic has all of the qualifications to take my place . . . or maybe better yet! I could appoint Sam Lacavoli! That would mean I don't even have to kill those bastards today. So what? Let them have the opportunity they've always wanted. Let them do their drugs. Let them make their fucking wars if they want. Why should I give a shit anymore?

Don Francisco felt it was quickly becoming a perfect plan.

Why did I wait so long? Why am I tormenting myself? Yes, my decision is made. It is done.

Don Francisco turned to look at his wife.

So she's grown old and fat, but I still love her. Her life has not been easy all these years living with a womanizing bastard like me. I can make it all up to her. I'll tell her my plan on the way home. She'll be so happy. Nicoletta and Carmella were right! I feel much better after going to church! He chuckled to himself.

"And so, my children, go in peace."

That's right, Father, I'll be going in peace. As soon as I get Nicoletta home, I'll call the Patrino and let him know that Sam Lacavoli has my blessing to become the new don. Then I'll meet with Lacavoli and grant him the surprise of his life!

He rose to push Nicoletta out to the waiting limo. As they exited the church, he saw the Turk jogging up the sidewalk toward him.

Thoughts ran quickly through his mind.

Turk and LaRocca have been faithful and loyal. Maybe they'll even want to retire with me. I could take them with me to Sicily. I can make them rich. They can live the rest of their lives like kings, he thought.

"I'll take da chair now, boss. How was church?"

"Turk, I can't wait to tell you how great it was!"

Don Francisco's eyes were beaming, and he was smiling from ear to ear. The Turk was confused and gave his boss a puzzled look as he rolled Nicoletta to the waiting limo. LaRocca rushed to open the rear door and began helping the Turk get Nicoletta inside. Seeing how much time it was taking, Don Francisco decided to walk around and enter the vehicle from the street side.

Parked half a block down the street was a white panel van. Sitting inside, two dark-skinned men had been intently watching the door of the church.

"There he is!" said the driver, starting the engine.

At first, he moved the van slowly in the direction of the limo.

"Now! Go now!" shouted the man in the passenger's seat.

The driver slammed the accelerator to the floorboard. The van responded instantly. Smoke billowed from the spinning tires that screamed out in protest as they bit into the dry pavement. The engine roared as the white van raced down the street at breakneck speed toward the limo. The passenger released the safety on the powerful automatic weapon he held.

The squealing tires and thunderous roar of the engine immediately caught the attention of LaRocca, the Turk, and Don Francisco. But everything was happening faster than the blink of an eye.

"Now!" screamed the driver. "Shoot now!"

The gunman squeezed the trigger. The staccato blasts from the powerful weapon broke the morning silence. Instantly, the Turk pushed Nicoletta's body to the floorboard of the limo and jumped on top of her just as a hail of shattered glass showered down over them.

Don Francisco was rounding the rear of the limo and had no place to hide. He had tried to make it to the door for cover, but the van was barreling down on them before he could get there. The van was careening wildly from side to side as the driver fought to keep it under control. The sound of bullets ricocheting and tearing through the metal of the limo filled the air. The erratic movement of the van was causing the shooter to have difficulty in hitting his target.

LaRocca, trying to reach the Don—who had crouched for cover behind the rear of the vehicle—was only a step away from the man he was determined to protect. In an instant, the van was alongside the limo, and the gunman was firing at close range. He located his crouching target, took aim, and squeezed the trigger again.

LaRocca dove into the violent hail of bullets in an attempt to shield the Don. Just as he knocked Don Francisco to the ground, covering him with his body, LaRocca felt hot, searing pain in his back as the bullets tore through his flesh.

Don Francisco's mind was screaming.

No! Not now! Not like this! Not on the street like a fucking dog! I have my plan—peace . . . peace . . . , he thought as he blacked out.

Don Francisco was lying on the pavement, bleeding and pinned down by the weight of LaRocca's heavy body. LaRocca tried to move, but the pain was too unbearable. He groaned as he heard the sound of the van's tires squealing around a nearby corner to make good its escape. He could hear women screaming and then the fading sound of a siren before he lost consciousness.

Chapter 12

T he persistent ringing of the telephone eventually stirred Eddie from a deep sleep. Megan was still slumbering soundly, undisturbed by the jangling of the phone next to her ear. He reached across her naked body and glanced at the clock as he picked up the receiver. It was almost one o'clock.

"Hello," he answered groggily.

"Eddie, there's big problems. The Don and LaRocca were just shot."

"WHAT? NO! Oh God, no!"

He bolted upright, stunned fully awake.

"How bad is it?"

"It's bad. Real bad. Things don't look good for the Don."

"Oh my god! I can't believe it! LaRocca—what about LaRocca?"

"He was hit pretty bad too, but nobody here knows anything yet. They're both still in surgery. Look, there's no fucking sense us bullshitting on the phone. Get your ass down here right away!"

"Yeah, right. I'm on my way. Hey wait, Dad! Don't hang up. Are you there?"

"Ya, I'm here."

"You didn't tell me which hospital!"

"Park Avenue."

The line went dead.

Slamming down the telephone, Eddie jumped out of bed.

"Megan! Megan!" he yelled.

Startled awake, she sprang up.

"What? My god, Eddie! What's the matter?"

He was yanking clothes off of hangers and struggling to get into them as fast as he could.

"No time to talk now. Hurry, Megan! Get dressed!"

"Get dressed for what? What the hell's going on?"

"Don Francisco's been shot! We need to get to the hospital right away. He may not make it."

"Oh my god, no!"

"Hurry, Megan!"

She jumped out of bed and began throwing on her clothes.

The hospital was located several blocks from the hotel on the same street. Driving like he was demon possessed, Eddie wildly cut in and out of traffic. His erratic driving frightened Megan out of her wits. She breathed a sigh of relief when he brought the Cadillac to a screeching halt in a No Parking zone in front of the main sidewalk leading to the entrance of the hospital.

He jumped out of the car and ran to the other side for Megan. Before she realized what was happening, he had pulled her out of the car. Clutching her hand in his powerful grip, he began running, almost dragging her behind him. As they neared the doors, they were both gasping for air.

They were panting as they passed several policemen milling around outside. The cops were watching the crowd that was beginning to congregate. A mob member stood on each side of the entry door, watching everyone who entered the building. Eddie couldn't help but notice that the two gangsters looked rather foolish the way they were dressed in the heat of the afternoon sun. Both men were wearing suits and ties, and they sported very Mafia-looking wide-brimmed hats. He thought they looked like guys playing the parts of gangsters in a B movie, imitating themselves.

Eddie and Megan gaited past the two mobsters and entered the large two-story lobby of the hospital. He went immediately to the information desk and approached a sweet-faced elderly lady dressed in the customary pink-and-white-striped uniform of the hospital auxiliary.

"Can you please tell me what room the Barratino family is in?"

The woman smiled at him pleasantly and looked at her charts.

"I'm sorry, honey. I don't see anyone by that name on my list. How are you spelling it?"

Duh! Eddie thought to himself. *How could I be so stupid? I must be getting senile!* "Never mind, ma'am. Would it be OK if I use your phone for a second?"

"Sure, honey, go ahead."

Eddie dialed the hospital operator. Within seconds, a page came ringing out through the loudspeaker system.

"Mr. D'Amico. Dominic D'Amico. Please call the operator."

A few seconds passed.

"Hi, it's me. Where the hell is everybody? OK, thanks. I'm on my way up."

She watched as he pushed the elevator button for the second floor. "We gotta go to room 200. It's some kind of private waiting room for the family. God, I'm dreading this!"

Reaching the room, Eddie braced himself for the worst and then pushed open the door. As he and Megan entered the room, they were immediately overcome with a sense of sadness and despair that permeated the room. Nicoletta was lying on a folding cot that had been placed against the far wall. Her hands covered her face. She was crying uncontrollably. Her daughters Angie and Margaret were at her side, stroking her head and whispering words of encouragement to her in Italian.

Carmella, dressed in street attire, had withdrawn to a corner of the room. She was sitting on a footstool, weeping. Feeling her friend's pain, Megan walked over to her with tear-filled eyes. She knelt down beside Carmella and put her arm around her without speaking. When Carmella saw Megan, the two friends embraced and remained locked in the comfort of each other's arms as they wept together.

Eddie walked over and nodded a greeting to Father Azzi, who was consoling Don Francisco's other two daughters Flora and Julia. They were listening to the priest and softly sobbing. Eddie silently embraced the two sisters and then walked over to the cot to pay his respects to Nicoletta and the other daughters. He knelt down next the cot, leaned over, and gave Nicoletta a long, fond embrace.

"I'm sorry, Ma," he whispered in her ear.

She looked into his face and began to wail.

"Oh, Edawardo, they shota your godfather! It'sa my faulta! It'sa my faulta! He no wanta go to church today. Those moolanjan disgustoso bastia shota mio Francisco!" she cried.

"I know, Ma. I know."

Tears began to run down Eddie's cheeks.

"Where's Sally?" he quietly asked Margaret.

"In the next room with the men," she answered, nodding her head in that direction.

As he approached, he detected an aggregation of men's voices penetrating the door. When he opened it, the room was filled with smoke and the pungent odor of their little dago rope cigars.

The room was large. It looked like some kind of meeting or training room. In the center was a row of folding tables. Seated in the chairs around the tables were members of the family.

Looking to the far end of the room, he spotted the Patrino and his two friends Don Cheech and Don Pasquale, surrounded by their bodyguards. By Mafia protocol, he knew that he must pay his first respects to the old dons.

As he headed in their direction, a large powerful-looking man with menacing eyes stepped in front of him and blocked his path.

"Rocco! He's OK! Let him pass," called out the Patrino.

Obediently, Rocco moved out of Eddie's way but eyed him suspiciously. The Patrino, mistakenly thinking Eddie was a made member of Don Francisco's family, said, "You will see that those who did this treacherous fucking thing to your godfather will get what they deserve."

Don Cheech and Don Pasquale had their eyes fixed on Eddie, waiting for his reply.

"You may be sure, Patrino, that those involved in this treachery will pay for their evil deed," said Eddie, giving them the answer he knew they all wanted to hear.

"Good. Very good. That is the way of our world," said Don Cheech.

"But don't forget. Not only those who pulled the trigger must pay, but also those who put out the contract. They all must die before you can consider this matter settled," said Don Pasquale with animosity in his voice.

The Patrino rose and looked out the window as he joined the conversation with his back to the others.

"They say it was the moolanjans. Have you heard any more news?

"No, Patrino. I just arrived. So far, I know nothing at all."

"Then go and find out what you can. When you know more, come back and see us," he ordered.

"Of course. As you say, Patrino."

As he walked away, he could feel the eyes of the three dons and their mobster entourage on the back of his neck. He headed back toward the folding tables. As he walked across the room, he spotted a chalkboard on the far wall. One of the boys had scrawled a message across it in big bold letters: THEY WILL PAY.

Dominic and Sally were having an intense conversation at the end of one of the folding tables. They were speaking in secretive, whispered tones. The other boys were playing cards and drinking coffee, trying to pass the time while they waited for news of their don's condition.

Just then, the Turk entered the room and made his way straight to where Sally and Dominic were seated. Eddie went over to join the three men. He extended his hand to Sally, but Sally ignored his gesture. Eddie withdrew his hand and, keeping his asperity to himself, thought, *Fuck you too, asshole!*

"Look, Sally, I know there's nothing I can say to make things any better, but I want you to know how sorry I am."

"Yah, yah, sure. Everybody's sorry."

"So what the hell happened? Your mother said the shooters were black. Is that true?"

"It's true, all right! Those no-good fuckin' spearchuckers did it! Turk saw them with his own eyes! Not only that, the fuckin' van they drove was One-Eyed Jack's."

"Wait a second, that doesn't sound right to me—" Eddie was cut midsentence by Sally.

"Hey! I don't give a damn how it sounds to you. Tell him, Turk! Tell him what you saw!"

"Tha's no shit, Eddie. It was dose no-good fuckin' moolanjans dat made da hit. Dey was drivin' dat white fuckin' van wid da pitcher of a one-eyed jack on the side. Dey came at us from outa nowhere, blastin' away wid a chopper! We never had a chance to do nuddin'!"

Eddie was shaking his head in disbelief.

"But it just doesn't make any sense at—"

"What's your fuckin' problem, D'Amico?" screamed Sally, poking his index finger into Eddie's chest. "Turk was there! He saw the whole fuckin' thing with his own two eyes!

"Yeah, well, sorry, but I don't buy it! Just think about it a minute! One-Eyed Jack's too fucking smart to use his own vehicle on a hit like this. Somebody set him up."

Dominic interceded. "Come on, Eddie. Wise up. The Turk knows what he saw. He saw the driver and the shooter. They were black. They were Jack's boys!" said Dominic emphatically.

"And you'd better start fuckin' buyin' it, Eddie! It happened, they did it, and my old man is in there fuckin' dying proof of it!" yelled Sally. "Turk said it was those degenerate fuckin' niggers. That's all the proof I need! What do you need? A fuckin' building to fall on your head?"

"You're always so damned contrary, Eddie! No matter what anyone says, you always think you're so much fucking smarter," snapped Dominic.

"Look, I'm not trying to start anything here. I just thought you guys were smarter than this. I know One-Eyed Jack's not that stupid! Just stop and think about it for one fucking minute. If any of you were gonna make a hit, would you use your own fucking car? No. Absolutely not!"

Sally jumped in. "You'll see how stupid he is! As soon as things get squared away here, he's history! I'm gonna show Mr. One-Eyed Jack motherfucker how stupid he is! He dies!"

The Turk piped up, "Yah, tha's no shit! I got a real fuckin' score to settle wid dat scumbag!"

"You guys are the ones with one eye! Are you all blind? You'll be playing right into the hands of the clever cocksucker who wants you to come to this conclusion. Some smart bastard planned it and knew you guys would fucking fall for it. Wake up!

All of you need to give this shit some serious thought before you go off half-cocked and take out Jack. My bet is you'll be killing an innocent man!"

"We don't have to think about it anymore, Mr. Smart-ass Fucking Professor! Jack's goin' down!" said Dominic, pounding his fist on the table.

"I'm outta here! But remember, my bet is you're all dead fucking wrong!"

His blood was boiling as he made an abrupt exit. He just wanted to find Megan and get the hell out of the hospital. When he threw open the door to 200, she came running over to him. She took his arm and hugged it in both of hers, pulling him down so she could whisper in his ear.

"Oh, Eddie! I can't believe what's happening here! It's worse than a nightmare!"

Without responding, he pulled her head to his shoulder and tenderly stroked her long blonde hair.

"Eddie, you have to come and help me talk to Carmella. She's a basket case!"

Carmella was still sitting in the corner, staring at the floor and sobbing quietly.

"Eddie, she's blaming this whole thing on herself. She thinks she's responsible for him getting shot!"

"What? Why in the hell would she think that?"

Megan pulled him farther away from the others and whispered in his ear.

"She says he didn't want to go to church today, but she talked him into it."

"Oh my god! That is a tough cross to bear!" he said sympathetically.

Suddenly a thought went through his mind that he knew he needed to share with Carmella. With Megan still hanging on to his arm, he walked over to the corner and pulled Carmella to her feet. She yielded to his touch and passively stood up. He placed his hands on her shoulders and shook her gently.

"Carm, please. Pull yourself together. Listen to me, Carm. Look at me and listen."

She raised her head and looked at him through glazed, bloodshot eyes.

"You've got to be strong. You can't blame yourself for what happened today. Somebody was out to get him, and if it wasn't today at church, it would just be somewhere else, another time. You've gotta stop beating yourself up and listen to me for a minute. Whoever was responsible for this really wanted him dead. They would've found him sooner or later."

Her sobs were slowly subsiding, and he knew she was beginning to hear what he was saying.

"See, Carm, no matter what happens in our lives, we've got to remember it's God who's in charge, not us. It was God's plan that your father went to church today, not yours. It was God's plan to have him meet his horrible date with destiny today. Now pull yourself together! You're the spiritual leader in your family. They need you to be strong now."

His words had comforted her. A sad, wistful smile appeared on her tear-streaked face. She embraced him.

"Thanks, buddy, I needed that," she said, using her father's pet name for him.

Megan was awestruck. She had just seen a spiritual side of the man she loved that she never knew existed. Megan believed in God. She considered herself a religious person. Eddie's words had touched her.

Everyone's eyes turned toward the door as it opened, and a doctor and nurse entered the room. The silver-haired doctor was still wearing his surgical gown spotted with blood. His face mask hung limply around his neck. The nurse was holding a clipboard in her hand.

Appearing very professional and robotic, the nurse announced, "Mr. LaRocca has been settled into an intensive care room, and he's resting comfortably. Our records indicate that he has no family here in town."

She paused and glanced at her clipboard to make her point. Everyone in the room was staring at her, listening to her every word intently, anxiously awaiting news about Don Francisco.

The priest spoke up, "But, Doctor, what about Mr. Barratino?"

"I'm sorry, Father, we only attended the surgery of Mr. LaRocca. I believe Mr. Barratino is still in surgery. I'm sure his surgeon will be in to see you as soon as he's finished."

"Would any of you like to see Mr. LaRocca for a few minutes?" asked the nurse. Eddie and Father Azzi answered her question affirmatively, in unison. "Doc, how is he? Is he going to be OK?" Eddie asked as they walked down the hall.

"Well, we feel he's out of danger for now. The surgery went as well as could be expected. He was struck by four bullets. One passed through him, and we removed two." The doctor paused. "The fourth bullet, however, presented a problem. It lodged itself very close to his spinal column. We feel it is much too risky to remove it. We decided it would be best to leave it alone."

"But he is going to be OK, isn't he, Doctor?" asked the priest.

"Well, he lost a lot of blood, but he's an amazingly strong man. I'm sure that with the proper care and rest, he should have a full recovery."

They had reached Lorenzo's room. The doctor reached up and slid the room number out of the brass holder screwed onto the door.

"Please keep it short. He's still groggy from the anesthesia, and he does need his rest. Just a few minutes, OK, gentlemen?"

"OK, thanks, Doc," Eddie replied.

Father Azzi went directly to the far side of LaRocca's bed. He pulled out his rosary and, moving his lips, began to pray silently. Eddie looked down on LaRocca.

Funny, he thought to himself, *when those terrible eyes are closed, he doesn't look so frightening.*

He leaned over LaRocca. "Hey, big guy," Eddie said lightly.

LaRocca's eyelids flicked and then opened slightly, revealing his serpentlike eyes. Glancing past the priest, he motioned Eddie closer. He tried to speak, but his mouth was dry, and his lips were parched. Arduously, he managed a gruff whisper.

"The Don . . . what about the Don?"

"We don't know anything yet, Lorenzo. He's still in surgery."

"Fast . . . it was fast, Eddie. I tried . . . tried to take . . . take it all myself. Couldn't get to 'im in time."

"Take it easy, Lorenzo. Don't try to talk now. But I need to ask you one question. Just move your head. Those men, the shooters, were they black?"

With a slight nod of his head, LaRocca indicated yes. He painfully lifted his right hand to cover one eye.

"OK, OK. I understand, Lorenzo. Now get some rest. I'll be back to see ya later."

LaRocca fecklessly reached out his big ham hock of a hand, and Eddie gave it a friendly squeeze. A single tear ran down from LaRocca's eye. The priest was still reciting his rosary as Eddie left the room.

Eddie was walking back to room 200 when he heard a loud, angry voice echoing from down the hall. When he turned the corner, he came face-to-face with the source of the disturbance. It was Tony Banducci, Don Francisco's attorney.

Tony was ranting heatedly, addressing LaRocca's doctor and two men who Eddie assumed were detectives.

"Look, I don't give a damn about your investigation! What are you, guys? Animals? The man just came out of surgery! He almost died!" berated Banducci.

Eddie realized that Tony was trying to head off the detectives, who were apparently on their way to interrogate LaRocca.

"Nobody, but nobody, talks to him until his doctor gives the OK! And I'm warning you, Doctor, if anyone—I mean *anyone*—disturbs my client and affects his recovery, I'll have your ass! You screw up, and we'll own you, your house, and your Porsche! When I get done with you, your newspaper boy will have a better-looking financial statement. Have I made myself clear, Doctor?"

"Yes, perfectly clear," the doctor answered tightly.

The attorney wasn't merely bluffing or showboating. He knew the doctor wasn't going to put himself on the line for his gangster patients. Banducci was sure he would make the detectives wait. Fearing he might put himself in a compromising position, the doctor had no problem siding with the attorney. Besides, he didn't really give a damn who shot the big ugly son of a bitch anyway.

The detective stood their ground against Banducci's onslaught.

"You know, Counselor, the sooner we get the information we need, the quicker we can work this case and find the people who did this.

Don't you wanna see justice served for your clients?" asked one of the detectives sarcastically.

"Hey, mister, I'm the attorney here. I'll take care of seeing that justice is served for my clients. Besides, this is family business. We take care of our own."

"Yeah, that's what I'm afraid of. We usually get to investigate more dead bodies after you guys take care of your own! You do know, of course, that murder is a crime in this state, don't you, Counselor?" asked the flinty-eyed detective, zinging back.

"Hey man, read my lips. Fuck you!" Banducci yelled into the detective's face.

Tony Banducci spun around and left the detectives and the doctor speechless and staring at each other.

Man, what fuckin' balls that Tony Banducci has! Eddie thought. He made a mental note to start using Don Francisco's attorney as his own.

Eddie headed back to room 200 to stand the life-and-death vigil for the Don. As he pulled the door open, he bumped into Sally coming out.

"Hey, Sally, I just saw LaRocca. Looks like he's gonna be OK."

"Yeah, so I heard. I'm on my way to see him," Sally said in a dispassionate tone.

Since he had last been in the room, someone had brought in a bunch of vigil candles, which were now burning silently on a table. People were kneeling in front of them, praying. Each person immersed in their own thoughts. The atmosphere was heavy laden with an invisible blanket of sorrow that covered the room like a cloud of smoke.

Eddie's eyes rested on Megan. She looked exhausted and drained. He walked over and knelt on the floor next to her.

"I take it there's been no news about the Don?" he whispered.

"No, not yet. Why is it taking so long?" she murmured back.

"I don't know, but the longer we wait, the more I worry. It can't be good."

Megan lowered her head and closed her eyes. Eddie rose to his feet and walked over to a window, where he stared out silently, deep in his own thoughts. Suddenly the door burst open, startling everyone. It was Sally. With no regard for the tranquil and somber mood of his family, he selfishly and impatiently bellowed out his own feelings.

"You mean the doctor hasn't been in here yet? What the hell's taking so long?"

His rude outburst upset Nicoletta. She began to cry again. Her daughters helped her to her feet and walked her back to the cot. Then the door opened, and a nurse came in.

"Salvatore Barratino. Is Salvatore here?"

"Yeah, that's me."

"Mr. Barratino is out of surgery. He's coming out of the anesthesia, and he's asking for his son and someone named Eddie."

"I'm his son. I'll go first," Sally said tersely.

"I'm going with you, Sally. He asked for me too," said Eddie.

"Fuck it! OK, then, let's go!" snarled Sally.

"Wait, Sally! I'm coming too," said Carmella feistily.

"He didn't ask for you! Wait here with the others!" Sally ordered.

His mean-spirited response angered her. She glared at him defiantly with tiger eyes. The nurse was growing impatient with their bickering. Eddie felt the hair rise up on the back of his neck.

"Like it or not, she's coming with us, Sally! End of story! Come on, Carmella, let's go," said Eddie, reaching for her hand.

As they walked down the long hallway, it immediately became apparent which room was Don Francisco's. Outside the door, two uniformed policemen stood chatting.

Just as the nurse reached for the handle, the door opened, and a doctor emerged. In his usual crude manner, Sally ignored an appropriate greeting and started speaking his mind.

"So what's the story, Doc?" he asked in a demanding and surly manner.

The doctor disregarded Sally's bad manners and responded in a friendly and professional voice.

"Well, Mr. Barratino, we have done all that we medically can for now."

"So what the hell is that supposed to mean?" Sally demanded.

"Your father was struck by three bullets that did a lot of damage. They caused some severe internal bleeding. I'm pretty sure we have the bleeding under control now, but you need to know—"

"Look, I'll tell you what I need to know!" interrupted Sally, "I have to see my father! You and I, we'll talk later." He rudely pushed past the doctor and entered the room.

"Doctor, I apologize for my friend, but please finish what you were saying. What do we need to know?" asked Eddie.

"Well, during the operation, Mr. Barratino went into cardiac arrest. We almost lost him. For a man his age, he appears to be in excellent physical condition, and he seems to have a driving will to live to have even made it this far. Naturally, we'll be monitoring him very closely. But his heart has suffered severe trauma. The bottom line is whether or not his heart will be able to recover from that trauma. That's my immediate concern, so I must advise you to keep your visit very brief. Go see him for a few minutes, and try to keep your brother or your friend in there calm. We need to make sure nothing upsets or excites him. Quite honestly, you may want to call his clergy," he said sympathetically.

Carmella started to break down. Eddie took firm hold of her arms to steady her.

"Come on, Carm. Get it together. You can't let him see you like this. You heard the doctor."

In the room, Sally was leaning over his father.

"Pa, Pa, it's me. Sally. Can you hear me?"

Don Francisco slowly opened his eyes. He tried to respond, but he couldn't speak. He feebly pointed to a plastic water pitcher beside the bed. Sally raised his father's head and held the cup while the Don weakly sipped from the straw. "Sally . . . you are my son. You carry my name," he said frailly.

Suddenly Don Francisco began to cough and choke. He was visibly in pain as he struggled to hold back the urge to cough.

"You must promise me . . . that you will not rest until I am avenged."

"I promise, Pa. I promise. I give you my solemn oath. I will hunt the bastards down to the ends of the earth. When I find them, I will kill the motherfuckers that did this to you!"

Don Francisco gave Sally a fading smile.

"Good, Sally, good. That is what I wanted to hear you say . . . ," he said, gasping for breath.

Don Francisco began to cough. Still holding the cup, Sally tried to give him more water. He waved it away with a feeble gesture of his hand.

Don Francisco sensed he was running out of time.

"Is Eddie here?" he asked hoarsely.

Sally nodded.

"Go, then . . . call him . . . you wait outside. Hurry."

Don Francisco was feeling very weak. He knew he was going to die. He closed his eyes, and his mind cried out.

Fuck you, Death! I spit in your face. But give me one more minute—just one more minute. I have something I must tell Eddie.

When Eddie and Carmella entered the room, they could feel the pall of death. It hovered over them like a black cloud. Don Francisco's rich, deep tan had vanished. It was replaced with the ashen pallor of impending death.

Carmella went swiftly to her father's side. She picked up his hand and began to pray. Eddie went to the other side of the bed, pushing the bed tray out of the way so he could get closer to the Don. He took his godfather's outstretched hand into his. Full of unbridled emotion, he kissed the back of the Don's hand.

"I love you, Godfather," he said.

Tears began to slide down Eddie's cheeks. Don Francisco weakly tugged on his hand in an effort to pull him closer. As the Don began to speak, his words were so inaudible that Eddie had to put his ear next to his lips to hear what he was saying.

"You know, Eddie . . . I have always loved you . . . like you were my own . . . son," he whispered.

Tears welled up in the Don's eyes and rolled down his pale, sunken cheeks.

"I know, Godfather, I know. I have known ever since I was a young boy," wept Eddie, clutching his godfather's hand in both of his.

"Good . . . remember our pact . . . it's all yours . . . take care of my family . . . I love you, . . . buddy.

Don Francisco could talk no more.

"Oh, Papa! My Papa! I love you! I love you, Papa!" Carmella cried out to him.

He looked at her through filmy eyes and managed a smile. She knew he had heard her.

Then Carmella panicked.

"Papa, hang on! Make your peace with God, Papa. Please, Papa . . . ," she begged.

With life ebbing out of him, he gently squeezed his daughter's hand, bidding her farewell. His eyelids began to flutter. He gasped for a breath.

"Forgive me, Father . . . for I . . . have sinned," he whispered weakly.

With tears flowing freely, Carmella gasped a sigh of relief.

The great and powerful Don Francisco Barratino closed his eyes and died.

Chapter 13

Carmella and Eddie opened the door to Room 200 in a benumbed state. Their frozen, bereaved faces instantly telegraphed the terrible message. *He's gone.* Crying and wailing filled the room. Pandemonium reigned.

Megan's eyes filled with tears as she ran to Eddie and embraced him.

"Come on. Let's get the hell out of here. I can't stand any more of this!" he whispered in her ear.

"Oh God, me either."

Inconspicuously, they slipped away, unnoticed. Making good their escape from the loud disorder of the distraught mourners, they ran to the elevator. When the doors opened, it was apparent that word of Don Francisco's death was already out. Throngs of reporters and Barratino family members were clamorously filling the lobby. Eddie grabbed Megan by the hand and led her to the far end of the room, where they ducked out a side door to avoid the disorderly, swelling crowd. Breathless upon reaching and entering the car, Megan exhaled a grievous sigh as Eddie wheeled the car in a sharp U-turn and sped away from the hospital.

Believing they were going back to the apartment, Megan was surprised when he turned the car in the opposite direction as they pulled onto the main street. She felt the desire to ask where they were going but sensed his need for silence.

When they neared the outskirts of the city, Eddie turned onto a road that led out into the countryside. Now late afternoon, the sun blazed like a great ball of orange fire, hanging suspended in the sky just above the horizon. He lowered the car windows, allowing the fresh air and warm breeze to brush across their faces. The gentle wind dried the salty wetness of his tear-drenched face, and the sweet, pleasant fragrance of the countryside wafted through the car, delivering its calming effect.

After driving several miles through beautiful farm areas, Eddie slowed the Cadillac. Megan watched him curiously as he looked for something alongside the road. Suddenly, he pulled the car off the pavement and brought it to rest in front of an old wooden gate that was hanging loose from its weathered, rusty hinges. Still he said nothing. They hadn't spoken to each other since they left the hospital.

As he turned off the ignition, he wrapped both arms around the top of the steering wheel and put his face down, burying his head between his arms. The pulsing of his body revealed his great sorrow. She was yearning to console him but instinctively knew that she was helpless. Nothing she could say or do could remove the hurt and sense of loss he was feeling. Patiently, she waited.

After a few moments, his body stilled. He wiped his face with the backs of his hands and, taking in a deep breath, opened the door and got out of the car. Megan sat motionless and silent in her seat.

Eddie walked around the car and opened her door. Still not speaking a word, he held out his hand for hers. She took his hand and stepped out. He led her to the old wooden gate. Lifting it off the ground, where it had settled into the tangled overgrowth of wild brush, he managed to push it open just wide enough to allow their bodies to pass.

They walked beneath several large old trees, treading across bright green wild clover that covered the ground. Several feet inside the gate, a dirt pathway exposed itself, offering them easy passage through the weeds that had overgrown the fields on either side.

The two walked in silence hand-in-hand down the path lined with noble old trees whose branches provided a canopy of shade, obscuring the bright blue sky. A light breeze whistled softly through the leaves of the trees. Wild birds, resting on the majestic long branches, chirped their welcome as the couple passed where two age-old boulders sat side by side, as if waiting for their arrival. Still without sharing a word, he let go of her hand and went to sit on the smaller of the two boulders. She couldn't help but wonder why he chose the smaller one, now seemingly dwarfed by the size of his body.

She stood for a time, quietly watching him in his solitude. Megan knew he wanted her to be there with him, yet instinctively, she knew that she should say nothing.

The sun was beginning to fall behind the horizon. Moment by moment, its brilliant orange mellowed, bidding good-bye to another day. Exhausted, Megan walked over to a great weeping willow tree. She sat down to lean back against the brawn of its massive old trunk. From the corner of her eye, something caught her attention. Near the base of the tree, two sets of aged and worn initials had been carved in a rough and childlike manner: F.B., and underneath, E.D.

The carvings had silently spoken volumes. Tears filled her eyes. She turned her gaze to the man she loved. His back was still toward her. His body was pulsing again, only stronger this time. The larger, empty boulder beside him also cried out a silent message of sorrow for Don Francisco Barratino. The vacant old boulder was now nothing more than a lonely shadow against the dusk of the setting sun.

Chapter 14

D on Francisco's murder was already creating problems within the Barratino crime family. The question of who would replace him was on everyone's mind. Before his body was even cold, they began to meet in small clandestine groups discussing and debating their choices. It would have been so much easier if Don Francisco had simply retired. Then he would have named his own successor. Given him his blessing. The matter would have been settled. Now, with Don Francisco's death, they must try to reach an agreement among themselves.

The old-timers' choice for their new don was Dominic D'Amico. He had been with Don Francisco a long time. As the Don's counselor, he had proven himself to everyone, including those in the national syndicate, to be cunning and smart, as well as loyal and a true Mafioso. Dominic had balls. He had made his bones many times over during the wars of the old days. Over the years, he had become acquainted with all of the other dons in the country, and he had earned their respect. Yes, Dominic D'Amico would be a perfect choice.

But there was also Sam Lacavoli. Some considered him a good choice. He had always wanted to be a don. He was younger and supported taking the family into drug trafficking and expanding their borders. With him as don, the family would grow. With him in charge, everyone would make more money. But Lacavoli's ambitions and greed would surely lead the family into wars. Don Francisco had brought about peace. Everything had been going just fine until his death.

Over the years, the Don's son, Salvatore, had made his wishes perfectly clear to everyone. He had always expected to take over the family business when the time came.

Many of the older family members had discussed this possibility among themselves. They had unanimously agreed that if the day ever came when Salvatore took over as don, they would retire. Not one of them had any respect or use for Sally. They saw him as unqualified and a threat to the honor and reputation of the family. He had never made his bones; and he wasn't even Sicilian. His impulsiveness, along with his violent and unpredictable nature, would, no doubt, get the family in trouble with other families—not to mention the law. They all agreed it would be better for them to pack it in rather than remain in a family with the explosive Salvatore Barratino as their don.

It had never been a secret how the old Mustache Petes felt about Sally. Even he knew that they did not trust him to be head of the family. But he didn't give a damn. In his opinion, the old-timers were nothing more than a bunch of old dagos with dried-up balls and hearts of chickens. They were all over-the-hill, content to rest on their past laurels and their money.

In his own strange way, Sally loved his father. But now he was gone. Life goes on, and the world of the Mafia keeps turning. With Sally as don, the family would have a fresh, new beginning. He would start wars and invade territories. He would show them all. He was the son of the king. He was a Mafia son. In his mind, that made him a Mafia prince.

Everyone knows the prince always succeeds the king. He had made up his mind that nobody was going to stand in the way of what was rightfully his. Oh sure, he knew the arguments that they would use against him. This business about him being adopted and not having pure Sicilian blood running through his veins. His view was this: To hell with all those phony, outdated ginzo customs and traditions. It was all a bunch of crap, as far as Sally was concerned.

Then there was the shit about him making his bones. What was the big fucking deal about killing someone? It was easy enough. In the days of the old-timers, there were plenty of wars. A lot of people to kill. It wasn't his fault he was raised in a time of peace. It was only timing. Just bad fucking luck. He'd had no one to kill. But he only needed a chance. He'd show them about balls. He'd prove to them how big his were. They'd be so big he'd have to walk bowlegged—maybe even carry them in a wheelbarrow. He mulled those thoughts over and over in his head.

Night had fallen. It had been an exhausting day for Sally. He relived the day's events. After his father was pronounced dead at the hospital, he had gone back to the farm with the others. Chaos took control outside their home. At least the big iron gates protected the family's desire for solitude. Without them, they would have been overrun with hundreds of well-meaning and meddlesome people. Nicoletta had become hysterical when she entered her home. Her husband was dead, but the sense of his presence in the house was overwhelming and more than she could bear. Unable to calm her, Sally finally had to call in the doctor to sedate her.

Behind the wheel of his car, he headed home, just finishing his late meeting with the undertaker, Giovani Garbelli. He was feeling numb and grief stricken over his father's murder that morning. Suddenly, tears began to run down his cheeks. There was so much he wished he could have changed. He shook his head in an effort to erase the thoughts from his mind.

Garbelli was a longtime friend of his father's, and Sally allowed him to make most of the decisions regarding the funeral arrangements. Because of his father's belief in the old-world customs and traditions, Don Francisco would be laid out in his own home. The viewing was scheduled for the next day at 7:00 p.m.

Sally had selected the most expensive casket. Nothing but the best for his father. Don Francisco would be laid to rest in an ornately gauche gold casket lined with burgundy-colored velvet.

As he drove, Sally's mind started spinning again. He was trying to put his thoughts in some kind of order. But his mind wasn't cooperating. It flashed out short little mixed-up blurbs: *After the funeral, find that fuckin' nigger . . . kill the dirty motherfucking scumbag . . . attorney . . . Banducci, Tony Banducci . . . the will. Wonder how much the old man was really worth . . . who gets what . . . let the girls have the property . . . all I want is the fuckin' cash . . . I'll be the don . . . I'm the son, it's my fuckin' right—that's the way my father would have wanted it.*

Sally pulled into the garage of his new ranch-style home. His wife, Connie, was in the kitchen helping their daughters bake cookies. Sally's two daughters were the only people in his life he truly cared about. If there was one ounce of feeling, an iota of love in his cold, unfeeling heart, five-year-old Gina and seven-year-old Marie owned it all.

"Hey, look, Daddy! Look what we made for you!" Gina exclaimed proudly, with a broad smile on her chubby little face.

"Wow! They look great!" he said.

He picked up one of the warm morsels from the plate. Smiling, he shoved the whole cookie into his mouth.

"Mmm . . . dey daste dood too," he said trying to chew and talk at the same time.

Connie waited patiently for him to finish his moment with the children.

"Are you hungry, Sal? Things have been so screwed up I didn't cook. I didn't know what time you'd be home."

"Nah, who could eat? I got so much shit on my mind I don't know if I'm comin' or goin'. I just wanna go to bed. Tomorrow's gonna be a real ballbuster of a day."

"I know. I'm dreading it," Connie replied.

"Come on, girls. Give Daddy a good-night kiss."

He lowered himself down and put one knee on the floor. The girls dutifully ran to him. They each gave him a hug and a kiss.

Sally was almost to his bedroom door when Connie called out.

"Sally! Wait a sec!"

She ran to him and handed him five slips of paper. They were telephone messages.

"Look at these, Sal. Pretty weird, huh? They're all from the same person—Senora Marisa Danielli. Every time she called, she said it was very important for her to talk to you right away. I think it has something to do with your father. Do you know who she is?"

"Yeah, sure. I know her. Nobody important—just some old widow bitch."

"Well, what does she want from you?"

"Whaddya think? I can just fuckin' imagine. My old man's been givin' her money every month for as long as I can remember."

Sally raised his voice into a high falsetto and mimicked the woman speaking.

"'Oha, Salvatore, I'ma so sorry abouta Don Francisco's deatha. Oh, bya da way, don'ta forget mya money every montha!' Screw her! All this benevolent bullshit's gonna stop when I'm the don."

"Sally, why don't you stop being so damn heartless for a change. I'm sure your father had good reason for giving her the money. And besides, you don't even know what she wants to talk to you about."

"What the fuck could an old woman like that possibly have to say that would interest me?"

Connie was irritated by his attitude.

"Well, she's going to keep calling. What should I tell her?"

"I don't give a shit! Tell her I died and went to hell!"

He crumpled the message papers in his hand and tossed them into the air.

"Here! Put these in the trash. I'm going to fuckin' bed."

He was sleeping soundly when the telephone rang. He looked at the clock. It was 6:00 a.m.

This better be good, he thought as he picked up the receiver. "Yeah, hello."

"Whatsa matter, Salvatorie? Why you no calla me back? Youa biga shota now that your father a morta?

She caught him off guard with her ballsy, early-morning censure. Having no better answer, he found himself lying.

"I got in too late last night to call you back. What do you want from me?"

"No, Salvatorie. It'sa what do you want froma me. I'ma gonna give you a gift."

He was losing his patience and becoming irritated with the old woman's game of mystery. It was too early in the morning to be playing verbal sports. He was just about to slam the phone down when she drew his attention.

"You listena me, Salvatorie. I'ma gonna tella you who killeda Don Francisco, bon arme."

"What the fuck are you talking about?" he yelled, jumping to his feet.

His outburst woke Connie. Alarmed, she bolted upright in the bed.

"What's going on?" she prodded.

"Shut the fuck up, and mind your own business!" he ordered.

He turned his attention back to the caller.

"I don't know what kind of game you're playing, but it doesn't matter. We already know who did it."

"No, Salvatorie. Thisa game you talk about, theya play a game ona you! You only know whata they wanta you to thinka you know," said Senora Danielli with conviction in her voice. "Whata I know, I heard witha my owna ears. I evena showa you some proof."

"OK, OK. So tell me then. Tell me now. Who? Who did it?" he demanded.

"No. You cornea to my house. Then I willa tella you the whole story anda givea you the proofa."

"I'll be right over. You wait," he said, hanging up the phone with one hand and reaching for his pants with the other.

"Was that the old woman?" Connie asked.

"Never fuckin' mind!" he snapped.

"Sally, I hate when you act like this! You're acting like a big asshole!"

"So fuckin' sue me!" he yelled as he slammed the bathroom door.

He was making good time through the early-morning rush-hour traffic. He knew where Senora Marisa Danielli lived. He had gone there on several occasions with his father when he dropped off the small manila envelopes for her. Sally had always known the envelopes contained money. He just never knew how much or why.

He recalled that Senora Danielli was a tall, aristocratic-looking woman. Even now, in her later years, she was still attractive. Sally remembered thinking that she must have been a knockout in her day. The woman had always been a mystery to him. He wondered if his father had been fucking her and if the envelopes maybe contained money for the ass he was getting.

He was now driving through the streets of the old neighborhood in which he had been raised. The neighborhood had gone to hell. Poor minorities of all races had moved into the area to take advantage of the cheap rents for the old homes. The houses were all deteriorating. Sally knew they were owned by slumlords, who, like vultures, took the rents and let the homes crumble and ruin.

The contents of knocked-over trash cans were strewn all over the streets. Junk cars were left abandoned in vacant lots, stripped of their motors, tires, and every other removable part. Most of the windows in many of the houses were broken or boarded up.

What a fuckin' mess, he thought. *I can't believe I used to live here!*

He turned into an alley, swerving to miss a pack of emaciated dogs scrounging for food in an overturned garbage can. Senora Danielli's house was halfway down the alley. It stuck out like a radiant stream of light in the middle of darkness. She had kept it well maintained. It sported a new coat of fresh white paint. All around the house, an array of colorful summer flowers tried valiantly to stave off the stench that permeated the area, but with little success.

Sally parked the car and walked around to the front door. When he reached the entrance, he peered through the screen door.

"Senora Danielli?"

"It'sa open, Salvatorie. Cornea in."

From the screen door, he could see her standing in the kitchen at the sink. The place was immaculate, with every little thing in its own orderly, assigned spot.

"Buon giorno, Salvatorie. Sita down. I madea you somea coffee."

"Good. I can use it."

Oh, great! I left the house without even brushing my teeth, he thought as he ran his tongue across them.

He sat down at the small table on which she had set two cups and saucers and a plate of homemade biscotti. He watched her through suspicious eyes as he sipped his coffee, waiting for her to speak.

Senora Danielli began telling her story. She explained how every Sunday after church, it was her custom to go to her cousins' house. She cooked and cleaned for them once a week. She told Sally she made them the same meal every week—spaghetti and meatballs. Yesterday when she arrived, they were drunk and still drinking heavily. She had seen them drunk before, so she didn't think much of it. She told Sally that her cousins could barely eat when she served them because they were so drunk. After dinner, she washed the dishes and cleaned up the kitchen as usual and then went through the house and emptied all the wastebaskets. Usually, she took the trash out when she left for the evening. But that night, she came back into the house to pick up her car keys, which she had forgotten on the kitchen counter. Her cousins did not hear her reenter the kitchen, and she overheard them toasting each other for killing Don Francisco. They were laughing and bragging about the brilliance of their plan. They talked about putting black makeup on their faces so they would look like moolanjans. She heard them talking about how they stole One-Eyed Jack's van. Then she began to fear for her life, realizing her newfound knowledge could prove to be deadly. She knew that if they found her listening, they would kill her. With extreme caution, she quietly slipped out of the kitchen door before she was detected. But a thought occurred to her as she was leaving. On a hunch, she went to the laundry area, which was located in the garage. She found something there that she took to give to Sally as proof that her story was true.

"Here. A gift fora you, Salvatorie," she said, handing him a brown paper bag.

Sally reached in the bag and pulled out a dirty, wrinkled T-shirt. He studied it for a moment. Around the collar were some black smudges from the makeup the killers had used. Touching the shirt gave Sally a strange and eerie feeling. The hair on the back of his neck stood up.

He trembled inside. He knew that he held, in his hand, the garment that the murderer had worn when he killed his father. With the shirt in his hand, he had no doubt that Senora Danielli was telling the truth. She had given him the names of his father's killers, as well as the proof.

"Senora, I have to ask you. Why would you give up your own cousins? They are your own flesh and blood."

"I tella you why, Salvatorie. Youra father, the great Don Francisco wasa truly a man of great honor and respecta. Whena my husband, Fico, workeda for youra father, he wasa his bodyguarda. Fico, he loveda your father. But thosea were terrible times. There were many wars, and many people died. Onea night, your father and Fico wasa cornea outa the funeral home. Somea no-good bastardo startsa shooting ata your father. My Fico, bon arme, he'sa very brave man. He stepsa in front ofa your father and startsa shooting back. He kills the somonabitcha. But he'sa catch three bullets ina chest. Those bullets werea meanta for your father. My Fico, he'sa die before the ambulance comes."

Sally listened intently as she continued.

"Wella, whena that happened, I'ma in a mess. My Fico, he'sa gone. I'vea gotta two daughters—one'sa seven and the other'sa eight. I'ma going crazy. Whata I gonna do? The day after mya Fico's funeral comesa the biga black car. Your father comesa to tella me nota to worry. He saysa he'sa gonna take care a me asa long as I live. And justa like a guardian angel, he did. You believea me whena I tella you, Salvatorie, nevera once, not in alla these yearsa did he evera forgeta my envelope. Whena my girls grow up, he pay toa senda botha them to the college. Now one'sa nurse anda my oldest daugher, she'sa lawyer. Alla this because ofa your father, bon arme."

She had told her story without emotion. But after she ended, great tears of grief filled her eyes and streamed down her cheeks. In all of his cynicism, even the hard-hearted Sally was moved by her story. His eyes grew shiny behind a film of tears he tried to blink away.

"So you aska me abouta giving upa my cousins? Ha! That'sa nothing! Ifa I coulda bringa back your father, I woulda givea upa my owna heart. Dona Francisco, he wasa greata man. So youa see, Salvatorie, I givea you my owna flesh anda blood because they area no-gooda bastardos. They killed a saint. They deservea to die. You makea me a promise, Salvatorie. You killa those no-gooda bastardos. You makea them pay!"

Sally found himself liking this woman. She understood about honor and respect. She understood loyalty.

"I promise you, Senora Danielli. My father's murder will be avenged."

"Gooda, Salvatorie, gooda," she said, wiping the tears from her eyes. He nodded his head and left, carrying the brown paper bag.

Chapter 15

S ally raced down the alley of the old neighborhood and headed for the farm. Rethinking Senora Danielli's story was sending him into an ever-hotter boiling rage. He wanted to see his father's killers dead. He wanted it so bad he could taste it. But he knew he must figure out a plan. He would be the one to decide how and when, and he would catch them by surprise with a sly and cunning scheme.

As he drove, he realized that there must be many more stories like Senora Danielli's. He felt proud of the way his father had honored his promise to her for all those years and was amazed that his father never seemed to forget those who were loyal to him. He had always loved and respected his father, but somehow, he had never seemed able to express or prove his feelings. As usual, he justified for himself that it wasn't his fault. He knew exactly whom to blame.

That fuckin' Eddie D'Amico was always in the way! He was in the middle of me and my father ever since we were kids, he thought to himself. *Always obeying my father's every word like a fuckin' little kiss-ass.*

Now that his father was gone, he wanted to get even with Eddie too. But he knew that Eddie was smart. He was the only one who had seen through the hoax of his father's murder. Besides, he was well liked and respected by all of the family members. But, Sally realized that if he wanted to become don, he would have to get along with Eddie, at least for now. He would need to use Eddie's brains. At least for a while. Then he'd get even with him somewhere down the road, when he didn't need him anymore. Sally liked his plan. He would bide his time. He would wait and pick the right opportunity.

He entered the compound and drove around to the rear door of the barn. No one was around. There was a strange, empty stillness inside the massive structure. But he could feel the ghostly presence of his father as he silently entered the huge great room.

He quickened his step and headed straight to a coat closet. Sliding several hung jackets out of the way, he pushed a hidden button on the side wall of the closet. Sally smiled as he heard the concealed door at the rear slide open. The light automatically went on in the secret room beyond the closet. He entered and admired his father's planning as he viewed the extensive Barratino arsenal.

There must be enough weapons in here to outfit the National Guard, he thought, chuckling to himself.

Sally surveyed the room's contents for a moment. Then he walked over to a case that contained a vast array of handguns. Not finding what he was looking for, he went to another case. Off to the side was a highly polished box. It reminded Sally of the box his mother used to store her special silverware. But this box contained exactly what he was looking for. A small-caliber semiautomatic pistol, complete with a silencer. His eyes widened and lit up in satisfaction.

Ah, perfect, he mused.

Sally took his time, looking the gun over carefully with slow deliberation. He loaded the weapon and screwed on the silencer. He looked around the room for a target. Finding none, he fired into the wall.

Phssst. It was almost soundless. The weapon sent its deadly missile deep into the wooden plank. Sally was elated. This deadly quiet little instrument had given him the answer as to how. His plan was almost complete. All that remained was choosing the right time.

Sally drove around to the front of the house. The undertaker's van was parked in the driveway. Men were unloading the vehicle, carrying things into the house to set them up for the viewing later that evening. Sally wanted to make sure he was satisfied with the arrangements Garbelli was making. Then he would spend a little time with his mother and sisters before mourners arrived.

Garbelli's people had cleared all of the furniture from the front parlor, where Don Francisco's casket would be placed. One entire wall had been covered with a floor-to-ceiling burgundy drape that would serve as a backdrop for the casket. Huge, expensive floral arrangements filled the perimeter walls of the parlor. Flowers had been arriving faster than the undertaker's staff could place them. Many lay in waiting, covering the front porch and a good portion of the driveway.

Ornate brass stands with connecting burgundy-colored ropes had been set up to define a walkway for the hundreds of mourners expected to come and pay their respects. Outside the ropes, the entire concourse was lined with elaborate floral arrangements. Sally admired the well-planned pathway. Visitors would file in and walk past Don Francisco's casket and then circle around and leave, exiting through the same wide double doors through which they had entered.

Sally was pleased with Garbelli's work. He felt it was exactly the way his father would have ordered it.

Don Francisco's body arrived at three o'clock. Sally watched as the casket was rolled into place. His sisters stood by, huddled together, sobbing quietly. A fat old female beautician, who had followed the casket in, began making last-minute touches to Don Francisco's hair and makeup. Sally felt a lump swell in his throat as his sisters sobbed loudly while they watched the woman work on their father.

Sally approached the casket and stared at his father's face, marveling at how magnificent he looked. Thanks to the makeup the woman had applied, his face was again a rich tan. Don Francisco was dressed in his favorite white linen suit with a black tie. Sally slowly shook his head, finding it difficult to believe that he would never hear his father's voice again.

His thoughts were interrupted by his mother's voice calling to him from the top of the stairs. Nicoletta had finished preparing for the dreaded evening and needed help descending the steps. She was dressed in typical Italian mourning attire—a long black dress, with her head and face covered by a long, black lace veil that reached to just below her shoulders. The white handkerchief she held in her hand stood out in sharp contrast against all of the blackness of her clothing. She appeared to be extremely calm.

As Sally helped her near the casket, all of a sudden, she began to flail her arms and wail, screaming out, "Oh, Francisco! Mio Francisco! Why, God, oh why, God, dida you takea mio Francisco?"

Her daughters ran to help Sally restrain her as she tried to throw herself into the casket with her husband. Nicoletta continued to shriek and moan loudly. They all cried together.

❖   ❖   ❖

It was four forty-five. Since most of the Barratino soldiers would need to be stationed around the compound, controlling security at the gates when the visitors began to arrive for the seven o'clock viewing, Dominic had instructed them to pay their respects at five o'clock. The gangsters began to straggle into the parlor. They walked slowly past the casket. Each of them stopped at the head of the casket to kneel and make the sign of the cross as they prayed.

Some of the boys touched Don Francisco's hand. Others stopped to bend and kiss his face. A few whispered their good-byes to their don. Many of them wept openly, unashamed of their feelings and love for him.

By six o'clock, most of the men had left to take their security posts. The Patrino arrived with Don Cheech and Don Pasquale. The Patrino went alone to Don Francisco's casket. He spoke a few words in Italian and then leaned over and kissed his dead friend's lips.

Following the Patrino, Don Cheech and Don Pasquale kissed Don Francisco's cheeks and touched his hand. Together the three Dons briefly paid their sorrowful respects to Nicoletta and Don Francisco's children.

Shortly before seven o'clock, the immediate family took their seats in the white folding chairs Garbelli had set up in the parlor. They sat facing the casket and the walkway so that the other mourners could offer condolences as they filed past.

Promptly, at seven o'clock, the big iron gates swung open. They came in by the scores. It was a bizarre mix of people. Politicians, widows, priests and nuns, labor leaders, bankers and leaders of the business world. They had all come to pay their respects. To say good-bye to the rich and powerful man who had touched their lives. This enigma of a man. This ruler of a crime family, now laid out to rest with the same pomp and ceremony as would be given a president or a king.

They all filed by his casket. Many of them had just shared in the celebration of the Don's birthday. Each one carried with them their own secrets as to why they came. Only they would know their true connection with Don Francisco. Only they would know how this man lying dead before them in the big gold casket had touched their lives. Only they would know the reasons that made the tears fall from their eyes as they looked down at the great man's cold, unmoving body.

They came, and they continued to come. It was nearly midnight when the last of the mourning visitors left. The family was exhausted. Tomorrow would be another long, emotional day for them. Tomorrow morning at ten o'clock, Don Francisco would be buried at Holy Angels Cemetery. Tomorrow, Don Francisco would take his last ride.

Chapter 16

It was well after midnight when the boys finished securing the compound. They headed for the barn to join the others. Some of the men were having a late-night snack. There was still a large amount of food left. Dominic had ordered lavish trays of Italian rolls and cold cuts, huge bowls of iced shrimp, and dozens of rich pastries. And of course, there was no shortage of liquid libation, which created a mood much different in the barn than it had been in the house.

The somber sorrow these Mafia men had all felt as they passed by Don Francisco's casket had vanished. The men's sorrow had been replaced with alcohol-induced anger and vengeance. Now there was family business to think about and deal with. The most important matter at hand was who would take Don Francisco's place as the new ruler of the family. It was a decision that needed to be made posthaste.

Most of the men had been plotting in their own minds how to get their revenge. How they would kill One-Eyed Jack Shepard, and at the same time, trying to decide who would be the best choice to step into Don Francisco's empty shoes.

It was a strange and unusual circumstance to have the Patrino, Capo de Capos, at a meeting such as this. As patriarch of the national crime syndicate, it was understood that as a matter of respect, he would control the meeting and discussion regarding Don Francisco's successor.

The Patrino ordered silence. He looked around the room to be satisfied that none other than trusted Barratino family members were present before he spoke. Eddie D'Amico was there, but none of the men challenged his presence. Not even Sam Lacavoli. He had his own greedy agenda, and he wasn't about to chance angering the Patrino.

"We have spent much time planning our revenge. But now it is time to discuss other more important things. We will have time for our revenge soon enough."

The Patrino paused and looked around the room. He had the undivided attention of all the men.

"Dominic, I have talked to many of your people. You were Don Francisco's counselor for many years. You are their unanimous choice to become the Don of the Barratino family. What say you now?"

Dominic rose from his chair and cleared his throat.

"With all due respect, Patrino, I am honored. But I would rather stay as I am. I feel I will be more valuable as consigliere to the new don. That is, Patrino, if the new don wants me to stay on in my position. I am satisfied being a consigliere. I have never aspired to become a don."

Dominic D'Amico was lying through his teeth. Little did anyone in the room know that he was laying the groundwork for his own cunning and devious plan. In fact, he had already secretly planted the sinister seeds that were already bearing the fruit of his evil scheme.

Eddie had watched Sally as the Patrino talked to Dominic. Sally hadn't batted an eye. He listened silently with a frozen, unemotional look on his face. Eddie thought it was strange. He couldn't believe that by this time, Sally hadn't thrown one of his usual raging tempter tantrums.

The room was deathly quiet. The Patrino turned his attention to Sally.

"Salvatore. You want to lay claim to your father's position. You claim it is your right as his son. But you are aware of the rules of our world. Only a full-blooded Sicilian can become a don. And unfortunately, you have not even made your bones. Because of these things, you cannot be considered.

The Patrino was speaking to him in a kindly and understanding tone. Sally glared at the Patrino but remained tight-lipped. Sam Lacavoli broke the silence.

"Look! If Dominic says no, then I should be next in fuckin' line. Don Francisco and I discussed this for years. He knew I always wanted to take over the family when he retired. He had already given me his blessing!"

"You're a lying cocksucker, and you know it!" Sally exploded.

"What the fuck do you know, asshole? You have no right to be a don. You haven't even made your fuckin' bones! You don't know shit! You're still wet behind the fuckin' ears!" Sam chided.

Sally rose from his chair and walked toward the sofa where Sam Lacavoli and his brother, Nick, were sitting. In his hand, he carried a rumpled brown bag. Sally stood in front of Sam, smiling evilly. Sam sneered at him.

"You're gonna be surprised at how much I know, you no-good motherfucker," Sally said calmly before spitting in Sam's face.

Just as Sam was about to jump up, Sally quickly pulled out the deadly little revolver and put it in Sam's face.

"Sit down! You and I are going to settle this making-my-bones shit right now!"

Suddenly Sam Lacavoli knew that Sally was on to him. He knew he was a dead man. Everyone else in the room could see it on his face. They watched in shocked silence, wondering if Sally had suddenly gone crazy.

"Open your mouth and say 'ahhh,' motherfucker!" Sally ordered.

Lacavoli, brave till the end, spat at Sally.

"Fuck you, Sally. I'll see you in hell."

"Yeah, but you go first, you rotten cocksucker!"

Sally raised the pistol to Sam Lacavoli's forehead and pulled the trigger. *Phsst.* Sam Lacavoli's brains splattered on the wall behind the sofa.

Nick Lacavoli and the Patrino's bodyguard, Rocco, both went for their guns.

"Don't anybody make a fuckin' move," yelled Sally. "Don't even fuckin' breathe!" he said, brandishing his gun.

Sally threw the rumpled bag on Nick's lap.

"Open it!" he ordered. "Pull it out!"

Nick pulled out the T-shirt. As soon as he saw it, he knew he was a living dead man.

"Let's all listen, boys. Nick's got a story to tell us. Don't you, Nick?" Sally asked as he jammed the silencer deep into Nick Lacavoli's ear. He reached into Nick's jacket and pulled the gun from his shoulder holster.

When the Patrino saw the T-shirt, he immediately placed his hand on Rocco's arm, signaling him to take his hand off his weapon. Sally ripped the T-shirt from Nick's hand and threw it to Dominic.

"Take a look at the collar, Dominic, and pass it around," he snapped.

Everyone sat in stunned silence, disbelieving of Sally's actions. They all waited in shock to see what was so important about the T-shirt that it caused Sally to blow Sam's brains out.

Nick didn't want to die. He sat there wondering how Sally had gotten Sam's shirt. He couldn't believe that somehow Sally had found out about their evil deed. With the gun still jammed in his ear, Sally gave him an order.

"Get on your knees, motherfucker, and start fuckin' talkin'!"

Nick quickly obeyed. He was beginning to tremble, fearful that his life was coming to an end.

"I'm fuckin' waitin'!" Sally screamed, jamming the silencer harder into Nick's ear. "Tell us everything, and I'll let you live!"

Nick was more than glad to accept Sally's offer. He wasn't ready to die.

"We did it. We killed Don Francisco. I drove. Sam was the shooter."

Nick paused. He didn't know how much more Sally expected him to say. Everyone else in the room stared at each other in disbelief.

"Come on, you rat bastard. Keep talkin'! Who else?"

"Cavelli! Vincent Cavelli! It was all his idea!" Nick cried. "He's the one who contacted Sam. Cavelli instigated the whole fuckin' thing! He said we should knock off the Don and take over the family so we could start dealing in drugs and take over the niggers' territories. He said we'd all get rich!"

There was no stopping Nick now. He was still trembling and singing like a canary, hoping that the treacherous Sally would honor his promise and spare his life.

"Cavelli promised us if we went to war with the moolanjans, he'd send down some of his soldiers to help us. That's it! That's all I know, Sally. Please, Sally! Please! Don't kill me! You promised! You all heard him! He promised!" he said, looking around the room pleadingly.

Sweat was running profusely down Nick's face. Sally's fit of rage had subsided. He stared at Nick through stone-cold eyes. With the passing of his anger, he was beginning to feel pleasure in tormenting Nick Lacavoli. The power of holding Nick's life in his hands felt intoxicating.

"There's no more! Honest! I told you everything! I told you everything I know, Sally! Please! Please don't kill me!" Nick begged.

Entreatingly, he looked around the room again, but the other men stared at him with cold, unsympathetic eyes.

"Come on, you guys all heard him! He promised! He promised me if I told 'im, he wouldn't kill me! Somebody! Talk to 'im! Come on! Make 'im keep his word!"

Everyone ignored his pleas.

"Whose idea was it to blame the moolanjans?" Sally asked.

"Cavelli. Cavelli planned it all . . . He said there was someone else in on it too. Someone from our family. But he didn't tell us who. Sam said Cavelli called him Mr. X . . . but honest! That's all I know! You promised, Sally! Come on, you promised!"

"Mr. X, my ass, you no-good motherfucker! The only thing you're good for is to die!"

Sally immediately put the silencer to Nick's forehead and pulled the trigger. *Phsst.* The soft, hissing noise propelled its deadly bullet into Nick Lacavoli's head. Nick's brains were splattered all over the wall behind him, next to his brother's.

Sally smiled. Proud that he had avenged his father's murder before he was even buried.

He had shocked every man in the room. Not only by his actions in killing the Lacavoli brothers on the spot, but with the speed in which he, alone, had uncovered their devious assassination plot.

Many of the men instantly changed their minds about Sally's ability to run the family. Even Eddie D'Amico started to wonder if he had underestimated the Mafia son's intelligence.

Maybe, just maybe, some of Don Francisco's brilliance and cunning had rubbed off on his son, thought Eddie.

The gang members quickly surrounded Sally. They were patting him on the back and congratulating him. All of them completely ignored the two dead men and the mess their splattered brains had made. This Mafia world was strange. So strange. Sally's killing two people had just catapulted him to the status of a hero. Death meant nothing in this world. What was important to them was the fact that Sally Barratino had tasted blood. Don Francisco was dead, but his son had avenged him. Now you can rest in peace, Don Francisco. Your Mafia son has kept his promise to you.

The proud look was still on Sally's face. He was treasuring his shining moment in the sun. All of the men were anxiously asking him questions.

"Come on, Sally, tell us, how'd ya find out?" asked one of the guys.

"Yeah, Sal, spill it. What tipped you off?" asked another.

"Those rat bastards had everyone fooled but you," said still another.

"Yeah! We never liked those two scumbag brothers anyway!"

"Mangia, it was great! You made your fuckin' bones and did your father's killers at the same time! That's what I call a real fuckin' score!" said one of the guys.

Everyone was talking at once. Sally was in his glory. But Dominic knew there was still important business to settle. He shouted at the men to quiet down.

"Come on, boys! It's late, and we've got important things to finish up here!" yelled Dominic.

The voices started to subside. But the men didn't look happy. Their curiosity had gotten the better of them. They still wanted to know more. They wanted to know how Sally had figured out that the Lacavolis killed the Don. Most of them were suddenly thinking that Sally must be one smart son of a bitch like a chip off the old block.

"Wait just a fuckin' minute, Dominic. I wanna get one more thing settled here before you move these rotten scumbags," said Sally.

He turned to face the Patrino.

"Patrino, I think this settles the matter of me making my bones."

The Patrino and the other two dons smiled and nodded their agreement.

"And, Patrino, you can see I have the support of the family. Now, do I have your blessing?"

Sally caught the Patrino off guard with his question. The Patrino wanted some time to think. Besides, there was still the question of Sally not being a full-blooded Sicilian.

"Salvatore, you go ahead and clean up. Get rid of those treacherous bastards. I will talk this over with Don Cheech and Don Pasquale in private. By the time you are finished, I will give you my answer."

"So be it," said Sally.

The three dons went into Don Francisco's office. Sally immediately took charge and began shooting orders. He called out to Tough Tony Battista.

"Tony! Get Nappy and Billy B. Go find something to wrap those cocksuckers in and get them the fuck outta here! Take 'em to the junkyard, and make sure you put 'em in a fuckin' car that's ready for the press! Before you leave, make sure you call Carlucci, and tell him you're bringin' him a couple o' packages. Tell him to meet you at the junkyard at the crack of dawn. I don't want any fuckin' mistakes! You understand?" Sally said threateningly.

Nodding, the three men all jumped up to follow his orders.

"Turk! Get someone to help you take that sofa outta here. Cut the fuckin' thing up and burn it in the trash incinerator. Take that fuckin' rug and burn it too!" he ordered.

"Vinnie, go find some shit in the kitchen to clean their rotten blood off the wall. In fact, acid-wash it and paint it! Capire?"

Eddie D'Amico wanted to leave. He wanted to run. He was feeling sick to his stomach. He had just witnessed two Mafia murders. He felt like he was falling off the edge of the line he walked and into the pit of "their world." While the Patrino met in private with the other two dons, he decided to step outside and get some fresh air. His whole world had changed drastically in the last couple of days. After what he witnessed tonight, there would be no turning back. There was nothing he could do about it. But he'd seen and heard too much already not to stay. He was curious to hear the Patrino's decision.

Rocco was calling everyone back into the barn. When Eddie returned, he saw that all of Sally's instructions had been carried out. The Patrino was standing by the pool table. He was waiting for the room to quiet down before he spoke.

"Our decision has been made. The matter of Don Francisco's murder is not over yet. Before we can consider this matter closed, Vincent Cavelli must be killed."

The Patrino walked over to Sally and put his hand on his shoulder.

"Once you have taken care of your business with Cavelli, you will have our blessing, Don Salvatore."

Sally and the Patrino smiled at each other.

"Consider it done, Patrino." Sally lifted the Patrino's hand and kissed his ring.

Sally had no qualms about ordering Vincent Cavelli's execution. As a matter of fact, he was looking forward to having the person responsible for plotting his father's murder killed.

"Turk, you take care of this. I want you on the next plane to Chicago—"

Dominic interrupted.

"Just a minute, Sally. Don Francisco and I were together for over forty years. He was more to me than just my don. He was my best friend. I claim the right to avenge his death. Let me kill Cavelli. For me, it is a matter of honor."

"Dominic, it's been too many years since you whacked somebody out. Let Turk handle Cavelli," Sally argued.

"Listen, Sally. Killing is just like riding a fucking bicycle! Once you've done it, you never forget how. Remember, I was making my fucking bones when you were still kicking the slats out of your fucking crib! This is a matter of honor between Don Francisco's memory and me," said Dominic passionately.

"OK, OK, Dominic. I understand. You win."

"Good. Then it is done. I will be on the next plane to Chicago."

Chapter 17

As was their usual habit on Saturday morning, Eddie, Nick the Greek, and Chicky were at the public market having breakfast at Jimmy's Restaurant. A constant when they were together was the spicing of their food with diverse conversational topics that knew no bounds. The particular subject at hand this morning: broads. The Greek was ribbing Chicky about his disappearance from the Don's birthday party the previous week.

"So, Chicky, I heard all about you fuckin' guys getting lucky after the party, but not one of you so-called friends had the decency to come and find me! So you guys just grabbed the broads and took off? Why'd you leave me stranded like a chooch?"

"Well, Nicky, you know what they say. A stiff prick has no conscience!" teased Eddie.

"Yeah, well, if that's the case, our friend Chicky here must not have any conscience at all. His dick is standing at attention all the time waiting for some broad to either salute it or kiss it!"

Hey, fuck you, Greek," said Chicky, blowing a puff of cigarette smoke toward him. "At least I use the front door when I get laid. Not like you and the rest of your paisanos!"

"Well, the good thing about the back door is ya don't have to worry about havin' to pay for any bambinos!"

As the three men continued to joke around with each other, Judge Carlivatti appeared at the table and pulled out one of the worn wooden chairs.

"Is this some kind of high-level summit meeting, or can anyone sit in?"

"Hi, Carm! I've been meaning to call you, but with all of the turmoil after the Don's death, I never got around to it," said Eddie. "I heard you got lucky, and I've been dying of curiosity to know what the fuck time you finally got home last Saturday night!"

"Well, you're a little screwed up with your time of day. You see, it should have been, what time did I get in Sunday morning!" corrected the judge smugly. "Anyway, I don't remember the exact time, but I can tell you this. If I lived on a farm, the cock would have been crowing!"

"Oh sure, and I'll bet your wife would have been doing some real crowing if she knew what your cock was doing that night!" teased Chicky.

"Yeah, Carm, where did you tell Rosie you were?" asked Eddie.

"What do you guys think I told her? Are you forgetting I'm a judge? I have sworn to protect and hold high the noble principles of truth and justice. So of course, I did the right thing. I was honor bound to tell Rosie the truth."

His friends were aghast at the very thought of his self-confession.

"Come on, Carm, are you shitting? You told her the truth?" asked Nick with a shocked look on his face.

"Sure. I simply explained to her that after the party, a bunch of us guys decided to get together . . . and play cards!"

They were all laughing at the judge's comeback when Jimmy, the restaurant owner, tapped Eddie on the shoulder.

"Hey, Eddie, ya got a phone call."

He strode across the white tile floor to take his call.

"Hello."

"I figured you'd be there," said a baritone voice on the other end.

"Yeah, I guess I'm pretty easy to find on Saturday mornings. So what's up, Bee?"

It was Eddie's undercover detective friend, Lou "Bee" Stinger.

"We need to talk. Now."

"OK. The usual place?" asked Eddie.

"Yeah, that'll do."

"I'm on my way," Eddie said and hung up the phone.

He returned to the table to say good-bye to his friends.

"Wish I could stick around and bullshit, but I gotta get going. Carm, you and Chicky decide who's gonna pay for my tab, or I'll have to tell your wives that the only thing you guys were playing after the party was a game of hide the wiener!"

"Hey, man, you don't have to resort to blackmail. What'sa matter? You a little short on cash today? Don't worry, I'll pick up your tab," said Chicky, laughing.

Eddie walked quickly to his car. Bee Stinger's telephone call had sparked his curiosity. He knew that Bee wouldn't have made a special effort to track him down at Jimmy's unless it was important. He began the long drive across town, heading for their meeting place in a small seldom-used park near the bank of the river.

As he drove, Eddie reflected on the last night he had been alone with Megan. He recollected their sexual interlude at the apartment, and the memory began to turn him on.

Megan had returned home right after the Don's funeral. Eddie was missing her and suddenly felt the need to hear her voice. He had tried to call her several times over the last few days but had only gotten through to her answering machine. He thought it was strange that she hadn't returned his calls. He reached for his car phone and dialed her number.

"Hi, babe, did I wake you?"

"Oh, hi, Eddie. No, I wasn't sleeping. As a matter of fact, I was just sitting down to write you a letter."

"A letter? That sounds pretty formal. What's wrong with the telephone?"

"Well, I've had a lot to think about, and I decided a letter would be the best way for me to say the things I need to tell you."

He could sense from her tone that something wasn't right.

"Come on, Megan. Let's have it. What's wrong?"

"Well, to tell you the truth, it's you and me, Eddie. We're what's wrong. After I got home and sorted it all out, I've come to the conclusion that it will never work out for us. I realize now that I let myself get carried away with all my selfish fantasies and desires. I was thinking with my heart and not my head. You see—"

She was shattering his emotions and his ego. He cut in.

"Wait! What the hell are you saying! Are you telling me you don't love me?" he yelled.

"No, I'm not saying that. Please calm down and listen to me. I love you more than I can find words to express. But that's exactly my whole point. I can't be head-over-heels in love with you and let myself get involved in a one-way relationship. I think you and I have different definitions of love. I don't believe you know how to love, Eddie. I mean really love and be faithful to someone in a relationship. You and I just live in two different worlds."

"Megan, that's not true! I've done a lot of thinking about this myself. Maybe we've had different values and dreams, but believe me, I'm tired of the kind of life I've been leading. I do love you, and I need you to help me make the change."

"But for how long, Eddie? A week? A month? How long will it last? I need a lifetime commitment. I've already made enough mistakes. I've been through two screwed-up marriages, and I'm not going to walk into another one with my eyes wide open. I can't let myself get tangled up in another mess where I end up getting hurt again. Life is too short for me to waste what's left on one more bad deal."

"Listen, baby. You've got to understand. I made up my mind. I'm ready to get off the merry-go-round I've been riding on. I wanna live a normal family life, and I can do it if you just give me the chance!" he pleaded.

"That's what you say now. But let's face it. We both know you've done plenty of screwing around and cheating on your wife. As much as I love you, the fact is, you're a whoremonger at heart, and I don't believe you can change, even if you wanted to."

"Megan, honey, look, all I'm asking for is a chance. I love you, baby. I really want things to work out for us. I want it as much as you do. We've already wasted half our lives. Just say you'll give me a chance. All you have to do is give it a try Megan, and you'll see. I promise I won't disappoint you."

"I don't know, Eddie. I want to, but I'm not sure. I mean, I'm just not sure I can trust you."

He could tell from the tone in her voice that she was wavering, so he kept pushing her for the answer he was looking for.

"All I'm asking for is a chance, Megan. Is that too much?"

"If I give you the chance, Eddie, you have to understand right up front that I'm not going to be treated like one of your bimbos. Sure, I'll admit I had a good time when I was there with you, but I can't be someone you wear on your arm and just show off like one of your expensive wristwatches or something. You know, you can be very charming when you want, but I think you can also be chauvinistic, and even conceited, and I really doubt that you can change that. It's a part of who you are."

"No. That's not true! For you, Megan, I can change. And I will. I promise!"

"Oh, damn you, Eddie! I really want to believe you, but I'm afraid. I wanna say yes, and I want to be with you forever. But I mean it! If I ever find out that you used me or lied to me like you've done to Danni, then I'm gone, and there will be no discussion. So if you can live with that, then perhaps I'll give us a chance."

Eddie breathed a sigh of relief.

"Of course I can live with that. I promise you, Megan. I'll change whatever I need to to make you happy."

"OK, then, what about Danni?"

"I'm going to get things all squared away with her today, and I'll call you tonight."

"Eddie, please, make sure you do what's right for her."

"Oh, now you're starting to sound like Carmella," he laughed. But don't worry, baby, I will. I'll take care of everything, and I'll do right by her. I love you, Megan."

"I love you too, Eddie."

As he hung up, he felt a new admiration for the strength of character she had shown in their conversation. He respected the fact that she stood up to him with her feelings. She had moxie. He vowed to himself to do his best to keep the promises he had made.

Eddie was nearing his rendezvous point with the detective. He turned off onto the narrow gravel road leading to the small park. As he pulled into the unpaved parking lot, he saw Bee sitting on a bench under the shade of a massive oak tree. He was casually reading a newspaper.

Bee Stinger was an enormous muscular man with craggy facial features, rather small cauliflower ears and penetrating, dark eyes. In his youth, he had been a professional wrestler, much to the dismay of his Jewish parents, who had always wanted him to become a doctor. Finally, in an effort to please them, they came to a compromise through which he gave up wrestling and began a new career in law enforcement.

Eddie and Bee became close friends after Eddie had helped him by using his political influence to have him assigned to the detective division. Over the years, Bee had earned a sterling reputation as a tough and honest cop.

"Hi, big guy! What's up?" Eddie asked pensively.

"Well, my friend, it's not what's up but what's been goin' down. There's been a lot o' shit in the wind this past week. I've told you before, but you keep ignoring my advice. This time, the feds are watching you like a fucking hawk. They're sayin' you're much too tight with the family to be the Mr. Clean you make yourself out to be. They're feeling pretty sure you're up to your ass in the mob's activities. There's a lot of investigation goin' on."

Eddie sat silently, without expression, listening to his friend.

"Trust me, Eddie. The heat is on. The feds' investigation of the Barratino family has now spread to Chicago. They've brought in more people to assist in the investigation, 'cause two other things have come down since the old man was bumped off last week, and they think they might have some connection with the Don's death. Ya know, the other night in Chicago, Vincent Cavelli was shot as he was going into his restaurant."

"Hey, hold it! Hang on a minute!" Eddie interrupted. "Just what the hell does this Cavelli guy have to do with any of this? Or with me?"

"Aw, come on, Eddie, cut the bullshit, will ya? You know, as well as I do, he's the don of one of the Chicago families."

Bee was wondering just how much Eddie really did know and whether he was conning him now. He searched Eddie's face for some kind of reaction, but he just sat staring at the detective with a deadpan expression on his face.

"So anyway, this Thursday, we get a telephone call from the Lacavoli brothers' cleaning lady who happens to be their cousin. She reports that when she went to clean their house on her usual day, it looked like they had just up and disappeared. All their clothes and both the cars were there, but it looked like they hadn't been home in days."

"Now you've lost me. What's all of this got to do with Don Francisco's murder? And more importantly, what the fuck has any of this got to do with me?"

"You can get inside that compound. Every time they turn around, some fuckin' new thing surfaces that points right in your direction. If you're not a member of the family, then why the hell would you have a code to go in anytime you want? And what about the disappearance of the Lacavoli brothers? The smart money's betting they had somethin' to do with Don Francisco's death, and maybe they've been rubbed out. You know, retaliation. Some of the investigators think maybe you were the one to put out the contract."

Eddie's face grew red with anger. Jumping to his feet, and with eyes flaming, he exploded his response.

"Me! What a fuckin' crock of shit! You don't believe I'm in on any of this, do you?

"Hey man, take it easy. What do you want to do? Shoot the fucking messenger? If I believed you were in all the way, I wouldn't be sittin' here talking to you. I'd be investigating your fucking ass. I know your ass ain't lily white either. And I don't know where you fit into this thing, but I'll tell ya the truth—when I look at all of the circumstantial evidence, I think you know a hell of a lot more about the Barratino family business that you let on. Anyway, the feds know there aren't a lot o' rocket scientists in that business, so they're comin' to the conclusion that you might be the brains behind a lot of this shit!"

Bee got up and threw a muscular arm around Eddie's shoulder, leading him toward their cars.

"Look, my friend, I'm telling you all of this for your own good. Back away from the fuckin' family. Your godfather's gone now. I know how you felt about him, but if you don't take my advice, you're gonna find yourself in the kind of trouble you can't fix, even with your connections."

"Stop worrying, I tell ya. I've got nothing to do with any of this shit! And I'm sorry I blew up at you, Bee, but it really pisses me off! Look, I'm really grateful for all you have done for me.

Chapter 18

Driving home after his meeting with Bee Stinger, Eddie was agitated, and his mind was racing. He had planned to settle the divorce thing with Danni today, but now the thoughts of being investigated by the FBI had stolen his attention and disrupted his agenda.

This is just fucking great timing! he thought. *I finally think I'm putting my life in order, and there's more bullshit to deal with. On top of it all, if Megan finds out about this, she'll think I was lying when I told her I wasn't one of them. And now with the feds on my ass, how the hell do I go and get the Don's money out of Switzerland?*

With only a short drive left to his house, he decided to put aside his other problems and concentrate on how to get Danni to agree to give him a divorce.

He began justifying his motive. *I'll take good care of her financially. She can have the house . . . the Cadillac . . . a generous monthly allowance. She won't have to work . . . I hope we can remain friends.*

He pulled into the driveway and entered the house, feeling ready for the confrontation. He had selected this particular day, knowing Ashley was spending the weekend with a friend. Searching through the house, he could find Danni nowhere. His gaze caught sight of the empty portable phone cradle.

Of course, he thought, *she's sunning herself by the pool.*

Danni had always been a sun worshipper and was proud of her rich, dark tan. Eddie opened the sliding glass door that led out to the expansive raised patio. The midmorning sun was already sending fiery hot rays earthward. He noted to himself that it was going to be a scorcher.

Walking to the edge of the patio, he looked down into the lower-level pool area and saw Danni lying on a padded redwood chaise lounge. A set of earphones covered her ears, and small white egg-shaped cups were placed over her eyes.

Eddie stood silently for a moment, admiring the beauty of her well-formed body. She had removed the top of her bathing suit, and her oil-basted breasts and body glistened sensually in the sunlight. His eyes fell to the scant piece of red cloth between her legs. Under it, the movement of her right hand was so slow it was barely discernible. Intrigued by Danni's self-manipulation, he continued to watch with interest.

It had been over two years since they had made love or slept together. He had often wondered whether she indulged herself in some form of self-gratification to quell the fire of passion that he knew must burn inside of her from time to time. Now he had his answer.

Watching his wife pleasure herself was beginning to turn him on. Eddie felt a pleasant swelling between his legs, and a sense of desire began to fill his body. He was confused as to which course he should take. Leave Danni alone to fulfill her own fancy or go down to her and play it by ear. The titillating aching in his groin made the decision for him.

He approached her quietly and stood motionlessly above her. She hadn't heard him arrive, but after a moment, she sensed his presence. Unstartled, she removed the cups from her eyes with her left hand. Her right hand remained faithful to its endeavor as she squinted in the bright sunlight, trying to focus her vision. She scanned his face and then closed her eyes and continued on with her pleasure as she spoke to him.

"What brings you here? Did you want me for something?"

"Well, uh, yes," he answered awkwardly.

The fact that his appearance at her side did not disrupt her sedulity only served to excite him more. His eyes remained riveted on her sensually moving hand.

"I hoped we could talk about us this morning."

"Well, I suppose we can do that, but as you can see, I'm a little preoccupied right now," she answered spitefully.

He was dumbstruck. Her actions were out of character for her and made him feel uncomfortable. He was at a loss as to what to say or do next. Suddenly, Danni withdrew her hand from under her bikini bottom and sat up. She stared into Eddie's eyes for a moment and then stood and tantalizingly removed the bottom of her bathing suit. She picked up a clear plastic bottle from the edge of her chaise and poured a generous amount of its tanning oil onto her fingertips.

"This part of my body was consuming me this morning," she said as she began massaging the oil between her legs.

He was still speechless. Danni's eyes moved to the bulge in his pants. His eyes were glued to the methodical rhythm of her hand between her legs.

"If you want, we can talk after you do something for me first," she said in a husky voice. "This craving is driving me crazy. I could use your help. I won't even ask you to make love to me. I know you can't do that. But I'm sure you can do to me what you do to those whores you sleep with. No love, no commitment, just pure animal pleasure. Just fuck me."

He was fully aroused and couldn't control the burning desire that now overwhelmed him. Danni unzipped her husband's pants and began stoking his hardness. She dropped to her knees and teased him with her hot, moist tongue.

As Eddie began peeling off his shirt, Danni rose, helping him remove his clothes until he stood naked before her. She picked up the suntan oil and poured it liberally over his body, slowly rubbing it into his chest and stroking him gently with her oily hands. They embraced, sensuously undulating their hot, slick bodies tightly against each other.

Danni took him by the hand, grabbed her towel, and led him to a patch of grass. She lay down on her back and spread her legs wide. With both hands, she gently teased her hard pink nipples, watching Eddie's reaction. His manhood stood fully erect, eager to satisfy its own desire.

Danni moaned and, spreading her legs wider, drew up her knees. She raised her arms to him in open invitation. Without hesitation, he lowered himself onto her. The taste of the oil was bitter in his mouth as he ran his tongue around her nipples. Excitedly, he drove himself deep inside of her.

"Yes, yes," she pleaded. "Harder, harder. Hurt me."

The forceful energy of their physical passion continued until their bodies were spent from exhaustion. Dripping with oily perspiration, they remained locked in carnal unison until the heat from the sun on their naked bodies became unbearable. He pulled Danni to her feet, and holding hands, they jumped into the refreshing water of the pool.

Cooling their heated bodies after their strange sexual escapade in the yard, they moved to the protective shade of the patio. Danni turbanned her hair, wrapped a colorful beach towel around her body, and entered the house. Eddie waited patiently, alone with his thoughts, for her return. It had been so long since they had had sex; he had forgotten what a good fuck she was.

At least getting laid sure seemed to put her in better spirits. I hope she stays that way so we can get this shit over with. He rubbed his hand across his bare chest. *Geez, I need a fuckin' shower.*

Inside the house, Danni was stirring a pitcher of iced tea. *Funny he picked today to wanna talk . . . The very day I made up my mind to give him his fucking divorce he's been begging for.* She giggled out loud. *He's gonna shit when he hears what I have to say!*

She returned to the patio, carrying the pitcher and two frosted glasses.

"You thirsty?" she asked, smiling.

"Yeah, like a blotter."

Anxious to get to the point, he gulped the glass of cold liquid and immediately began explaining his ideas for the financial arrangements he was prepared to offer. As he spoke, he felt encouraged as Danni smiled and nodded her head, seemingly in approval. Finished, he paused, waiting for her reply. Danni calmly rose from her chair.

"Look, we both need a shower. This oil all over me is making me nervous. We'll finish this when I come back down."

"But . . . b—"

"No *buts*, sonny boy. Go take a shower. You'll feel better," Danni said sharply, ending the conversation as she walked into the house.

Her mood was too good to spoil, and wanting to meet his objective, Eddie quickly showered and returned to the kitchen table to wait for her. Danni was taking her time. He had finished the whole pitcher of iced tea and was growing intensely impatient. He wondered if she was purposely trying to piss him off.

When Danni entered the kitchen, she looked refreshed and extraordinarily attractive in a short pink terrycloth robe cinched at the waist.

"Are you hungry?" she asked sincerely.

"No, thanks."

"Gee, that's funny. As I recall, you always used to crave food after sex. What happened?"

"Nuthin'. I just want to get our situation resolved, that's all. The whole thing has really been bothering me."

"Why the hell should you be bothered? As usual, you'll get your way."

Her statement surprised him.

"You mean you'll agree to the divorce?" he asked, hoping she couldn't detect the excitement in his voice.

"Yes, I'll agree," she answered with a sly smile on her face.

Eddie suddenly realized that she was toying with him. He sensed that she knew how badly he wanted the divorce, and that she was going to try to take total control of the situation.

Fuck her. She's not going to beat me at my own game.

"Oh, come on now, Eddie. You don't think you're going to get off the hook with me that easy, do you? You've humiliated me plenty, and I've put up with your bullshit for a lot of years. So now you're the one who's going to pay for a change. You can have your divorce, but with conditions. Let's go into the family room, where we can be more comfortable." She walked away, and Eddie obediently followed her.

Danni sat down and curled her legs up under her on the white leather sofa. Eddie chose a straight-backed chair across the room.

"OK, Danni, we're comfortable, so start talkin'. What's the fuckin' problem? You want more money?" he asked, trying to control his growing irritation.

"Relax, Eddie, relax. No, I didn't mean pay in a financial context. I must say, to your credit, that you have always been generous with the money. In fact, I consider it to be one of your biggest faults. You think you can buy with money what you are incapable of giving with your time and consideration. Your financial terms are fine with me, and I know you'll live up to them because I know one thing about you—you're a man of honor when it comes to money. But you see, there are other ways that people can pay for things that aren't as easy as just writing a check."

"Well, what the hell is it, then? What else do you want?" he asked with a puzzled look on his face.

"You are going to give me back my self-respect at the expense of your own. You're going to be my own private whore."

"What the fuck are you talking about?"

"Giving you this divorce is against my better judgment. From my point of view, it will only mean that we are unmarried in the eyes of man. I took an oath before God that I would be faithful to you until death do us part. I intend to uphold that vow until the day I die. So you see, Eddie, in my eyes and in God's, you will always be my husband."

Smiling evilly with dagger eyes, Danni pulled out a white plastic device from the large pocket on her robe. A shocked expression came over Eddie's face when he saw it in her hand.

"Do you know what this is, Eddie? This is how much you degraded and humiliated me, sonny boy. You stripped away my self-respect when you forced me to use this thing to satisfy my physical needs!"

Danni turned on the vibrator and waved it in the air. The humming noise continued as Eddie disconcertedly dropped his eyes to the floor and squirmed silently in his chair.

"Would you like me to show you how it works?" she asked, rubbing it gently between her legs.

He refused to look at her.

"No! I know how the fuckin' thing works!"

"Damn it, Eddie, look at this! I want you to see how easy you were to replace! My friend here doesn't lie, or cheat, or go out and fuck other women!"

Eddie was speechless. Danni was forcing him to feel some of the humiliation that he had caused her to endure over the years. The vibrator was still humming in her hand as she pointed it at him repeatedly to emphasize her remarks.

"Here's the bottom line, sonny boy. I was a virgin when I married you, and I'll never be an alley cat like you. After our divorce, I don't intend to go into bars and pick up men when I feel the need for human physical satisfaction. So here's my deal. You can take it or leave it. You'll get your divorce on the condition that if I have the desire or need for your body, you'll come when I call. You'll be my on-call whore, so to speak."

She paused to let her offer sink in, smiling and enjoying the humiliation she knew he was feeling. He was furious that she had filled him with guilt. He could not respond to her.

"Well, come on, what do you say? Do we have a deal? You get what you want, and I'll get what I need when I need it."

Eddie sat speechless, staring at the floor.

"What's taking so long for you to decide? You know you enjoyed our little encounter today. I'm still a good fuck, aren't I? Or are you worried about little Megan?"

She stunned him again. He couldn't believe that she knew about Megan.

Dannie laughed out loud. "What's the matter? Are you surprised, Eddie? When I heard she was in town and would be at that party, I figured you two would cook something up and you might come asking for your divorce. Yeah, that's right, sonny boy, I've had some time to think about all of this. So just tell me, what's wrong with fucking around on Megan once in a while? It never bothered you to screw around on me all these years! Hell, by this time, you must be an expert at deception. She'll never know. All you have to do is lie to her the way you lied to me," Danni asserted with a sarcastic smile on her face.

Fuming with rage, Eddie jumped up and quickly crossed the room to where she was sitting. Gnashing his teeth, he stood before her, staring into her flashing brown eyes. Tight-mouthed, he snarled, "OK, Danni, you've got yourself a deal. Let's just get the fuckin' divorce done!" he said, thinking to himself that one more lie to Danni wouldn't matter.

Chapter 19

T he high shine on the long hallway floors of the hospital glistened, reflecting the glow from the fluorescent lights above. Eddie was carrying a small black suitcase and checking the room numbers on the doors as he passed. He stopped at number 536. Pushing open the door, he found Lorenzo standing at the sink shaving. Lorenzo LaRocca looked pale and much thinner than usual. He smiled at Eddie through the reflection in the mirror.

"Hi, Eddie!" he said in his usual gruff and wheezing manner.

"Well, today's the big day, my friend. How you feeling?"

"I feel great, but stayin' in dis hospital's worser dan doin' time in da joint!"

"Ah, come on, Lorenzo, are you saying you liked prison better than the hospital?"

"Hah! It's just one o' dose figurines of speech. But I'll tell ya one ting for sure, da fuckin' food's better in prison!"

They both laughed as Eddie handed him the suitcase.

"I brought you the clothes you asked for."

LaRocca's face became somber as he took the suitcase and sat down on the edge of the bed.

"Look, Eddie, I'm not too good wid da words, but der's some tings I wanna say to you. All my life, I followed da code o' loyalty and respect. While I was in dis white prison, you showed me you're really a true friend. You know, wit all da flowers and havin' my favorite food sent in every day. And now payin' da bill for me. I want ya ta know you got me as a friend for life. Any cocksucker which fucks wid Eddie D'Amico answers to LaRocca from now on," he said, holding out his big hand for Eddie to shake.

Deeply moved, Eddie took LaRocca's huge strong hand in both of his and squeezed responsively.

"Look, Lorenzo. About the hospital bill. There's something you really need to know. The money for the hospital comes from Don Francisco. Even from his grave, he has taken care of you."

For a moment, LaRocca looked puzzled. Then a huge droplet spilled from his eye and ran down his freshly shaven craggy face.

"I'm glad ya tole me dat, Eddie. I been feelin' so fuckin' guilty dat I failed 'im. I jus' wish I coulda saved 'im. But I swear I did my best! I tried ta take da bullets for 'im, but it just wasn't in da fuckin' cards."

LaRocca was distraught. Eddie tried to change the subject.

"So hey, what are your plans? Have you decided?"

"Yeah. I gave it a lotta tought. Sally's da don now, and he's a Barratino. I tink da boss woulda wanted me to stay wid da kid and take care o' him. I know Sally could never be a pimple on his ol' man's ass, but outa respect for Don Francisco, I'm gonna stick around, as long as he does da right tings. But ta tell ya da truth, I probly won't stay long, knowin' that little prick like I do."

"Well, whaddya say, Lorenzo? Let's get the fuck out of here. I've got your pardon right here," said Eddie, handing Lorenzo the paid hospital bill.

"Was dere anyting in it about my good behavior?" smiled the Enforcer.

"Shit, no! As a matter of fact, it says right there that you were a big pain in the ass!"

"Good! Dat's da way it's supposed ta be. LaRocca, a big pain in everybody's ass," he grinned.

The door of the room opened just as LaRocca finished dressing. A smiling young nurse, accompanied by a male orderly pushing a wheelchair, entered the room.

"Well, Mr. Lorenzo, all of the paperwork is done, and Roger here will take you down to the front door when you're ready," said the nurse cheerfully.

"Look, Nurse. Da name's LaRocca, and dat pansy is not gonna take me nowhere, understand? LaRocca's gonna walk outta dis place by himself. Ya got dat?"

The young nurse, intimidated by LaRocca, looked petrified. She began to stammer.

"B-b-but, Mr. Lorenzo, hospital rules say y-y-you must be transported t-t-to the door."

In the blink of an eye, LaRocca grabbed the young orderly and stripped from him his hospital scrubs along with his underwear. Roger was left standing naked from the waist down with a look of disbelief on his blushing red face. Roger immediately crossed his knees and slapped both hands over his dangling privates. Then as if he were a feather, LaRocca bodily picked up the stupefied orderly and sat him down in the wheelchair.

"Jus' so ya know, Miss Nurse, dese will be down at da front door," he said, holding up Roger's clothes. "You push 'im down dere. He looks like he needs da rest. Come on, D'Amico, let's get outa dis fuckin' place!"

The nurse, not knowing what to do, stood staring, dumbfounded. Eddie was fighting back the urge to burst out laughing as they quickly left the room.

They exited the hospital and saw the Don's Silver Cloud Rolls-Royce was parked at the curb. The Turk was casually leaning against the fender. As soon as he saw Eddie and LaRocca, he ran up to take the suitcase from Lorenzo.

"Hi ya, pal!" said the Turk as the two men gave each other a short embrace.

"Hey, tell me, Turk, ya been takin' care o' tings while I been in da stir?"

"Naw, I left dem all for you ta do when ya got outa da joint. I didn' want ya ta get fuckin' bored when ya got back."

The Turk opened the rear door of the Rolls for Lorenzo to enter.

"Hey, what da fuck! Ya gone nuts or sometin', Turk? Get in da fuckin' front. I'm drivin'!"

The Turk smiled and winked at Eddie, happy to see that his friend was his old self again. LaRocca turned to Eddie before getting into the car.

"Remember, Eddie, what I said in dere goes. I'm behind ya now all da way. Anyting ya need, anyting at all, ya just call LaRocca."

"Thanks, Lorenzo. I'll remember that."

As Eddie walked to his car, he recounted LaRocca's words and realized that LaRocca meant he would even kill at his request. The thought was chilling, yet somehow empowering.

Eddie checked his watch as he reached his car. It was eleven o'clock. He decided he would have plenty of time to see Mr. Fontagrossi before his two o'clock meeting at Tony Banducci's office for the reading of Don Francisco's will.

Mr. Fantagrossi, a retired printer and former counterfeiter, still did special jobs for the family. The elderly man still lived in the old Italian neighborhood and worked in the garage behind his home.

Eddie drove slowly down the street, looking for the old, run-down house. He pulled into the driveway and parked in front of the garage. As he exited his car, a tired-looking, overweight dog sauntered over to greet him and sniff his leg. Eddie loved dogs and couldn't resist stopping to pat the greasy head of the old pooch before entering the garage.

Mr. Fontagrossi was sitting at a worn wooden desk covered with papers. Eddie noticed that he was stooped over with age as he rose off his chair and gave a toothless grin. He brushed a lock of his long gray hair from his smiling eyes with a dirty, ink-stained hand.

"Ah, Mr. Carlos, so nice to see you! I have your order all ready."

The old man shuffled over to a file cabinet and took out a small manila envelope and a box of business cards. He cleared a spot on his desk and emptied out the content of the envelope. Before them lay a New York State driver's license with the name "Edwardo Carlos" bearing a picture of Eddie's face.

The printer watched for Eddie's reaction over the top of his spectacles, which were balanced precariously on the tip of his nose. Eddie picked up the phony license and studied it carefully. He smiled his approval.

Mr. Fontagrossi turned the box of business cards around to reveal the sample taped to the outside of the box. It read, "EDWARDO CARLOS, Diamond Merchant, Zurich—Rio de Janeiro—New York," along with fictitious phone numbers for each city.

"You've done a fine job, Mr. Fontagrossi. How much?"

"Well, Mr. Carlos, since you are an old friend from the neighborhood, let's say three hundred." He looked into Eddie's eyes to see if there was a reaction.

Without a word or hesitation, Eddie reached into his left pants pocket and brought out a roll of money. He snapped off the rubber band and counted out three one-hundred-dollar bills.

"This is for the good job," he said, handing over the money to the old man. "And this is for your silence," he added as he gave the printer two more hundred-dollar bills.

"Thank you, Mr. Carlos. You're a gentleman."

Mr. Fontagrossi stuffed the money into the top pocket of his ink-stained leather apron as he motioned with his hand the twisting of a key in a lock on his lips, and then with a dramatic gesture, he threw away the imaginary key. Eddie nodded approval with a smile and left the garage.

He arrived at Tony Banducci's office early. Eddie and the attorney were seated in the wood-paneled conference room when the receptionist ushered in Carmella and Sally. As soon as Sally saw Eddie, he went ballistic.

"What the fuck is he doing here?" Sally screamed at Banducci.

"Hey! Calm down, Sally. Your father appointed Eddie executor of the estate. It's all here in the will, and it's perfectly legal."

"Well, it ain't fucking legal with me! I don't know how you did this, D'Amico, even worming your way into the fucking will!"

Sally was shaking in anger and screaming at the top of his lungs.

"Sally, please stop yelling. Let's just get this thing over with," pleaded Carmella.

"This asshole probably conned the old man out of all his money. I bet the old bastard left everything to him! You fuckin' get it over with without me!" yelled Sally as he headed for the door.

"Hold on, Sally! Just wait a minute, will ya? Your father left me nothing in the will! So why don't you just sit down and listen," Eddie said sternly.

"Don't you ever fuckin' tell me what to do, D'Amico," Sally yelled, pointing a menacing finger at him. "If you're not in the will, then you've got an ace up your fuckin' sleeve. But you just remember this. I've got your fucking number, and someday you're going to pay for all the bullshit you've given me all these years. Read the fucking will without me!" Sally ranted as he left the room, slamming the door behind him.

"Wow! What a temper! Is he always like that?" asked Banducci.

"Yes. Always," said Carmella, "Only sometimes, he's even worse. I swear that when he acts like this, he's possessed by Satan himself."

"Well, then, let's get on with it, shall we? What about your mother and sisters, Carmella?"

"Oh, they're not coming. My mother isn't into this at all, and my sisters would just like me to get them each a copy of the will."

"All right, then. As the executor, Eddie already knows what it contains. It's a relatively simple will when you consider—"

Suddenly the door flew open, and Sally bolted back into the room.

"Stop! Stop fucking everything!" he ordered. "I'm going to hear what's going on in here! Now start again from the beginning."

Tony Banducci read the will, explaining that Nicoletta had received a lifetime estate in their home and all of the property at the farm, plus one vehicle. All of the other cars and real estate were to be divided between the children. All of the money in bank accounts was to be divided equally between Nicoletta and the children. Nicoletta and Carmella had been designated to handle the division of the Don's personal effects. The executor was charged with setting up a lifetime family trust for each member of the family within sixty days.

"Hold it! Wait just a fuckin' minute! So tell me, Tony, where does the money come from to cover the trusts?" Sally asked through clenched teeth.

"I don't know, Sally. You'll have to ask Eddie. He's the executor, and he's handling that end."

"There ya go! I told ya! I knew it! I fucking knew it!" Sally screamed, pounding both fists on the table. "I knew this cocksucker would have an ace up his sleeve. Then you tell me, D'Amico. Where's the fucking money coming from for the trust?"

"Well, Sally, if you'll calm down, I'll tell you. Your father and I had some business dealings and made some good investments together. The money will come from his end," Eddie lied.

"Oh yeah, and let me guess. You're the only fucking one that knows how much his end is, right?"

"The amounts are substantial. With proper investments, the trust will be perpetual, and—"

Sally was livid and interrupted with a threat.

"Let me tell you something, asshole. I don't believe your cock-and-bull story for one fucking minute. Somehow you managed to pull some kind of scam on me. You listen to me, D'Amico, and you listen good! I'll figure this out and pay you back in fuckin' spades. Someday, I'll even the score!"

Sally glared at Eddie with a sinister look on his face.

"Remember my words!" he yelled as he stormed out.

Chapter 20

The deep, professional sound of the captain's voice awoke Eddie with a start.

"We will be arriving in Las Vegas in ten minutes. Flight attendants, please prepare for landing."

Eddie looked at his wristwatch.

Good, he thought, *I'll be on time for my meeting with Ace LaBelle.*

An attractive flight attendant approached and removed the magazine from his tray.

"Seat and tray up," she said, smiling as she peered deep into his eyes.

An expert at reading body language, Eddie had watched her make a play for him during the entire flight. She had given him constant signals. Smoldering eye contact, the slight brush of her hand against him every time she passed or brought him anything. It was no surprise to him when she finally made the purposeful comment that this flight would be a layover. He had to admit that she had him thinking. He watched admiringly as she walked down the aisle talking to the other passengers in first class.

He turned his attention to the view of Las Vegas outside the plane window. Any other time, he would have jumped at the opportunity to give her a jump, but he had more important things than a piece of ass on his mind this trip.

The smooth-talking captain was a good pilot. He lightly greased the massive plane onto the runway as if it were a feather. A pilot himself, Eddie mentally gave the captain a 10 for his perfect landing.

As he neared the exit, he stopped to retrieve his tan leather hanging bag from its compartment. The flight attendant was standing at the door, bidding the departing passengers farewell. As Eddie approached her, she smiled pleasantly and handed him a small folded piece of paper.

"Here are some numbers that are sure to bring you some luck in Vegas. Thanks for flying with us. Have a pleasant stay."

Eddie smiled back, and with only a nod of his head, exited the aircraft. He felt his curiosity getting the better of him as he entered terminal. He paused to open the folded paper. On it was written "Sandy Marcus—Airport Inn," and below the writing, she had drawn two happy faces with a heart on each side.

I'll bet she knows how to make a guy smile, he thought as he crumpled up the note and started to throw it into a trash container. But before it left his hand, he thought better of his decision and stuck the balled-up piece of paper into his pants pocket.

The terminal was humming with activity and jam-packed with people. He knew very well the layout of McCarran International Airport and easily worked his way through the throngs of people. As he neared the bottom of the escalator, he heard his name being called. He looked around the shoulder-to-shoulder crowd, trying to find who was summoning him.

"Eddie! Eddie D'Amico, over here!" the male voice called out.

He spotted waving to him from a distance Johnny Johnson, a limousine driver for the casino. Johnny pushed his way through the crowd and took the hanging bag from Eddie as he stepped off the escalator.

"Hi, J.J. How's the world been treating you?"

"The world's been treating me great. It's those fucking dice that are killing me!" he laughed. "Where's the rest of your luggage?"

"That's it. I'm traveling light this trip."

The afternoon sun was blazing. As they exited the terminal, Eddie felt the blast of hot air on his face.

"Wow! It's a scorcher here!"

"Not to worry, Eddie. I've got a couple of your favorite imported beers iced down for you in the car, and the casino is as cool as an iceberg."

"J.J., you're a good guy. Did you remember to pick up my package?"

"Yep! It's locked in the glove compartment."

The Tropicana's gray-and-maroon limousine with, the recognizable license plate marked "Trop 1," was parked at the curb with the trunk lid open. Johnny opened the rear door, and Eddie slid into the cool interior, reaching immediately for one of the cold beers.

"OK, Eddie, I'll have you at the casino in a flash."

"I need you to take me over to the executive aviation area first. LaBelle Aviation, to be exact."

"No problem, boss," said Johnny with a trace of New York accent still in his voice.

When they reached the private aviation area, Johnny's gray-blue eyes looked at Eddie through the rearview mirror.

"I'll wait for you. How long will you be?"

"I may be a while, and I don't want to tie up the limo. Just do me a favor and put my package inside my hanging bag. Have them hold it for me at the bell desk until I check in."

"Sure thing."

Eddie handed Johnny a fifty-dollar bill and stepped out of the limo in front of a large metal building. The sign over the door read "LaBelle Aviation." He pushed open the glass door, walked across the thick gray carpet to an ebony reception counter where a well-dressed middle-aged woman greeted him.

"I have an appointment with Mr. LaBelle. I'm a little early," he said as he handed her the business card that read "EDWARDO CARLOS, Diamond Merchant."

"I'll tell Mr. LaBelle you're here," she answered and disappeared down a hallway.

In her absence, Eddie wandered around the front office, looking at the many autographed pictures of entertainers and dignitaries who had flown in Ace LaBelle's aircraft.

"Right this way, Mr. Carlos."

She led him to the end of the hallway and stopped at a closed door.

"Go right in," she gestured.

As Eddie entered, Ace LaBelle rose from his desk and walked around it to greet him. He was a tall, fit-looking man, appearing to be in his late fifties. He made an impressive and professional appearance, dressed in a white shirt and tie.

"Nice to meet you, Mr. Carlos. Please have a seat," he said, motioning to a large gray chair in front of his highly polished ebony desk.

"Your message said you want to charter a jet. Where is it you want to go?" asked the pilot.

"To Milan, or rather, somewhere near Milan."

Ace LaBelle looked surprised and gave Eddie a somewhat suspicious glance.

"I'm sure you must be aware that there are much less expensive flying options, Mr. Carlos. Is there something else that maybe we should be discussing?"

"Well, as a matter of fact, yes. But first, let me tell you that I'm a close personal friend of Kimo. He recommended you to me."

"Ah, Kimo. How is the old scoundrel?"

"Couldn't be better. He's just kicking back and spending most of his time at his place in Maui, fishing, drinking beer, and chasing women. Kimo has handled all my other charters, but he doesn't have the equipment for the charter I need. So he gave me your name. He told me you're an excellent pilot and said you can be trusted."

LaBelle appeared to be flattered.

"Go on. Tell me about this charter you need."

"I'm in the wholesale diamond business. An opportunity has presented itself where I can buy a large number of diamonds at some real bargain prices. The diamonds are coming from a well-established and very reputable firm in Switzerland, but because of the price, I am somewhat suspicious of their true origin. Most importantly, I don't want to take the chance of my luggage being checked if I have to go through customs. I considered purchasing them and having them shipped, but that would be much too risky. They could be lost or stolen in transit."

"Well, Mr. Carlos . . ."

"Please, call me Eddie."

"OK, Eddie, so far, you haven't told me anything that would make me refuse the charter. That is, provided you agree to my financial arrangements."

LaBelle's eyes twinkled with obvious interest in Eddie's proposal.

"Let me give you a little more detail. As a pilot, myself, I'm aware of the type of information you'll need to know, and I understand that your flight books would not show any small, out-of-the-way airports or strips in that area. My plan is to take a commercial flight to Milan, rent a car, and scout out a suitable field that we can use for our purpose. When I locate a field, I'll leave the rental car there, arrange for transportation back to Milan, and fly back to the States. You, then, will fly me back to that field, and you will wait for me while I drive into Switzerland to make my purchase. I'll return the rental car to Milan and arrange for transportation back to your plane. I get to come back with my diamonds, and you come home with a pocket full of cash money. We both win."

Ace LaBelle was smiling from ear to ear.

Kimo was right, Eddie thought. *Ace had a streak of larceny in him a mile long and would do anything for money.*

"Well, Eddie, it sounds like you've planned it well. It's workable as far as I'm concerned. Now all we have to do is agree on the financial arrangements."

Ace reached into his desk drawer and pulled out a brochure.

"These are the regular rates for my aircraft. On a deal like yours, you pay me double the normal rate, plus a five-thousand-dollar bonus for let's call it my cooperation. I'll estimate the flying time, and you can write me a check in advance for the normal charges, which on paper will show a legitimate transaction. For our little side deal, you pay me cash before we leave Italy, including all of the waiting ground time. If you can live with those terms, then you and I have a deal."

Eddie stood up and reached out his hand.

"Done. I'll leave for Milan tomorrow. When can you make the flight?"

"As soon as you bring me a check. Is that soon enough?" Ace asked laughingly.

Eddie gave him a thumbs-up sign.

"Now I just have one small favor to ask of you, Ace. Can you call a taxi for me?"

The cabdriver let Eddie out at the front entrance of the Tropicana. He was well known to most of the hotel's employees. He had been a VIP customer of the hotel for years. In return for his patronage and generous tipping, he received royal treatment. The service personnel greeted him as if he was a member of their family and responded promptly to serve his every wish.

Upon entering his room, he went immediately to his closet. His garment bag was hung just as he had requested. He searched its inner pockets and found the small brown paper-wrapped package that Johnny had picked up for him. Tearing off the paper, he revealed a small white box that contained a black velvet pouch.

From the bathroom, Eddie took a dark green hand towel and spread it out carefully on the bed. He emptied the contents of the pouch onto the towel. Diamond look-alikes of all sizes glittered, reflecting magnificent splendor. Eddie smiled as he stared at the expensive-looking phony diamonds. He chuckled to himself, thinking about how they looked so valuable and yet were so absolutely worthless.

He removed a jeweler's loop from his pocket and picked up one of the larger stones, studying the replica carefully.

Ah, this is perfect. A perfect phony, he thought, chuckling to himself.

Another piece of his plan was in place. Anxious to get on with it, he went to the writing desk and began making out a list.

1. Airline ticket—Milan, a.m.
2. Call Switzerland bank—get cash ready.
3. Establish Nevada residency—quickie divorce.
4. Call Megan—start packing.
5. Rental car—Milan.
6. Sandy—airport inn?

Just as he was reaching for the phone to begin making his calls, it rang.

"Hey, big guy, what's the idea of not taking your usual suite I always have set up for you?"

It was the outgoing, attractive Lisa Powers, his casino hostess.

"Geez, Lisa, I just needed a place to crash for the night. It seemed like such a waste to use the big suite."

"You let me decide that. Are you trying to take my job?" she kidded. "Seriously, Eddie, we just want you to have the best. Why don't you move into the suite?"

"No, thanks, Lisa. Hell, you can hardly call this room roughing it. I'll be fine."

"OK, but listen, if there's anything at all that you need, just page me. And as usual, don't bother checking out. I'll take care of everything for you."

He stared at the telephone for a moment. Staying at the Tropicana was always a pleasure and a real ego trip for him. He wished he could stay longer this trip.

The big 747 was less than an hour away from landing in Milan. It had been a smooth flight and quite fortuitous for Eddie. Seated next to him in first class was an Italian contractor named Frederico Fellini, who was returning to his home in Milan. When the two men exchanged business cards, Eddie was careful not to give him one of his phony cards. While chatting during the flight, the two men realized they had a lot in common. They developed a friendly relationship and enjoyed each other's company. During their conversation, Eddie questioned the happy-go-lucky Italian about whether he knew of any airstrips on the outskirts of Milan. Frederico mentioned that he knew of one north of town near the Swiss border. It had been used by the Germans during the Second World War and was currently being used as a base of operations for glider pilots.

When Eddie expressed great interest in seeing the airfield, Frederico insisted that he spend the night at his villa, and he would personally take him there to see it the following morning. Eddie could hardly believe this stroke of luck had befallen him. He genuinely liked the gregarious portly Italian and gladly accepted his offer.

The red Ferrari was speeding past the green Italian countryside at breakneck speed. Frederico was behind the wheel laughing and joking about Eddie's fear of his reckless driving. The car suddenly made a sharp turn down a long driveway lined with tall Italian cypress. Soon the magnificent villa of Frederico Fellini came into view. The Ferrari slowed to a stop in front of the massive hand-carved double entry doors.

"Wella, howa you like it, Mr. D'Amico?"

"It's incredible! How many rooms in there?"

"Shita, I don't know. I never bother to count."

They entered the three-story-high foyer. A huge crystal chandelier hung majestically from the ceiling. For as far as the eye could see, the floor was covered with a white marble matrix laced with rose-colored accents. To the right was a winding staircase with ornately hand-carved railings.

A short, heavyset woman dressed in black appeared.

"Maria willa show you toa your room. I'lla go and makea sure we have a fine feast tonight."

"Frederico, I'm speechless. Your home is beyond words."

"Ah, so if itsa beyond words, don'ta say anything. Just enjoy! Tonight we havea nice mongiotti, and tomorrow I'lla takea you to the airfield. Go, nowa rest. I'lla call you when itsa time to eat."

Eddie nodded and followed Maria up the long staircase. The woman silently led him to a room in the rear of the villa. He glanced around the expansive room, admiring its ornate Old World charm and the richness of the furnishings. He decided to shower first, and then he fell onto the canopy-covered bed and soon dropped off to sleep.

His newfound friend awakened him with a boisterous call to come downstairs for dinner. Frederico proved to be true to his ancestry; he was an exceptional host. He had his cook prepare a special seven-course meal for his guest. The two men ate in true Italian style—not until they were full, but until they grew tired. After several hours, they became weary from their overindulgence of food and wine. Exhausted, they retired to their rooms.

Eddie lay in bed thinking about how much he liked his new friend. Since meeting Frederico, some new thoughts about his plan were forming in his mind. Frederico had generously offered Eddie the use of one of his vehicles, which meant that Eddie would no longer need a traceable rental car. But first, he would need to check out the airstrip and make sure that it would meet the necessary requirements to land Ace's Lear jet. He closed his eyes and drifted into sleep.

He awoke early with excitement and anticipation of getting on with his plan. He dressed and slipped quietly downstairs, figuring Frederico would still be sleeping. When he reached the first floor, he heard the sound of loud baritone singing. He followed the sound and discovered it was coming from the other side of heavy wooden double swinging doors that led into the kitchen. As he peeked inside, he saw Frederico making breakfast.

"Ay, Eddie! Buon giorno! How do you like your eggs?"

"Over easy," Eddie replied, chuckling at his friend's gusto.

"Overa easy ita is. So, my friend, how dida you sleep?"

"Like a fucking log, of course. I drank too much of your homemade wine."

"The wine, she'sa good for you. Ita makesa your salami nice anda hard!" said Frederico, gesturing with a stiff arm.

"Hey, Frederico, tell me something. Do you have a nickname, or does everyone always call you Frederico?"

"Wella, that depends. Mya mother, she callsa me son. Mya kids, theya calla me Papa, anda my ex-awife, shea callsa me no-gooda son of a bitch! But my friends, theya calla me Rico. You cana calla me Rico too, Eddie."

As they ate breakfast, the two men discussed staying in touch with each other and agreed to meet in Las Vegas in the near future. When they finished eating, they drove to the airfield. Eddie could not believe his eyes. It was perfect. The runway was in good condition and plenty long enough. He got all of the field information he needed from the base operator. Ace would simply have to arrive during daylight hours. There were no runway lights, and without them, a night landing would be extremely dangerous and out of the question.

His new friendship with Frederico was proving to be invaluable. If all went well, he could even shorten his trip and finish his plan sooner if he could just convince Ace to come to Italy without the down payment check he requested.

The men drove back to Frederico's villa, where Eddie placed a call to Ace LaBelle and explained his new idea. The pilot was cooperative and receptive to the change in plan. He agreed to do the necessary paperwork and would make arrangements to arrive at the airstrip late the next afternoon.

Next, Eddie dialed the number to the bank in Switzerland. He wanted to advise the bank that he would be arriving the next morning and verify that the arrangements for him to pick up the cash were in order.

"Yes, Mr. D'Amico, I'll put you through to Mr. Dorfman."

Jackpot! Eddie thought as he hung up the telephone.

He would need to leave immediately and drive to Switzerland in one of Rico's cars. It would be late when he arrived, but he could surely find a room, get a good night's sleep, and be at the bank bright and early the next morning. After he got the money, he would drive to the airfield and meet Ace for the return flight home. He would leave the car at the airstrip, and Rico had volunteered to pick it up later. It was a perfect plan.

He went upstairs to collect his hanging bag and to make sure that Don Francisco's paperwork, the bankbooks, and the phony diamonds were all in order. He stuffed them all back into the money belt he was wearing around his waist.

Frederico was waiting for him at the foot of the stairway. Together they walked out to the huge garage that housed eight cars. Frederico selected a set of keys from a key board and motioned for Eddie to follow him to a sporty royal blue Pantera. Eddie took the keys, and the two men embraced.

"Go witha God, mya friend," said Frederico, his eyes moist and glassy.

"I can't find the words to thank you enough for all you've done, Rico. Now you have to promise me something. When we meet in Vegas, you will be my guest. No arguments. Is that a deal?"

"So be it. It's a deal. When I comea to Vegas, I'lla play anda you'lla pay!" Frederico said, laughing.

The two men embraced again before Eddie climbed into the racy little car. He was on his way to Switzerland and Don Francisco's fortune.

The road wound its way through picturesque villages and rolling green pastures. Off in the distance, ominous snowcapped mountaintops towered high above the landscape. Eddie was overwhelmed at the beauty of the Swiss countryside.

The road he was traveling was winding and constantly ascending, but the powerful little Pantera was undaunted and effortlessly climbed the grade. He reached his destination shortly before nightfall and drove around the downtown area until he located the bank so he would know exactly where to go in the morning. Down the block, he spotted a department store that was still open. He swung the Pantera into a nearby parking lot. A short time later, he emerged from the store carrying a rather large, nondescript brown suitcase and a small stainless steel attaché case. He placed them in the trunk of the car and cruised the downtown streets looking for a place to stay.

He checked into a quaint chalet-appearing hotel located only a few blocks from the bank. His room was rather dwarfish, but it was exceptionally clean. Although he was feeling a little nervous and edgy, his stomach reminded him he hadn't eaten since breakfast. He ordered room service and decided to take a shower to try and calm himself down while he waited for his food to arrive. Just as he was drying off, he heard a knock on his door. Wrapping the towel around his waist, he opened the door, and a pretty young girl smiled at him and boldly looked him over with curious eyes as she pushed the food cart into the room. Normally calm, collected, and in control of his situations, for no explainable reason, he suddenly found himself embarrassed under the young girl's scrutiny. He nervously signed the bill and fumbled through his money for a tip.

When the girl left the room, the full weight of the events since Don Francisco's death seemed to descend upon him all at once, smothering him with the importance of their significance in his life. Suddenly he felt as though he was in over his head and couldn't breathe. The thoughts in his mind were whirling around like some kind of out-of-control kaleidoscope. He sat on the edge of the bed, pulled a beer from the ice bucket, and guzzled it down.

Tomorrow is the big day, he thought. *It will all just begin tomorrow. The frightening and awesome responsibility of all that money.*

Nervously he took the bankbooks from his money belt. He held them tightly in his hands, and tears began to fall from his eyes. He was beginning to feel crushed by the magnitude of what his godfather had thrust him into.

Wake up! Wake up! It's all a bad dream, his mind was screaming out. *Oh, Godfather, you made a mistake! This is all more than I can handle*, he thought.

The Don's voice was ringing in his ears: "I personally have no fear of death . . . all you have to do is supply the bank with proof of my death . . . you must be very careful what you do . . . I can count on you to see that your godfather's wishes are carried out . . . I could do no more even if you were my own son."

"I miss you, Godfather. I loved you more than you ever knew. I wish I had never seen these fucking books and that you were still alive!" he whispered aloud.

Eddie buried his face in the pillow and wept until he was completely cried out and drained. Then he struggled to sit up, and he took a deep breath. Suddenly a sense of peace began to engulf him, as if in some mystical manner he had been fortified with power and strength from just the memory of Don Francisco.

The nervousness and anxiety he had been feeling was flushed away symbolically by his tears of remorse over the Don's death. Eddie felt renewed and refreshed.

"Don't worry, Godfather. I will keep my promise to you. I won't let you down," he said aloud, reaffirming his pledge to himself and to the silence of the dimly lit room.

He looked at the now-cold food he had ordered and pushed the room service cart out into the hallway, his meal untouched. Then securing the door to his room, he began preparing for the trip he would make to the bank in the morning. He carefully reviewed Don Francisco's documents one last time and then meticulously arranged the papers, the bankbooks, and the black velvet pouch of faux diamonds in the stainless steel attaché case. Satisfied that everything was in order, he phoned the front desk and ordered a wake-up call. He fell asleep soon after his head hit the pillow.

Early the next morning, Eddie entered the bank appropriately dressed in a gray three-piece business suit and a dark burgundy tie. On the outside, he appeared calm and self-assured; but on the inside, his stomach was in knots. He still hadn't eaten since breakfast the day before. His case of nerves had completely destroyed his appetite. He felt a little foolish and intimidated walking into the bank carrying the large brown suitcase along with the attaché case.

He was taken aback when he entered the front doors. The lobby of the bank, high-ceilinged and very tastefully furnished, looked more like some exclusive men's club of older times. Other than the security stationed at the doors, there were no tellers, bank employees, or customers in sight. There was only one enormous very expensive-looking desk to one side of the room, where a matronly woman was seated.

"Yes, sir, how may I assist you?" she asked as he approached.

"I have an appointment to see Mr. Dorfman," he said, setting down the large suitcase and handing her a business card from his suit pocket.

She scrutinized the card that read "ED D'AMICO and ASSOCIATES, Builder, Developer, Design and Engineering. Then she peered over the top of her Ben Franklin spectacles at the open page of her leatherbound registry book.

"Ah, yes. Please have a seat, Mr. D'Amico. Mr. Dorfman will be right with you."

She pressed a button on the intercom and announced Eddie's presence to Mr. Dorfman. Eddie heard no response. With an aloof air, the woman acknowledged him no further but simply busied herself with paperwork on her desk. Eddie suddenly realized that he had been unconsciously tapping his foot on the floor and tried to still all movement of his body immediately. Then he felt perspiration beginning to seep from the pores of his armpits. He tried to recall whether he had applied his antiperspirant that morning.

Footsteps on the marble flooring drew his attention to the direction of an approaching man. He was of small frame with a long, thin face. His eyes appeared magnified behind the thick black horn-rimmed glasses that dominated his face. His suit reminded Eddie of the kind he used to wear as a kid when Don Francisco took him out with the boys.

"Mr. D'Amico?"

Eddie nodded and stood to greet the man.

"So nice to meet you. Please follow me to my office."

The little man turned on his toe as if performing a military maneuver and marched quickly away. Eddie picked up his suitcase and attaché and followed close behind him.

Mr. Dorfman's office was at the end of a very long hallway. It was incredibly imposing, particularly for such a small man. Eddie thought the size of the room made Mr. Dorfman look like an optical illusion, and the humor of his thought made him feel a little more at ease.

"Mr. D'Amico, I think you'll be pleased to know that I've made all of the arrangements as you requested. We will, of course, follow customary procedures, so we shall begin with your documents. May I see them please?"

Eddie removed the documents from the attaché case and handed them to the banker. Mr. Dorfman carefully perused the paperwork. Then without looking up, he pressed an intercom button on his desk.

"Heidi, please come in here."

Immediately, a door at one side of the office opened, and a lovely blonde-haired, blue-eyed woman entered. Eddie kept his eyes on her, but she never once looked at him.

"Heidi, these documents are ready to go to security for the file check."

She took the documents and left the room. Eddie realized he was tapping his foot again, and felt angry at his lack of self-control.

"Excuse me, Mr. Dorfman, will you explain the procedures to me?" Eddie asked.

"Yes, of course. Heidi will have the documents, the signatures, and the thumb print verified against our security files. Now I will begin asking you a series of questions to which your answers must confirm the legitimacy of our business here today."

Mr. Dorfman's quiz took about ten minutes and consisted of questions regarding the Don's secret code information and password acknowledgments. Eddie was comfortable through the questioning and confident that all of his answers were correct since Don Francisco had provided him with all of the necessary information. Just as they finished, Heidi knocked once on the door and entered, returning with the paperwork. Mr. Dorfman looked at each page and announced that all verifications were in order before handing them back to Eddie.

Curious to see what the verifications looked like, Eddie flipped through the papers and saw that a customized bank stamp with the word VERIFIED and the date was placed below Don Francisco's signature and thumb print.

"Now, Mr. D'Amico, if you will just follow me, it has all been prepared for you in a counting room."

Mr. Dorfman led Eddie down the hallway and down a flight of stairs. At the bottom, two armed security guards were stationed outside a prison-type barred gate. Upon Dorfman's order, the gate slid open to one side, and one of the guards followed them in and positioned himself just outside the solid steel-doored counting room.

"I'm sure you will find everything in perfect order, Mr. D'Amico. I personally checked it all myself. When you are finished, just press the button, and Hans here will escort you out of the bank," said Mr. Dorfman.

"Thank you, Mr. Dorfman, you've certainly handled everything to perfection and most professionally."

"Mr. D'Amico, if I can be of any further service to you, please do not hesitate to contact me."

The guard opened the door to the small vaultlike counting room. Eddie's eyes grew wide. He could hardly believe what lay before him. Piled on a steel table inside the room were stacks of money in one-hundred-, five-hundred-, and one-thousand-dollar denominations, and these stacks only represented a portion of Don Francisco's fortune.

The solid steel door slid shut, and then Eddie heard a clicking sound that he thought must be the locking mechanism.

"Oh my god, Don Francisco. Holy shit!" he muttered to himself.

Eddie sat down on the hard steel bench at the table and felt his palms begin to sweat. Nervously he stared at the piles of money and began wondering if he had miscalculated. He looked at the suitcase he had thought might be a little large. Now he wondered if it would be too small to hold all of this money. Beads of perspiration were forming on his forehead. Without thinking, he wiped his face with the sleeve of his suit, and the fabric showed its saturation of his sweat. He waved his arm through the air in an attempt to dry the sleeve, hoping it wouldn't leave a visible ring or stain. He pulled out his handkerchief and mopped the rest of his brow from which the sweat was now pouring. He desperately wanted to loosen his tie and rip the collar of his shirt open, but instead, he started feverishly counting the money.

Just as Mr. Dorfman had assured him, it was all there. He breathed a loud sigh of relief and then methodically started placing the stacks of bills into the suitcase as if he were putting together a puzzle, trying to make all of the pieces fit. His concern over the suitcase being too small was justified. There were several stacks of money that would not fit. He managed to jam the remainder of the bills into the attaché case and snapped it shut.

Eddie's heart was pounding as he pushed the call button for the guard to open the door. Just as the door clicked and began to slide open, a horrible thought crossed his mind. He hadn't tested the weight of the suitcase, and he was terrified that he might not be able to carry it.

The guard was now fully visible but was not looking at Eddie. He stood at attention just outside the door facing the hallway. Eddie placed a firm grip around the handle of the suitcase and took a deep breath. With one strong pull, he lifted the suitcase.

Thank God I got it off the ground! he thought.

As he exited the counting room, he thanked Hans, trying not to grunt his words under the strain of the heavy suitcase. Then he thought about the flight of stairs he would need to climb, and for a moment, he felt it was hopeless.

Get hold of yourself. This is only mind over matter. You can do this. Just get to the car. Just get to the car, he chanted over and over in his mind, trying to psyche himself up.

Eddie was thankful that Hans preceded him on their journey to the bank's exit, so he couldn't detect what a stressful effort it was for him to carry the heavy case up the stairs. As Hans neared the front entrance of the bank, the security guards stationed there opened the doors. Hans silently escorted Eddie to the waiting Pantera.

The fortune finally locked safely in the trunk, Eddie slid into the driver's seat and started the engine. He put the car in gear and pulled out into the traffic, while at the same time tearing his tie from his neck and unbuttoning his shirt. He was less than half a block from the bank when he let out an earsplitting yell of joy and relief.

Eddie couldn't wait to get to the airstrip and head for home. Even though his stomach was now overcome with hunger pangs, he had a song in his heart as he cruised along in the sports car down the twisting turns of the mountainous road.

God forbid I should have an accident with all of this money in the car, he thought.

He envisioned the car rolling down the mountainside, the trunk flying open and thousands upon thousands of large denomination bills floating through the air into the fathoms of the crevasses below. He lightly pressed the brakes and dropped the gear to slow the Pantera down.

Suddenly, he felt his heart palpitating, and he began to feel faint. He struggled to keep from blacking out and started looking for a place to pull off the narrow road. Around the next bend, he spotted a view overlook. He quickly turned into the parking area and brought the car to a stop next to the large telescope that was mounted near the edge of the drop-off. He laid his head back and closed his eyes, trying to regain his composure. He opened the door and took a deep breath of the fresh mountain air.

Seeing no one else around, he decided this was a good time to make some necessary adjustments to his baggage. He opened the trunk and removed all of the money from the attaché case, except for the amount he would need to pay Ace, and arranged it carefully in the various pockets of his hanging bag. Then he began to transfer money from the suitcase to the garment bag, making sure it was equally distributed for weight and appearance.

Feeling stronger now, he was just about to reenter the car when he heard the sound of tires pull onto the gravel parking area. As he glanced around, the police car came to a halt just behind the Pantera. The officer instantly emerged from his vehicle and strode directly toward Eddie with his hand resting on his revolver.

Oh, dear God, what now? he wondered.

He felt his knees weaken.

"Good morning, Officer. Beautiful day, isn't it?" Eddie asked, trying to keep his voice calm.

"Yes, it is, and this is the most beautiful view from this mountain. I stop here every morning when I start my shift. It just puts me in a good mood, ya know what I mean?"

"Yes, sir!" he responded, feeling blessed and relieved.

Eddie walked to the edge of the lookout and made small talk with the policeman while he admired the magnificent view of the bright green valley outstretched before them.

"Well, time to get back to work. That's a beautiful car you're driving. Where are you headed?"

"To Milan to visit an old friend," Eddie responded, his adrenaline flowing strong.

"Good for you! Enjoy your visit and drive carefully. This road can be a little dangerous, you know."

"Yeah, thanks, Officer. Hope you have a great day!"

As soon as the policeman moved his car, Eddie pulled out ahead of him onto the road and started down the mountain again. After a few minutes, he noticed the police car following closely behind him. He began to perspire and tremble inside.

Shit! He knows what I have in the trunk, he thought, paranoid over his cargo.

All at once, the flashing lights of the police car came on. Just as Eddie was trying to make a snap decision whether to pull over or step down on the accelerator to try and make a getaway, the police cruiser pulled out and whizzed past the Pantera at high speed. Eddie heard the siren start up as the officer continued on down the mountain ahead of him.

Once again relieved, he tried to push all of the stressful events of the trip from his mind. He decided this would be a good time to plan out some of the trusts he would need to set up as soon as he got back home, but he couldn't concentrate. He could only think of food and wondered how much longer it would be before he could get something to eat.

It was late afternoon when he arrived at the airfield. He felt happy and excited when, in the distance, he could see the white Lear jet parked near an old hangar that was being used as an office. As he got closer, he panicked when he noticed a red Ferrari sitting next to the jet. He knew it had to be Frederico's. Then he saw Frederico and Ace standing together conversing just inside the door of the hangar.

Oh my god! What the hell is Rico doing here now? If they've compared notes, I'm dead. They each know me by different last names! How the hell will I ever explain this? he wondered fearfully.

He drove past them, acting as if he hadn't seen them, and decided to park directly next to the loading compartment of the jet. Its door was opened and waiting. Eddie jumped out of the car and began loading his luggage into the plane. Just as he finished, Frederico and Ace walked around the tail section.

"Hey, Eddie, you have a gooda trip?" asked Frederico.

"Rico, my friend, everything went well. Very well. I can't thank you enough for the use of your car."

Eddie searched the faces of both men, trying to discern whether there was any doubt in their eyes. He could detect none.

"Nicea airoplane you gonna flya home in, eh?"

"Yeah, Rico, some plane!"

"I take it everything went OK?" asked Ace.

"Couldn't have been better," Eddie replied. "But I've been so busy. I haven't eaten, and I'm starving. Are we ready to go?"

"Waita justa minute!" shouted Frederico as he ran toward his Ferrari.

In a moment, he returned carrying a medium-sized basket.

"Here, I bringa you this. I thought you woulda be morte di affam. Here isa somea homea-made bread witha the besta cold cuts anda the nicea provolone. Mangiare, mangiare, and enjoy!"

"Bless you, Rico! You're a saint!" exclaimed Eddie as he took the basket of food and handed Frederico the keys to the Pantera.

"I keep ina touch and seea you soon ina Las Vegas, eh?"

"Yes, Rico, and I'll do my best to equal your hospitality and generosity."

The two men embraced fondly. All of Eddie's fear and stress disappeared as he boarded the jet. He realized that luckily, his last name must have never come up between Ace and Frederico.

Ace followed Eddie into the rear of the plane while the copilot completed the preflight.

"So tell me. Did you get the diamonds?" Ace asked excitedly.

Eddie smiled and nodded knowingly as he opened the stainless steel attaché case and took out the black velvet pouch. He reached up and turned on the overhead light before pouring a few of the fake jewels into the palm of his hand. They glittered brilliantly under the light, reflecting splashes of rainbow colors.

"Holy shit!" exclaimed Ace. "They're beautiful!"

"Yeah, but I'm afraid I've got some bad news for you, Ace. Since I don't have any checks with me, I'm going to have to pay you all in cash!"

"Aw shit, Eddie, that's terrible news," Ace said, laughing and holding out his hands as Eddie filled them with the money from the steel case.

"You know, Eddie, I knew I liked you from the minute I saw you," said the pilot as he stuffed the cash into his flight bag. "Let's go home, partner," he said as he headed for the front of the plane.

After quickly devouring the contents of the food basket, Eddie settled back in his seat and slept all the way home to St. Louis.

Chapter 21

F ive weeks had passed since Eddie's return from Italy. As soon as his divorce was finalized, he and Megan flew to Las Vegas and were married in a quickie Nevada-style ceremony. After honeymooning in the City of Lights for two days in an elegant two-story suite on the top floor at the Tropicana, they returned to St. Louis and finished moving Megan into Eddie's penthouse apartment at the 111 Park Avenue Hotel.

Eddie had wanted to take Megan on a honeymoon cruise, but he was consumed with making good his promises to Don Francisco. His mind was fully occupied with devising a scheme for laundering the huge amounts of money, and he needed to start setting up the family trusts.

The day after returning home from Italy, he had placed all of the cash in safe deposit boxes at four different local banks. Now all that remained for him to do was to try to convince the old-time mobsters to cooperate with him and go along with his plan. Trying to figure out the perfect solution for laundering the money had been giving him anxiety attacks. He felt a sense of depression and remorse over the fact that Don Francisco had pushed him unwillingly over the edge and into the world of the Mafia. With each passing day, he was becoming more entangled in its dangerous and sinister web.

Eddie stretched, awakening slowly and feeling drugged by a night of heavy sleep. He lifted his head to peek over Megan's still-slumbering body and squinted to focus on the nightstand clock. Its red digital numbers glowed a soft silent message. It was 5:20 a.m. He knew the alarm would go off any minute. Not wanting to disturb Megan, he reached over her and disengaged the setting.

He eased his body out of the bed and stood for a moment, admiring the beauty of his new wife's finely chiseled features and her sensuous full lips. He couldn't resist bending over to tenderly kiss her forehead before heading for the shower.

Megan was still sleeping as he poured his first cup of coffee. It was 6:00 a.m. Eddie went to his briefcase, which was standing open on the kitchen counter, and searched through its contents. He pulled out a piece of yellow legal paper on which he had written ten names. The list consisted of old-time family members that Don Francisco had helped to set up in business.

Eddie had invited all of the old mobsters to meet with him in the hotel later that night so he could lay out his strategy to them for laundering the money. Each man would play a major role in his plan, and he would need the full support of all of them for his scheme to be successful. He had some serious reservations as to whether he could convince ten old and stubborn, hardheaded Italians to buy into his plan. In the event the old men chose to be uncooperative, Eddie had a couple of aces up his sleeve, but he believed that if they had any brains at all, they would find his offer profitable. He knew that they would be foolish to refuse him, but as additional insurance, he had figured out a way to back them into a corner, using their dislike and distrust of Sally as leverage if they wouldn't agree to his plan.

A long time ago, Eddie had made it a practice not to go into a meeting unless his desired outcome was already a forgone conclusion that had been predetermined in a smoke-filled room or on a golf course or over a martini. He was resolute in his decision to control these old Mafioso and make his plan work at all cost. He was banking on the fact that things were not going well within the Barratino family since Sally's takeover as don. Against the wishes of the ten old-timers, Sally had moved into the territories of the black Mafia, competing with their drug and numbers rackets. As most of the old mobsters had predicted, Sally's actions had started a war with One-Eyed Jack Shepard and the black Mafia, and Sally's arrogance in refusing to listen to his advisors, as well as his lack of experience, were causing him to lose the war.

To further complicate matters for the Barratino family, Vito Cavelli had sworn to avenge his brother's death and had moved in some of his soldiers from Chicago with orders to kill Sally on sight. Finally realizing that he had bitten off more than he could chew by involving the Barratino crime family in a mob war on two fronts at the same time, Sally feared for his life and went into hiding.

Eddie was hoping that the men on his list had enough hatred for the bloodthirsty Sally that it could be used to his advantage during his negotiations with them. Satisfied and comfortable with his plan of attack for the meeting that evening, he closed up the briefcase and headed for the elevator.

It was now 6:20 a.m. He knew that his recent lack of attention to his own company business was causing serious problems, and he was getting farther behind each day with important matters that needed his attention. Today he was anxious to get on the road to check the progress of his construction projects and then get to his office and wade through the piles of paperwork that had been building up on his desk.

As he exited the building to the rear parking lot, the crisp air of the fall morning invigorated him. He breathed in deeply and exhaled slowly, watching the warm breath escape from his mouth like smoke from a cigarette. Feeling motivated and energetic, Eddie walked at a brisk clip toward his white Ford station wagon parked at the far corner of the lot. As he turned the key in the door lock, he heard a popping sound, immediately followed by the shattering of glass. Instinctively, he jerked open the door and dove into the car atop thousands of pieces of glittering jagged glass that had exploded from the driver's window of the car. Just as his body fell heavily to the floorboard, the windshield shattered, raining a hail of broken glass down on top of him.

Fearing to move from his temporary place of safety, he lay frozen in fear. His heart was beating so wildly that it ached inside his chest. He was panting heavily, trying to figure out who would be trying to kill him. Only one name came to his mind. Sally Barratino.

After several minutes that seemed like an eternity to him, he sat up slowly and peeked out through the jagged edges of the windows. His eyes carefully searched the rooftops of the surrounding buildings, but he could spot no one. Finally, hoping the coast was clear, but not taking any chances, he jumped out of the vehicle and began running as fast as he could toward the safety of the hotel, dodging in and out of parked cars, using them as protection along the way.

He burst into his apartment, shaking uncontrollably. Hoping Megan was still asleep, he closed the door quietly and then quickly double-bolted it before running to the phone in the guest bedroom. With a trembling finger, he dialed Bee Stinger's pager number, left a message, and hung up. Within seconds, his telephone rang back. Eddie grabbed the receiver on the first ring, praying it hadn't awakened Megan.

"Yeah, Eddie, what's up?"

"A fucking sniper just tried to kill me!" Eddie whispered excitedly.

"Are you shittin' me? What the hell happened?"

"I was getting into my car in the parking lot, and some motherfucker started shooting at me!"

"Did you see who it was?"

"Are you crazy? I just dove for cover!"

"So then what? Did you report it?"

"Fuck no! I've already got enough heat on me! I just ran back up to my apartment, and you're the first person I called."

"Well then, if you don't want it reported, what do you want me to do?"

"The fuckin' shooter's probably long gone by now, but can't you just come by and check the rooftops on the QT? Maybe you can find some clues."

"OK, I'll be right over."

Bee rang the door chimes just as Eddie had finished washing the glass out of his hair and getting dressed. Eddie looked through the peephole in the door before opening it.

"Get in here, Bee, and bolt the damned door behind you," Eddie whispered, holding his index finger to his lips and pointing toward the master bedroom.

The detective acknowledged the signals to be quiet and followed Eddie as he strode quickly and nervously over to the bar. Bee watched him toss down several shots of anisette to steady his nerves while he told his story.

When Eddie had finished, Bee asked in a hushed voice, "Tell me something, Eddie. Do you have a piece?"

"Are you joking? What the hell would I want with a gun? I haven't even shot one since Don Francisco used to take me shooting with him when I was just a kid. I admit I just had the shit scared out of me this morning, but I don't know if I'm ready to start packing a piece like some kind of hoodlum."

"Yeah, well, no buts about it. This is serious shit. You're better off being safe than sorry, or maybe even dead. Here. I brought you a present," said Bee, displaying a small automatic Beretta in an ankle holster.

"Is that one of your guns?"

"You ask too many questions. Remember, I'm the detective. I'll ask the questions. Would I be giving you a piece that could be traced back to me?"

"Yeah, maybe you're right. Then thanks for the present, but what the hell am I gonna do with this peashooter when the son of a bitch is shooting at me with a high-powered rifle from a rooftop?" Eddie asked.

"Hey, you never know with these guys. The next time, he might try to get you at close range, and if that happens, you'll be glad you have that peashooter. Come on, Eddie, let's take a ride."

"Where the hell to? Ya know I've got a business to run. How the fuck can I go anywhere when I've got some asshole trying to kill me?"

"I've had it with this whispering. Come on, let's get outa here so we can talk. I'll drive you by your jobs, and then we'll go bang off a few rounds at the shooting range. I wanna see if you can hit something with that peashooter."

Before leaving, Eddie quickly looked in on Megan and, thankfully, found her still sleeping soundly.

The quick succession of hollow-sounding gunshots echoed through his protective ear covering. Eddie watched as Bee pushed a button on the wall beside him, and the target of a full-sized male image suspended on a cable and pulley contraption began to move slowly toward them.

Eddie proudly examined the bullet-riddled face of the human-shaped target and then removed his ear guards and set them down alongside his small but deadly Beretta. Bee patted Eddie on the back and grinned.

"Shit, my friend, you just impressed the hell out of me! You're a real natural! Look at that poor son of a bitch," Bee said, pointing at the paper target. "For a guy who hasn't shot a gun since he was a kid, you're a dead shot!"

"Yeah, well, I'd better be a dead shot if I don't wanna be shot dead! I just hope this little peashooter can stand up to a high-powered rifle on a rooftop!"

"If it's Sally who's out to get ya, it won't matter whether you have a peashooter or a cannon. He could just decide to set a timer somewhere for you and blow you to bits."

"Ya know, Bee, that's what I always liked about you. You're so reassuring. What a fucking comforting thing to say! Could you just keep that shit to yourself before I wanna go slit my wrists!"

"Hey, my friend, you never listen to me. I've been telling you to keep your distance from the mob. I told you you've been too close to the family for too long. Anyway, it's common knowledge there's no love lost between you and Sally."

Bee's comment caused Eddie to recall Sally's last threat to him at the reading of Don Francisco's will in Tony Banducci's office.

It was almost five thirty when Detective Stinger dropped Eddie back off at his apartment. *Good*, he thought, *I'll have plenty of time to take a relaxing shower and change before my eight o'clock meeting with the mobsters.*

He began calling out to Megan, but she did not reply. Upon entering the bathroom, he noticed a note taped to the mirror. She had gone to the movies with Carmella.

The hot shower felt soothing. In his mind, he began reviewing his strategy for the meeting. Considering himself a master of manipulation and control, Eddie had made up his mind to put his study of social behavior into effect. He would be intentionally fourteen minutes late entering the meeting. He knew that his planned tardiness would not be enough to make anyone leave, but it would subliminally put him in the ultimate position of control by virtue of the fact that all the others would be waiting for him to arrive. They wouldn't consciously realize that his ploy would make him the single most important person to attend the meeting.

At precisely twelve minutes past eight, he left his apartment and got into the elevator, carrying the metal briefcase. He walked down a long corridor, paused under the sign that read "Napoleon Room," and took a deep breath before he flung open the door.

He was immediately greeted by the familiar strong odor of little dago rope cigars. The instant he entered the room, the gruff, powerful voice of Romy Marchetti called out angrily.

"You're fucking late, D'Amico!"

"Yes, Romy," he answered politely, looking around into the faces of the men seated around two brown folding tables. "Forgive me, gentlemen, and please accept my apologies. I received a very important long-distance telephone call just as I was leaving to meet with you," he lied.

Eddie could sense the electrical energy and hostility that permeated the room. Ten pairs of eyes glared at him suspiciously. He knew he needed to take immediate control.

"Gentlemen, let me set the tone for our meeting by telling you that I know, beyond a shadow of a doubt, that the information I am going to share with you is true and factual, so please do not insult me by contradicting or denying what I am about to say."

He now had raised their curiosity levels to exactly where he wanted them. Each of the men was staring intently at him, giving him their undivided attention.

"Gentlemen, I come to you tonight not as an adversary but as a friend with good intentions. I have but one purpose in mind. To fulfill a promise that I made to Don Francisco, *buon arme*, just before he died.

I am going to offer all of you a proposal that will be to our mutual benefit, but I am here to tell you that I intend to keep my promise to the godfather with or without your cooperation—"

"Why don'ta you get to the fuckina point?" yelled out Lucky Carlucci.

The rest of the men grumbled at Lucky and waved him off. Ignoring his outburst, they motioned for Eddie to continue.

"By now, I think most of you are aware that Don Francisco appointed me executor of his estate—"

"Biga fuckin' deal! Whata does any of thisa shit havea to do witha us?" asked Enrico Cappiano, the shoe manufacturer.

"Shut up and let him talk!" someone yelled out.

"Thank you," Eddie replied to his unknown benefactor.

"Gentlemen, I have full knowledge of the fact that Don Francisco was a silent partner in each of your businesses. I know that for many years, you were paying him green money that amounted to 50 percent of your profits . . ."

All of the men began to whisper among themselves. Eddie realized by their actions that they thought he was trying to shake them down. The wrecking contractor, Rocky Nucci, became openly hostile.

"We don'ta give a shit whata you thinka you know! Don Francisco's dead!" he yelled. "Alla fuckin'a bets are off now!"

"Wait a minute, Rocky! Let me make something perfectly clear!" Eddie interrupted. "Your deal with Don Francisco doesn't end unless I say it does, and as long as I'm alive, his interests are going to be protected!"

"Hey, so it'sa no biga deal. Maybe you gotta die," said Lucky through clenched teeth.

Lucky's comment suddenly made Eddie realize that any one of the men in the room had the power to put a contract out on his life. He wondered if perhaps one of them had with the attempt that was made on his life that morning.

"Firsta let usa hear about thisa mutuala benefita bullashita. Leta him finish," one of the men called out.

"Not me. I've heard enough. I'm fuckin' outa here," said Romy Marchetti, rising from his seat.

"Go ahead and leave, Romy, but if you do, your actions could jeopardize every man in this room," said Eddie. "My plan calls for 100 percent participation from all of you. Without it, there's no deal."

Freddie Flowers spoke up and gave the others a warning glance. "Sita down, bonehead, anda listen. Everybody shuta up. Come ona, geta to the point, D'Amico."

"OK. Here's my dilemma. Don Francisco left a considerable amount of cash for me to set up trusts to take care of his wife and kids. Where I need your help is laundering this money. If you agree, then I will meet with each of you twice each year, and I will give each of you half of whatever amounts you feel you can safely launder in cash, and I'll give you the money up front. As you can see, by me giving you the cash in advance, I have complete faith and trust in the fact that you are all men of honor. After you receive the cash, you will begin to receive invoices in the mail from phony companies that I will set up. The invoices will show products that you use in your business every day. All you have to do is treat the invoices like regular payables. Post them to your ledgers, write a check in that amount, and mail it to the address shown on the invoice. What you do with the cash is your business. Just think about it, for years, you had to fuck the government and rip off cash to pay Don Francisco. With my plan, you will keep 100 percent ownership in your businesses and still fuck the IRS, but this way, you get to keep the cash for yourselves. You see, Don Francisco is reaching out from his grave to still be your partner in a different way. Only this time, he will be giving money back to you for all your years of loyalty and respect. And you, in return, still give him honor by making sure his family will be properly taken care of just like he took care of all of your families when he was alive. Now has anybody got any questions about this?"

"Yeah," said Mario Terranova, the music store owner. "What if we don't play ball with you?"

Irritated by Terranova's tone, Eddie decided to become more forceful.

"The answer to that question is very simple. Should you decide to refuse to honor Don Francisco's memory and help me carry out his last wish, then I must consider you adversaries, in which case I will have no choice but to inform Sally of his father's arrangement with each of you, and you can have him sucking your blood for the rest of your lives. We all know how Sally operates. He'll probably up the ante, and if you don't pay, he won't think twice about sending you to Carlucci's press. So what do you say, gentlemen? Let's not stick it up each other's ass. If we play ball together, we all win."

Some of the men grumbled, feeling defensive over his threatening remarks. They huddled together and began to talk among themselves. Eddie waited patiently, watching some positive nods of their heads and overhearing a few promising words here and there.

The mobsters remained huddled together in discussion for quite a while, and Eddie was becoming impatient and concerned that his plan might not come together after all. Finally, Freddie Flowers stepped forward to speak.

"Eddie, we thinka what you havea proposed isa fair fora all of us. Oura only risk willa be ina fucking the governament, buta we've had to live witha that for years. As men ofa honor, we will do the righta thing anda respecta the memory of oura friend, Don Francisco. We willa play ball witha you. But we havea onea more question. How longa willa thisa laundering last?"

Eddie let out a veiled sigh of relief.

"I don't know, Freddie. It will continue until all of the money is laundered, and I can't even begin to figure that out until we each get together and decide how much we can clean up each year without bringing attention to what we are doing."

"Itsa no matter howa long ita takes. We'da be fools not to takea the deal, anda besides, ata oura ages, we no wanta to deal witha Sally. He's a loose fuckin'a cannon!"

The atmosphere in the room changed immediately. All of the men stood and voiced their agreement.

"Gentlemen, gentlemen! Please, I need your attention for one more minute," he said, silencing the group. "One word of caution. I cannot stress to you enough the need for secrecy regarding our arrangement. If Sally ever finds out about our deal, it will mean big trouble for all of us."

"Hey, itsa no problem, D'Amico. Sally fucksa with us, we just arrange for him to visit hisa father," answered Lucky.

"Good. I'm glad we are all in agreement. Now that our business is concluded, what do you say we go to the bar and celebrate the liberation of your businesses and the big money you'll all be putting in your pockets? Tonight the drinks are on Don Francisco!"

Everyone was pleased with the outcome of the meeting. They headed to the bar together, laughing, joking, and shaking hands with Eddie along the way. But even though Eddie was relieved and happy that the old mobsters had accepted his plan, he felt a sense of foreboding. He couldn't help but wonder whether he would soon be having a drink with the person responsible for making the attempt on his life.

Chapter 22

Eddie apprehensively slid in behind the wheel of his station wagon and turned the key in the ignition. Just as the engine roared to life, the windshield exploded, pelting him with shattered glass. Stunned, he reacted by covering his face with his hands. He felt the warmth and wetness of his own blood as it ran between his fingers and into his eyes. Trembling with fear, he tried to scream, but no sound would come from his mouth.

Everything seemed to be happening in slow motion. Suddenly, rage filled his mind. He pulled out the Beretta from his ankle holster and began firing wildly through the windowless opening at the faceless figure looking down at him from the nearby rooftop. He pumped the trigger continuously until the hammer came down on an empty chamber. *Click. Click. Click.* The repetitious clicking sound sent a wave of fear through every inch of his body.

The shooter then boldly rose to his full height, standing behind a parapet on top of the building. Raising his powerful weapon to his shoulder and taking careful aim through the crosshairs. Eddie was paralyzed in his upright position, staring with a frozen fix upon his attacker. As if he had superhuman eyesight, Eddie could see the faceless shooter's finger tighten slowly around the trigger, and he motionlessly watched as the trigger was squeezed. He could hear the sound echo through the air as the weapon discharged. Again he tried to scream, but to no avail.

Suddenly, Eddie's body bolted upward, awakened and startled by the sound of someone pounding on his door. Jumping up from the chair he had fallen asleep in, he felt moisture of perspiration on his clothes, and beads of sweat across his brow began to trickle down his face. When he reached the door, he cautiously peered through the peephole into the smiling face of Bee Stinger. With a sigh of relief, he slid open the dead bolt and opened the door.

"Come in, Bee."

"Geez, what the hell's wrong? You look like you just saw a ghost!"

"Shit, man, I'm a nervous wreck! I keep having a nightmare about the shooter every time I fall asleep. I just dozed off watching TV, and it happened again. Damn it, Bee, you've gotta catch that bastard, or he won't have to get me with a bullet. I'll die of a heart attack first!"

"Yeah, well that's why I'm here. But you know, we've got nothin' to go on. He didn't leave a trace of evidence on that roof. I was hoping you might be willing to give me a little more help with this investigation. You aren't shittin' me. You must have some ideas about who's behind this contract that's out on you."

"I've already told you a hundred fucking times, Bee, the only one I can think of is Sally Barratino!" Eddie lied, thinking of the old mobsters.

"So, then, what's going on with Sally and you all of a sudden? Let's talk about this."

"Let's talk while I shave and clean up. I'm taking Megan and Carmella out for dinner tonight."

Bee followed Eddie into the master bedroom and sat on the edge of the bed. Eddie spoke to him through the reflection in the bathroom mirror as he started to shave.

"Sally and I don't even talk to each other since Don Francisco died. How would I know anything? All I know about Sally is what I read in the newspaper or hear on the news, like two or three of his men were gunned down over the past couple of months," said Eddie as he grabbed a towel and wiped the soap from his face.

"You don't even pay attention. It's worse than that. He's lost six men," corrected the detective. "And now between Cavelli and One-Eyed Jack, he's been getting his dick knocked off but good!"

"What a shame. As far as I'm concerned, it couldn't happen to a nicer guy," sneered Eddie as he put on a clean shirt.

"Yeah, rumor on the street says he's running out of muscle."

"That's the only part that bothers me, Bee. To be perfectly honest with you, I'd really hate to see some of Don Francisco's old-timers go down, like LaRocca and the Turk."

"See! There you go again! Those guys are button men, nothing more than paid killers! How the hell can you say you care about people like them?"

"You just don't understand the way it works. I was raised around all those guys. In their minds, they're soldiers in a war. They're men of honor. The only people they harm or kill are other family members just like themselves who made the same kinds of choices. When they kill, it's nothing personal. Just business."

"Nothing personal, pal. This is just fucking business. Bang, bang, you're dead, asshole!" mimicked the detective.

"I guess from your perspective, it's a fucked-up way for me to look at things, but that's how I was brought up."

"Just listen to yourself! What a sick justification for murder! I swear, you fuckin' dagos all lose something in the translation!"

Eddie picked up his blue cashmere wraparound topcoat.

"Come on, Bee, walk me out. I gotta go, or I'll be late picking up the girls."

As they exited the building, both men consciously scanned the rooftops as they walked through the parking lot. Eddie stopped alongside a gray vintage Cadillac sedan in mint condition.

"You driving this?" asked the detective with a puzzled look on his face.

"Yeah, it's my old man's pride and joy. I borrowed it from him and stashed my wagon. I figured by switching vehicles, it might keep the trigger-happy bastard from finding me as easy."

"Good thinking. But don't let switching cars give you a false sense of security. If the shooter starts tracking you, it probably won't be long before he realizes you've changed cars. Just be careful. If I were you, I wouldn't even trust my own mother."

"Well, that's one thing I don't have to worry about. She died when I was just a little kid, remember?"

"Yeah, I know," said Bee, looking a little embarrassed. "It was just a figure of speech. You know what the fuck I mean."

Eddie shot an apologetic wink at Bee. "Sure, Bee. Just do me a favor, will ya? Catch the dirty bastard. I'm not ready to die yet."

"Hey, pal, I'm doing all I can without calling on the help of the force."

"I know. Thanks, Bee. Thanks for caring. You've been a good friend."

Bee nodded knowingly and waved as Eddie slid into the Cadillac, started the smooth-sounding engine, and drove away.

As Eddie neared the farm, a bright full moon illuminated the compound, casting a ghostly white glow over the long black silhouettes of the enormous trees. Eddie pulled into the driveway and guided his father's old Cadillac over to the silver pedestal. Lowering the driver's window, he entered his secret code and watched as the big white iron gates guarding the Barrratino estate slowly swung open.

As he approached the house, the only light visible to bid any welcome was a dimly lit porch lamp. The windows of the old Victorian mansion that once radiated a cheerful amber glow were now all dark and foreboding. Strongly sensing the absence of Don Francisco, Eddie was suddenly overcome with an eerie cold chill. He wondered how Nicoletta made it through each dark and lonely night, her huge home now filled with only memories and a pitiful emptiness.

He firmly tucked the box of long-stemmed red roses under his arm and grabbed the fancily wrapped gift of chocolates he'd bought and headed for the door. When he rang the bell, the familiar door chimes sounded the tune of "O Sole Mio." It was Don Francisco's favorite tune, and it reminded him of happier days at the Barratino home. The memory lifted his spirits a bit.

Carmella answered the door, looking prim and conservatively attractive in her street clothes. She gave him a warm smile and welcomed him into the brightly lit foyer.

"Eddie! It's so nice to see you. Come in!"

"Hi, Carm. You know, I gotta confess something to you," he said and then leaned over and teasingly whispered in her ear, "You're a gorgeous broad, and pretty sexy when you're not wearing your nun's habit."

Carmella giggled and gave him a sisterly peck on the cheek.

"Oh, Eddie, you really shouldn't have," she started as she reached for the candy and flowers.

"Well, geez, Carm, I, uh, didn't really. I mean, I brought these for your mother."

Momentarily embarrassed, she pulled back her hands, and a crimson blush crossed her cheeks.

Suddenly, the thought crossed his mind that nuns probably never have the pleasure of receiving gifts of roses and candy. He wished he had been more thoughtful of her.

"Sorry, Carm. Guess I screwed up," he apologized.

"You did exactly the right thing, Eddie. Mama will absolutely love these. I can't tell you how much she needs this and how happy she'll be!"

She affectionately took his arm and pulled him toward the kitchen where Megan and Nicoletta were sitting at the table.

"Mama! Look who's here. Your favorite godson!"

"Hi, Ma. Don't get up. Here, these are for you," Eddie said, placing the gifts in front of her.

"Ah, Grazia, grazia, Edwardo!"

With some difficulty, Nicoletta rose from the table and reached for him. After a long hug, she stepped back, placed both hands on her hips and looked him over with questioning eyes.

"What'sa matter witha you? You go skinny."

"No, Ma, I'm just working hard, that's all."

"Wella, you bride isa gonna fatten you up now. I teacha her how toa makea the sauce and the raviolis!"

"That's right, honey, I've learned a lot from her today," said Megan as Eddie greeted her with a loving kiss.

"Good! It's about time you started keeping me in the style of food to which I am accustomed," he joked. "Are you girls ready to go?" he asked, checking his watch. "We have reservations, you know."

"Edwardo, wait. You comea back anda visit witha me, huh?"

"I will, Ma. Soon. I promise," he vowed giving her another hug and a kiss on the head.

"And, Edwardo, you don'ta work so hard! Too mucha beeziness isa no good! Alla for what? You takea the time anda enjoy your beautifula new wife. No bea likea your godfather. OK?" she cautioned, her eyes turning red and glassy.

"Mama! Don't eat all the chocolates. Save one for me please!" Carmella begged, trying to change the subject.

Eddie led Megan and Carmella out of the kitchen. With a heavy heart full of sadness for Nicoletta, he helped the two women into the car. As they drove to the restaurant, Carmella sensed his concern for her mother and assured him that Nicoletta would be fine.

Eddie had chosen a popular French restaurant well known for its gourmet food and high prices. Megan and Carmella were delighted when they learned where he was taking them.

As they entered into the elegant ambiance of the building, soft, romantic music surrounded them. They were escorted to a grand booth on a raised level that offered privacy and comfort in its candlelit setting.

A waiter appeared, acknowledging Eddie as a familiar customer.

"Good evening, Mr. D'Amico. May I serve cocktails?"

The three placed their orders, and the waiter took his leave.

"He didn't bring us menus, Eddie. We have no menus," remarked Carmella.

"Not tonight, Carm. I took the liberty of ordering a special seven-course dinner for my two special women on a very special night. I promise you won't be disappointed," said Eddie.

Sipping their cocktails, they engaged in reminiscent conversation of their high school days together. One old story led to another as they enjoyed each course of the exquisite dinner Eddie had arranged for. Now sipping their after-dinner espressos laced with sambuca, Carmella's curiosity could wait no longer.

"OK, you two, we've finished a spectacular dinner. Don't you think it's time you share with me the reason for it? Come on now, I can't stand it!" she pleaded excitedly.

Eddie reached out, and the three of them joined hands.

"You're right, Mother Superior, but this dinner was really Megan's idea. She has something to ask you."

"Well, then, Mrs. D'Amico, what are you here to ask me?"

Megan's eyes became moist and twinkled in the soft glow of the candles. She looked as if she wanted to speak, but the words were too difficult to say.

"What's the matter, honey? Is something wrong, Megan?" Carmella asked softly.

"No, Carmella. Nothing's wrong. Finally, everything in my life is right! I'm happier than I've ever been! I just wanted to share with you that God has answered a prayer for me that I've been praying for all my life."

Megan paused for a moment and smiled lovingly at Eddie.

"You see the two of us?"

Carmella nodded. "Megan, I've never been happier for both of you! Is that it? Are you two going to be on a forever honeymoon and that's what we're celebrating?"

"Well, yes, that too, but soon there will be three of us! I'm going to have a baby!" Megan shrilled.

"Oh, dear gracious Father in Heaven!" exclaimed Carmella. "What wonderful news!"

"The only thing that can make it more wonderful is if you'll agree to our wish for you to be the baby's godmother. Will you, Carmella?" asked Megan with tears of happiness streaming down her cheeks.

"I'd be honored. God bless you both!"

Eddie lifted his espresso cup to proclaim a toast.

"Here's to baby Carm and the best godmother a child could ask for!"

They clicked their cups and drank.

"Baby Carm?" Carmella asked.

'You see," said Eddie, "if the baby's a girl, we're naming her Carmella, and if it's a boy, we're naming him Carmen, after Carmen Carlivatti, whom we're asking to be the godfather, so we'll have a baby Carm either way!"

"Then here's to our new blessing!" toasted Carmella.

"Now wait, Carmella, there's more. I think my husband has something else to tell you," Megan said with a look of suspense on her face.

"That's right, Carm," said Eddie. "You know that you and Megan are my two favorite girls in all the world, and tonight we're celebrating Megan's dream come true."

Carmella looked at him questioningly.

"Well, I'd like to make a wish tonight that your dream will also come true. You see, I've never forgotten about the dream you've had since before you were even a nun. You always wanted to open a special home for orphans and abused kids. I know how hard you've tried all these years to obtain the funding through the church, but so far, that hasn't happened."

"But, Eddie, it's not going to happen anytime in the near future. You're right, it's been my dream, my top priority, but apparently, it hasn't been God's will."

"Well, Carm, I never asked you, but I always wondered why you never asked your father to help you make that dream come true."

"Oh, Eddie, you don't know how many times I prayed about doing just that, but I always disagreed with my father's way of life, and I felt it would be too hypocritical of me to use his blood money."

Carmella buried her face in her hands. Eddie reached for her wrists and gently pulled her hands from her face.

"Listen to me, Carmella. You know in your heart that your father used his influence and a great deal of his money to help a lot of people. People in need, Carmella. He never forgot them. He took care of them until the day he died. Still, he reaches out from his grave to help others. Now let him help you take care of those children that need you so desperately."

She looked at him with disbelieving eyes.

"Eddie, I, I can't believe . . . I mean, you don't know how much money—"

"Carm, you've always told me to do the right thing. I've always done my best to follow your advice. Now it's time for you to do the right thing. Trust me. I do know how much money it takes, and thanks to your father, it's all arranged. All you need now is the blessing of the church!" he said excitedly.

Carmella closed her eyes tightly, and a single tear appeared at the corner of one eye. She made the sign of the cross over the front of her head and body as Megan and Eddie watched her anxiously. Then she opened her eyes and exclaimed with delight, "This is the most heavenly night of my entire life!"

Eddie raised his espresso cup to propose another toast, but Carmella placed an interrupting hand on his wrist.

"Eddie, tell me that Sally has nothing to do with this," Carmella said with serious concern in her voice and a frown on her face.

Her plea had taken Eddie by surprise.

"Carm, no. Why in the world would you think that?"

"He's just so treacherous. I know all about the wars he's started and the people he's had killed. I couldn't bear the thought of him being any part of this."

"Carm, I swear. Sally doesn't know anything about this, and he has nothing at all to do with it. Sally and I don't even talk to each other. If he had his way, he'd probably like to see me dead."

He regretted the words as soon as they left his mouth.

"That's just it. I'm convinced he's possessed by the devil, and I'm ashamed of the fact that he's my brother. All of my life, I've thought of you as more of a brother to me, and God forgive me, but I actually pray that the police will catch him for something that will send him to prison for the rest of his life! He's dangerous and evil. He wouldn't think twice about killing anyone who gets in the way of what he wants!"

"Hey, come on, lighten up, Carm. Forget about Sally. Let's just focus on the good news. You need to start making plans to open the Barratino Children's Home!"

She thought for a moment, and a sweet smile replaced the frown on her face.

"I'm sorry. You're absolutely right! This is a night I'll cherish forever! How can I ever thank you, Eddie?"

"Don't thank me, Sister. All the thanks goes to God and Don Francisco."

"Then I'd like to offer the final toast to both of my fathers, since the two of them have made the dreams of best friends come true!"

There was a biting nip to the cold night air as they stepped out of the warmth of the restaurant. The three of them huddled together as they waited for the valet to retrieve the vintage Cadillac. When it arrived, Megan jumped into the front seat as Eddie held open the rear door for Carmella. He tipped the valet and quickly slid in behind the wheel. Megan snuggled in tightly next to him and kissed his cheek as he pulled the shiny old car out from the porte cochere.

Just as Eddie pulled out onto the street, the rear windshield of the car exploded, hailing shattered glass all over Carmella and the rear seat. With a quick glance over his shoulder, Eddie yelled, "Duck! Get down on the floor, Carm!" Then the window of the driver's door exploded with a popping sound, spewing bits of glass across him and Megan.

Eddie slammed his foot down on the accelerator and steered wildly with his left hand as he pushed his screaming wife downward in the front seat with his right hand. The powerful engine roared when Eddie realized that the sniper must be behind them to the left. The tires squealed as he snapped the wheel to the right, and the car careened crazily across the road. Headed for a yard, the Cadillac raced across the lawn and through a large hedge, bouncing forcefully as it jumped a curb and hit the street on two wheels. Eddie kept his foot jammed down on the accelerator pedal, and the sturdy old car sped down the dark side street. Nearing the next cross street, he spun the wheel to the left, sending the car on two wheels as it slid around the turn at breakneck speed.

A few blocks farther, he felt they were out of danger and eased his foot off of the accelerator. He looked for the next alleyway, pulled in, and stopped the car. Megan was in a fetal position on the front floorboard of the car, whimpering and shaking. No sound came from the backseat.

Eddie reached for Megan and attempted to pull her up onto the seat, but she flinched at his touch and pulled away from him, crouching as far as she could under the dashboard. He pulled himself onto his knees to look behind the front seat.

"Carm. Carm," he called out gently in a trembling voice.

He could see her body pressed flat to the floorboard behind his seat. A sick feeling of terror washed over him, and he yelled out her name.

"Carmella!"

Slowly, she lifted her head and turned her eyes to look up at him.

"Oh, dear Mary, Mother of Jesus, what happened?"

"Carm, are you OK?"

"I think so. Where's Megan?"

"She's here, Carm. I need to help her. Please get up, and be careful of the glass," he cautioned as he brushed away some glass and helped her back onto the seat.

Turning his full attention to Megan, who was still whimpering huddled in a small quivering balled-up position under the dash, he began lightly fingering her hair to shake out pieces of glass. He took her shoulders into his hands and tried to lift her as carefully as possible.

"Megan. Megan, honey. Talk to me, baby. Come on. It's over now. Come up here, let me see if you're OK."

Her whimpers evolved into audible words.

"Oh my god, oh my god," she kept repeating tearfully.

Eddie pulled her up into his arms and held her close to him as he carefully felt her body. His eyes recklessly searched over her for visible wounds until he satisfied himself that she was not bleeding. He looked back at Carmella. She sat motionlessly with unseeing eyes, her hair blowing softly across her face from the cold night wind coming through the gaping windowless opening behind her. He knew he needed to get the women to a safe, warm place as he felt a shiver from the chilling air race through his own body.

He jumped out of the car and jerked open the rear door.

"Come on, Carm, get in the front seat with Megan. You'll be warmer," he urged.

Carmella took his hand, and looking at him through glassy eyes, she asked, "It was Sally, wasn't it?"

"I don't know, Carm. Just hurry! We need to get the hell out of here!"

The three of them huddled together in the front seat, feeling little of the warmth coming from the car heater Eddie had turned on full blast. The icy night wind rushed over them, cutting through their clothing like a knife and chilling their bodies to the bone as he drove down the street looking for a pay phone.

He pulled into a closed but well-lit service station, parking the Cadillac close to the building in such a way that the missing windows could not be easily noticed.

"Sit tight, girls, I'll call a cab, and we'll be home before you know it."

Eddie ran to the pay phone and called for a cab. Then he dialed a number that he had called many times before. The living quarters at the barn in the Barratino compound.

"Yeah," the gruff voice answered.

"Lorenzo, it's Eddie. I need your help, man."

"Ya got me, just say da word. Whadya need?"

"I'm on my way to the farm with Megan and Carmella. We're in a cab, so can you meet us at the front gate?"

"Yeah, I'll watch for ya."

As Eddie approached the car to wait with Carmella and Megan for the cab to arrive, the reality of the attack gripped him. He looked at his father's treasured vintage Cadillac in horror, and dread swept over him.

"Shit, my old man's gonna be pissed!" he muttered aloud.

The hedge he had barreled through had badly dented the front of the car, and the once-beautiful paint job no longer gave the sparkling reflection of its polished years of loving care.

Eddie forgot about his preoccupation with the car when he noticed Carmella and Megan in the front seat, shivering with their arms around each other, trying to stay warm. He ran to the passenger door just as the taxicab pulled into the parking lot.

"Come on, girls, come on! Let's get the hell out of here!"

The three of them welcomed the warm comfort of the cab as they drove along in silence toward the farm. Each of them reflecting alone on their personal memories of the attack. Sally's hateful face was embedded in Eddie's mind's eye.

The no-good bastard had no consideration for these women. What a fucking animal! If anything happens to Megan or the baby because of this, I swear I'll kill the scumbag myself! he thought.

With her head snuggled into his shoulder, Megan was praying to herself.

God, please God, protect Eddie. I love him so much. Please God, tell me he hasn't lied to me and he really isn't one of them! I'm having his baby. You've blessed me so! Please don't let me become a pregnant widow! Please, God, hear my prayer!

Carmella caressed the small crucifix she wore around her neck as she thought silently to herself, *Let this be the last straw for my brother! We'll call the police as soon as we get home! I know Sally was behind this evilness and hatred. Maybe this time there will be enough evidence to lock him away forever!*

As the cabbie pulled into the driveway and approached the huge gates, they began to swing open. The headlights of the taxi fixed upon LaRocca's huge figure standing straight ahead in the middle of the driveway.

"You folks gettin' out here?" the cabdriver asked in a cracking voice, his eyes glued on LaRocca's frightening face.

"We sure are," Eddie said with a sigh as he shoved cash over the shoulder of the driver.

"Hey, buddy, thanks!" responded the driver as he quickly counted and discovered his generous tip.

LaRocca escorted the women to the limo waiting to drive them to the house.

As they drove the rest of the way, Eddie shared his thoughts with Megan and Carmella.

"Carm, I want Megan to stay here with you tonight."

"But, Eddie, where are you going?"

"Don't worry, baby. I'm not leaving without you. I'll stay in the barn with the guys tonight."

"Eddie, you're coming in to call the police, aren't you?" asked Carmella.

"No way, Carm! No cops. Not yet. I promise I'll get to the bottom of this, but I've gotta check a few things out first. We're gonna keep this quiet for now, OK?"

"I can't believe you're saying that! This is the perfect opportunity to—"

Carmella stopped midsentence, realizing that she might be saying too much in front of Megan and LaRocca.

"To what? Perfect opportunity to do what?" questioned Megan somewhat angrily.

"Oh, I don't know, Meg. I'm just upset over what happened, but I trust your husband knows what's best. Come on, honey, let's go inside and let Eddie handle this how he wants. I know he'll do the right thing," she finished, giving Eddie a warning look over her shoulder.

Once the two women were safely locked inside the house, Eddie jumped into the front seat of the limo next to Lorenzo.

"So what's da problem, Eddie? What da fuck happened?"

"Wait till we get to the barn, Lorenzo. I need a stiff drink first."

They settled into their safe haven. Eddie poured himself a vodka rocks and headed for the sofa. Before he sat down, his mind vividly recalled the night he watched as Sally blew the brains out of the Lacavoli brothers in this same spot.

Just a different couch, and now Sally wants to blow my brains out, Eddie thought. "Where's Sally?" Eddie blurted out nervously.

"Whad are ya, kiddin'? He's holed up out at da junkyard. Been der steady since da heat got turned on. I been guardin' him, but tonight he gave me da night off."

Eddie changed his mind about sitting on the sofa and moved to a chair. He began relating the events of the sniper attacks against him to LaRocca, leaving out any mention of his conversations with Detective Stinger. The Enforcer listened attentively until he finished.

"Dis doesn' sound right. Who'd be lookin' ta knock you off?"

"I think I know, but I'm not really sure. I thought you might have heard something through the grapevine."

"Naw, I ain't heard nothin'. You oughtta know better den me who ya mighta pissed off enough to wanna see ya dead."

Since making his deal with the old Mafioso, Eddie had ruled them out.

"The only person I know who hates me enough to want me dead is Sally," said Eddie, watching for some reaction from LaRocca's serpent-like eyes.

LaRocca remained expressionless and waited for Eddie to continue.

"I'm hoping with your connections, Lorenzo, you can nose around and see what you can find out. I'm at the end of my rope with this shit. I wonder if I oughtta call one of my cop friends," Eddie said, still looking for a reaction from the Enforcer.

The word *cop* had finally stirred some emotion in LaRocca, who angrily jumped to his feet.

"No fuckin' way! Dat ain't gonna happen. If you do dat, den you and LaRocca can't do no business! I won't be no ratfink snitch for you or nobody else!"

"Hey, take it easy, Lorenzo! I didn't mean to insult you. We're just not talking my language here. What do you suggest I do?"

"Look, man, you didn' pay good attention to our little talk at da hospital. I told ya anybody dat fucks wid you, fucks wid LaRocca, remember? Did ya tink I was jus' talkin' outa my asshole?"

LaRocca continued his furious ranting.

"Mingya, Lorenzo! OK, OK! Calm down, will ya? I gotta figure out what to do about this, and I'm runnin' out of time!"

"Hey! It's like dis, D'Amico. You came here to me looking for help. So now your problem is my problem! LaRocca's word and repatation is at stake here, so if ya want my help, we do tings my way. Da way I see it, ya got two choices. Ya keep fuckin' around and do nothin' till da mudderfucker whacks ya out, or we do it my way, and LaRocca gets da prick first, capeesh?"

"And what if it's Sally?" asked Eddie, shocked by LaRocca's matter-of-fact offer to kill someone for him.

"See, ya didn' pay attention again! I told ya at da hospital dat I stay wid Sally as long as he did da right tings. If he's da one behind da contract on you, den as far as I'm concerned, he's dishonorin' and disrespectin' his fadder's wishes. If he's tryin' ta kill ya, he ain't doin' da right ting in my book cause we all know dat Don Francisco loved ya like a son. If Sally's doin' dis, den he ain't no different den anybody else da Enforcer handles. You gotta make da choice, D'Amico. Who dies? You or da other guy?"

Chapter 23

S ally found himself in danger of losing everything. Since starting the wars in an effort to enlarge and strengthen the family, both in manpower and money, his plan had cost him a number of men, creating a growing discontent among the members. As predicted by the old-timers, it became increasingly apparent that Sally did not have enough experience to run the family. The support he previously usurped from the older Mafioso by avenging his father's murder had waned. He had abandoned all of their advice and forged ahead trying to take over the territories of the black Mafia and the Cavelli family. They, in turn, were looking to rid themselves and the world of Sally Barratino.

Now fearing for his own life, Sally had gone into hiding to reconsider his war strategy and regroup the remainder of his force. He still maintained the full power of his position as don over the younger family members, and he intended to take full advantage of that. Sally's priority in life was to win whatever he wanted, no matter the cost.

Knowing his own life was in jeopardy and worried about the safety of his wife and children, Sally made sure the word was on the street that he had moved out of his house. His new residence was located in a rolling field in a remote area on the outskirts of town. Sally had turned the junkyard, owned by Lucky Carlucci, into a virtual fortress.

The property was enclosed by an electrically charged chain-link fence topped with layers of circular strung barbed wire. Old trucks had been strategically parked around the fence's perimeter. The vehicles were equipped with hidden security cameras and armed with high-powered machine guns. The only access to the property was through heavy black iron gates at the end of the long graveled driveway entrance. Only those who knew the secret code could be buzzed into the junkyard stronghold. Sally stayed holed up there day and night except for an occasional secret rendezvous, from time to time, with his wife and children.

Deciding to concentrate on the Cavelli family, Sally had ordered Jimmy "the Brute" to Chicago to spy on Vito Cavelli. The Brute knew his job well and returned with a detailed account of Vito's daily activities, showing him to be a creature of strict habit.

Cavelli reportedly arrived at his restaurant in the Italian village every morning at precisely six thirty to count the previous night's receipts. Vito was always accompanied by the same two bodyguards who made breakfast for him while he made the count. Then the three men would leave the restaurant each day between 7:30 and 7:45 a.m.

Vito's consistent daily schedule was exactly what Sally needed to know in order to implement his plan. The news he had received two days earlier through the Mafia grapevine created perfect timing for Sally. Word came to him that longtime family member Billy "the Bomber" Ziccari, had just been released from a long stint in prison. The Brutes new mission was to pick up Billy and bring him directly to Sally.

Sally was pacing the floor inside the junkyard's old concrete building he had newly remodeled. He had appropriately appointed the large gathering room for its intended usage. The interior walls were walnut paneled. Two card tables and a pool table stood on the dull black slate floor. A large formal conference table with twelve high-backed burgundy leather chairs dominated the far corner of the room.

Watching a boxing match in another corner of the room, LaRocca, Vinnie Barratino, and Cappy were sprawled out on the three overstuffed sofas arranged around the television set. Dominic and the other boys were playing poker across the room.

"Where the fuck is the Brute?" asked Sally, speaking to no one in particular as he continued his impatient pacing.

All of them otherwise preoccupied either shrugged their shoulders disinterestedly or grunted an unknowing response.

A few minutes later, the door opened; and Jimmy "the Brute" entered, followed by Billy "the Bomber." Everyone in the room turned their attention to focus on the Bomber.

His head was as smooth and hairless as a billiard ball, and he had swollen, puffy cheeks under brown eyes that were rimmed with red. His large, noticeably flabby gut extended well beyond the waistband of his pants. The overweight Billy "the Bomber" stood on display as Sally strode across the room to him.

"Tell me, Jimmy, are you sure you got the right fuckin' guy here? He doesn't look like a bomber to me. Looks more like a fat-ass fucking dud!" Sally chided as he patted the soft overhang of Billy's stomach.

Everyone in the room remained silent and stared at the Bomber.

"So, Billy, what have you got to say for yourself?" asked Sally.

The Bomber shrugged his shoulders.

"I asked you a question! Can you talk, or did they cut your tongue out in prison?" Sally demanded.

"Sure, I can talk," Billy replied.

"So talk to me, then."

"What do you want me to say, Sally?"

"Look, stupid, this ain't a fuckin' quiz show! Did Jimmy tell you about the job we've got to do?"

"Yeah, he told me."

"How many jobs like this have you done before?"

"Plenty. More than I can count. But you know I've been in the joint for fourteen years."

"What the hell does that mean? Just give me a straight fucking answer! Can you do the job or not?" asked Sally, becoming increasingly irritated.

"Yeah, yeah, sure. Maybe it won't be a piece of cake, but I'll figure it out. I can do the caper," said Billy.

"That's good, Billy. Very good. This job is important. You see, if you cut off the head of a snake, the rest of the body dies, and that's what I need—to get the Cavelli family out of my hair once and for all."

Dominic stood up from the card table and interrupted.

"Sally, I think you're making a big mistake. If we fuck this up and miss Cavelli, he'll join forces with other Chicago families and move an army of men in here against us and wipe us out. With your father gone, our family doesn't have the power or respect to stop such an alliance," cautioned Dominic.

"My old man is dead!" Sally lashed back. "I make the decisions now, and my decision is final! Besides, Billy here says he can do the job. He's done plenty of others for the family, and it's just like riding a bike. You never forget how to do it."

"But, Sally, fourteen years in the slammer is a long time. A guy gets rusty if he doesn't—"

"Hey! We're not havin' a fuckin' debate over this! I've made my decision, and it's done! Anyway, I'm sending the Turk and the Brute with him. They'll stand guard and make sure he's not disturbed so there won't be any mistakes!"

Sally pulled an evelope out of his pocket and handed it to the Bomber.

"Here's a few grand. When the job is done, you get the rest. Buy what you need, and get double everything because I've got another job for you after this. Can you make it happen with Cavelli this Saturday morning?"

"No problem, Sally. This'll be a piece of cake," Billy the Bomber replied, not looking at Sally. He was peering into the envelope and thumbing through the hundred-dollar bills that were jammed into it and smiling from ear to ear.

In the dark wee hours Saturday morning, Jimmy "the Brute," the Turk, and Billy "the Bomber" walked in the shadows of the dimly lit alley behind Cavelli's restaurant. As they neared the rear door they planned to enter, two large alley cats sprang out of a nearby dumpster, crying out in protest at the intrusion of their feast. The Bomber, so startled by the incident, began to perspire and stood trembling as the Brute worked on the lock to gain entrance to the building.

The Turk suspiciously watched the Bomber wipe the perspiration from his face.

"Jimmy, go in there with him and stay with him. Make sure everything gets done right," whispered the Turk.

Jimmy nodded, and the two men entered the restaurant. The beams from their flashlights flickered as they made their way through the kitchen. They walked down a hall to the hostess station and paused to look around the room. Behind the counter on which the cash register sat was a door marked "Office."

"There it is!" whispered the Bomber.

Jimmy "the Brute" picked the lock, careful not to leave any telltale mark of forced entry. Once inside the office, the two men moved quickly. They pulled the sofa away from the wall and the Bomber tore away an edge of the material lining on the back. He began stuffing several bundles of dynamite into the opening. The Brute watched with amazement.

"Holy shit, Billy! How much powder you puttin' in there? Mengya, it looks like enough to blow up a fuckin' battleship!" whispered the Brute.

"Yeah, yeah, I know. But I wanna make sure I get the fucker."

The dynamite sticks set, the Bomber connected the small digital timing device and began to set the timer.

"Hey, Jimmy, what time you got?" asked the Bomber.

"Two fifty-five," the Brute answered.

The Brute held his flashlight beam steady on the timer. The Bomber's face was close to the device and the Brute could see that sweat was streaming down Billy's puffy cheeks. His eyes blinked nervously, and his lips were twitching as he programmed the mechanism.

"Come on, man, what's taking so long?" Jimmy whispered.

"Hey, cool it, Jimmy. I got it now. It's all set to explode at seven in case he arrives a little late."

"OK, if it's done, let's get the fuck out of here!"

They pushed the sofa back against the wall and securely locked the office door as they left. They quietly made their way out of the restaurant and joined the Turk, who was still standing guard in the alley. The Brute relocked the heavy rear door with his special device, and the three men stealthily crept away from their deed well done to where they had hidden their car.

"Whaddya say, let's go to the airport and get some breakfast. I'll buy, and we can hang around there and watch the morning news before we head back," suggested the Bomber.

The three mobsters seated themselves in a comfortable booth near an overhead television in the airport restaurant. They covertly discussed the job they had completed while they consumed their enormous orders of food. The Turk and the Brute teased the Bomber unmercifully over the fright and nervousness he had displayed. For hours they joked and laughed and continued to drink coffee while they eagerly awaited the eight o'clock news.

The news program came and went with no report of any explosion.

"Hey, no boom-boom, man," said the Bomber.

"What the fuck happened!" Jimmy asked, looking at the Bomber.

"Nothin' happened. Relax. They probably couldn't get the story to the station on time," laughed the Bomber.

"Yeah, maybe you're right," said the Brute.

"You's guys better be right, 'cause I'm tellin' ya, if somethin' ain't on dat fuckin' TV by nine o'clock, you're in deep shit, Billy!" barked the Turk.

The next hour seemed like an eternity to the three conspirators. The nine o'clock news came and passed with no mention of a bombing.

"That's it! We're outa here! Come on!" ordered the Turk.

The three men got in the car and headed back toward Cavelli's restaurant. They drove down the narrow alley and found everything just as they had left it. No explosion had taken place.

"When Sally hears about this, you got a real fuckin' problem, Billy," said the Turk.

"What do you mean I got a problem? What about you, guys?" asked the Bomber, his eyes darting nervously between the Turk and the Brute.

"Billy, what the fuck do you think went wrong?" asked the Brute, scowling and waiting for his reply.

"It's nothin', I tell ya. Nothin'. Just a loose fuckin' wire, that's all. Yeah, that's all it can be," said the Bomber in a shaky voice.

"Let's get to a fuckin' phone. We gotta call Sally," said the Turk.

Jimmy the Brute lost the coin toss and had to make the phone call to Sally. After being given the news of the failed plan, Sally's fury was unleashed, and the Brute was glad to be so many miles away. Finally, Sally stopped yelling and lowered his voice to a stern growl.

"Listen, Jimmy, and listen to me real good. You guys go back in there tonight and fix whatever that idiot fucked up, understand, and you tell that fat slob that if he screws up again, he's a dead man, capeesh?"

The line went dead.

The three men went back to the airport and settled into chairs in one of the waiting areas. They dozed off and on during most of the day, trying to catch up on some sleep so they could complete the job after midnight. Shortly after nightfall, they headed back into the airport restaurant to have dinner. Halfway through their meal, the evening news came on with an upfront story of a bombing at Cavelli's restaurant. Film crews were at the scene trying to report on the chaos in the background.

A short time later, the phone rang at the junkyard stronghold. LaRocca answered the call.

"For you, Sally. It's da Brute."

"Yeah, Jimmy, what's up?"

"I'm at a pay phone, and I gotta talk fast! We gotta catch a plane outa here in a hurry!" panted Jimmy excitedly.

"What the fuck's going on?" demanded Sally.

"OK, OK, I'm trying. Sally, you're not going to believe this. Are you sitting down?" asked the Brute.

"Get to the fucking point!" screamed Sally.

"The dumb cocksucker must've screwed up the a.m./p.m. time. The bomb went off tonight!"

"What the—"

"Please, Sally, let me finish! I gotta make the plane and get the fuck outa town. We'll be back in a couple o' hours, and I'll give ya da whole skinny, but geez, the place is a mess, just like an atomic bomb went off. It looks to me like a lotta people bought the farm," said Jimmy breathlessly.

Sally slammed down the receiver.

"Hey, change the fuckin' channel now! Get the Chicago news station!" Sally yelled. "We got a major fuckin' problem!"

Dominic turned the dial and found the Chicago channel. An attractive anchorwoman was announcing the bombing.

"Massive explosion at the popular Italian village restaurant. Preliminary reports indicate at least eight people are dead and an unknown number are seriously injured. Two of the dead have been identified as the parents of Vito Cavelli, reputed mob boss of one of Chicago's crime families. Tragedy has been plaguing the Cavelli family. A short time ago, Vincent Cavelli, another reputed crime figure, was killed by a sniper when entering this very same building. Police believe that shooting and this explosion to be mob related and may be connected to the murder of Francisco Barratino, a once-powerful crime figure in St. Louis. We will bring you updates on this story as they are available, and now this—"

Sally screamed out in fury. He picked up the telephone and flung it with herculean force at the television. The men in the room ducked to keep from being hit by flying glass as the TV exploded from the impact. Its shattered remains were hurled to the far corners of the room.

Sally's face was beet red and twisted in rage.

"That dirty, no-good degenerate motherfucker! Did you hear what that stupid idiot did?" he screamed at the top of his lungs.

"Sally, let's hope one of the unidentified bodies was Vito's," said Dominic wisely.

That thought had not previously occurred to Sally, and the idea of it seemed to calm him down momentarily. A slight smile crossed his face. In his loathsome and nefarious way, he obviously had not one iota of concern or remorse for any of the innocent victims of his bungled caper.

"Yeah, yeah sure. You're right, Dominic. There's still a very good chance we got the rat bastard by accident," Sally chuckled. "OK, let's get back to the business of what to do about those fuckin' spearchuckers."

He sat in his chair at the head of the long mahogany conference table. LaRocca, Dominic, Cappy, Tough Tony Battista, and Billy "B" Bellini pulled out the heavy wood and leather chairs and took their usual places at the table. Sally's younger cousin, Vinnie Barratino, began to pull out a chair to join the others.

"Hey, Vinnie, what the fuck are you doing?" asked Sally.

"What does it look like I'm doing? I sitting fucking down," Vinnie answered with a puzzled look on his face.

"Not here you ain't. You got no business listening to what we're gonna be discussing here. You're still just a punk kid."

"Kid! Whaddya mean kid? I'm twenty-five fuckin' years old!"

Sally smiled at his cousin.

"No shit, Vinnie. You're that old? Seems like only yesterday you were fifteen," Sally taunted.

"Well, can I stay, then?"

"Nah, I've got a very special job for you to do."

Vinnie beamed, anxiously waiting to hear what his special assignment would be.

"First, get rid of that television or what's left of it, and make sure you clean up all the glass."

Vinnie looked around the table into the faces of the other men. They were all smiling at Sally's needling of his cousin. Vinnie became embarrassed, then angry.

"That's it! That's fucking it! You call that a special fucking job? You treat me, your cousin, like a piece of shit? Just like . . . just like, a . . . a . . . a fuckin' stooge!"

"You are a piece of shit, Vinnie. But there is one more thing."

Sally laid five one-hundred-dollar bills on the table.

"Go to the discount store and buy another TV. And bring me the receipt! I wanna make sure you don't knock me off for the change," Sally said, smiling.

"That's it, Sally. Now you've really done it. Now you're questioning my loyalty?"

"Let me tell you somethin', Vinnie. When I want loyalty, I look in the fuckin' mirror, you got that?"

Sally got up and put his arm around his cousin.

"See what I mean, kid? You just don't get it yet. You can't even take a little fuckin' ribbing without going to pieces. You gotta grow some balls, kid. Here, this is for the lesson," Sally said as he stuffed a hundred-dollar bill in Vinnie's shirt pocket. "Just stick with me, kid, and I'll have you rolling in dough. Now go take care of what I told you to do."

Sally slapped Vinnie on the back.

Full of resentment and humiliation, Vinnie dropped his head and lowered his eyes to the floor. He couldn't bear to see the smirking smiles on the faces of the other men.

"Yeah, OK, Sally," Vinnie said obediently.

Privately, he despised Sally more and more each day. As he finished sweeping up the broken glass and headed out to accomplish the special assignment his cousin, the Don, had given him, he envisioned getting even with Sally and vowed secretly to himself that one day he would run the family.

An hour and a half later, Sally and the boys were still planning their strategy against One-Eyed Jack Shepard and his black Mafia members when the door burst open and Vinnie came running into the room.

"He's alive! The cocksucker's alive!" he shouted breathlessly. "I saw him! I saw 'im wit my own eyes!"

"Hey, slow down! Who's alive?" asked Dominic.

"Cavelli! I saw him on TV!"

Sally jumped to his feet and grabbed Vinnie by the shoulders, shaking him as he yelled in his face.

"Talk fast, asshole, and start from the fuckin' beginning! I want the details!"

"OK, OK! I was in da store buyin' the new TV like ya told me, and ya know how they have all the T Vs turned on? Well, I was waitin' for my change—I mean, your change, and all of a sudden, dis special report comes on about the bombin', and there was Cavelli right on da TV! Da reporter tried to get 'im ta talk, and Cavelli slaps da mike right outa his hand and whacks da guy right in da face! Dat's da story—he's as alive as we are!"

Sally was seething with rage.

"Well, Dominic, so much for your theory!" snapped Sally.

"Yeah, that stupid-ass bomber has just added to our problems in spades," said Tough Tony Battista.

"Don't worry, 'cause I'm gonna make that cocksucker pay in spades," said Sally through clenched teeth.

"What're ya gonna do now, Sally?" asked Vinnie with excited anticipation.

"Well, Vinnie, it's like this. With Cavelli still breathing, we've got a lot of things to figure out here. We shouldn't be making important decisions like this on empty stomachs, so I want you to go down to Spinelli's and pick up some nice cold cuts. Make sure you get that good provolone and plenty of bread."

"Yeah, and don't forget the olives and dried tomatoes," added Tough Tony with a chuckle.

"We got enough wine and beer?" Vinnie asked meekly as he dutifully took the money from Sally.

"Just pick up some more anyway," Sally ordered.

The mobsters took their places at the conference table and began plotting their new methods of attack and defense. When Vinnie returned with the food an hour later, the room was filled with smoke, and the ashtrays on the conference table were overflowing with ashes and cigarette butts, most of which lay smoldering in their heap.

"Hey, it's about time! What took you so long?" Sally asked in an admonishing tone. "Vinnie, get this table cleaned up, will ya? How can we eat with this mess?"

They had no sooner started to eat than Jimmy "the Brute" came in, followed by Billy "the Bomber," and the Turk.

"Well, look here, boys, the three fucking stooges are back!" shouted Sally.

"Listen, Sally," the Brute began.

"No! You listen, Jimmy! I sent you and the Turk to take care of things for me, and you let this fuckin' idiot blow up half the city! You kill a bunch of people, but you miss the one guy you're supposed to hit!"

"No fuckin' way, Sally. Me and the Turk held up our end. We did just like you told us. We got him into the building and covered for him. We don't know nothin' from nothin' about settin' a bomb! You're the one that hired him, so you better ask him what the fuck went wrong."

"You know, Jimmy, I guess you're right. You guys did what I told you, so my beef is with him," said Sally calmly as he looked toward Billy.

Sally's tranquil tone and control of his anger came as a surprise to the others.

The Bomber's red-rimmed eyes began blinking nervously.

"Say, Billy, are you hungry? Would you like something to eat or drink maybe?"

The other mobsters around the table looked at each other questioningly, wondering whether Sally had lost his mind all of a sudden.

"Yeah, I'll take a beer. I'm as dry as a popcorn fart," Billy answered.

Sally nodded to Tony, and he handed the Bomber one of the cold beers. Billy reached out for it with a trembling hand and guzzled it down with one swallow, ending his libation with a loud, disgusting burp.

"So, Billy, tell me, do you have the other timing device and the dynamite you were supposed to buy for the next job?" Sally questioned.

"Yeah, I got 'em. Out there in the bag in my car."

"Jimmy, go out and get the stuff. Bring it in here so Billy can show me what he did in the restaurant."

The Bomber started to feel a little more at ease with Sally's passive demeanor.

"Hey, Sally, can I have another beer?" asked the Bomber.

"Sure, Billy, help yourself," Sally answered pleasantly.

The Bomber grabbed another beer and sat down at the table with the boys.

"Geez, Sally, I'm glad you're not so pissed at me. I know what went wrong, so it won't happen the next time."

"Ya know, Billy, somethin' tells me you're right. I know you won't mess up for the next job."

The Brute returned carrying a worn tan-colored canvas bag, which he set on the Bomber's lap.

"OK, Billy, show me how you put the bomb together. I wanna understand what happened."

"OK, Sal, where do you want me to set it up?"

"Right here on the table, pal."

"Hey, Sally! Have you lost your fuckin' mind! You gotta be kidding! I'm gettin' the fuck outa here!" said Dominic emphatically.

"Relax, Dominic, relax. It's safe, isn't it, Billy?"

"Yeah, sure. It's as safe as being in church," said the Bomber, laughing.

Billy the Bomber proceeded to set up his bomb to the distress of the other men in the room. Sweat was visible on the faces of the mobsters as they tensely watched him connect the sticks of dynamite to the timing device. Sally, on the other hand, appeared comfortable with one foot up on a chair and his arm resting on his knee. He was smiling at the Bomber as he watched calmly, seeming to enjoy the apparent agony on the faces of the other men.

"Well, there it is. All set to go, or should I say blow?" laughed the Bomber.

Sally walked over and whispered in Vinnie's ear. Vinnie smiled and left the room. Sally then walked over and stood in front of the Bomber.

"OK, Billy, now show me how you set the timer. Let's say you wanted it to go off at midnight, which is about an hour from now. What would you do?"

"Well, the first thing is to set the time of day."

The Bomber looked at his wristwatch.

"The time is eleven fifteen. So you push this one here for twelve o'clock, like this. Then you push this little button to activate the timer, but I won't do that because it will arm the bomb. But anyway, when you push that button, this little red light goes on and it's all set to go off in forty-five minutes. That's what I did in the joint, Sally. I don't know what went wrong."

"I know what went wrong, Billy. You're a dumb fucking asshole!" roared Sally.

"What? What went wrong?" asked the Bomber stupidly.

"You! You went wrong, you crazy fuckin' idiot! You don't even know the difference between night and day! Boys, put him in that fuckin' chair over there," said Sally, pointing.

Tough Tony and Billy Bellini pushed the Bomber into the chair, keeping their hands firmly on his shoulders. Just then, Vinnie returned to the room carrying a length of rope and some silver-colored duct tape.

When the Bomber saw what Vinnie was carrying, he suddenly realized what Sally had planned for him.

"Tie him up!" Sally ordered.

"Please, Sally, please! I'm sorry! Here, take what's left of the money," the Bomber pleaded as he reached into his pocket and produced the envelope.

Tough Tony yanked the envelope out of his hand and threw it to Sally. The Bomber's eyes began blinking uncontrollably, and white mucus ran from his nose into his mouth.

"Sally, have mercy! Please have a heart!"

The Bomber's hands were tied behind his back.

"Stand him up," Sally ordered.

Sally then picked up the bomb and taped it to the Bomber's chest.

"Now remind me, Billy, was this the little button I should push to arm the bomb?"

Looking into the Bomber's face and smiling, Sally pressed the button, and the red light went on. Immediately, the red digital numbers on the clock began their countdown.

"Yeah, Billy, it's working perfectly. It says forty-four minutes and fifty-two seconds. I'm proud of you! You didn't screw up this time," said Sally with a broad grin on his face. "Take this creep outside and put him in a car that's ready for the press, and make sure you tie his feet securely."

The Bomber began to cry, and a large puddle of water appeared at his feet from him urinating in his pants.

"Sally, I'm sorry. Please, Sally, please," he whimpered.

"Don't worry, Billy. You only have forty-two minutes and ten seconds more to be sorry. Then you don't have to be sorry anymore."

The Bomber's legs went limp, and he began to faint.

"Get this fuckin' slob outa here! He's too stupid to live anyway.

Jimmy the Brute and Tough Tony dragged the Bomber from the room, the toes of his shoes trailing along the floor.

Upon the return of Tough Tony and Jimmy the Brute, a deadly quiet cloud of anticipation filled the room. As the minutes ticked away the short and final time the Bomber had left to live, all the men tried to look at their wristwatches unnoticed. At twelve o'clock, a muffled explosion shook the windows of the building, signifying Mafia-style justice.

Sally, watching the reactions on the faces of his gang members, took a bite of cheese he was holding in his hand.

"Ya know, this is great provolone!" he said with a broad smile on his face. "You guys oughtta try some."

Chapter 24

Eddie sat upright in his bed, once again awakened by the same reccurring dream.

It had been two weeks since the would-be assassin had made the last attempt on his life.

He lay back on his pillow and pondered his plight.

Don Francisco's voice was reverberating in his mind: "Things must be done with someone you can trust beyond a shadow of a doubt."

His mind cried out in anguish. *I know, I know, but who? Who shall it be?*

How ironic it was, he thought, that less than a year after Don Francisco's death he should find himself in the very same predicament he was in the day Don Francisco died. "So, then, Godfather, who do I have to trust with the knowledge of your great fortune?" he said, speaking out loud to himself.

Eddie blamed himself for the situation he now found himself embroiled in. His greed had caused him to make the wrong choices. Now those decisions were threatening his life.

With eyes wide open, he had entered a game played only in the world of the Mafia, where the stakes are high and life and death are the chips used for the ante, but he knew for him the die had been cast—there would be no turning back or retracing his steps.

Like quicksand, the Mafia world had swallowed him; now he had no choice but to stay in the game to the bitter end.

His frightening thoughts had caused beads of perspiration to form on his brow; his heart was beating frantically in his chest. Upset with himself, he jumped out of bed and walked around the bed to see if he had awakened Megan.

She was sound asleep. Lost in his thoughts, he walked from the bedroom and aimlessly began to pace the living room floor. Feeling a chill go through his body, he walked over to the marble fireplace and lit the gas log. Instantly, the dark room came to life bathed in a warm and comforting golden glow.

Pleased with himself, Eddie watched with interest as reflections from the fire began to mystically bounce and dance merrily, embracing all that it touched with a warm golden hue.

He stood motionless by the fireplace, enjoying the relaxing warmth by the fire, mesmerized by the hypnotic power of the flickering flames.

Suddenly, he felt another anxiety attack begin to overcome him as the problem he was now facing began to flash through his mind.

Oh, Godfather, what a mistake I have made, he lamented to himself. Why did I allow you to throw me into your world of death and evil? Now death is knocking on my door just as it was on yours. I know for your family's sake, I must act quickly and decide with whom I am to share our secret with before I meet your fate and unwittingly take our secret to the grave with me. I have thought of everyone and come to the conclusion it must be Dominic. I have no other options. It must be him. He is my father. Even though we don't get along, at least I know I *can trust* him."

After making his decision, he felt as if a great weight had been lifted from his shoulders; he let out a sigh of relief and began to relax. Feeling cold and tired he lay down on the white bearskin rug, enjoying the softness of the fur and the warmth of the fire. As Eddie tossed and turned, the once-magnificent bear lay silent, staring at him out of unseeing eyes, its large pointed teeth visible in its ferocious gaping mouth. Eddie rolled on his back, using the bear's head as a pillow, and fell soundly asleep.

"Eddie, Eddie," Megan called out softly as she gently shook his shoulder.

In spite of her gentle manner, he woke up with a start.

"Easy, baby, easy. It's OK," she said softly as she knelt down beside him.

He looked up into her face, noting that her long blonde hair had fallen forward, covering her cheeks, making it appear that her liquid blue eyes and lush full lips had been surrounded with a golden frame.

His emotions took him by surprise. He suddenly sensed the fire of passion burst hot and all-consuming inside of his body. He was excited and pleased with the emotions coursing through his body. For months, his fear of dying and the stressful preoccupation with his problems had rendered him impotent. While the fire of desire was raging within him, he was determined to take advantage of it and prove his manhood. He reached up to Megan and tore the robe from her body. Megan was caught by surprise, but his aggressive behavior had aroused her.

The flickering fire of desire lying dormant within her during the celibate period quickly erupted into a flaming volcano of passion. She became increasingly more excited by the selfishness of his behavior, realizing that for him, she was nothing more than a sexual object to be used by him to fulfill and satisfy his own singular desires.

Once their animal desires were fulfilled, they remained still, gasping for air, the sweat on their naked bodies reflecting the colorful dancing flames of the fire.

She reached for his hand as she spoke. "Wow, honey, that was great. I've never done it that way before—I mean, so physical and rough. I can't believe how it turned me on," she gasped elatedly.

He smiled and gently kissed her on the cheek. "Ya, me too. It's been a long time since we made love."

Exhausted, they fell asleep wrapped in each others arms, the warmth from the fire engulfing them.

Eddie awoke and carried the sleeping Megan into the bedroom and gently laid her on the bed, covering her nakedness with a blanket. As he turned, he glanced at the red glowing numbers on the clock resting on the nightstand.

Hmm . . . plenty of time, he thought to himself. It was Saturday, and he had made up his mind to go to the market.

Since that last attempt on his life, he remained in his apartment, fearful of leaving its safety in the event the sniper might be on a rooftop waiting for him to leave.

Nonetheless, today he had made up his mind to venture out regardless of the consequences. His self-inflicted reclusiveness was driving him crazy.

Making love to his wife after weeks of abstinence was just the tonic he needed to lift his spirits.

With a spring in his step, he headed toward the shower, feeling fresh and exhilarated. Suddenly a thought occurred to him that he paused in midstride, turned, and walked into the living room, heading toward the marble-topped bar.

Sitting down on a stool, he picked up the receiver of the telephone resting on the corner of the bar. Deep in thought, he paused for a moment and stared at the instrument resting in his hand. *What the fuck. I have no other choice*, he thought and dialed a number.

"Ya," the voice on the other end of the line answered tersely.

"I know it's a little early. Are you up and around yet?" asked Eddie apologetically.

"Ya, I'm up. You just caught me going out the door. What's up?"

"I need to talk to you as soon as possible. It's important."

"OK, are you calling from home?" the voice asked.

"Ya, I'm home."

"OK, I'm heading to town now. I'll be there in about a half an hour."

"OK, thanks. A half an hour is fine."

"All right, then," said Dominic D'Amico as he hung up the telephone on his son.

Eddie had to rush. He took a quick shower and shaved. He had just finished putting on a dark blue jogging suit when the door chimes sounded. He carefully closed the bedroom door behind him and briskly walked to the entry to open the door for his father.

Dominic was his usual dapper self, dressed in a camel hair coat and sporting a dark brown wide-brimmed hat; on his hands was a pair of expensive brown leather gloves.

Eddie always felt uncomfortable and intimidated in the presence of his father, and today was no exception.

"Thanks for coming," said Eddie, appearing to be nervous.

"Ya, no problem. Is this going to take very long? I gotta lot of shit to take care of this morning."

"No. Not at all, just a few minutes, and then you can be on your way."

"Good," Dominic answered.

As they walked into the living room, Dominic paused and sat down on the sofa. His piercing eyes were fixed on Eddie as he placed his gloves and hat beside him. Unbuttoning his coat, Dominic continued to stare at Eddie.

"Well, what the fuck is so important?" Dominic asked, breaking the uneasy silence.

"Would you like some coffee or something?"

"Nah, thanks, my teeth are floating already."

"OK, then give me a minute. I'll be right back. I've gotta go get something."

Dominic nodded an acknowledgment as he picked up a magazine off the coffee table.

Eddie quickly walked to his study and closed the door behind him. He walked over to the bookcase and removed some books, revealing a small round wall safe. Quickly spinning the dial, he carefully entered the combination. Opening the safe, he removed a white envelope he had prepared several days before. Not knowing to whom he would entrust the envelope, he had not written any name on the document. After closing the safe and replacing the books, he quickly walked over to his desk and printed the name "Dominic" on the envelope.

Returning to the living room, he pulled up a footstool and sat down facing his father. Dominic sat silently waiting for his son to speak, his eyes fixed on the envelope Eddie was holding in his hand.

"Look, I'm worried, very worried that the cocksucker trying to kill me might not miss the next time. If that happens, I need somebody I can completely trust to take care of something for me." Eddie took a deep breath and paused, studying his fathers' reaction.

"What kind of things?" asked Dominic, his piercing brown eyes searching Eddie's face.

"Do you remember the day at the Don's birthday party you asked me what him and I had talked about that morning? Then you blew your fuckin' top when I wouldn't tell you?" Eddie paused, waiting for a reply.

"Ya, ya, I remember. So what?"

"Well, that day, he told me he was worried that somebody might be trying to kill him and asked me to take care of some things in the event of his death. Well, he was right, and now with the shooter trying to kill me, I'm in the same fucking predicament he found himself in, so now I have to prepare for the worst. If I die, I need someone I can trust to carry out the plan I devised for him."

"You're my father, and I know I can trust you. But before I go any farther, do you agree to help me, no questions asked?"

"Ya, ya, sure, why not? You're my son, and he was my best friend. Sure, I'll help," said Dominic, appearing to be less antagonistic.

"OK. Good, then. I was hoping you would say that, so here's the deal. I've made it as simple as I can." He handed his father the envelope that he had continued to hold in his hand. "In that envelope is a key to a safety deposit box along with some instructions and the name of a bank. There are three other deposit boxes involved in my plan, but the keys for those boxes, along with further instructions, are all locked in the first box for which I have just given you the key."

"There is one way, and one way only, that you can use that key I have just given you, and that is by providing the bank with a certified copy of a death certificate proving I am dead. You will also need the death certificate for other things that are explained in the second box. Any questions?"

Dominic thought a minute. "Ya, just one. What if you don't die? Then what am I supposed to do with this?" he asked, holding up the envelope.

"Well, while I'm alive, that envelope is absolutely worthless to you. When they catch the shooter, you can return it to me or keep it as a memento of this discussion. It's your choice."

"OK, good enough," said Dominic, nodding his head to indicate he understood his son's request. "That's it then?"

"It is as far as I'm concerned," replied Eddie. "I hope that envelope is something you will never have to use."

"Ya, me either, but you know you can depend on me," said Dominic, rising as he spoke. Dominic paused at the door. "Does anyone else know about this?" he asked, holding up the envelope.

"No, not a living soul—just you and me," Eddie replied. "I must confess, I thought about asking you for your pledge of secrecy, but I didn't want to insult you by asking such a thing. You're my father. If I can't trust you, then who could I trust?"

Dominic listened intently as Eddie spoke, nodding his head in silent agreement with his son's words.

"Thanks, Dad, you don't know what a load this is off my mind," said Eddie as they shook hands.

Dominic smiled, putting the envelope in his pocket as he walked out the door. Another piece of his plan had just fallen into place.

Chapter 25

His meeting with Dominic had caused Eddie to arrive at Jimmy's Restaurant later than usual.

As he walked through the well-worn wooden door, he could see the restaurant was already full of people. Pausing for a moment, he glanced around at the white porcelain-topped tables and could see that they were all occupied. He did a double take when he spotted Lorenzo LaRocca seated alone at the boys' favorite table in the far corner of the room, his face buried in a newspaper.

Eddie walked toward the table, his footsteps muffled by the thick layer of sawdust covering the floor.

Sensing Eddie's presence, LaRocca looked up and smiled as he saw his friend.

"Morning, big guy, do you mind some company?" asked Eddie, sitting down at the table, not waiting for a reply.

"Fuck no, Eddie," answered LaRocca, folding the paper as he spoke and throwing it on the chair beside him. "What da ya want? I'll buy ya breakfast."

"Thanks, anyway, I'll get it. When the girl comes around, have her bring me a cup of coffee."

Lorenzo nodded as he picked up his fork to finish his breakfast.

Eddie walked over to the cafeteria-style service counter and got in-line behind two grizzly-bearded farmers dressed in blue coveralls and beat-up straw hats. "Morning, fellas," Eddie smiled. "Morning to you, sonny," one of the men replied, his corn cob pipe still in his mouth. When he arrived back at the table, a cup of steaming hot coffee was waiting for him, white wisps of steam silently signaling the impending danger of its heat. Eddie made a mental note to himself to approach the steaming cup with care.

"Where's all your cronies dis mornin'?" asked LaRocca as Eddie sat down.

"Ya know something, I was just wonderin' the same thing. But tell me, what's going on with you, guys? What the hell are you doing here? The story on the street is you guys are all held up at the junkyard waiting for things to cool down."

"Ya . . . dat's right, we was, but tings changed overnight. It's a whole new fuckin' ball game now."

Puzzled by his friend's remark, Eddie asked, "So what the hell happened that could have made things change so quickly? Did you guys all call a truce or something?"

"C'mon, Eddie, you gotta be fucking kiddin'. You know Sally better den dat. Tell ya one ting, you won't guess in a million fuckin' years what he's went and done."

Lorenzo had piqued Eddie's curiosity. "Well, I wouldn't put anything past him, so tell me, what's he done?"

"OK, are ya sittin down?"

"Well, I think so," Eddie chuckled.

"Get dis, Sally's hired a bunch of missionaries to help us wit da war."

"Missionaries—what do you mean missionaries are going to help Sally fight the war?" asked Eddie, puzzled by LaRocca's comment.

Irritated by Eddie's lack of understanding, LaRocca continued. "Der soldgers, real fuckin' soldgers—professionals who fight wars for money."

"Oh," Eddie laughed, "I understand now. You're talking about mercenaries, you must be kidding, Sally had hired mercenaries?"

"Yep, dat's da guys, real soldgers—dey even dress in dose goofy fuckin' camouflage clothes."

Eddie remained speechless as LaRocca continued talking.

"Eddie, I'm telling ya somethin', dez guys are real motherfuckers."

LaRocca paused a moment to look carefully around and lowered his voice to a whisper. "Dey gotta arsenal of weapons bigger den da fuckin' marines. Dey even got tank-destroying cannons. I seen da shit wit my own eyes. Dey said dey ripped it off from Uncle Sam when dey was in da service." LaRocca's face grew pensive.

"Ya know somethin', Eddie, I bin in dis business a long time, but I never saw a bunch of crazy bastards like des guys in my life," LaRocca said in a serious manner. Finished with his story, he sat back in his chair, waiting for his friend's reaction.

Eddie was dumbstruck at Sally's cunning move. "I can't fucking believe it," he replied, shaking his head. "Maybe we've all been underestimating Sally. He's got to be the first don in history to hire mercenaries to help fight a family war."

"Well, you believe it, Eddie. You just fuckin' believe it. As a matter a fact, pretty soon you'll be able to see dem wit your own eyes," said LaRocca, looking at his wristwatch. As he continued, "I'm supposed meet dem here. Dey should be walkin' in anytime now."

"Hmm . . . why would they come here?" Eddie asked cynically. "That sounds a little strange to me."

"Hey man, believe me, dez guys are not stupid. Der here to buy a truckload of food for der hideout."

"Hideout, they have a hideout? There not staying at the junkyard?" asked Eddie in amazement.

"Nope, no junkyard for dez guys. Der setting up a camp in some deserted barn dey found way out in the boondocks somewhere."

"Man, this is really something, but I must say it all sounds pretty bizarre to me," Eddie said as he put his empty plate on top of LaRocca's. "But listen, let me change the subject for a moment. I was glad when I saw you here because I planned to call you today anyway. It's about your offer of help with my problem . . ." He paused, trying to choose his words carefully; he did not want to offend his friend. He continued. "I can't tell you how much I appreciate your offer to help me, or how deeply grateful and touched I am by it . . ." He paused again. "But the truth is I'm just not like you guys. I don't have the balls to have someone killed, not even if my own life is at risk. I'm—" LaRocca held up his hand and interrupted him.

"Forget it, say no more, but I'll say dis. You got more balls den you think you have. It took real moxie to say what you just did. Consider da case closed, and just remember I'm always here if ya need me."

"Thanks, my friend, I appreciate that," said Eddie, offering his hand. Eddie studied LaRocca's face as they shook hands. It remained expressionless.

Suddenly, Eddie felt an urge to leave the table. "Excuse me, I gotta go tap a kidney," he said as he rose from his chair.

LaRocca nodded and picked up his newspaper.

Returning from the restroom, Eddie entered the dining area just in time to see Turk Scotto and a tall athletic-appearing man wearing camouflage-colored fatigues heading toward LaRocca's table.

Eddie couldn't help but notice that the tall stranger walked with a crisp military gait as if he was marching in some unseen parade. *Well*

I guess it doesn't take a rocket scientist to figure out that guy is one of the mercenaries, Eddie thought as he headed to join the three men.

Arriving at the table, he paused a moment behind his chair and looked into the long tanned face of the mercenary. The soldier's light brown hair sported a short military cut; his sparkling liquid brown eyes looked Eddie over from head to toe. The mercenary exuded an aura over his persona that made Eddie like the man on sight. "How ya doin', Eddie? Say hello ta Duke," said the Turk with a wide smile on his face.

Duke immediately rose to his feet and took Eddie's outstretched hand in a powerful viselike grip. He smiled, showing yellow nicotine-stained teeth.

"My pleasure, Eddie," he said in a soft, pleasant voice that betrayed a slight Texas drawl.

"Likewise, Colonel," said Eddie with a broad smile on his face as his eyes focused on the emblems on Duke's shoulders. The soldier, going along with Eddie's military comment, stepped one pace backward and saluted smartly. "Colonel Lieutenant David Donnelly at your service, sir!" he snapped out. Their eyes locked together, and both men began chuckling at Duke's military gyrations as they both sat back in their chairs.

Yep, I like this guy, thought Eddie as Duke began the conversation.

"So tell me, Eddie, do you have a last name?" He smiled slightly.

Before Eddie could reply, LaRocca answered for him. "D'Amico, our friend here is Dominic D'Amico's son," LaRocca said with a sense of pride in his voice.

"Ah, so Dominic's your father. Very interesting. So tell me, Eddie, are you also in the "family" business?" Duke quipped.

"Fuck no, not me, I'm a brain surgeon," joked Eddie, half laughing.

Turk broke into the conversation. "So, Eddie, tell me sometin. Der's a rumor on da street dat somebody's been trying to wak ya. Who in da fuck did ya piss off so bad dey would wanna knock ya off?" Before Eddie could respond to the Turk's comment, Duke jumped into the conversation. His demeanor had suddenly changed; his eyes grew cold, and his voice was curt and all business.

"So tell me, Doctor, what's this all about?" asked the soldier tersely. "If you have some kind of problem, perhaps I can be of some service to you . . ." He paused. "For a price, of course."

"Well, it's true, Duke. I do have a real fuckin' problem. Some son of a bitch has been taking potshots at me with a rifle."

"That sounds serious. Well, you have a standing offer. All you have to do is pay me, point me in a direction, and somebody is going to die," said the mercenary in a menacing tone.

"Ya, I just hope I'm not the one who dies," replied Eddie, rolling his eyes at Duke as he spoke.

"What time we supposed ta meet your guys?" LaRocca asked, looking at his wristwatch. Duke looked at his large black sports watch. "They should be loaded up by now."

"Well den, what ya say we get movin," said the Turk matter-of-factly.

Everyone rose from the table. Duke Donnelly stuck out his hand to Eddie. "Nice meeting you, pardner." He smiled as the two men shook hands; he then put his free hand on Eddie's shoulder and continued, "Listen, I'm dead serious. If you need some help with your problem, call me," he ended in a concerned tone.

"Thanks for the offer, Colonel. I'll keep it in mind. It was nice meeting you. I hope we can do it again sometime," said Eddie sincerely.

Turning to face Turk and LaRocca, Duke said, "So long, you guys. Listen, you be careful out there. Don't go getting yourself killed." With that, he turned and headed toward the door.

Eddie had been impressed with Duke Donnelly. *Yep, there's something about that guy I like, no matter what he does for a living,* he thought to himself as he stepped out into the brisk morning air.

*   *   *

After leaving the restaurant, Eddie felt the wind cut through his sweat outfit like a knife. He shivered and quickened his pace toward the car.

Thoughts of Duke Donnelly and his band of mercenaries were racing through his mind. *My god, Jack Shepard and his men won't stand a ghost of a chance against the mercenaries' military armament. They'll be slaughtered like sheep,* his thoughts continued as he entered his car and began driving. *I've got to do something fast.*

He reached down and picked up the telephone and realized he was so upset he couldn't get the phone numbers he needed in their proper order. Exasperated, he opened his glove box and pulled out his address book to get One-Eyed Jack's number.

He dialed the elusive number, and a syrupy sweet sounding voice answered, "One-Eyed Jack's, can I help you?"

Eddie's response to the woman's friendly demeanor was vitriolic and to the point. "Is Shep there?" he asked, ignoring his demeanor.

The woman remained pleasant. "That depends on who's calling, honey." Her voice purred politely.

"Tell him it's D'Amico, Eddie D'Amico."

"OK, baby, I'll see if he's here," she lied, knowing full well he was in his office in the next room. In a matter of seconds, a rich, powerful baritone voice resonated over the receiver. "Well, hello, brother, to what do I owe the honor?" asked One-Eyed Jack Shepard, an obvious tone of respect in his rich, melodic voice.

"You'll know soon enough, Jack, but we need to talk now—like in right now," Eddie conveyed his sense of urgency by the tone of his voice. Jack got the message. "OK, my man, right now it shall be. Where?" asked Shep.

"Hmm . . . shit, let me think a minute . . ." There was a long pause before Eddie finally responded. "In the old neighborhood, the Baptist church on the corner of Scio and Lyndhurst streets. And, Shep, come alone. Don't tell anyone where you're going. I don't want people to know that we've met. I already have more fucking problems than I can handle as it is."

"Ya, brother, so I heard, so I heard," said Shep knowingly. "Let's say twenty minutes—does that work for you?"

"It works for me. Twenty minutes it is," answered Eddie.

The large interior of the old magnificent church was nearly dark. Eddie paused for a moment to let his eyes grow accustomed to the dim lighting.

A row of candles on large brass stands flicked valiantly, trying to illuminate the cavernous expanse of the old building.

Eddie was startled by a noise behind him.

Ever fearful for his life, he spun around, quickly crouching behind one of the nearby pews, his hand freeing the Beretta from its ankle holster at the same time.

His eyes were now accustomed to the light. With a sense of relief, he recognized the imposing silhouette of Jack Shepard's huge frame filling the doorway that led upstairs to the choir balcony.

Ignoring the gun in Eddie's hand, the big man nodded an acknowledgment without saying a word. He turned and began walking up the long narrow staircase to their covert meeting place. Feeling foolish, Eddie returned the Beretta to its holster and followed Jack Shepard up the stairway.

As the big man emerged from the confining quarters of the narrow staircase, he turned and held out his hand toward Eddie. The two friends shook hands. Eddie began to speak before their hands had separated.

"Jack, you've got real fucking problems, and I mean real problems." The big man smiled, showing lethal white teeth. "So what else is new, my man? Shit, problem is my middle name."

"Ya, maybe it is, but not this kind of problem. This is real serious shit, man. You and all your people are in danger."

"From who, that little no-good piss-ant Sally?" he asked sarcastically. "If that little pip-squeak leaves that fortress he built for himself, he's a fucking dead man. If I don't get him, Cavelli will," he finished in an angry tone.

"Shep, listen to me, Sally's really got an ace up his sleeve. He's already left the junkyard and is living back home. He's not running anymore. He's going to attack, and attack big. He's hired a bunch of former Green Beret mercenaries to take you and Cavelli out, and that's no fucking shit."

"Man, you've got to be fuckin' kidding me," replied the big man in amazement.

"I wish I were. I could hardly believe it myself when I heard about it, but I met the leader this morning at the market. It's all true, so help me."

"Supposedly, these guys even have heavy military ordinance with them. Shit, Jack, I don't care how brave you are, you can't afford to risk fucking with these guys. There's no way you can win. They're all trained professionals. It's the business—they kill for a living.

"I'm telling you, my friend. I'm really concerned for your safety, and your days are numbered unless you do something in a big damn hurry." He let out a sigh.

Eddie had gotten the big man's attention; he too now appeared to be concerned. "Well then, what do you suggest I do?" he asked petulantly.

"Shit, man, fuck if I know . . ." Eddie paused a moment. "Maybe it would be better to call a truce and hammer out a deal with Sally." As an after thought, Eddie continued, "Better a deal than dead."

"Hmm . . . you may have something there. Let me think about that. Look, I'm going to stay here awhile and do some serious thinking."

Jack Shepard called their meeting to an end by rising. He gave Eddie a long affectionate hug. "Thanks, my man, I owe you."

"You don't owe me anything, Shep. Whatever you do, just do it quick. Make the right decision, and most of all, be careful," said Eddie as he turned and walked toward the darkened stairway.

Jack Shepard sat back on one of the oak pews mulling over the disturbing information he had just received. He has a lot of respect for Eddie. They had been friends for a long time; he had always regarded him as someone who could be trusted.

Hmm . . . maybe Eddie's right, he thought. *Call a truce with Sally, divide the territories, and put an end to the senseless killing.*

Satisfied with his decision, he left the old red brick church and headed to his office to get Sally's phone number and make him a proposal. Sitting behind the worn wooden desk in his office, the big man decided to try catching Sally at home.

He dialed Sally's number; a woman answered, "Hello."

"Connie, this you?"

"Yes, this is Connie," she answered, not placing the voice.

"Well then, hello, Connie, this is Jack Shepard, how have you been?"

"Oh, oh, hello, Jack," she replied, taken by surprise. "I'm fine, thank you for asking . . ."

"Connie, it's very important I speak to Sally. Do you know how I can get a hold of him?"

"Well, as a matter of fact, he's out in the yard playing with the girls."

"Can I talk to him?"

"Well, that I can't guarantee, but I'll see if he will come to the phone," she answered honestly.

"Thanks," he answered.

Jack Shepard waited for what to him seemed like an eternity. Sitting in silence, nervously wondering if Sally was going to take his call. His question was finally answered when Sally's voice blasted in his ear.

"Well, well, the big man himself. What the fuck do you and I have to talk about, Mr. Big Shot?"

Jack Shepard wasted no time getting right to the point.

"A truce, Sally. I'm calling to suggest we call a truce. No more shooting or killing for thirty days. Then you and I can sit down and iron out our differences."

"A truce. All of a sudden you want a fucking truce. What's the matter, tough guy? Are you running out of men or balls?" chided Sally.

"Look, man, lets get one fuckin' thing straight. Jack Shepard's got bigger balls than anyone you've ever met in your lifetime. I'm just trying to be practical, that's all!"

A long pause ensued while the deceitful Sally's mind raced, trying to formulate a plan that would use One-Eyed Jack's offer to his advantage.

Hearing no response, Jack Shepard began speaking into the silent instrument. "Hey, listen, man, just forget I called. All bets are off—"

"No, no, just wait a fucking minute. I was thinking, that's all. Maybe you're right, it wouldn't hurt to see if we can make a deal. All we can lose is a little time. The war will always be there if we can't get together," said Sally philosophically. "Thirty days, you say. A truce for thirty days, starting when?" Sally asked.

"When we hang up the phone," Shepard answered. Then continued, "We'll let things cool down for a few days, and I'll call you in a week to set up a meeting on some neutral ground."

"OK, Mr. Black Man, you got yourself a thirty-day truce."

"You listen to me, Sally. I would stake my life on your father's word, but I don't trust you as far as I can throw you. No motherfuckin' tricks, understand!"

Sally's temper flared. "Listen, you black motherfucker, I gave you my word. I'm a man of honor. I'm not doing this because I like your black fuckin' ass. I just don't want any more of my people getting killed, if we can make a deal, that's all," shouted Sally as he slammed down the phone.

Chapter 26

His meeting with Jack Shepard had upset Eddie. His overactive mind imagined the terrible consequences that could befall Jack Shepard and his men if they engaged in warfare with the skilled mercenaries. His thoughts of such an impending disaster made him nervous and edgy. Instead of going home as he planned, he decided to go to the firing range for a while to relax. Lately, that seemed to be the only place he felt comfortable and safe.

He tried firing the Beretta for a while, but today the magnitude of the problems complicating his life would not leave his mind. With a restless spirit, he put away his Beretta and decided to go to the small customer lounge for a cup of coffee.

He walked to the coffee machine and waited impatiently while the hot liquid filled his cup. Spotting a large well-used overstuffed chair in the corner of the room, he decided to sit down and try to relax. Deep in thought, he took another sip of the hot liquid and closed his eyes.

He reflected back on the full schedule of events that he had experienced that morning, his victory over the impotence that had plagued him for weeks. His unsettling meeting with his father—in the event of his death, Dominic would have access to Don Francisco's fortune. Then there was LaRocca's bizarre story and his meeting with Duke Donnelly and Jack Shepard. Reliving everything all over again caused him to be overcome with exhaustion, and he dozed off.

The dark gray carpet in the room masked the sound of a man's footsteps silently approaching him.

"What's the matter, Eddie, don't you have a bed at home?" the voice asked. Startled, Eddie jumped, spilling the hot liquid on his privates as he quickly rose to his feet.

"What are you, some kind of fucking sadist or something? You just scared the shit out of me," complained Eddie to his friend Bee Stinger, with a tone of irritation in his voice.

The detective was laughing in spite of Eddie's anger, but try as he might, he could not control his behavior over the humor of his friend's unexpected reaction.

"Look, I'm sorry, man. I didn't think. I guess I should have known better. I know how jumpy and uptight you must be," said Bee, still chuckling.

"Who, me uptight? You've got to be kidding. What the fuck do I have to be uptight about? Doesn't everybody have someone running around trying to whack them out," said Eddie, smiling at his own black humor.

Suddenly turning serious, Eddie asked, "So tell me, Bee, do you have any thoughts about who may be behind this thing?"

"Shit, no, I've told you more times than I can count we have nothing at all to go on, but you don't help matters either. All I ever get from you is it must be Sally," answered Bee.

"Look, stop being a fucking bonehead, will you. Don't you think that if I knew anything I'd tell you? It's my fucking life that's at stake here. Let's just drop it, forget I asked," snapped Eddie angrily.

"Look, I'm sorry. I know what you must be going through."

"Do you? That's just wonderful. How the fuck could you or anyone else know what it feels like to be a fucking sitting duck, that anytime, any place, some son of a bitch can get you in his crosshairs and blow your fucking brains out?"

Upset with their conversation, Eddie began walking toward the trash container to throw away the cup he still held in his hand.

The detective, feeling bad over his friend's plight, put his big arm around Eddie's shoulders and walked silently with him to the receptacle. "Do you want to bang off a few rounds before you go? You can show me how good you're getting. We can do ten matches of ten rounds each for ten dollars a match. Come on, what da ya say?" asked the detective.

"Naw, I'm much too irritated to shoot now. I'd rather just go home."

"Oh, come on, you've been telling me how good you are. Now stay and show me," insisted the detective.

The opportunity to show off his shooting skills to his friend suddenly appealed to Eddie. He nodded his agreement, and the two men walked to the firing range. Eddie watched as his friend fired off his final ten rounds with a smile on his face.

"OK, Bee, that makes two you won." He raised his arm, his hand palm up, as he spoke. I won eight—that's eighty bucks you owe me. Only green money, no checks," he joked. Eddie was now in a better mood.

"Goddamn, Eddie, that was great shooting. You wound up being a crack shot," commented the detective dejectedly as he dug in his wallet for the money.

"Let's look at it this way, Bee: I had a lot of incentive to want to learn quickly," Eddie wisecracked.

He stuffed the money in his pocket as he shook hands with his friend. "See ya around Bee," he said as he walked toward the door leading to the parking lot exit.

The detective remained riveted in place, shaking his head from side to side as he watched Eddie walk out the door.

*   *   *

"Honey, I'm home, don't pay the ransom. I escaped," Eddie quipped as he called out. "Ya, sure, Mr. Wise Guy, I'll bet you escaped. The question is, from where?" said Megan as she entered the room dressed in an old green flannel robe and carrying a feather duster in her hand.

"So where have you been? I thought you would be coming right home after the market," she asked, giving him an affectionate peck on the cheek.

"Well, I intended to, but I had a stop to make and then ran into Bee Stinger at the firing range."

"God, Eddie, you and that firing range—why don't you give that pistol of yours a break for a while," she said scoldingly. "I'll bet you forgot you were supposed to be at the Carlivattis' house tonight at seven for Christina's confirmation party."

"*Holy Shit!* You're right, I did forget. Did you get her a gift?"

"Of course I did. You didn't expect for a minute that I'd wait for you to do it, did you?" she responded smilingly.

"Nah, I didn't guess you would have," he answered, amused at his wife's remark.

"I'm going to take a nap. Otherwise, I'll be worn out tonight and won't be able to be my charming and entertaining self."

Megan threw the feather duster at him.

"OK, Mr. Prince Charming, take your nap, but would you use one of the slaves quarters? I'm cleaning our bedroom," she joked.

Continuing on with her humor, he answered, "Of course, Lady Megan, I am easy. Your wish is my command. To the slave quarters it shall be." He turned and blew her a kiss as he entered the guest room door.

*   *   *

The dashboard clock read ten forty-seven as Eddie backed out of Judge Carlivatti's driveway. Chilled, Megan pulled up the collar on her white mink coat and snuggled in closer to her husband.

"You know, it was a strange mix of people at the party, didn't you think so?" Megan asked. Eddie turned and smiled as he answered her question.

"Well, maybe to you it may have seemed that way, but it was no different than I would have expected it to be."

"Yes, I suppose you're right. To you it would all seem perfectly natural, but to me it was strange to see your cronies from the market and the old neighborhood crowd rubbing elbows with all those judges and political bigwigs. I guess I'll just never get used to your lifestyle."

"Why not, Megan? Those big shots are no different than anyone else. They all put on their pants the same way, and to the best of my knowledge, they only have two balls just like everyone else."

"Oh, stop it, Eddie. You just love using all those street analogies, don't you?" she smiled as she punched him gently on the arm.

Megan enjoyed herself at the party and was in a talkative mood. "You know, it was a pleasure to see Joey Cariola again. He's always so funny and clever. He seems to have something humorous to say about everything, but he did say something I didn't understand. Eddie, what did he mean when he said he worked for Carmen?"

"What he meant is that he's Carmen's bailiff. Joey takes care of the daily court calendar and is Carmen's man Friday."

"Oh, I see. Well, anyway, I had the opportunity to get to know him a little better tonight. He seems like a very nice man."

"He is. He's a great guy. Carmen loves him like a brother. He's been with him a long time," said Eddie.

The station wagon moved smoothly over the brightly shining wet pavement. The two passengers alone with their thoughts enjoyed the comforting warmth of the car's interior and the soft, relaxing music emanating from the radio.

It was Megan who broke the silence first. "You know, Eddie, Christina appeared to be strange to me. I can't quite put my finger on it. She seems intelligent enough for a young girl ten years of age, but I got the feeling something was odd about her. I don't know, maybe it's just my imagination."

Eddie smiled and placed his hand on her leg. "You know, baby, you're pretty perceptive. Carmen had her tested, and they tell him she's emotionally withdrawn, whatever that means."

"Hmm . . . interesting," said Megan. "Too bad. She's such a sweet girl."

They were nearing the hotel when Megan again broke the silence. "You know, I had quite a talk with Danni tonight. She was very cordial and civil, but she did make one strange comment. What did she mean when she said there's still a debt you owe her that you haven't paid yet? I thought you've been very faithful in sending her checks out on time each month."

Eddie's mind flashed back to his last meeting with Danni and the unwritten bizarre terms she attached to their divorce agreement. He wondered if the time would ever come when she would expect him to make good on his promise.

After a slight pause, he answered his wife's question. "Hell, I don't know what she was talking about, Megan. Maybe she was just trying to break your chops or something," he lied.

Suddenly Megan squealed with delight. "Oh, Eddie, the baby's kicking like crazy. Hurry, hurry, feel right here." She took his hand and guided it to her stomach. "Do you feel it, do you feel it?" she asked excitedly.

"Yep, maybe it's trying to break out of there."

"Oh, Eddie, you're still calling our baby an *it*. Don't you want me to try and find out what we're going to have?"

"No, not me. I'd rather be surprised. I'll be happy with whatever God decides to bless us with. You can find out, though. Just promise not to tell me, OK?"

She put her arms around him and kissed him on the cheek as he guided the vehicle into the hotel parking lot.

The telephone was ringing as Eddie opened the apartment door. Switching on a light, he headed for an ornate white-and-gold provincial-style telephone sitting on top of a marble table located in the entry hall.

"Who could be calling at this hour?" Megan commented, looking at her wristwatch as she opened the door to their bedroom. Ignoring her question, Eddie quickly walked over and picked up the receiver.

"Hello," he said into the mouthpiece.

"Are you still awake? I got some real good news for you," said Dominic D'Amico excitedly.

"Really, what kind of good news?" asked Eddie, caught by surprise by the tone of excitement in his father's voice.

"I got 'im for you. I got the dirty cocksucker whose been shooting at you," replied Dominic.

Eddie was shocked by his father's words; he became overcome with excitement, but a burning doubt gnawed in the pit of his stomach. Could it really be true? Did he even dare believe it was possible? Question after question kept popping into his mind at all the same time.

"Are you sure? You're not shitting me, are you? Who is it? Is he with you now? How'd you find out?" Eddie continued to blurt out one question after another in rapid succession without pausing to wait for an answer.

Dominic finally had to stop him in midsentence. "Hey, hold it, hold it! One question at a time. First things first, yes, I'm positive he was the one. Yes, he's with me now," said Dominic with a chuckle in his voice.

"Hey, wait a minute. You said he was the one, and he's with you now. Where? Where is he right now?"

"In the trunk of my car," Dominic answered matter-of-factly.

"Is he dead? Did you kill him?" asked Eddie nervously.

"Look, no more questions, no more answers. You'll soon know everything, but I will tell you this—you're going to be in for the surprise of your life. Just be in front of the hotel. I'll pick you up in about forty minutes. Oh, one other thing—don't tell anyone about this call, especially your wife, *capishe?*"

Eddie was beginning to speak when the line went dead. Bursting with excitement, he headed toward the bedroom to share the good news with Megan. As he neared the door, he realized that if he told her anything now, it might prove later to be a big mistake. He decided to heed his father's warning until he was sure of what really took place. Clearing his throat, he slowed his pace and attempted to control his excitement. He paused for a moment at the door and nonchalantly walked into the bedroom. Megan was seated in front of her dressing table, brushing her long golden hair.

"Well, who was that on the telephone?" she asked.

"Look, baby, I can't tell you too much right now because I don't know the whole story myself," he answered, "but I can tell you this—if the information I just received is true, it's good news, very good news. And when I get back, I'll tell you everything."

"God, Eddie, you're acting so weird," she said, smiling at her husband's obvious exuberance. "You're going to tell me about what? Where are you going now?"

"Someone's picking me up. I don't know where I'm going. Just trust me, I'll be home shortly, and then I'll tell you the whole story. But before I can do that, I have to find out all the details myself. Right now all I know for sure or can tell you with any degree of certainty is if what I was just told is a fact, you and I are going to be ecstatically happy."

"OK, OK, Eddie, I get the point," she laughed, enjoying her husband's upbeat mood. "But now you've got me so curious and excited I'll be waiting on pins and needles until you come home. You better get back here the minute you can, that's all I ask."

"I will. You got a deal, baby, I promise."

The heavy weight of his problems and the pressure and stress that it had caused had covered him like an invisible blanket of gloom for months. As he told Megan the good news, he suddenly began to realize that his father's call had caused his spirits to soar in the hope his long ordeal might finally be over. Not wanting to be questioned by his wife anymore, he made up his mind to wait for his father in the lobby. He walked over to Megan, who was sitting silently, watching his every move.

"I love you, baby," he said, putting his arm tenderly around her. "I can't wait for our baby to come so we can start to be a real family," he whispered in her ear.

"I love you too, Eddie," she said as she rose and began grinding her body tightly into his. Eddie pulled away.

"Wait, baby, let's not start something we don't have time to finish."

"I know, Eddie. I'm sorry, it was bad timing on my part, but sometimes I become overwhelmed with passion."

"Well, put your motor on pause. I'll come home as soon as I can, and push your On button, and we can pick up where we left off, OK?" he laughed.

"I guess it will have to be OK. I have no other choice, but it won't be easy laying around in bed with my motor on pause. Maybe I'll have to take things into my own hands." She smiled demurely after delivering her double-meaning quip.

"You're really something. The longer were together, the more I love you," he said sincerely. He kissed her tenderly on the cheek and headed for the door.

"I'll be waiting for you, honey. Hurry home. I'm anxious to hear the news," she called out as he closed the door.

When Eddie arrived in the lobby, he still had some time to kill. He walked over to a small seating area in front of the darkly tinted windows and sat down on a large comfortable tan leather chair. Laying his head against the pillow, he closed his eyes.

My god, he thought, *I'm glad I called LaRocca off. If he had killed the mysterious shooter, the attempted assassin's blood would now be on my hands.* He shuddered at the thought.

Through the dark windows, he saw a car ease up to the curb and looked down at his watch. *If that's Dominic, he's right on time*, he thought as he rose and walked out into the chilly night air.

Recognizing Dominic's big late-model Cadillac, he walked over and jumped in the front seat. He immediately began firing questions at his father.

"OK, enough is enough. So tell me, who was it? Or who *is* it, whatever the right fucking word may be," asked Eddie with a sharp edge on his voice.

"You'll soon see, but all in good time," his father answered, taking his eyes off the road and smiling at his son.

"What the fuck are we doing here, playing some kind of kid game or something? What's the big deal about telling me now? Don't I have the right to know who it was that hated me enough to want me fucking dead?" said Eddie, growing angry at his father's secrecy.

"Look, in a few minutes, you'll hear the whole story. Just cool your fuckin' jets for a while, and soon I'll tell you everything you want to know," answered his father, patting him on the leg as he spoke.

"OK, OK, have it your way. Just tell me this, is the cocksucker dead? Answer me that one question."

"Yes," answered his father. "Soon you will see that your worries are all over from today on. The shooter will never bother you again. There, does that satisfy you?" asked Dominic.

"OK, then, just one more question—is he really in the fucking trunk of this car? Answer me that one," asked Eddie, wanting to know but afraid of hearing the answer.

"Yes, I told you the shooter is in the car. I'll bet in your wildest dreams you never would have thought you'd be in the same car with the degenerate bastard that tried to kill you," said Dominic, laughing heartily at his own statement.

"Ya, you're right, you can say that again," said Eddie, chuckling at the sick humor of the night's bizarre turn of events.

Well, better you than me, you sick bastard. You tried to kill me, instead you got yours, so fuck you, whoever you are. I hope you burn in hell, thought Eddie to himself.

The big car moved quietly through the dark country roads. Eddie settled back into the comfort of the red leather seat. His father had saved his life; he'd keep his mouth shut and let him do things his way, he thought as he closed his eyes and tried to relax.

"Where are we going?" he asked without opening his eyes. "The junkyard," his father answered. *But of course,* he thought. *Where else would we be going with a dead body in the trunk of the car?* Soon the person who had been trying to kill him would be part of a metal bale going to the smelter, never to be heard from again.

Eddie's mind was working overtime; he found himself having trouble dealing with the fact that he felt not an iota of remorse or one shred of guilt that someone had been killed because of him.

His overactive mind was sending him disjointed thoughts. *I didn't order it . . . I'm not involved . . . There's no blood on my hands . . . Fuck, it was either him or me . . . Better him.* Eddie began to look at his father with newfound respect. *Maybe I misunderstood him all these years,* he thought. *When the chips were down, he came through for me . . . he killed to protect me . . . I have to mend my fences with him . . . get along better . . . try to establish a relationship.*

Dominic slowed down and pulled off the paved road and onto the long gravel driveway leading into the junkyard. He skillfully maneuvered the car around the deep water-filled potholes and ruts in the driveway.

Arriving at the waiting security pedestal, Dominic swung the Cadillac to the left side of the road, lowered the window, and punched in his secret code number.

The large black iron gates began to swing open. Dominic, who had remained silent for most of the ride, turned and spoke to Eddie as he waited for the slow-moving gates to open.

"Well, in a few minutes, you'll know the whole story—who was shooting at you and why." He smiled knowingly at his son.

"Good, I can hardly fucking wait," said Eddie truthfully.

"I'll bet you can't, I'll bet you can't," replied his father, smiling at his son as he spoke.

Once inside the junkyard, the road narrowed and wound between the shadows of old rusty vehicles that had been stripped and abandoned along both sides of the road.

A full moon created strange—and weird-looking silhouettes of the junked vehicles piled on top of one another. They indicated a bizarre portrait of a junkman's art that was clearly etched against the moonlit sky.

Dominic drove toward the area where the huge press was located guided by the long steel crane boom positioned alongside of the press. He parked the Cadillac next to a pile of stripped-down cars that were slated to be crushed in the monster press the following day. He then reached under his seat and retrieved a long black flashlight. Handing Eddie the car keys, he opened his door and exited the car.

"OK, Eddie, you wanted answers, I'm going to give you answers. Open the trunk, and I'll tell you the whole story.

Bursting with curiosity, Eddie anxiously put the key in the lock and lifted the trunk lid. The trunk light automatically went on, illuminating the interior. Eddie gasped and reeled backward, shocked and flabbergasted at what he saw.

The trunk was empty!

Fuming in anger, he spun around, berating his father with a verbal tirade of profanity as he turned. Once he was facing his father, he stopped in midsentence instantly, dumbstruck and confused when he saw Dominic with a gun in his hand aimed directly at his chest.

Unable to comprehend his father's actions or intentions, he again verbally lashed out at Dominic. "What the fuck is this, some kind of sick joke or something? What are you doing with that fucking gun pointed at me?"

"You really don't get it, do you?" said Dominic as he switched on the flashlight and directed the powerful beam into his son's eyes.

Eddie was momentarily blinded by the light but managed to keep it from impairing his vision by holding his hand between the beam and his eyes. Once his eyes had adjusted to the glare of the light, he could see that Dominic's face was slightly illuminated by the reflection of the powerful beam off the chrome bumper of the Cadillac. Through his half-closed eyes, Eddie was amazed to see that his father's facial features had become distorted and twisted into a frightening evil mask. In spite of the fact his father was standing before him with a gun aimed directly at his heart, Eddie was in denial and could neither fathom nor accept what was taking place.

Dominic, recognizing his son's inability to comprehend the predicament that he was in again, asked the same question. "You still don't get it, do you. You're supposed to be so fucking smart, and you still haven't figured things out yet, have you?"

Eddie stared blankly into his father's face and remained silent.

"So tell me, Eddie, what is it about this gun that you don't understand? What is it about the fact I'm going to kill you that you don't understand!" snarled Dominic.

His words finally managed to break through his son's disbelief, bringing the reality of the danger of his situation crashing down on him. Eddie's hot temper flared; he became angry rather than fearful. As though a light had gone on in his head, he began to understand the bizarre series of events that had ultimately brought him to this place tonight. Only one piece of the puzzle still remained unanswered in his mind—the reason *why*.

"So it was you. I can't believe this. It was you all the fucking time shooting at me, your own son," Eddied exploded out of control, screaming forcefully at his father. "Why, just tell me why. What have I ever done to you that was so terrible that you would want me dead? What are you, a fucking animal? Is that what you are, a no-good fucking animal?"

Dominic could see that in his anger, Eddie was completely ignoring the revolver that he was holding in his hand and appeared to be preparing to lunge at him. As a precaution, he took several steps backward and brandished the gun menacingly.

"Sit the fuck down," Dominic ordered angrily, motioning to the rear bumper of the Cadillac.

Dominic's observation of Eddie's body language had been correct. Eddie had considered rushing him before he had a chance to fire, but now that Dominic had moved backward, the distance would be too great for him to cover without getting fired upon at point-blank range, which could prove to be fatal.

Without any options left, he sat down on the bumper of the car as his father had ordered. His mind racing with thoughts: *I've got to play this cool . . . engage him in conversation . . . try to make him relax . . . catch him off guard . . . maybe get a chance to jump him . . . what the hell, nothing to lose . . . going to kill me anyway . . .*

"So tell me, you still haven't told me why you want to kill me. What have I ever done to you?" asked Eddie calmly.

"Ha, me trying to kill you, whata joke—the last thing in the world I wanted was you dead, but your question tells me one thing. You still don't get it, do you? I had you in my crosshairs more times than I could count. Killing you was the last thing I wanted to do."

"Then why? What the fuck is this all about? If you didn't want me dead, why would you shoot at me just to miss? Have you gone fucking crazy or something?" asked Eddie with a tone of disbelief in his voice.

"I was shooting at you to miss, to scare the shit out of you, not to kill you, you dumb bastard. I figured that when you got worried enough about dying, you would have to come to me and turn over control of the Don's fortune. This morning, when you called me and gave me that envelope, you played right into my hands, giving me access to the money and signing your own death warrant at the same time.

"I told you in the car the shooter would never bother you again. That's because, my son, tonight you are going to die. Nobody will ever bother you again!"

Eddie ignored Dominic's sinister comment and was intent on keeping him talking, waiting for the right opportunity to make his move.

"So it's the money—it's always been about the money. But tell me something, the money was supposed to be a secret. How'd you ever find out about Don Francisco's fortune? He told me that only the two of us knew of its existence," said Eddie in a more subdued manner.

Dominic appeared to be more relaxed now that Eddie was not acting in a threatening way.

"I found out by a fluke accident, really," Dominic answered calmly. "He had been drinking rather heavily one day, which was unusual for him. I had to go to his office for some bullshit reason and found the safe open. He was in his chair sound asleep in a drunken stupor. Seeing an opportunity to find out how much cash he was hoarding, I searched the safe. That's when I found the bankbooks. It was at that moment I realized that the no-good bastard had been holding out on me big-time for all these years. He had me do all the dirty work, and the greedy cocksucker fed me crumbs while he kept all the big money for himself. I decided right then and there I wanted what was rightfully mine, so I devised a plan to frighten him, to have him worry about dying. I knew he wouldn't want to take all that money to the grave with him. He'd want to see that his family got it and to ensure that would happen. I figured he'd have to give someone close to him the books and control of the money just in case he got whacked. I was sure that after nearly forty years together, and me remaining faithful and loyal to him, knocking off anyone who got in our way, I would be his logical choice to trust with the money. I had made up my mind that once I had my hands on the money, I was going to kill the fuckin' ungrateful son of a bitch and keep it all for myself. My plan would have worked, but even then, he screwed me and gave you the money instead of me. I've racked my brain ever since—why you and not me?" said Dominic in a pensive manner.

Meanwhile, Eddie's thoughts were racing a mile a minute. *Hmm . . . he looked relaxed . . . need to keep playing along with him . . . keep him relaxed . . . the Beretta, got to get to the Beretta . . . oh my god, what's the chance one of us is going to die tonight.*

Dominic broke the silence. "So now you know the whole story. There should be no more questions left for you to ask. So tell me, Eddie, are you ready to die?"

"Have you really lost your mind? How could you even ask such a stupid fucking question, who in the fuck is ever ready to die, especially at the hands of his own father?"

Dominic laughed. "Father, hah, what a fucking joke. Do you think I'm stupid? Me your father, what a crock of bullshit. All I am to you was the farmer who planted the seed. All these years, you cared more for him than you ever did me. Killing you will be easy for me. It'll be no different for me to do than when I set him up to be killed by the dumbass Lacavoli brothers. In my world, it's just fucking business. Killing you tonight will be just fucking business."

Eddie realized he was running out of time. More thoughts began to fill his mind. *I got to stall him . . . got to think of something . . . but what . . . I don't know this crazy cocksucker holding a gun on me . . . he's like a stranger . . . yes, that's it . . . a fucking stranger . . . stall . . . stall for time . . . time is on my side, not his . . . stall . . . get him relaxed . . . maybe . . . maybe . . . I'll have the courage to try something . . . ,* he thought.

Eddie wanted to keep him talking. "So OK, killing me is just business, but if it's going to be so easy, at least finish your story. There's one more thing I want to know before I die—if you knew about the money, then it was you who plotted everything, and if that's true, then are you also Mr. X?" Eddie asked calmly.

Dominic laughed. "Ya, I'm Mr. X. Those Lacavolis were stupid. I just used them to run interference for me with the Don so I wouldn't be suspected of anything. My plan was working perfectly too. I got so close I could taste it. I almost had it all right in my hand. Then you got in the way. I knew things were falling apart for me when you and the old man had your cozy little meeting the morning of his birthday party. It was after your meeting with him that I ordered him to be killed the next day. As stupid as they were, the Lacavolis did me a favor by snuffing him out for me."

Dominic laughed. "That asshole Lacavoli was telling the truth when he told Sally about a Mr. X being in the Don's family before Sally whacked him. That's why I had to kill Cavelli myself. I couldn't take a chance that by accident someone from our family might find out that I had been having meetings with Cavelli." Dominic let out a sigh and smiled evilly at his son. "But it's all over now. I finally got my hands on the money. Thanks to you, the only thing left for me to clean up now is killing you. If it's any consolation, I'll have to leave your body where it will be found, so I can get my hands on the death certificate I need. There will be no ride to the smelter for you."

Eddie realized his time had run out. *The eyes, the eyes are the window of a man's soul. Watch the eyes*, Don Francisco's voice screamed out to him silently.

Dominic's eyelids were blinking nervously. Eddie sensed he was about to fire.

"Wait, wait, one more question," screamed out Eddie, startling Dominic. "Did you know I had a gun?" he continued to scream.

His yelling had broken Dominic's concentration for a split second; it was the opportunity Eddie had been waiting for. *Now, now*, he thought as he dove to his right, his body disappearing into the darkness. After hitting the ground, Eddie continued to roll away from Dominic's position, pulling the Beretta from its holster at the same time. Once the Beretta was firmly in his hand, he halted his evasive movements and came to rest on his stomach, his face buried deeply into a puddle of muddy water.

Dominic had been caught off guard by Eddie's quick movements. Startled by the yelling, he wildly fired four shots into the darkness in rapid succession.

Eddie lifted his face out of the water in time to see the flashes from Dominic's gunfire and immediately panicked. His vision was severely impaired by the water and mud that had filled his eyes in his dive for cover. He frantically tried to clear his vision with the back of his free hand, but to no avail. Blinking and squinting, he could barely discern Dominic's silhouette through the opaque film that covered his eyes.

Dominic, still holding the powerful flashlight in his hand, made a perfect target.

My god, if I could only see, Eddie thought. *It would be an easy shot. I'll only have time for one shot. If I miss, I'm a dead man.* He rose slightly from his prone position, trying to see his target better and get off a shot.

Dominic saw Eddie's movement and directed the beam from the light into Eddie's face, further diminishing his ability to see.

Dominic fired two more times. Eddie felt a burning sensation in his left ear as one of the bullets careened by his head. Fearing he would not have the opportunity to fire again, Eddie pulled the trigger of the Beretta three times. Another gunshot followed his own, but he was unable to see the flash from Dominic's revolver.

With the flashlight still in hand, Dominic dropped to his knees and fell facedown onto the ground, his body covering the flashlight, once again turning the scene into total darkness.

Gasping for breath and with his heart pounding wildly in his chest, Eddie slowly rose to his feet. He began coughing and gagging as nausea overcame him. The realization that he had just killed his father suddenly began to overwhelm him, and he began to vomit.

In a stunned stupor, he walked over to the Cadillac and opened the rear door. In a state of shock, he slumped into the backseat, leaving the door open. The cold night air and the wetness of his clothing caused shivers to course through his body, and he began to shake uncontrollably.

His thoughts were of himself and his plight. He felt confused and alone like some pitiful wretch who had been ostracized and abandoned by the rest of the world. The reality of killing someone, let alone his own father, had diminished his ability to act or think. Like a zombie, he lay on his side, shaking and staring into space out of unseeing eyes. His thoughts were consumed with the vision of his father's dead body lying in the mud only a scant few feet away.

Suddenly, the sound of nearby footsteps sloshing through the mud startled Eddie out of his self-pity respite. *Oh, I can't believe this. He's still alive . . . he's coming to kill me*, he thought to himself.

Panic stricken, he jumped out of the car with pistol in hand and slammed into the large body of Lorenzo LaRocca. LaRocca lifted Eddie off his feet and forcibly yanked the Beretta from his unyielding hand.

"Easy, Eddie, easy. It's OK, it's OK, you're safe now. It's all over," said LaRocca.

The sight of LaRocca's powerful presence had a calming affect on Eddie; now he was feeling protected and safe. Questions began to race through his mind once more.

"So tell me, Lorenzo, what the hell are you doing here? Did you know he was going to kill me?" Eddie asked through chattering teeth.

"Ya, I figered dat's what he was gonna do, but I couldn't figer out why," LaRocca answered, shaking his head.

"Man, I'm so fuckin' confused how'd you know?" chattered Eddie.

"Well, dis mornin' he comes out to farm and spends da day in de old man's office goin' over boxes of stuff. I don't pay too much attention to 'em, and den I see him leave around dark. He comes back later an' musta snuck in 'causes I don't hear or see him. Around eleven o'clock, I'm in my room laying on de bed readin' when da light on de phone goes on, wonderin' who da hell is in da buildin', real easy like I pick up da phone to listin. I recognize your ol' man's voice tellin' you da cock-n-bull story dat he waxed da guy dat was shootin' at ya. I knew he was lyin' cause LaRocca would have heard somethin' if dat had happened, and besides, he was out at da farm all day. How could he get da shooter when he spent da whole day and half da night in de ol' man's office? Well, anyway, I knew right away he was up to no fuckin' good when I heard him tellin' ya dat big bullshit story. I figured you were in some kinda trouble, so I kept listenin'. Near de end of his story, ya remember he told ya not to tell anyone specially your wife? Dat's when I knew for sure he was gonna kill ya. He didn't want anyone to finger him as bein' da last one to see ya alive. Knowing you were a dead man, if he got ya alone somewhere. I followed him, but I was still screwed up about somethin'. Why in de hell did he wanna kill ya?

"I don't know, Lorenzo," Eddie lied. "But please finish your story. If you followed him, what took you so long to get here?"

"Well, after he picked ya up and headed out dis way, I dropped way back, knowin' der was nutin out here but da junkyard. Dat made me doubly sure he was gonna whack you tonight. But of all da rotten fuckin' luck, I got stuck by some train dat passes by once a fuckin' year. To tell ya da trute, I figered dat when I got here, I was gonna find ya dead.

"Well, if he had his way, I would have been dead," Eddie said through chattering teeth. "Thank God I managed to get off a couple of shots before he finished me off. But to tell you the truth, I don't know if I'll ever get over killing someone, let alone my own father," said Eddie in a dejected manner.

"Well den, I've got some real good news for ya. You didn't kill your ol' man. LaRocca did. Didn't ya notice he fell forward on his face when he went down? Dat was because of da slug I planted in da back of his head."

Eddie tried to respond but remained speechless.

"Well, anyway, dat's dat. It's all over now. Only he knew why he kept trying to kill ya, and he ain't gonna be talkin' to anyone anymore. Look, Eddie, da keys are in my car. I'll stay and take care of tings here.

You go home and just forget what happened tonight. If he'd of killed you, I da killed him anyway. So you see, when your old man got outta bed dis mornin', he was doomed to die."

Eddie was choked with emotion; he fondly gave the big man a hug and slowly walked in silence toward LaRocca's car.

Chapter 27

E ddie D'Amico was rinsing his coffee cup at the kitchen sink when the telephone rang. He glanced up at the wall clock. It read six thirty. *I wonder who can be calling this early?* he thought as he picked up the telephone.

"Hello."

"Mornin'."

Eddie recognized the raspy voice of Lorenzo LaRocca.

"Oh, hi, Lorenzo, what's up?"

It was their first contact since the fateful night at the junkyard when Dominic D'Amico was killed.

"So tell me, sometin' Eddie, ya gonna keep my car forever, or ya gonna give it back someday? You've had it over a *week now*!"

"Well, to tell you the truth, Lorenzo, I have been seriously considering giving it back to you," joked Eddie.

"Good, dat's good. I'm glad to hear dat. Where is it now?"

"In the parking lot behind the hotel," answered Eddie.

"Ya goin' to da market today?"

"Yes, as a matter of fact, I was just walking out the door."

"Den why don't ya bring it here and pick me up. I'll go to da market wit ya. When you're ready, I'll drop ya off home," said Lorenzo.

"Sounds like a plan to me. I'm on my way."

"OK den, I'll see ya soon," answered Lorenzo as he hung up the phone.

When Eddie arrived at the Barratino farm, Lorenzo was at the front gate waiting.

Eddie pulled in the driveway and circled the big Lincoln around so that it was facing the road. He remained behind the wheel as Lorenzo walked toward the car. The big man walked over to the driver's side and pulled open the door.

"Shove over, I'm drivin'," he ordered. Silently, Eddie slid over to the passenger side of the vehicle. Lorenzo guided the car out of the driveway, heading south in the direction of the market. Eddie broke the silence.

"Lorenzo, I can't tell you how grateful I am for what you did for me the other night. You saved my life."

"Ah, forget it. I told ya in da hospital dat day, if ya ever needed me, I'd be der. Now let's drop it. What done is done," the big man answered.

"OK, then, just a couple of questions. What did you do with Dominic's car?"

"Dumped it ina real deep lake ina abandon gravel pit," answered Lorenzo matter-of-factly.

"Do you think they'll ever find it?" Eddie asked.

"Probly not, but I wiped it clean, if dat's what ya worrin' about."

Eddie grew silent.

Oh my god, what an idiot I am. I should have been worried sick over the fact my fingerprints were all over Dominic's car, he thought to himself. He chalked up one more debt of gratitude that he owed Lorenzo. Thoughts of Dominic's car made him relive the terrible chain of events that transpired the night his father died in the junkyard. He was deep in thought when Lorenzo broke the long silence.

"Did ya hear da news dat yesterday dem crazy fuckin' mercenary whacked Vito Cavelli?"

"What, no shit. No, I haven't heard a word. How'd they do it?" asked Eddie with a surprised tone in his voice.

"For dem nuts, it was easy, real fuckin' easy. Dey waited outside his house, and when his limo picked him up in da mornin', dey blew up da fuckin' car wid some kind of tank-destroying missile, and addios, Vito Cavelli and his two body guards," finished Lorenzo.

"Man, oh fucking man, Sally may just pulled his ass out of the fire after all. I must confess, I really didn't think he was smart enough to pull it off," said Eddie, a look of amazement on his face.

"Now all that stands in his way from having it all is Jack Shepard," said Eddie.

"Ya, well, dat's been all taken care of too. Dey called truce a week ago—no more shootin' for tirty days. Now we'll just half ta wait to see what happens wid da moolanjans," said Lorenzo.

Eddie sat silently as Lorenzo circled around the market looking for a parking space. Finding one, he skillfully maneuvered the big Lincoln into the tight space.

"Man, whata fuckin' zoo dis place is today," commented the big man as they walked toward Jimmy's Restaurant.

"Ya, it's like this every week, but we got here kinda late," answered Eddie as he looked down at his watch. Entering the restaurant, Eddie glanced around the room and saw there were no empty tables.

"Looks ta me like we're fucked. Ders no place ta sit," said LaRocca.

Before Eddie could answer, a voice called out from across the room.

"Eddie, Eddie, over here," said Chicky Blandino, who was standing on a chair in the back of the restaurant waving his arms.

Eddie acknowledged Chicky by waving back. Turning, he began walking across the sawdust-covered floor toward his friends' table, the huge-framed Lorenzo LaRocca following close behind him.

As he neared the table, Eddie could hear the sound of loud, boisterous laughter coming from a corner area of the room off to his right. Curious, he looked toward the sounds and saw that a large number of black men were crowded around several tables enjoying themselves and having a great time. Eddie recognized the figure of One-Eyed Jack Shepard wearing his trademark black eye patch.

Arriving at the table, Eddie greeted each man at the table individually. They were Chicky Blandino, Nicky the Greek, Judge Carlivatti, Councilman Elwood Doyle, Joey Cariola, Bee Stinger, and the judge's driver, Sam Zerilli.

"What a motley-looking crew this is. Who called this meeting together?" quipped Eddie as he motioned to Lorenzo to take the lone unoccupied chair. "Go ahead, sit down, Lorenzo. I'll go find another chair," said Eddie, walking away from the table.

"Hey, Lorenzo, you're going to ruin your reputation hanging around with that guy," joked the Greek.

"Ya, I know, but whataya gonna do, he's gotta have one friend," the big man joked back.

Eddie returned carrying a chair.

"OK, move your fat asses over," said Eddie to Sam Zerilli.

After Eddie was seated, Lorenzo rose to his feet. "I'm starvin'," he exclaimed. "Whataya want, Eddie? I'm buyin'."

"I don't care, surprise me," Eddie replied.

"Bring him a dish of pasta. You'll be safe with that. D'Amico's a pastaholic," joked Sam Zerilli. Councilman Doyle began telling jokes, and everyone's attention at the table turned toward him.

Bee Stinger, who was sitting next to Eddie, leaned over to whisper in his ear.

"Did you hear that Sally got Cavelli yesterday?"

"Do they have proof it was Sally?"

"Of course not, but who else could it be? He'd better have a good alibi. I'm sure he'll be brought in for questioning."

"It's no skin off my ass. I hope he rots in hell."

"Hey, you guys, pipe down. I want to tell you a funny story," said Chicky, tapping a glass with his fork.

"Maybe Eddie's heard the story already, and that's why he has LaRocca with him as a bodyguard today," said Chicky, blowing a large cloud of smoke into the air and laughing.

"I don't have any idea what the fuck you're talking about, but please continue on. I know our friends can hardly wait to hear one of your lame bullshit stories," joked Eddie.

"Don't listen to D'Amico. This is not a bullshit story, it's all true, so help me, God," said Chicky, making a sign of the cross over his heart and raising his right hand in the air.

"Well, anyways, I know you guys all know Don Reilly, the builder—you know, the one that used to be a good friend of D'Amico's. You all noticed I said 'used to be,'" laughed Chicky.

"Tell me why you said 'used to be,'" Eddie joked back.

"I'll tell you why . . . *laughter* . . . because . . . *laughter* . . . because you're in big trouble with him," said Chicky, who was now laughing so hard in anticipation of his story he began to cough and choke. Chicky was laughing uncontrollably; his laughter became contagious, and soon the others at the table were laughing along with Chicky, without knowing what they were laughing over.

Finally, Chicky composed himself, wiped the tears from his eyes, and was about to begin his story again when LaRocca returned carrying a large serving tray.

Chicky looked over at LaRocca and, pointing his finger at the tray in the big man's hands, started laughing uncontrollably again.

"Look, look," he cried out, continuing to point at the tray.

When the others saw the source of Chicky's laughter, everyone around the table once again began to laugh along with the silly Chicky.

In the middle of the tray, in all of its' magnificent splendor, stood a monstrous dish piled high with spaghetti and crowned with four large meatballs. With a deadpanned face, LaRocca carefully placed the huge dish of pasta in front of Eddie, handed him a fork and spoon, and began shaking cheese over the spaghetti.

Eddie stopped laughing long enough to spear a meatball with his fork and jam the whole meatball into his mouth.

Slowly the laughter subsided, and the judge looked over at Chicky and spoke. "C'mon, Chicky, are you ever going to get to your damn story? We haven't got all day, you know," said the judge with a broad smile on his face.

"OK, OK, I'm trying, I'm trying," said Chicky, blowing a cloud of smoke across the table from his newly lit cigarette.

He began his story again, looking at Eddie as he spoke.

"Eddie, do you remember that stripper you fixed Don Reilly up with a while back?" Chicky asked.

"Sure I do. Her name's Peaches. Her stage name was Peaches and Cream. Don's been fucking around with her for months, so what's the big deal?" answered Eddie.

"Well, you might not think it's a big deal, but his wife certainly does," answered Chicky, smiling and chuckling to himself.

"Well, anyway, Don's spendin' a lotta time with this broad and coming home in the wee hours of the morning. Then he starts making mysterious business trips out of town. His wife's no fuckin' dummy and begins accusing him of fucking around on her. Well, Don's got no real money of his own. The big money all belongs to his wife from an inheritance," continued Chicky. "So she threatens to throw him out on his ass if he don't straighten out. Don knows if that happens, he'll be dead broke and a bum. Now he ain't gonna let that happen. She's got him scared to death, so he dumps this Peaches broad."

Chicky now had everyone's attention. He took a hit from his cigarette and continued.

"Well, the crazy bitch isn't about to go away that easy, so she starts harassing him by calling the house at all hours of the night and hanging up." Chicky, enjoying his story, was smiling broadly and giggling as he continued. "Don's going nuts and doesn't know what to do. His wife tells him if the calls don't stop, he's gone. Suddenly the calls do stop for a couple of weeks, and Don begins to breathe easy again." Chicky was now laughing as he spoke.

"Now the story really gets good," he laughed. "A couple of nights ago, Don's worst nightmare happened, the ditzy bitch pulls into Don's driveway about three in the morning, blowing her horn and gunning her motor. Don gets up and goes to the window and sees her yellow

Eldorado convertible and almost has a heart attack. He turns on the porch light, goes outside, and then sees she got the top down and is sitting behind the wheel bare-ass naked ..." Chicky paused for effect. The men around the table began to chuckle.

Chicky blew a cloud of smoke high into the air and continued.

"Well, Don motions her to leave. She motions him to get off the porch and come to the car. Meanwhile, she keeps blowing her horn. Finally, she backs out of the driveway, and Don breathes a sigh of relief, but suddenly, he realizes something's wrong. The crazy bitch is backing clear up the street. Don's house is on a curve at the end of a street. The dipshit broad keeps backing up to the end of the street that faces his house. Then she floors the car and, with her horn blowing, heads towards his house balls out. Don panics. He realizes she's gonna try to run him over, so he jumps off the porch and begins running for his life to hide behind the garage." Chicky was now laughing so hard at his story he could barely speak and paused to catch his breath; everyone around the table were shaking their heads and chuckling.

"Come on, man, get to the fuckin' end. I can hardly wait to see what da ditzy broad does," said LaRocca laughingly.

"Well, anyway, here she comes, pedal to the metal. She sees Don disappeared, so she makes a slight course correction, comes barreling through the hedges, and smash into the bay window, where a baby grand piano is sitting. Motor roaring, she knocks the piano across the room and drives that fucking Eldorado so far into the house the only thing stickin' outside the house is the trunk."

A roar of laughter crossed the table, which caused Chicky to pause a moment.

"Wait, wait, there's fucking more," said Chicky, holding up his hand as he wiped tears of laughter from his eyes. Slowly the laughter subsided, and he continued on with the end of his story.

"Well, by this time, Don knows he's a dead fucking duck and goes running back into the house. Just as he reaches the living room, the floor joist suddenly gives away, and Don, the Eldorado, the piano, and most of the first floor winds up in the basement. By the time help arrives, his wife is gone, but she leaves him a note taped to the bathroom mirror. The note says, *To Mr. Bum, I call you that because that's what you're going to be when my lawyer gets done with you. See you in court, Asshole."*

LaRocca was laughing raucously. "Some broad, what balls. I wonder what family she's wit?" he exclaimed.

Eddie, trying to catch his breath, attempted to speak.

"So tell me, Chicky, what the fuck has all this got to do with me?" he asked, still chuckling.

"Oh, ya, I forgot to tell ya," Chicky began, breaking out into laughter again. "Reilly's blaming you for everything, and he says it's all your fault because you introduced him to the crazy bitch. He's telling everyone he's going to shoot ya on sight," said Chicky, bursting into laughter again.

Eddie and Lorenzo immediately sobered up; neither of them saw any humor in Chicky's last remark.

A hand on his shoulder startled Eddie, causing him to jump out of his chair.

"Hey, easy man, easy," Jack Shepard said, smiling at his friend's reaction.

"Ya, it's easy for you to say," answered Eddie. "What's up?"

"Can I see you outside for a minute?" the big man asked.

Eddie nodded, and the two men headed toward the door.

"So what is it with all of you guys?" asked Eddie, gesturing toward the group of black men milling around in front of the restaurant waiting for Jack Shepard.

"Nothing, nothing at all. We're just going out to East Park and have a little fun." Jack saw the puzzled look on his friend's face and continued.

"These guys play on a slow-pitch ball team I sponsor, that's all. Now thanks to your suggestion, we have a truce with Sally, so we're going to have a little practice, barbecue some steaks, and drink a little beer."

"Sound like fun," answered Eddie.

"Hey man, why don't you come with us. As I remember, you were a pretty good ballplayer in your day."

"I'd like to, but I'll take a rain check," Eddie answered, shaking his head. "I have some business to take care of," he lied.

"Well, I got to get going. I just wanted to thank you for your heads-up about Sally's mercenaries and the suggestion regarding the truce. Matter of fact, I'm meeting with Sally in a few days to discuss the details for a permanent truce, but he's going to be in for a real surprise."

Jack's last statement piqued Eddie's curiosity.

"Surprise, what kind of surprise?"

"I'm hang' it up, Eddie. I'm done. I've got all the money I need. I'm tired of all the bullshit and danger that goes with this business. Sally can have it all. I'm going to retire," said Jack.

"Hey man, that's great news, Jack. I think you're doing the right thing."

"Ya, me too. Well, I gotta get going. Thanks again, brother. Let's get together real soon for a few toddies!"

"I'd like that. I'll call you," said Eddie.

The two men shook hands. Eddie stood motionless for a moment and watched as Jack Shepard turned and walked toward his waiting men.

Arriving at East Park, Jack Shepard turned into a gravel driveway. The four vehicles behind him followed.

Jack guided the white van toward a large pavilion situated near a ball field. He brought the van to a halt next to a grouping of tables located inside the pavilion. With the zeal and enthusiasm of much younger men, the member of Jack Shepard's black Mafia donned their baseball shoes and headed for the ballfield.

Jack, with the assistance of two teenage helpers began unloading the van and carrying the food to one of the nearby tables. Letting his two helpers continue the unloading, he walked to the edge of the pavilion and watched the activity on the field with a broad smile on his face.

I'm glad to see them having so much fun, he thought. *The war with Sally had made the past few months a living hell for everyone. Yep, I'm doing the right thing. Sally can have it all. I'm done.*

Jack turned to go back and assist with the unloading when his eyes caught a movement at the edge of the woods behind the left field. He paused to stare toward the movement and then blinked his eyes, not believing what he was seeing. Seven men dressed in camouflage clothing and carrying automatic weapons were coming toward his men on a dead run.

"Run! Run for your lives!" Jack screamed out to his unsuspecting men. "We've been double-crossed by that fucking Sally. *Run! Run!"* he yelled out again as he ran toward his van for a weapon. Before he could reach the van, the staccato sound of the automatic weapons firing filled the air.

He turned his head as he ran and saw some of his men drop on their tracks as they were shot in the back while they attempted to flee to safety. Jack dove into the van and emerged carrying a machine gun in each hand. He ran back toward the ballfield firing, the weapon as he ran.

He found cover behind a heavy steel support beam and continued to fire back at the mercenaries. Two of the mercenaries fell dead from the barrage of Jack's bullets. Seeing their comrades' fall, the other mercenaries dropped to the ground and concentrated their fire toward Jack.

Jack's gunfire had allowed some of his men to escape while the assassins became preoccupied with silencing the gunfire coming from the man behind the steel post.

The weapons in Jack's hands were empty. He threw them to the ground and stepped out from behind his cover.

With his hands at his sides he walked toward the ballfield shaking his head in despair at the carnage before him. The mercenaries slowly rose to their feet and started walking toward him, the muzzles of their guns pointed at his chest. The groans of men in pain floated across the ballfield, breaking the silence.

Duke Donnelly was now standing in front of Jack, noting the eye patch. "Jack Shepard, I presume?" he said.

Jack ignored his antagonist's question and continued to gaze at the results of the massacre. Dead men were everywhere; others were groaning and writhing in pain. Tears began to stream down Jack's face from his one good eye.

"So you call yourself a soldier. You're nothing more than a degenerate motherfucker who guns down unarmed men in the fucking back. You are the worst motherfucking scum of the earth I have ever run across in my life," screamed Jack, shaking his fist in anger at Duke Donnelly as he spoke.

"Go ahead, you bastard, finish your job," Jack yelled out, spitting in Duke Donnelly's face.

Duke lashed out with his free hand and slapped Jack Shepard across the face.

"No, Jack, I'm going to let you live. My assignment was to put you out of business," stated Duke calmly as he wiped the spit from his face. "But if you start up again, the next time you won't be so lucky."

Duke Donnelly, without waiting for a reply, turned and began to walk away. He paused, and turning to Jack, he said, "Oh, by the way, the reason I didn't kill you today is because of your friendship with Eddie D'Amico." Signaling to his men, he spoke, "OK, c'mon, let's get out of here. Pick them up," he ordered, motioning to the two fallen mercenaries.

As he watched the departing assassins, Jack Shepard fell on his knees on the grass.

Oh my god, oh my god, all this death for nothing. In a couple of days, Sally was going to have it all anyway, he thought.

Jack Shepard placed his head in his hands and began to weep violently.

Chapter 28

The mercenaries loaded the bodies of their fallen comrades into the back of a vintage black van as Duke jumped in behind the wheel.

"C'mon, hurry up and get in," he barked. "The cops will be here any minute."

The men immediately obeyed his orders, running behind the already-moving vehicle and diving headfirst through the open doors. Duke headed toward their hideout, taking special care not to exceed the speed limit. Everyone remained silent on the long ride back to the hideout, each man deep in their own thoughts.

The more he relived the incident in the park, the worse Duke Donnelly felt. *I've never done anything like this before*, he thought. *Jack Shepard was right. I deserved everything he called me . . . why did I let Sally talk me into it . . . Ah fuck, what's done is done.* Duke pulled off the pavement onto a dirt road running between two fields that were overgrown with weeds.

They bumped along, swerving from side to side as Duke skillfully attempted to maneuver around the deep potholes that lay in their path. Without warning, the road abruptly ended in front of an old dilapidated barn. Duke brought the van to a halt and began barking orders before his feet hit the ground.

"Bury them, Make sure they're deep. Get everything loaded up, and when you're ready to leave, torch this place. Any questions?"

"No, sir!" said one of the men as he saluted smartly.

"OK, good. I'm going to change clothes and go get the rest of our money from that little prick Sally. I'll catch up with you tonight at Checkpoint Charlie." The men saluted and trotted away to carry out Duke's orders.

The sun was high in the sky as Duke pulled alongside the silver pedestal and entered the code Sally had provided him. Entering the compound, he followed the winding dirt road and stopped in front of a concrete block building that housed Sally's office.

Pausing at the heavy metal door, he pressed the large button located alongside the door. In a moment, he could hear an electronic buzzing sound that indicated the automatic door locks were being released.

"Push, Duke. It's open now," said a voice coming from a hidden speaker. He knew the owner of the voice was able to see him by means of a concealed camera. Duke entered the room and realized the voice belonged to Sally's cousin Vinnie Barratino, who was now standing in front of him.

"Hi, Duke, how'd things go this morning. Did ya get it done?"

"I'm a professional, Vinnie. I always get the job done," Duke replied in an arrogant tone.

"Great, Duke, great. I'm sure Sally will be happy to hear the good news," Vinnie responded, a broad smile on his face. "Sally's in his office with Cappy and Billy B."

Duke nodded and walked to the door of Sally's office. He paused a moment and knocked. Without waiting, he pushed open the door and entered the room.

He was surprised to find the room surprisingly bright basked in sunlight from a large window behind Sally's desk. Off to his left, Billy B and Cappy were sitting at a small table playing cards. Two chairs stood empty in front of Sally's large metal desk.

Duke's trained survival instincts immediately began flashing warning signals to his brain. *If you sit in one of the empty chairs, you will not be able to watch the men behind you. Be careful, Duke. Be very careful.* Duke walked across the room toward Sally's desk, nodding an acknowledgment to the two men as he passed. He sat in one of the chairs, and his instincts were telling him he had walked into a trap.

Sally was the first to break the frigid silence.

"Well, Duke, did you take care of business? Did you get the job done?"

"Of course, I got it done," Duke snapped. "I always finish what I start."

"Good, good, that's great," said Sally, leaning back in his chair and smiling from ear to ear.

"So tell me, Duke, how many of those black bastards did you get?"

"What the fuck do I know, Sally, I didn't wait around to count," Duke answered, obviously irritated by Sally's question. As he spoke, he casually placed his hand in his right jacket pocket.

"What about Shepard, did you whack him?"

"No, he arrived with the rest of them, but he must've left," Duke lied. "But what the fuck is this anyway, twenty questions? Read the evening paper. You'll get all the facts you want. Now just give me the rest of my fucking money, and I'm out of here," barked Duke angrily.

"Sure, sure, Duke. I got it all right here for you," said Sally as he slid open a drawer on the right side of his desk.

Smiling at Duke, he slowly reached into the drawer. When he withdrew his hand, he was holding a chrome-plated revolver, which he pointed at Duke's chest.

"Surprise," Sally grinned. "You didn't really think I would pay you the kind of money you were asking for this caper, did you?"

Through stone-cold eyes, Duke looked squarely into Sally's face, seeming to be completely oblivious of the weapon menacingly pointed at him.

"Surprise, you say. No, nothing you do would surprise me, Sally. All I had to do is think of the lowest and most despicable fucking person on earth, and it fits your profile to a tee. I was expecting something like this from you. Anyone who would break a truce and order unarmed men to be killed has to be the worst kind of degenerate motherfucker in the world."

Duke's tirade was angering Sally. "Shut your fucking mouth, do you hear me?" Sally growled.

Duke ignored Sally's outburst. "I hate myself for allowing you to talk me into this fucking deal. If I had any sense at all, I should have killed you and rid the world of the scum that you are."

Sally had heard enough. In a boiling rage, he jumped to his feet.

"So, you fucking asshole, if you expected this, how stupid can you fucking be coming in asking for your money?"

"Well, Sally, that's a good question," Duke drawled. "You see, I brought a surprise to the party too." He removed his right hand from his jacket pocket and held it high in the air.

Sally was dumbstruck when he saw Duke was holding a grenade in his hand. Duke rose slowly to his feet.

"Who's the asshole now, Sally? I realized if you double-crossed Shepard, you would be double-crossing me too, so I brought you this little present. As a matter of fact, I even unwrapped it for you. You'll notice the pin is out." Duke was speaking in slow, measured tones with a smile on his face.

"Fuck you, Duke. You ain't scaring me none. You're still going to die," roared Sally.

"Oh, really. In that case, you and your boys are going to go with me, then. When this baby's released, it goes *BOOM*, and we all go together. Are you ready to die, Sally?" Duke said calmly, a smile on his face.

Duke turned to look at the men behind him. They were standing. Two more guns were now pointed at him.

"Fuck you, Duke. Shoot 'im, shoot 'im. Shoot the no-good cocksucker!" yelled Sally to his men.

"Fuck you, Sally, are you crazy or something? If he drops that grenade, none of us are going to get out of here fuckin' alive," cried out Billy B, fear emanating from his voice.

"Come on, Sally, he's right. Just fork over my money. I'll leave quietly and be out of your life forever." Duke was smiling; he could see from Sally's demeanor he was weakening.

"Go-wan Sally, do like he says. Give him his fucking money. Have you gone mad?" Cappy chimed in.

Sally was about to relent when his cunning mind conjured up an idea to beat Duke Donnelly and have it all.

Hmm . . . somewhere I read that grenades have a few seconds of delay before they explode, he thought to himself. *That's all I need, just a couple of seconds . . . Hmm . . . Cappy and Billy will die, but fuck them, that's their problem, not mine.*

Sally had made his plan; now it was time for implementation. Without warning, he jumped into action.

"Fuck you, Duke!" he screamed out, firing three shots in quick succession into Duke's chest. Duke reeled backward from the force of the big-caliber bullets.

Realizing he was a dead man with blood spewing from his mouth, he gasped his last words, "I'll see you in hell!" He dropped the grenade from his hand.

The instant Sally fired his last shot, he dove headfirst through the window behind him.

At the sound of Sally's first shot, Cappy and Billy made a mad dash for the door. But they were too late—a powerful explosion engulfed the room.

Sally was lying stunned outside on the ground under a blanket of debris and shattered glass. He lay motionless. Then slowly he began to move. With a great deal of effort, he rolled over on his back and painfully rose to a sitting position. Dust covered his face, and he was bleeding profusely from facial and hand cuts.

Sally smiled, revealing the blood that had covered his teeth. His eyes gazed at the damage his evil deed had caused.

"Fuck you, Duke Donnelly, I win!" he uttered throwing his head back and laughing maniacally.

Chapter 29

E ddie slammed the newspaper down on the table. "I can't fuckin' believe this. Two weeks since Sally murdered those guys in the park, and they aren't even looking in his fuckin' direction."

"Ya, I read da paper. Dey tink it's dose Nazi skinheads did it," answered Lorenzo.

"What a fuckin' joke," Eddie said disgustedly. He knows he must not say anything to Lorenzo about his plan to talk to Bee Stinger. He decided to change the subject.

"So tell me, Lorenzo, I can't wait to hear about this big fucking argument you had with Sally."

"Ain't nutin to tell. After he waxed does two guys, I tol him to stick his family and his job up his ass," the big man finished proudly.

"So what are you goin' to do now? It's not like you're a brain surgeon or somethin'," Eddie joked.

His friend was asking a question he had been asking himself many times over. All he knew how to do was break bones and kill people.

"Shit, Eddie, I don't know. Maybe I just go fishin' da rest of my life."

"Ya got the money to retire and do that?"

"Fuck no, but I'll figer out sometin'."

Eddie's questions were making him nervous. Talking about things he wasn't ready to deal with. Lorenzo rose from his chair and walked over to the coffeepot to fill his empty cup.

"Are we done playin' twenty questions? How about tellin' me why ya asked me ta come over," the big man said tersely.

Eddie was smiling; he could hardly wait to see Lorenzo's reactions when he saw what he had in store for him.

"C'mon, I've got some things I want to show you."

Eddie rose from his chair, Lorenzo at his heels. They walked through the parlor into the room Megan had made into a nursery. Lorenzo stopped and gazed around the room.

"Ya asked me over ta show me da baby's room?" he questioned, a puzzled look on his face.

"Not exactly," Eddie half laughed, flinging open the French doors and stepping out onto the balcony.

"Take a look," he invited, pointing to the five-story building across the street.

Emblazoned on the building, a new sign sang out proudly, "Barratino Children's Home."

"*Holy shit,* when did ya do dis?" Lorenzo exclaimed, awestruck.

"I've been working on it for months. It was an athletic club. It's got everything—a gym, running track, pool, it's even got a workout room. And best of all, the top four stories are rooms that will be great for the kids' living quarters."

"Well, it looks like ya made Carmella's drems com tru," Lorenzo said, patting Eddie on his back as he spoke.

"Wait till you see the top floor. I made it into a penthouse suite for Carmella and Nicoletta."

"Nicoletta, she's here too?

"Ya, she wanted to stay at the farm until Carm took her to the small French church right next door to the home. The church was built like a replica of Notre Dame, and Nicoletta fell in love with it, so she agreed to move in with Carm."

"Dat's really great. I da like to see da place sometime."

"You will. Nicoletta made gnocchi for us when she heard you were coming over."

"Man, dat 'ill be a treat. Nobude can beat her cookin'. What time we eatin'?"

"I don't know. They'll call us when it's time," Eddie answered, "but, we've got some things to do. I'm going to show you some stuff that's going to knock your jock off."

"What if I don't got no jock on, den what are you gonna knock off?" Lorenzo joked.

"Shit, I don't know, maybe your dick," Eddie replied laughingly.

Ever since Eddie had called him, Lorenzo was curious as to what Eddie was going to show him. He couldn't wait to see and hear what his friend had in his mind. Knowing Eddie, he could only imagine it would be something good.

Eddie walked to the far end of the apartment, paused in front of a seldom-used closet, and opened the door. Lorenzo was puzzled as he peered into the darkness over Eddie's shoulder. He watched as Eddie opened a newly installed door and stepped into the adjoining apartment. The big man followed. Eddie stepped aside, allowing him to pass. Lorenzo's eyes explored every corner of the room, the puzzled look remaining on his face.

"Well, what do you think?"

"What am I supposed ta tink? It's terrific!" Lorenzo answered, wondering why Eddie had taken him there.

"It's yours," Eddie said happily.

Silence. Finally, Lorenzo spoke.

"Ya gone nuts or sometin'? I can't afford a place like dis."

"Well, maybe not, but I can," Eddie laughed. "C'mon, let me show ya around."

Lorenzo was in a state of shock. He couldn't believe it was really happening. He obediently followed Eddie as he gave him a tour of the apartment.

"I set it up with the things you enjoy," Eddie voiced proudly. "Big screen TV for your sports interest, a steam unit in the bathroom, and this." He opened the door to a small fully equipped workout room. "C'mon, one more thing." He led Lorenzo to a large bedroom sporting a king-size bed. Overwhelmed, Lorenzo stopped at the entry door, trying to digest what was happening. He gazed into the room, frozen in his tracks.

"Hey, come over here and look at this." Eddie was standing in front of a mirrored closet nearly the length of the room.

Lorenzo walked over.

"Slid 'em," Eddie ordered.

Lorenzo slid the doors one at a time. His jaw dropped, and he began shaking his head from side to side.

"Naw, Eddie, no fuckin' way!" he exclaimed, his eyes fixed on the clothes neatly hanging on poles, the entire length of the closet. It was all there—sports jackets, trousers, topcoats and hats, and rows of neatly lined shoes.

Eddie's eyes remained fixed on the big man, taking great pleasure in his friend's amazement.

"Look, Eddie, I know ya mean well, but I can't tak dis stuff. I didn't do anyting to deserve dis."

"You got to be kidding me. You didn't do anything to deserve this, you say. Well, let me remind you, my friend, of a night not long ago in a cold, wet junkyard, I was a walking dead man. But for you, I wouldn't be here right now. I'd be six feet under."

Lorenzo understood the veracities of his friend's comments. Eddie was right—he would have been killed that night, and by his father, to boot.

"Look, Lorenzo, there's no discussion. This is a done deal, *capisce*?"

Eddie did not share all of the reasons of his overwhelming generosity. Had he and his father both died that night, there would be no one living with knowledge of the Don's great fortune. It would more than likely languish for decades entombed in the great vaults of that Swiss bank. *My god*, Eddie thought, *it had come so close to becoming a reality.*

Lorenzo was standing silently admiring the clothes. *Mangia, dat Eddie's got good taste*, he thought, deciding that if his friend was happy doing it, who the heck was he to argue?

"C'mon, big guy, follow me. We gotta take a walk. There's one more thing."

Eddie entered the hall from Lorenzo's apartment. They walked down to the elevator and out the back door and into the parking lot. Lorenzo was tagging behind his briskly walking friend. Eddie stopped quickly in front of a brand-new white Cadillac Fleetwood. Smiling, he asked, "Well do you like it?"

"Ya gotta be kiden, what's not ta like?"

Eddie realized he had just blown away Lorenzo. "Don't worry, my friend, the money I've spent on you for all this is chump change compared to what would've been lost if you hadn't saved my life. It's yours," he stated proudly as he slapped the keys into the big man's hand.

"Naw, no fuckin' way. Dis is way too much. I can't do dis."

"Oh yes, you can. You see, there are some strings attached. I want you to work for me. I'll pay you double what you've been making."

"Hey man, you're speedin', slow down here. How can I work for ya? I don't know nutin about construction."

Eddie laughed heartily at his friend's remark. *Of course, what else would he think*, he thought.

"No, no, nothing like that. I want you to take care of Carmella and Megan, drive them around once in a while—"

"Hol' dit, hol' dit, dat sounds lika cho-fer ta me, and Lorenzo LaRocca ain't gonna be no cho-fer for anyone."

"Hey, hang on a minute," said Eddie, smiling. "They both have cars. They won't need you all the time. See, I got you this pager." He held it in his hand. If they need you once in a while, they'll just page you. In the meantime, you hang out, play your horses, and do what the fuck you want, and still get paid."

Lorenzo realized it was a once-in-a-lifetime opportunity. His friend was making him an offer he couldn't refuse. Lorenzo was emotionally moved. He embraced Eddie fondly. Then opened the car door and started to enter.

"Hey, hold it, where the fuck you going?"

"To da farm and get my stuff."

"We gotta go across the street and eat yet," said Eddie, laughing.

"Oh ya, I forgot, let's go, den," said the big man sheepishly, putting his arm around Eddie's shoulder and walking by his side.

"Der just one ting, Eddie—no fuckin' monkey suits."

Eddie was in a good mood. Laughingly, he replied, "OK, no fuckin' monkey suits," he mimicked. Both men were enjoying the moment. They continued laughing as they walked across the street and into the home.

*   *   *

Four months had passed since the opening of the Barratino Children's Home.

Sally was riding high on the crest of his victory. In his mind, he was invincible. He had attained his dream of controlling all the organized crime activities in the city. Since the massacre in the park, he had immediately moved in and taken over control of Jack Shepard's territories.

With the annexation of the new areas and his newfound involvement in drug trafficking, money was rolling into the family coffers in huge amounts. But his newfound success was causing logistic problems for Sally. More men were required to oversee his burgeoning empire. After his dastardly deed in the park, other mobsters, like Lorenzo, had seen fit to leave the family, believing Sally had crossed the line of honor. This exodus of muscle left Sally with only a small number of greedy loyalists to manage his quickly growing holdings. Desperate, he began recruiting mobsters from families around the country, offering large sums of cash to those who would join his gang. Though Sally was an egotistical sycophant, he recognized he needed someone to replace the missing Dominic D'Amico as consigliere.

The man of his choice was Guido Luciano, a relative of the infamous Lucky Luciano clan from New York City. Guido was smart, ambitious, and greedy. He had no qualms about killing people on command; it made him, in Sally's mind, a perfect choice to fill Dominic's shoes.

* * *

Carmella was ecstatically living her dream. The home boasted over one hundred permanent residents and was growing daily.

Megan and Carmella had grown closer than ever, bound together by their love of children. She also assisted Carmella in tutoring and counseling the children in need of special attention. In Megan's mind, her life was perfect. She was happily looking forward to the arrival of her baby, which was due in two days.

Even Nicoletta was doing well, happy with her new life away from the farm. She kept herself busy cooking and making daily visits to the nearby church bringing food and pastries for the priest and nuns to enjoy.

She had appointed herself the matriarch and proclaimed Sunday as their day of unity. Nicoletta insisted they all attend the eleven o'clock service together. Eddie, not wanting to be the only male, would drag along the reluctant Lorenzo, who would grumble and complain but relent, knowing full well his reward would be a wonderful feast after the service in Carmella's penthouse.

Eddie, true to his word, had completely changed his lifestyle going to work each day at his construction company and coming directly home each evening. He missed going to his favorite haunts but enjoyed the serenity and peace of his new life. He looked forward to having Lorenzo eat dinner with him and Megan each evening. After dinner, they would retire to Lorenzo's apartment, watch sporting events on the television, and play endless games of high-stake gin rummy.

Fate had violently altered their lives and had wondrously brought them all together in this one place. Each of them reposing with contentment and pleasure in their newfound existence into which fate had thrust them. But unfortunately, fate is fickle and unpredictable. Things could change in the blink of an eye.

* * *

It was early Saturday morning; Eddie was sitting in his favorite chair reading the morning paper. He was startled by a knock on the door that separated Lorenzo's apartment.

"Hey man, ya up?" the muffled called out from behind the door.

"Ya, I'm up, it's open."

"Mornin', boss," he said, a broad smile on his craggy face.

"What the hell you so cheerful about so early in the morning?"

"'Cause I just read da paper, and I just hit a long shot at Santa Anita dat pay thirty-two ta one."

"I should have known," Eddie half laughed.

"Well, it's Saturday, whatda ya say we goin' ta Jimmy's? I'm starvin'."

"I want to grab a fast shower, why don't you go ahead and nail a table and I'll meet you there shortly."

"Ya, dat will work out better anyway. We'll have two cars. I gotta take your wife shop'en later."

"OK, then, I know one thing—I'm not going shopping with the two of you," he laughed. "I'll see ya there," he said, closing the door behind the big man.

When Eddie arrived at the restaurant, it was jammed as always and was a beehive of activity. Spotting Lorenzo at their usual table in the far corner of the room, he moved to join him. As Eddie made his way, he paused momentarily at tables along the way, shaking hands, slapping backs, and trading barbs with acquaintances.

The judge was the first one to notice Eddie when he arrived at the table.

"Hi, Eddie, look, I saved you a seat right next to me and Lorenzo. This way, you can sit between the good and the bad. Hmm . . . so let's see, what would that make you?" the judge pondered.

"The ugly," quipped the quick-witted Joey Cariola.

"Fuck you, Joey," laughed Eddie.

"Hey, I like dat, Joey, dat's pretty good—da good, da bad, and da ugly." Lorenzo paused, rising from his chair.

"Here, Eddie, let's change seats. I'm more uglier den you," he laughed raucously, enjoying his self-inflicted degradation.

Nicky the Greek and Chicky had been privately comparing notes over a woman that they both dated and bedded down. They paused long enough to join in Lorenzo's humor. Eddie had just finished his breakfast when Lorenzo whispered in his ear.

"Hey, look who in da fuck is headin' dis way."

Eddie turned his head slowly and followed the big man's eyes. He saw Sally and another man coming toward their table. *What the fuck does he want*, Eddie wondered.

"Well, good morning, guys," Sally said pleasantly, a smile on his face. "So what's the topic today?"

"Broads, it's always broads," Chicky offered, blowing out a cloud of smoke.

"Ya, that's because you can't think of anything else," the Greek chimed in.

"So to what do we owe this honor?" asked the judge frigidly.

"Oh, nuthin much, I just came over to bust Lorenzo's balls a little bit," Sally answered, his smile fading to ice.

"So tell me, Lorenzo, how do you like retirement? I hear you live in a big fancy pad at the One Eleven and that you even bought yourself a nice new car?"

"Ya, I saved up my money when I was workin' for your old man."

Sally noticed Eddie had buried his face in a newspaper, ignoring his presence at the table.

"Hey, D'Amico, I came over to introduce you to the man who took your father's place. Eddie lowered the newspaper and scoped the stranger standing silently beside Sally.

It was easily recognizable that the man worked out with weights. His muscles bulged under his clothing. Shiny thick black hair was combed straight back, revealing an overabundance of hair crème. He had sharp, chiseled features, and he peered at Eddie through menacing black eyes.

"Fellas, meet my right-hand man, Guido Luciano."

The men at the table coolly nodded acknowledgment. Guido extended his big hand toward Eddie, who ignored the hand and began reading the paper. Sally was not going to let Eddie get away with snubbing him in front of everyone.

He bore in. "Ya know, Eddie, it's strange the way your old man just disappeared like that, not saying good-bye to anyone, leavin' his clothes and other shit behind. Ya, really strange it is, all right. Tell me, did he ever send ya a postcard or call and tell ya where he was?" Sally was smiling, an evil look on his face. He was doing his best to antagonize Eddie into some kind of reaction. He succeeded.

Without warning, Eddie jumped to his feet, grabbing Sally by the throat with his left hand and delivering a crushing blow to his face with his right. Sally reeled backward. Before Guido could react, Chicky stunned him by breaking the heavy wooden chair over his head. As his knees buckled, Lorenzo slammed a powerful blow to his midsection, causing him to fall on his back. The Greek immediately jumped on his prone body and pulled his weapon from its holster. Cocking it, he stepped back and pointed it at the bewildered Guido.

"Fight!" someone yelled out.

"Who is it?" called out another.

"I can't see."

"Fuck 'em, let them fight," a gruff voice concluded.

Seeing that the boys had handled the threat of the powerful Guido, Lorenzo pushed Eddie out of the way. Sally was struggling to get to his feet. The big man grabbed him by the arm, and with his weapon in Sally's face, he warned, "Don't make any mistakes unless you're tired of breathing."

Sally pushed away LaRocca's arm. Undaunted, he ignored the brandished weapon and walked over to Eddie. He went nose to nose with him.

"Oh, don't worry, D'Amico, you'll pay for this. You'll hear from me again. I've got plans for you." Sally was smiling as he spat in Eddie's face and turned.

Lorenzo grabbed the gun from the Greek, removed the clip, and threw the weapon to the now-standing Guido.

"What the fuck's going on here?" Jimmy asked. "Are you guys nuts or somethin'?"

"Relax, relax, Jimmy, it's over. I'll pay you for the chair," said the judge.

"Man, Eddie, you really nailed that cocksucker," Joey chimed in.

"Did you guys see the way I busted that chair on that prick's head?" boasted Chicky proudly.

Lorenzo, with his arm around Eddie's shoulder, was shaking his head.

"Dat was a bad move, Eddie."

"Why?" Eddie snapped back. "He hates me anyway. One more thing's not going to change things."

Before Lorenzo could respond, his pager went off.

"Dat's your wife. C'mon, let's get da hell outa here before any more shit happens."

They said their good-bye's and walked toward the door followed by ribbing from their friends.

"Hi, champ."

"Hey, slugger, where ya goin'?"

Their friends were already rehashing the incident.

Lorenzo paused for a moment outside the door.

"Tell your wife I'll be waiting outside da back door."

Eddie nodded and walked away, seething in rage and deep in thought.

Arriving at his apartment, Eddie called out for Megan. She emerged from the guest bedroom she had converted into a nursery.

"Hi, honey, what brings you home so early?"

"Sally was there. I just couldn't stand the sight of the asshole," he lied, "You paged Lorenzo. He said he'll be waitin' for you outside the back door."

"OK, I'm just going to pick up some groceries. I won't be long. Ya know what, it's a beautiful day—why don't we take a nice ride out in the country when I get back?"

"I don't think so. You're due any day now. I don't want to be that far out in the boondocks. I have a real problem visualizing myself as Dr. D'Amico delivering my own baby in the backseat of a car," he laughed.

She giggled at his humor.

"Oh well, I guess you're right," she said dejectedly.

Sensing her disappointment, he suggested an alternative.

"I've got an idea—Mendon Ponds Park is not too far from the hospital. It's beautiful down there. I'm sure the flowers are in bloom, and you know how you enjoy feeding the ducks. How's that sound?"

"Oh yes, that sounds terrific, but lets talk about it when I get home."

"Be careful not to do any lifting. You're due any day now," he cautioned. "Let Lorenzo do it."

She laughed.

"C'mon, honey, you don't really believe I let him come in the store with me. Can you just imagine how I'd look with that monster lumbering around behind me?" she chuckled.

"Ya, I guess he is pretty frightening looking," he said with a half laugh.

"OK, I'm outa here, see you soon honey," she said giving him a peck on the cheek and walking out the door.

Lorenzo pulled up to the red zone in front of the store to let Megan out. He turned and smiled.

"I'll wait here for ya."

"Lorenzo, you're parking in a fire lane."

"No kiddin', do ya tink dey'll put me in jail?" He snickered.

"My god, Lorenzo, you're impossible. I won't be long," she said laughingly as she gave him an affectionate tug on his ear.

"Yep, dat's me, all right, Megan, Lorenzo de Impossible," he chuckled, watching her exit the car from the rearview mirror.

He picked up the ever-present racing form from the seat and began studying its contents. After a short while, he began glancing at the door. "What's takin' her so long?" he wondered. She finally emerged with her basket heavily laden with groceries. Setting aside his paper, he reached over and popped the lid of the trunk.

As he stepped out of the vehicle, he saw a dark green pickup barreling toward him at a high rate of speed. He instinctively slammed the door shut and jumped for protection behind the big car. At the same moment, the speeding vehicle hit a speed bump, went airborne, careened wildly to the left, and landed on the sidewalk. Lorenzo watched in helpless horror as the out-of-control vehicle struck Megan, sending her body high into the air. Her body slammed down onto the roof of the Cadillac with a bloodcurdling thud. She lay broken and bleeding a scant distance away from where Lorenzo stood frozen in place as the horrific scene unfolded before him. He quickly turned at the sound of screeching tires as the driver turned sharply upon entering the street and disappearing from view.

Lorenzo walked around to the passenger side of the vehicle and gently lifted Megan from the roof of the car. Unbridled tears were coursing down his cheeks, and he choked back the great waves of emotion that were racking through his body. He laid Megan's lifeless body at his feet. A huge crowd was beginning to congregate as he took off his white sports coat and covered her body. A sad and respectful hush fell over the gathering crowd.

Lorenzo could hear sirens nearing. He silently stood over her body; large drops of sorrow were falling from his eyes onto the concrete beside her. After giving his account of the accident to the police, he walked over to the illegally parked car and fell heavily behind the wheel. He picked up the telephone, sucking in deeply and exhaling as he dialed.

"Good morning," the voice answered pleasantly.

"Carmella," he gasped, unable to continue.

"Lorenzo, is that you? Are you all right? What's wrong?"

Trying to get hold of his emotions, he replied, "Carmella, sometin' real bad just hapened. You gotta tell Eddie, Megan's dead," he choked.

"What?" *Oh dear God, no, oh no, oh no.* What happened?"

"Hit-and-run." The line went dead.

Lorenzo was driving the short distance back to the hotel when the telephone rang.

"Ya." It was Carmella.

"I'm going to wait for you at the back door. I want you there when I tell him. God only knows what he might do."

"Yah, you're right. I'm only a few minutes away."

"OK, then, see you soon."

She pulled out a tissue and tried to dry the fountain of tears falling from her eyes. They met at the back door of the hotel. Lorenzo explained the gory details and the circumstances surrounding Megan's death.

"Oh my god, Lorenzo, there's no easy way to do this. There's nothing anyone can say or do to soften the blow."

"Well, dat's life. We all gotta go sometime."

"I know, but not like this," she said stoically.

"They were just getting their lives together, so looking forward to the baby and all. I pray God gives me the right words to say."

"Der ain't any right words in dis situation. C'mon, we better get goin' before da newspapers or de cops call Eddie."

"Oh, dear me, you're right, Lorenzo. I never thought of that. Let's hurry."

They went into the elevator and then walked down the hallway to the door of Eddie's apartment. Arriving at the door, they paused. "I'm dreading this," Carmella muttered. "You ready?"

He nodded.

She rang the bell.

Seeing his two friends, Eddie threw open the door, stepping aside to let them pass.

"Hi wha . . ." His voice trialed off when he saw the look on their faces and their bloodshot eyes. He now realized something was wrong. Megan was not accompanying them, and he stuck his head out the door and looked down the hall. He shouted. *"Where's Megan? C'mon, where's Megan?"*

"Eddie, there's been a terrible accident," Carmella began.

"Is she in the hospital? Tell me, damn it, is she in the hospital?"

"Eddie, please sit down," Carmella asked softly.

"Sit down, sit down, why should I sit down?" he bellowed.

Reality was beginning to set in for Eddie. He studied Lorenzo's face. The sorrow he saw there telegraphed his worst suspicions.

"She's dead? She's fuckin' dead, isn't she?" he roared.

Carmella lowered her eyes. She murmured the single word that drove the stark reality of the horrific news deep into Eddie's brain. "Yes," she answered simply.

That simple word sent Eddie off. He went berserk—throwing lamps, tipping over tables, and punching holes in the walls, at the same time crying out Megan's name.

Carmella and Lorenzo had not said a word since Eddie's outburst. Carmella was kneeling in front of the sofa with her head buried in the pillow. Lorenzo had gone over to the bar and was downing straight shots of Chivas Regal. They both looked over in Eddie's direction when they realized his ranting had ceased.

He walked over to Carmella, who had risen to her feet.

"Carm, now my baby's gone too," he said pathetically, tears rolling down his cheeks.

Chapter 30

Τ he sun was hanging low over the horizon. The flaming orange of its glow painted a beautiful mosaic on the still blue waters of the lake. A small aluminum boat rested quietly upon the lake's calm surface with two fishermen on board.

"You know Lorenzo, we've been sitting here for two fuckin' hours without one bite. You said this was a good spot," said Eddie D'Amico.

Lorenzo put down the racing form he was reading and answered. "Sa what da fuck ya gonna du, sue me? Dat's wat da guy tol me at da bait store."

"Ya, ya, but now I'm getting sick of this shit. Every time we go out, we never catch any fuckin' fish. This will make the third time in a row," lamented Eddie.

"Relax, Eddie, relax. What da fuck else ya got to do? Ya sold yur business. Yur a man of leisure now. Cool yur fuckin' jets and enjoy it," said his friend.

"Ya, I guess you're right. It is peaceful out here in the water. It gives a guy a chance to think."

"Ya, so what do ya tink about?"

"Well, I think about Megan a lot and wonder what it would have been like for me with her and the baby here. It's hard to believe it's been six months since she's been gone," Eddied finished, a tear running down his cheek.

"Ya, Eddie, I know what ya mean. I miss her too. She was one terrific lady."

"You know, Lorenzo, not a day goes by that I don't wonder if it wasn't some kind of setup and not an accident like the police said."

"Ya, but you remember da cops found a broken liquor bottle when da door of da truck flew op'en. Da are sur da driver was drunk."

"Ya, I know, but I can't help but wonder," said Eddie pensively.

"Oh, hey, I been meanin' to tell ya somethin' that I keep forgetting' to tell ya, so now I rember, an I'm gonna tell ya."

Eddie chuckled to himself at his friend's misuse of the English language. "So you going to tell me now?" he asked, a broad grin on his tanned face.

"Ya, sure, I'm gonna tell ya. Do ya remember dat guy, Guido Luciano, da one Sally got ta replace yur ol' man . . ." He paused, waiting for a reply.

"Ya, sure, I remember him. How can I forget that day!"

"Well, anway, I was talkin' to Tough Tony da oder day. Da caught him robbin' dough from da family outa da drug cash."

"Holy shit, he'll be a dead man."

"Ya, got dat right, but ders more, and it gets worser. Sally also found out he's porkin' his wife regular like."

"Man, I can't believe Connie would do such a thing."

"Well, she is. Da meet at da Exit 45 Motel. Sally's even got pictures of dem fuckin'."

"I know he's a dead man now. Holy shit! Guido will be history, but hell, what's another dead man to Sally? The real question is, what's he going to do to Connie?"

"Who da fuck knows what dat crazy cocksucker will do," Lorenzo answered with a sigh.

"By the way, I have something to tell you. I had a visit from Bee Stinger and another detective the other day . . ." Eddie paused for Lorenzo's reaction. Lorenzo rolled his eyes and became immediately concerned.

"No shit, what did ya want?"

"Nothing really. My father's disappearance is still an open file. They were just asking if I could think of anything that could help the case."

"Ya, so what did ya tell dem?"

"Well, I told them you were my neighbor and lived right next door and was sure you might be able to tell them something that might help them," said Eddie, chuckling as he spoke.

"Get outa here, ya fucker," Lorenzo laughed as he hit Eddie on the head with a fishnet.

"Come on, Lorenzo, let's get the hell outa here. We can't even catch our breath out here."

"Ya, I've had it too. Pull up de anchor."

Lorenzo and Eddie had been inseparable since Megan's death. Lorenzo had taken him under his wing and pulled him out of his depression and his binge drinking. He got him to get away from the self-imposed exile at his apartment by taking him to sporting events and the horse races. They enjoyed their evenings by playing endless games of gin rummy and cooking Italian food together. Thanks to Lorenzo, Eddie was slowly beginning to enjoy life again.

*   *   *

It was the morning after Eddie and Lorenzo's three-day fishing trip. Eddie awoke and looked at the clock on his end table—it was 6:00 a.m. Jumping out of bed, he put on his bathrobe and went into the kitchen to make his coffee. Cup in hand, he walked over to the French doors that opened onto the balcony overlooking the city. Ignoring the chill he felt from the cold winter air, he stepped out onto the balcony. Deep in thought, he remained motionless as he became covered with a white mantel of snow that slowly drifted down, turning the city white. Suddenly, he turned and went back into the living room and sat down at the bar, picked up the phone, and dialed a number.

"Ya," the sleepy-sounding voice of Bee Stinger answered.

"It's Eddie, did I wake you up?"

"You sure as hell did. What's up?"

"I've got something to tell you. It's important. Can you come over my place when you're up and around?"

"Well, I am *up now*! I'll jump in the shower and be right over." The detective slammed down the phone, obviously irritated by Eddie's early-morning call.

Eddie walked over to his favorite chair and turned on the television and dozed off. He awoke with a start at the sound of the melodious chimes sending out its message that someone was at the door.

"Good morning, pal," Eddie said as Bee entered the room.

"*Pal, my ass*, this better be good."

"It is. Did you have breakfast yet?"

"No."

"Let's go into the kitchen. Then I'll make you some. I haven't eaten either."

As Eddie cooked, he began telling the detective the story that LaRocca had related to him in the boat regarding Guido Luciano. The two friends were now sitting at the table enjoying the breakfast Eddie had prepared.

"What a dumb fuck this Guido guy must be. What did he think Sally would do if he found out, give him a medal or somethin'?" said the detective.

"Well, he won't give him a medal, but he will get some metal in the form of a bullet in the head. The way I understand it, he's going to try and set it up like a mob hit so no one will suspect him," Eddie finished.

"OK, pal," Bee said, rising from the table, ending their conversation.

"Thanks for the info, and the eggs. I'll let myself out." The detective turned and walked toward the door.

Eddie began cleaning up the kitchen. *Hmm* . . . , he thought, *if Sally whacks Guido and the police can prove it, Sally will be sentenced to death or life in prison. What a pleasant outcome that would be.* He smiled, enjoying the possibility of having Sally out of his life forever.

*   *   *

Sally, Tony the Turk, Jimmy the Brute, and Vinnie Barratino were sitting around the table having lunch in the back room of the Black Orchid. The men had been summoned there by Sally to discuss what he described as family business. Jimmy the Brute couldn't wait any longer and was curious to find out why Sally had called the meeting.

"So what's da deal, Sally?" he asked as he poured sambuca into his and Sally's glass.

Sally was never one to mince words and got right to the point.

"We gotta whack Guido Luciano," he answered with a smile on his face.

"Are ya kidin' or what!" exclaimed the Turk.

The others were shaking their head in disbelief.

"Do uses guys think I would kid about somethin' like this?" Sally replied.

"He's been stealing thousands of dollars from the cash we receive for our drug sales. I set him up, and he's ripping off half of what we take in for himself."

"*Holy shit!* I can't believe he'd be that stupid!" Vinnie exclaimed.

"But there's also something that pisses me off more than his stealing the money. I've been having him tailed to find out where he's stashing the money and found out he's been banging my wife on a regular basis." Sally threw a bunch of pictures on the table showing Guido and Connie both naked in bed.

"Here, look at this one." He flipped the photograph in the center of the table. "She's sucking his cock in this one."

Sally was obviously irritated sharing the intimate information of his marital problems with the men.

"OK," said Jimmy the Brute. "What's the plan?"

"We'll set it up to look like a mob hit. This way the cops will never suspect us."

"Ya, that all sounds good, but how we gonna pull dat off?"

"Easy, Turk, real easy. Guido and Connie do all their fuckin' on the outskirts of town at the Exit 45 Motel. I'll keep a tail on them, and when they go there the next time, they'll have company—me, the Brute, and the Turk. Jimmy drives, Turk will be the lookout, and I'll go in and whack the both of them," Sally stated matter-of-factly.

"Fuck, Sally, you're going to whack your own wife?" Vinnie asked, shaking his head.

"Why not, Vinnie, she's nothing more than a fuckin' whore now. Why shouldn't I have my revenge? Besides, whacking her will make it look more like a mob hit, like somebody was trying to get even with me." Sally smiled, pleased with his plan.

"Ya forget one thing—if we bust da door down, everybody will hear us," said the Turk.

A broad smile appeared on Sally's face. "They always reserve the same room. I rented the room and had a key made. There won't be any breaking down doors for us," he laughed.

"What about me, Sally?" Vinnie asked. "You got nuthin' for me to do?"

"Oh yes, Vinnie. You're going to be me. Can you still write my name like I do?"

"Ya sure, ya can't tell them apart, but what that got to do with anything?"

"Plenty, Vinnie, plenty," said Sally with a broad grin still on his face. "You're going to take a trip to Chicago, flying there and using my name to check into a hotel. You're going to be my alibi, but you must be very careful not to let anyone see you. Wear a hat, and pull it down over your face when you check in. Stay in your room and never leave it. Order room service, and when it arrives, leave the tip on the dresser and stay in the bathroom. You'll use my credit card, keep it open, and then all you have to do is walk out late at night wearing your hat, *capisce?*"

Sally finished, feeling he had a perfect plan. "OK, boys, that's the story. Now all we have to do is wait for the two of them to go to the motel and have their last fuck."

Sally was on his way home, pleased with all that transpired at the meeting with the boys. A broad grin covered his face when he thought of how surprised his wife was going to be when she found out he knew the little game she played to get out at night to have her little tryst with Guido. He was still smiling when he pulled into the driveway of his home. When Sally got up the next morning, he informed his wife he was going to Chicago on business.

"When are you coming home, honey?" Connie asked.

"Couple a days," he answered curtly.

"OK, have a good trip," she replied, kissing him on the cheek as he headed to the door carrying an empty suitcase.

Sally jumped into the car and headed to his hideout at the junkyard. He would stay there to make sure he wasn't seen by anyone since he was supposed to be out of town. He knew Connie would take advantage of his absence and go have her fuck session with Guido. Sally picked up the car phone and called Jimmy the Brute.

"Hello, this is Jimmy," the voice said.

"Jimmy, Sally. Get over to my house ASAP. The minute she leaves the house, come and pick me and Turk up at the junkyard, *capisce?*"

"Ya, I got it, boss."

"Good, I'll see ya later," Sally answered as he placed the telephone in the cradle.

Sally reached into the shoulder holster concealed under his jacket and pulled out the Beretta he had used to kill the Lacavoli brothers.

"You're going to be busy tonight, pal," he said to the silent pistol as he patted it and returned it to the holster.

It was six o'clock before the phone rang at the junkyard.

"She just left the house. I'm on my way. Ya better bundle up. Its snowin' like a motherfucker." And the line went dead.

The parking lot at the motel was completely covered with snow as Jimmy pulled in and parked next to Connie's car.

"That's it, they're in room number 11," said Sally. "Jimmy, turn the car around and back in. Turk, when I go in, you wait outside and keep your eyes open."

Inside the room, Connie and Guido were sitting on the edge of the bed naked; each held a large glass of scotch in their hand.

"So, Connie, you never told me how you manage to get out at night without Sally getting suspicious."

"Well, I'm not as dumb as you think," she chuckled. "During the day, when he's gone, I go to the shopping mall and do a little shopping. Then after dinner, I tell him I'm going to the mall to do a little shopping. Instead of the mall, I meet you here—we fuck our brains out—and return home, take the shopping bags out of the car, and show Sally what I bought that night."

Guido was laughing so hard he spilled his drink. "That's clever, very clever," he said.

Little did they know that Sally was looking for some tools and found the packages in the middle of the afternoon. When she returned that night and showed him the same packages, Sally knew she was fucking around with someone.

"Connie, why don't you come over and give our friend here a kiss," said Guido, pointing to the erection of his large penis.

"Sure. Why not, big boy?" She walked over and got on her knees in front of him and began pouring scotch on his erection and began licking it off. Growing excited, he grabbed her by the back of her head and jammed his manhood deep into her mouth.

On the other side of the door, Sally carefully and quietly put the bootlegged key in the door. He put his hand on the doorknob and turned it slowly. *Holy shit!* he thought to himself. *I hope the safety chain is not on.* Luck was with him.

With the Beretta in hand, he burst into the room and quickly closed the door. Connie freaked out seeing Sally enter the room and jumped to her feet, revealing her nakedness. Guido stood speechless, staring at Sally in disbelief.

"Well, well, look what we have here—a no-good, degenerate thief and a no-good fucking whore," Sally taunted them, smiling as he spoke.

"Lay down on the bed," he ordered Guido.

"Sally, but . . . but . . . ," Guido stammered.

"No *buts*, you dirty prick. You steal my money, and then you have the balls to fuck my wife."

Guido was now lying on his back on the bed. "Please, Sally, mercy, I beg you," he stammered.

Sally walked over to the bed and put the barrel up against the side of Guido's head and pulled the trigger. *Pssst*, the little Beretta responded quietly. Guido died instantly. Connie stood silently by and watched, too petrified to speak. She was crouched down, her arms folded across her breasts, trying to cover her nakedness.

Sally pointed the Beretta at Connie. "So what have you got to say for yourself?"

"Forgive me, Sally. Please, I'm sorry, please. You know I love only you."

"So you love only me yet you've been fucking him. What is it, was he a better fuck than me?

"No, no, baby, you're the best. You're the best, please forgive me. I'm the mother of your children. Who will take care of them if you kill me?"

"Ah, maybe you're right. Do something for me, and I might let you live."

"What is it Sally? I'll do anything, anything at all," she pleaded.

"Go over to the bed and start sucking on Guido's cock," he ordered.

She looked at him in disbelief, and without saying a word, she walked over to Guido's dead body and did as Sally ordered. Sally walked quietly behind her and put the Beretta a few inches from Connie's head.

"Fuckin' whore," he uttered as he pulled the trigger. *Pssst,* the Beretta spoke again, delivering its message of death one more time.

"You aren't fit to raise my kids, you fucking whore," he said to the unhearing Connie.

Sally walked over to the dresser and looked in the mirror. He noticed his hair was mussed and pulled out a comb and rearranged his hair. "Hmm . . . not bad," he said out loud, admiring himself in the mirror.

Sally pulled out his handkerchief and wiped the doorknob on the inside, cleaning off his fingerprints. Shutting all the lights in the room, he stepped into the frigid night air, pausing a moment. He wiped his prints clean from the outside doorknob.

"How'd it go?" the Turk asked.

"Great, just great," said Sally, a broad smile on his face.

The two men began sloshing through the snow to the waiting car.

Chapter 31

B ee Stinger arrived at the police station and looked at his wristwatch. *Plenty of time before roll call,* he thought. He walked over to the cafeteria, bought a doughnut and coffee, and sat down at an empty table. He noticed that the morning paper was lying on the chair beside him. Taking a bite from his doughnut, he opened the paper and was shocked at the headline. "I'll be a son of a bitch, Eddie was right," he muttered to himself. The headline read, "Gangland Execution at Motel." The detective jumped up and raced to the phone to call Eddie.

"Hello," Eddie said.

"Did you see the morning paper?" Bee asked.

"No, but Lorenzo just told me."

"OK," the excited Bee blurted out. "We'll talk later."

"OK," Eddie answered and hung up the phone.

Bee *hurled* his unfinished coffee and doughnut into the trash and raced to the chief's office. He flung open the door and, breathing heavily, stopped at the desk of the chief's secretary.

"Good morning, Bee, what's all the huffing and puffing about?"

Bee held up the newspaper. "It's about this," he replied.

"It better be good. He's busy as a one-armed paper hanger," Geraldine quipped, a pleasant smile on her face as she pushed the intercom button.

"What is it, Gerry? I thought I told you not to disturb me," Chief Lou Tacito's voice echoed through the speaker.

"Bee's here, he asked to see you."

"Send him in," the voice replied.

"So, what's up, Bee?" the chief asked his friend, a smile on his face.

"Lou, read this," said Bee, handing him the newspaper.

The chief looked up from the newspaper. "So what, are you worried about the gang war?"

"*HELL NO*, Sally Barratino either did it or set it up to be done."

Shaking his head and smiling, the chief asked, "So what are you, a fortune teller?" the chief chided.

"No, I'm not, but Eddie D'Amico might be," the detective answered.

"So what has D'Amico got to do with this?"

"Three days ago, Eddie told me Sally was planning on snuffing Guido because he was stealing money from the family, and to make matters worse, he was also banging Sally's wife."

"Hmm . . . are you telling me you believe that Sally would kill his own wife? That doesn't make sense."

"Lou, I'm telling you, Sally makes Satan look like an angel. He'd kill his own mother if she got in his way."

"OK, Bee, you came here for a reason, so what's on your mind?"

"Well, of course, we have to launch an investigation. Just go ahead and do our normal routine. What I'd like is your permission to let me quietly do some investigating on my own and see what I can dig up."

"All right, you got it. Be careful, and don't try to be a hero. And report your findings only to me." the chief put his hands on Bee's shoulder. "Remember, Bee, you're playing with life and death with this asshole. Don't take any chances."

"I won't. Thanks, boss," he answered as he headed for the door.

Across town, Sally walked out of his bedroom at the junkyard and into the kitchen.

"Morning, boss," Vinnie greeted.

"Pour me some coffee and run into town and pick up a couple morning newspapers."

"That's all you need?" Vinnie asked.

"Yep, just hurry back."

When Vinnie returned to the junkyard fortress, all of the boys were in the large family room playing poker. Vinnie immediately walked over to Sally and handed him a newspaper. After scanning the paper, Sally rose from his chair and stood up laughing.

"Hey boys, looks like we've got a problem. There's been a gangland killing in town. We'd better be careful."

Sally continued to laugh as he walked over to the fireplace and threw the newspaper into the roaring fire.

"Hey, Vinnie, call Giovanni Garbelli, tell him to call me. According to the newspaper, I got to arrange for a funeral," said Sally, roaring with laughter as he spoke.

Two weeks had passed since the chief and Bee Stinger had met regarding the two murders at the Exit 45 Motel. They were in Jimmy's Restaurant, at a small table located in a corner behind some produce boxes.

"Well, let's hear it, Bee. What did you find out?" asked the chief.

"Well, Sally seems to have an alibi. He allegedly was in a hotel in Chicago at the time the killings took place, but get this, nobody saw him enter or leave his room for the two days that he was supposed to be there. But that doesn't mean he didn't set up the hits—it only means he may not have pulled the trigger."

"Did he check in with a credit card?" the chief asked.

"Yes, he did, and I also had a handwriting expert check his signature, and it seems to be his."

"Well, let's convince a grand jury. Maybe we can get someone in the gang to spill their beans," said the chief.

"Well, there's something else Lou. The FBI has been bugging some of the phone booths that Sally is known to use, and the operator heard Sally explaining to the capo why he whacked Guido, who was a made man, and somehow the tape didn't record any of the conversation."

"Well, that shouldn't be a problem. Those stakeouts always have a two-man team to verify the information they receive," said the chief.

"That's the problem. When Sally made the call, the other agent was out taking a leak, which leaves only one man to testify. The FBI talked to the prosecutor, and that dog won't hunt," he said. "They'd never get a conviction . . ." Bee paused for a moment and continued, "But get this, Lou, the sheriff's office, for years, has been tearing off blank pages of their daily reports and stashing them away so they are in sequence. This way, they can go back to any given day and write in anything they want to, and it will be in perfect sequence with the reports of that day."

"Holy shit, you've got to be kidding me!" the chief exclaimed. "But what's that got to do with anything?"

"Well, the FBI is going to have the sheriffs department write up a report that they were involved with the bugging, and their man will verify he heard Sally explaining why he knocked off Guido," the detective replied.

"So what you're saying, they're going to frame Sally and his men, who are dishonest as hell, and the sheriff who gives the testimony will go to jail. If anyone ever finds out, I don't know, Bee, that's shitty police work to me," the chief ended, shaking his head.

"Look, Lou, who will ever find out we'd be doing the world a favor getting rid of that no-good motherfuckin' Sally. Did you forget the massacre in the park? Sally killed those men, and we couldn't pin anything on him. I say, let's get rid of the bastard. He'll either get death or life. For me, I hope it's death," ended Bee.

"I'll tell you, Bee, it's not anything I would want on my conscience."

Judge Carlivatti had just picked up his topcoat and was leaving his home to go out to the waiting limousine when he paused a moment to slip into his coat. As he neared the telephone, it rang, and he picked up the receiver. "Hello," he said into the mouthpiece.

"Good morning, Judge, I have a message for you," the voice said. "Sally wants to see you at the Black Orchid at six o'clock sharp. Don't be fuckin' late." The line went dead.

The judge knew that the call could mean nothing but trouble for him. He took out his handkerchief and wiped the perspiration from his face. Suddenly, the door opened, and his wife came into the room and saw him standing there wiping his face.

"What's the matter, Carmen? You're white as a ghost, do you feel all right?" she asked with concern in her voice.

"I'm OK. I must be getting the flu or something. I'll be fine," he replied.

He hurriedly kissed her on the cheek and headed toward the front door. Suddenly, he paused and turned.

"Oh, honey, I just remembered. I'll be working late tonight. I have to do some research for a sentencing tomorrow."

"What about dinner, do you want me to bring you something to eat?"

"No, thanks, honey. I'll send Sam out to get me something." He turned and walked down the sidewalk to the waiting limo.

He was sitting on the bench and could not concentrate on the case before him. All he could think about was his meeting with Sally that evening. Not wanting to be unfair to those on trial, he decided to recess the court. He glanced at the black clock hanging over the entry door. He decided to adjourn the court at twelve o'clock.

Walking toward the limo, he decided to go work out at the gym to kill some time.

"Where to, boss? Ya going home?"

"No, Sam, take me to the gym."

Sam was carefully maneuvering the limo through heavy traffic toward the health club. Arriving in front of the club, he double-parked the limo as the cop on the beat directed traffic around the vehicle. Sam jumped out of the limo and quickly walked around to open the door for the judge.

"Do you want me to wait?" he asked as the judge exited the vehicle.

"No, thanks, Sam, I'm going to grab a steam, get a rubdown, and take a nap," the judge replied.

"I'll take a cab home. Take the rest of the day off, and I'll see you at the usual time in the morning."

"Thanks, Judge. Hope you feel better."

The policeman stopped traffic as Sam moved the big limo into the driving lane.

Judge Carlivatti locked his locker and looked at his wristwatch; it read 5:40 p.m. He briskly walked out of the locker room toward the front desk and threw the keys on the counter.

"Good night, Tommy," he said to the attendant, who was busy rolling towels.

"Good night, Judge," Tommy replied.

As the judge walked out into the cold night air, snow was falling at a rapid rate. He shivered and pulled up the collar of his coat as he quickly walked toward the waiting cab.

"Where to, pal?" asked the driver as he shoved down the lever starting the meter.

"The Black Orchid Restaurant, do you know where it is?"

"Ya, sure do. Go there myself sometimes. The old lady loves their jumbo shrimp cocktail," replied the cabby.

The cabby pulled into the small shopping plaza that housed the restaurant. The judge paid the cabdriver and looked down at his wristwatch; it was six o'clock. *Good*, he thought. He paused a moment to notice it was snowing much harder. He began to shiver again and wondered if it was the cold night air or if he was shaking in expectation of the ordeal he was about to face when he met with Sally and his gang.

As he entered the restaurant, he paused a moment by the hostess's station to allow his eyes to grow accustomed to the dimly lit room. The only light in the alcove was coming from a floor-to-ceiling tree that was wrapped with small twinkling lights that bid a warm welcome to all those who entered the portals. The judge's eyes, now accustomed to the darkness, glanced around the elegant black-and-peach interior of the room. As he looked over toward the bar, he could see it was jammed with people. It was happy hour, and everyone was enjoying the free tastefully done spread Freddie always put out. Suddenly Freddie noticed the judge standing motionless in the alcove and began walking toward him.

"Hello, Judge, how are you? Welcome, welcome," said Freddie Bentivegna as he extended his arm and reached for the judge's hand.

"Hello, Freddie, I see you're busy as usual," the judge replied.

Freddie was a large-boned tall man, his curly hair was dyed brown, and his piercing green eyes seemed to look right through a person when he spoke to them. It was a well known fact Freddie loved women, and his sexual prowess was legend among the "in" crowd.

"Follow me, Judge. The boys are waiting for you."

The judge silently followed Freddie as they walked to the rear of the building. They stopped in front of a heavy black drape that hung from floor to ceiling. Muffled unintelligible voices were coming through the heavy drapes. Freddie looked up toward the ceiling. The judge's eyes followed his gaze. Mounted in the ceiling next to the drapes was a very small red light. Freddie pressed a button on the wall. Suddenly the drapes began to split in the middle and roll back toward the walls. The motor changed in pitch as the mechanism strained to open the heavy drapes.

Freddie turned and silently left, leaving the judge staring awkwardly into the room. He was amazed to see a gargantuan booth across the back wall of the room; both ends continued on against the side walls, leaving space for food to be served on the huge oblong table. Five men were staring at him as he entered the room. The men were dwarfed by the massive peach-and-black booth that could easily accommodate twenty people.

It was Sally who broke the silence first. "Hello, Judge, make yourself comfortable," he said, motioning to a seat across from him.

"Hello, Sally," replied the judge, looking at each of the men to acknowledge that his salutation was for them also. The men were eating family style from the large serving dishes in the middle of the table.

"Would you like some pasta fagioli?" Sally offered.

"No, thanks, I would just like to know the reason you asked me down here. My wife is holding dinner for me," he lied.

The other four men in the room were Vinnie Barratino, Jimmy the Brute, Cappy Capparella, and the Turk Scotto. All remained silent while they ate their food. The judge knew by the men's silence it was going to be Sally's show, and nothing but trouble for him was going to come from this meeting. Sally put down his fork, and smiling at the judge, he began to speak.

"Well, Carmen, you don't mind if I call you Carmen, do you, Judge?" he asked. "Remember, just like in the good ole days in the neighborhood."

The judge remained silent as Sally spoke and then responded, "Yes, of course I do. What's the old neighborhood got to do with anything?"

"Well, Carmen, quite a bit. I'm going to ask you a couple of other things and see if you can remember something about them."

As Sally spoke, Jimmy the Brute was looking around the table, trying to catch the attention of the other men at the table, a smile on his round, chubby face.

"Let's see if you remember this," Sally continued. "Do you remember when we were kids, your old man fell off a truck and couldn't work for a couple of years? Can you remember who paid all the bills at your house?" Sally asked.

"Sally, I don't know what the hell you're driving at. You know as well as I do it was Don Francisco," the judge answered in an irritated manner.

"Well, we're playing a game called 'remember,' Carmen, and when we're done, I'm going to ask you a small favor, *capisce?* Tonight is the night you're going to pay for all past favors," he said, his eyes flashing a menacing glare at the judge.

The tense silence was broken by a loud drawn-out fart by Jimmy the Brute. The Brute's timing was bad as Sally was trying to make a serious point with the judge. Sally exploded in anger and jumped out of his chair. "Get the fuck out of here, you stupid bastard," he yelled through clinched teeth. "And don't come back until you're called."

Jimmy the Brute rose immediately from his chair and walked toward the opening in the black curtains, a sheepish smile on his face. Though Jimmy left the room, the foul order of his presence remained.

"Now, Carmen, lets get back to business," Sally began. "Who was it that paid for you to go to college when you wanted to become a lawyer?"

"Wait just a fuckin' minute, Sally," shouted the judge as he rose from his chair, the street kid in him taking over. "I paid your father back for every fuckin' dime he gave me, plus interest."

Sally acted as if he didn't hear the judge's outburst. "And when you ran for judge, who was it that got all the union to support your election?"

The judge, now in a rage, leaned over the table and screamed in Sally's face.

"I never asked for any help from your father or the unions in any of my elections," replied the judge, now shaking in anger.

Turk Scotto leaned across the table. "Sit down, Judge," he said as he gently pushed the judge back in his chair.

All eyes were staring at the judge in disbelief, amazed that he had the balls to stand up to Sally the way that he did. Sally, a smile on his evil face, continued on as if nothing happened.

"Carmen, our sources tell me that the boys are going to be indicted for the murder at the motel."

"So what's your problem got anything to do with me?" the judge asked, his face still flushed in anger.

"Just this, Carmen." Sally was speaking softly in small, measured tones. "You are the presiding judge and make the decision who will be sitting on the bench if we go to trial. When you make the appointment, you make sure you choose someone who is going to see that everything goes our way every chance he can."

Sally was now standing staring at the judge with ice-cold, threatening eyes.

"It's impossible. I can't control—"

Sally broke in and didn't let the judge finish. "You just fuckin' fix it." Sally looked over to Cappy Capparella. "Show him the pictures," Sally ordered.

Capparella—a quiet, intelligent man who was the family's bookkeeper—reached inside of his jacket pocket and took out a white envelope and threw it on the table in front of the judge. The judge, with hand shaking, tore open the envelope. It contained six photographs of his wife and children. The pictures indicated they were taken with a telephoto camera and that his family was not aware they were being photographed.

"So, Judge, let's just say, with your cooperation, you're buying your family an insurance policy," Sally said, a broad smile on his face.

The judge understood the inference of the message and continued to sit silently, listening to Sally's threats.

"You fix it, Carmen. Otherwise, it's them one at a time, then you. Our source didn't know what they have for evidence, but I do know this," Sally continued. "Murder one carry's a death penalty, or at best life in the joint if we are convicted."

"But, Sally, be reasonable. Even if I wanted to, there is no way in hell a judge can influence a public trial so that it could change the result," pleaded the judge.

Cappy Capparella's quiet, steady voice broke into the conversation. "Look, Judge, all we are asking for is a little edge. It might make a difference for us with a weak case," Cappy concluded.

"First of all, Cappy, I cannot be the judge in this trial. Everyone knows I grew up in the old neighborhood and was tight with Don Francisco."

"OK," Vinnie called out, "say we buy that, but you can appoint a judge who shall, we say, be friendly towards us."

Sally rose again from his seat, obviously irritated with the judge's responses.

"Look, Carmen, this fuckin' discussion is over," said Sally. "If it's going to be between you and me and your whole family, guess who's going to lose?"

With that, the judge stood up and scooped the pictures off the table and looked at Sally in the eyes.

"Fuck you, Sally," he shouted as he spun around and headed toward the bar to call a cab.

As he walked toward the waiting cab, he couldn't help but wonder why during the entire meeting not one person professed any innocence to the murder of Guido and Sally's wife. Settling into the warmth of the cab, he realized he was trembling. He laid his head back and closed his eyes. The cab moved silently down the road, the sound of tires muffled by the fresh fallen snow. The cabdriver had tried to converse with his passenger, but to no avail. He resigned himself to the silence within the cab.

As Judge Carlivatti peered out the window of the cab, he watched the heavy falling snow make a white blanket over all it touched. Tears began to stream down his face, knowing full well there was nothing he could say or do that would change Sally's mind. For them, perception was reality; their heads were as hard as their hearts that beat within them like some unfeeling, uncaring human pump. He knew if he didn't cooperate in some way, serious reprisals would fall upon his family and himself. His life was ruined; the only chance of salvation was if Sally's information was incorrect and they were not indicted. He did not want to think of the other alternative.

Two weeks had passed since his meeting with Sally. The Judge had put thoughts of it aside, hoping for the best. The judge kissed his wife good-bye and began walking down the sidewalk to the waiting limo. He paused for a moment to notice the dazzling reflection of the sun off the clean, freshly fallen snow. Sam already had the limo door open, waiting for him to enter.

"Good morning, Sam," the judge hailed still a good distance away from the limo.

"Hi, Judge, beautiful morning," Sam called back, glancing around and giving the beauty of the morning his seal of approval.

Entering the limo, the judge made himself comfortable and placed his stainless steel briefcase on the seat beside him.

"Are you ready for your coffee?" Sam asked as he swung the limo into traffic.

"Sam, how could I start my day without my cup of black nitro you call coffee," joked the judge.

Sam moved his seat forward and began holding the limo on course with his legs as he twisted the top off the thermos bottle. With practiced skill, he poured the steaming liquid into the judge's cup, on which was printed "Number One Dad" in bright red letters. Without taking his eyes off the road, he passed the steaming liquid to the judge. The judge knew from past experience to let it cool down and set the cup down in the beverage holder in front of him.

"You want your paper now?" Sam called out.

"No, thanks, I want to enjoy the ride a little."

The judge continued to look out the window, enjoying the beauty of the fresh fallen snow that covered the foliage as the limo whisked by. He smiled as they passed a snowman with a Santa Claus head cocked to one side. *Hmm . . .* , he thought to himself, *only two weeks before Christmas.*

"Hey, Sam, you can give me the paper now."

Sam reached to his right and folded the paper and held it up for the judge to take. The judge opened the folded paper and leaned back in shock. His worst nightmare had become a reality. The large bold black letters screamed out the bad news, causing him to gasp for air.

"Four reputed Crime Lords Indicted for Murder." He unconsciously refolded the newspaper and set it on the seat beside him. He closed his eyes, and memories of his meeting with Sally began running through his mind.

Sam pulled up to the Hall of Justice, and in a daze, the judge exited the limo and ignored Sam's good-bye. He entered the massive marble and glass structure, walking down the halls to his chambers, failing to acknowledge or respond to the friendly salutations of those who passed him by. Arriving at his chambers, he went directly to his desk and sank into his large brown leather chair without removing his camel hair topcoat. He was in deep thought and looked up at the sound of the heavy metal door opening from his bailiff's office. Joey

Cariola entered the room. He was carrying the clipboard with the day's docket schedule under his arm and a cup of coffee in his hand.

"Morning, Judge," he said as he continued to walk toward the large mahogany desk.

Joey's voice startled the judge out of his reverie. "Good morning, Joey," replied the judge as he stood up and took off his topcoat. Joey handed the judge his coffee and began to lay out the judge's messages on his desk in order of importance.

"I'll be right back. I've got to hit the john." Joey nodded his understanding and walked over to the couch and slumped down. Joey had known Carmen Carlivatti for over forty years, and he could tell by his demeanor that something serious was on his mind. As he relaxed on the couch, his mind wandered back to an incident that had taken place at Christmastime the year before. He and the judge were having lunch when he confided in the judge that he was depressed over the fact he was in debt over medical bills he owed following his wife's death of cancer. He explained that he had used up his life's savings paying for treatments not covered by his insurance and still owed eleven thousand dollars.

The day after the lunch, Joey found a white-trimmed red stocking taped to his telephone. An envelope was folded and stuffed in the stocking. On the envelope was written, "To my friend Joey" in the Judge's usual meticulous penmanship. Joey had never forgotten the words on the card. "Sometimes in the hustle and bustle of our everyday lives, we forget to properly acknowledge and say thank you to special people that we care about. Thank you for your loyalty and devotion, and most of all for your friendship for all these years." A check for eleven thousand dollars was attached to the note. "Buon natale! Your Friend, Carm."

Joey was startled by the judge's hand on his shoulder.

"Hey, Joey, did you fall asleep on me?"

"Naw, I was just thinking of something. So what did you have to tell me?"

The judge sat down on the couch next to his friend and told him the story of his meeting with Sally and his men.

"So what are you going to do, Carm?"

"I wish I knew. To tell you the truth, I have seriously considered suicide. That's the only way I can save my family from harm."

Joey was shocked at his words and tried to speak, but his word came out in a high falsetto. "Your problems are my problems. It's always been that way," Joey choked out his response, rising as he spoke. The judge put his arm around his shoulders. "Come on, partner, we got work to do. Get me my robe," said the judge, looking at the clock on the wall.

The judge donned his robe and headed to the door that was the entrance to the courtroom, where Joey was standing. When he arrived at the door, he paused a moment; grabbed Joey's right hand in both of his and squeezed them tightly. He winked at Joey, a smile on his handsome face as he walked through the door into the courtroom and headed toward the bench with Joey's voice ringing in his ears. "Everyone, please rise, the Honorable Carmen Carlivatti presiding." There was a discernible tone of pride in his voice.

The judge was in his limo heading home. He was looking forward to lighting the fireplace, having a martini, and relaxing when the car phone rang. *Who the hell can this be?* he thought. *It's a private number that no one has.* He picked up the phone.

"Hello." He heard the crackling of interference on the line.

"Hello," he repeated.

"Hello, Judge, Sally said. It's time to shit or get off the pot. Do you have anything for me to tell him?"

"Vinnie, this is Vinnie, isn't it?

"Ya, this is Vinnie."

"Look, Vinnie, tell Sally there's nothing I can say that I haven't told him already."

"I wanna make sure I understand your answer. Are you telling me you're not going to help us?"

"I'm not saying that, Vinnie. What I'm telling you, my hands are tied. There is nothing I can do," the judge replied, a tone of frustration in his voice.

"Same fuckin' thing. We'll be in touch real soon." The line went dead.

The judge slowly hung up the phone, deep in thought, and settled back into the plush cushions of the limo. His brain was racing, many thoughts going through his mind at the same time.

He knew one thing for certain—he must deal with the reality this problem was not going to go away. His one real concern now was the lives of his family. He started to weigh his options, and only one came back time and time again. With him out of the way, there would be no reason for Sally to harm his family. Suicide was his only option now.

Chapter 32

It was 6:30 a.m., and Judge Carlivatti was slowly driving through the old neighborhood where he was raised. Thoughts of his younger days were running around in his mind. He had made some serious decisions on how he would bring his problem with Sally to an end. For some unknown reason, the spiritual side of him made him decide to come to the seven o'clock mass at Mount Carmel Church, where he was baptized and confirmed. Spotting the church, he eased his white Fleetwood Cadillac into the parking lot and entered the church. Walking over to the holy water, he dipped his finger into the bowl, making the sign of the cross as he walked through the inner doors and sat down in the last pew. He glanced around the sparsely filled room and kneeled down and began to pray. Finishing his prayer, he unconsciously began to speak quietly to himself. "Lord, forgive me for what I am about to do today. Unless you give me a miracle, I have no other choice, or they will kill my family."

With that, he rose and exited the church and walked back to the Cadillac. Seating himself in the car, he opened the glove box and removed a .38 caliber pistol and put it in his coat pocket. He had made up his mind that today he was going to die.

He drove around aimlessly, deep in thought, trying to remember if he had done all the things necessary to make his financial matters easy for his wife to handle when he was gone. He glanced at the dashboard clock; it read one fifteen. He decided to head for home. He would have dinner and see his family one last time. He had made up his mind to leave home after dinner and go to the parking lot at the Hall of Justice and do his dastardly deed.

He walked into the house and could smell the pleasant aroma of sauce cooking. As he walked into the kitchen, his wife was stirring a large pot of sauce that was simmering on the stove.

"Hi, honey," he said as he hugged her from behind, his arms encircling her stomach.

"Hi, Carm," she answered, turning her head and kissing him on the cheek.

"So what kind of pasta are we going to have tonight? Rigatoni, I hope."

"No, it's not rigatoni. It's something you like much better. Go look under the towel," she motioned with her hand.

He walked over to the towel and grabbed two ends like a magician would do and muttered "Abracadabra!" as he removed the towel at the same time.

She was watching his face intently to see his reaction when he saw the homemade gnocchi.

"Wow!" he exclaimed. "What a nice treat."

She smiled proudly as he walked over to her and wiped some flour from her face. Their eyes met and signaled a message they both understood. They hugged and kissed passionately. "Tonight," she whispered. "Tonight," she repeated as she grinded her body against his and stroked the hardness between his legs.

"Let's go upstairs," he said as he opened her blouse and kissed her breast.

"No, honey, I got too much to do now, but I promise you, tonight. I'm so horny I'll fuck your brains out."

He smiled at the crudeness. "Sounds like a deal to me," he lied, knowing full well he would never be able to take her up on her offer. Tonight, he had a date with destiny and death.

"I'm going upstairs to take a nap."

"OK, I'll call you when dinner's ready."

"Carmen, Carmen, wake up!"

He rose up with a start. "What the hell is the matter, Rose?"

"Oh, Carmen, I'm so worried. The school nurse just called and asked if Christina was sick. She is not in school today. I'm beside myself with worry." She was now crying uncontrollably.

"Maybe she's just skipped school." He knew it was a stupid thing to say the minute the words left his mouth.

"Damn it, Carmen, you know better than that." Her tone was harsh and irritated. "Chrissy would never do something like that. I just know something terrible has happened."

He knew his wife's instincts were right. *God, I hope she's not dead*, he thought, recalling Sally's threats. "Settle down, honey. I'll call Lou Tacito and have him get some men on it right away." He reached over to the bedside telephone and dialed Joey Cariola.

"Judge Carlivatti's office," Joey answered.

"Joey, it's me. We got a real problem. Christina didn't show up at school today."

"Oh my god! No!" Joey gasped. "It's Sally, isn't it?"

"Of course it is. Sally said he would kill the girls one at a time," said the judge, sobbing and choking out the words.

"Is there anything I can do?"

"Yes, call Chief Tacito and tell him about my meeting with Sally and have him get some men working on it. I'm going to have my hands full with my wife. She's flipping out already and doesn't even know anything about the Sally thing."

"OK, Carm, I'll come over to the house after I make the call." As an afterthought, he asked, "Do you really think he would harm her?"

"I really don't know. Sally's capable of anything. My one hope is he's just trying to scare me into helping him, which is impossible for me to do. I'll see ya later." The judge hung up the phone in the middle of Joey's next question.

The judge sat up, his feet dangling over the edge of the bed. He placed his head between his hands, his mind racing a mile a minute. *No sense killing myself now. What I was trying to stop has already happened . . . . I can only hope she's alive . . . . . If he's killed her, I must kill Sally immediately myself to save the others regardless of what happens to me.*

The judge went downstairs, dreading the thought of facing his wife, who by nature was very excitable and emotional. He was surprised to see her putting the finishing touches on dinner.

"Honey, put out an extra plate. Joey's on his way over." She nodded her head to acknowledge his request. She liked Joey and knew he was Chrissy's godfather and they shared a very special relationship between them.

The evening at the Carlivattis' home was very quiet and solemn. After dinner, the girls went up to their rooms. Rose took some sleeping pills and retired to her room. Carmen lit a fire, and he and Joey played gin rummy until the early hours of the morning.

Joey looked at his wristwatch. "It's late, I should get going."

"Why don't you just stay here tonight? There's everything you'll need in the morning in the guest bedroom."

"OK, I'm going to hit the sack, then. I'm exhausted."

"Ya, me too!"

"Good night, Carm."

"Good night, Joey."

A new day had arrived. Stephanie and Angela had left for school. Joey and Carmen were seated around a small oak table drinking coffee and watching the morning news; Rose was knitting a multicolored afghan.

There was no conversation; everyone was deep in their own thoughts regarding the disappearance of Christina. Time dragged on with hardly a word being said. The judge got up and walked into the kitchen to get another cup of coffee. He glanced at the clock hanging on the wall. It read eleven minutes after eleven. Just then, the telephone hanging next to the snack bar began to ring. The judge raced over and answered it, beating his wife to the instrument by a split second.

"Hello," he said anxiously, wondering who was going to be on the other end of the line.

"Carm, it's Lou."

Oh God, oh God, let her be alive! he thought.

Lou Tacito was a well-trained professional and understood the fear and torment that was eating away at his friend on the other end of the line.

"Carm, we found her, she's alive . . ." He paused, waiting for the news to sink in and a feeling of relief to come before giving him the bad news.

"Rose, she's alive! Thank God! Thank God!" he exclaimed joy and relief in his voice.

"Who is it, Carmen? Who are you talking to, what's going on?"

The chief could hear the turmoil and waited patiently for the judge to return.

"I'm sorry, Lou, my wife is flipping out on me. Please go on."

"Carm, there's more. I was going to come over and tell you in person, but I decided not to waste another minute to give you the news."

"Thanks for that, Lou. Please go on."

"Well, Carm, the bad news is she's been raped, and we are not sure yet, but it may have been multiple times . . ." The chief paused to let his message sink in.

"Oh no, oh no!" the judge uttered.

"What's he saying? Damn it, Carmen, give me that phone!" she screamed, pounding him on his back and trying to snatch the telephone from his hand. The judge was now extremely irritated at his wife's behavior.

"Hold on a minute, Lou, I've got to get my wife out of here."

"Joey, take Rose in the family room, give her a shot of brandy or something, and tie her in a chair if you have to."

"Rose, please go with Joey. I'll get all the information, and I'll come in and tell you . . ." He paused a moment to catch his breath. "Is that OK?"

"I guess it will have to be," she responded angrily.

Joey bent down and picked up her knitting off the floor where she had thrown it. He gently took her by the arm and escorted her to the family room.

"I'm sorry, Lou, my wife has been a basket case since this all happened."

"Shit, Carm, I can well imagine what the two of you have been going through," the chief replied in a sympathetic tone.

The judge pulled up a barstool and sat down, bracing himself for the sordid details he knew were about to come.

"Well, she has been beaten up pretty bad, but it's nothing that won't heal up. But you can well imagine she's had a very traumatic experience. She'll be fine physically, Carm, but I'm more concerned about the mental scars that will remain long after her wounds have healed."

The judge listened attentively as the chief continued on.

"Now that you know what's happened, let me tell you what else we know so far. Then I'll answer your questions, is that OK?"

"Of course, please go on. I'm so fucking emotionally drained I can't even think anymore."

"Understood," the chief began again. "I had her taken to Our Lady of Mercy Hospital. I remembered she was born there, and I thought it might be your preference."

"Yes, that's where I would want her to be. Angelo Di Maggio's our doctor, and he's on staff there."

"Great, Carm, I knew Angie and you were good friends, so I took the liberty of calling Angie. As a matter of fact, he's with her right now."

"Thanks, Lou, you're right on target and have done just fine." The judge was getting impatient and wanted to hear the rest of the details so he could get to the hospital to see his daughter.

"Well, Carm, they grabbed her on the way to school. It was two men—a white guy and a black guy."

"What?" interrupted the judge.

"Please, Carm, hang on, let me finish." The judge remained silent, and the chief went on. "They took her to an old gravel pit about fifteen miles west of town. There's an old block building about a mile from the highway that used to be a scale house, and that's where she was raped. She fought back like a tiger, and that's when they beat her up."

"Did both men rape her?"

"She didn't know after the white guy raped her. She tried to escape, and the black guy caught her and knocked her out . . ." The chief paused to get a response from the judge.

"God, Lou, she's just a baby. Do you know how many times she was raped?"

"It's hard to tell, but the preliminary report indicates more than once," the chief responded in a sympathetic tone.

"Carmen, when are you coming in here to talk to me? I can't stand all this for another minute," she screamed out in a high, shrill voice.

"I'm just hanging up," he lied.

"We're almost done, Carm," said the chief. Hearing Rose's outburst, he continued on.

"They left her half naked on the floor of the building. I don't know if they intended for her to die of exposure or not. In any event, they underestimated her courage and will to live . . ." He paused a moment. "Carm, she walked nearly a mile from the scale house half naked and in stocking feet. It was a fucking miracle she made it. If she had fallen or stopped to rest, she'd have frozen to death. As luck would have it, a county plow truck happened to be driving by headed for their shop. The driver spotted her, ran over, and carried her to the warmth of the truck's cab. The guy was great. He wrapped her in his coat and gave her some hot coffee. The fact is, he probably saved her life. He called the sheriff's department from his radio, who I had already contacted about the kidnapping. They immediately sent a cruiser to get her and rushed her to the hospital. You know the rest." The chief was relieved the discussion was over.

Silence remained on both ends of the line.

The judge broke the silence. "That rotten, no-good, degenerate bastard Sally, he should burn in hell. Thanks for all your help, Lou."

The judge hung up the telephone, not waiting for a reply. The judge started to rise from the barstool and began to feel faint and dizzy. He grabbed for the countertop, trying to steady himself and hoping the feeling would pass.

"Carmen, what the hell's taking so long? What's he doing, reciting the Congressional Record," she screamed out.

"I'm coming, Rose! I'm coming!" *God, I'm glad Joey's here*, he thought. He knew the information he was about to share with her was going to blow her mind.

He began to slowly walk toward the family room on wobbly legs. He entered the room and took a seat next to his wife on the sofa. Joey was sitting next to her on the armrest, holding her hand. The judge was searching his mind for the best way to break the terrible news. She noticed his hesitation.

"Goddamn it, Carmen! Start talking. What the hell are you waiting for?"

She broke his concentration, and he began to blurt out the story just as the chief had explained it. When he began to tell her the sordid and disgusting details of the rape, something snapped in her mind. She jumped to her feet, pulling her hand from Joey's firm grip, yelling, and screaming. She raced across the room over to the windows facing the street and began tearing down the red crushed velvet drapes, at the same time pulling a handful of hair from her head. Joey reached her first and wrapped his arms around her waist. She spun around in his grip like a running back shaking off a tackle, leaving Joey standing there in stunned disbelief, holding her black silk blouse in his hand. Escaping Joey's grasp, she ran to the fireplace and picked up a large brass peacock resting majestically on the mantel, and spinning around like a discus thrower, she hurled the heavy brass object through the front window. Judge Carlivatti, still feeling faint and weak, made a feeble attempt to grab her as she ran past him, picking up anything she could get her hands on and throwing them around the room.

Crying hysterically, she was grabbing and tearing at her body with her nails, making long red marks wherever she touched. Realizing that her blouse was gone, she reached up and, with one swift motion, ripped off her brassiere revealing, her full white breasts. Joey ran over to her and grabbed her by the hand, but she jerked free from his grasp and ran to the other side of the room, her breasts bouncing like nipple balls as she ran. The judge, now on his feet, made a diving tackle and drove her to the floor and landed on top of her. She tried to throw him off, but he managed to restrain her and keep her pinned down.

He yelled out to Joey, "Hurry, call Dr. Di Maggio. He's at Our Lady of Mercy Hospital. Tell him our problem and to get here ASAP."

Joey was at the wheel of his black Dodge van trying to keep up with the ambulance that was transporting Rose Carlivatti to the hospital. Joey looked toward the passenger's seat; the judge had his eyes closed.

"Carm, you awake?"

Joey received no answer.

As they entered the doors of the emergency entrance, Judge Carlivatti spoke for the first time since leaving his home.

"Joey, I want to go right up and see Chrissy. Would you mind taking care of the paperwork for admitting Rose? Just answer what you can, I'll fill the rest out later." The judge headed for the elevator without waiting for a reply. He arrived at the elevator just as the doors began to close.

"Going up," he called out.

A thin, frail white arm shot out between the nearly closed doors. With a swift, deft movement, the arm pushed against the rubber stops, and instantly the doors reversed direction and began to open. The judge was surprised to see the arm belonged to a white-garbed nun, who was smiling at him, obviously proud of her accomplishment with her duel with the closing doors.

"Thank you, Sister," said the judge, a forced smile on his drawn face.

"You're welcome," she answered with a slight nod of her head, giving the handsome stranger a motherly smile.

"What floor?" she asked.

Holy shit, I don't know, he thought to himself. "Four," he lied.

The judge went back down to the admitting office. Joey was sitting at the desk, filling out Rose Carlivatti's paperwork. The judge put his hand on his shoulder.

"Thanks for today, my friend,"

"No problem, Carm, what are friends for?"

The judge glanced at the clock.

"It's three thirty, do you want to meet me later at Rocky's for some tripe?"

"I'd love to, but I got some business I need to take care of," Joey replied.

"OK, then, why don't you plan on coming to the house tomorrow. We'll watch some football, I'll order in a pizza, and we can drink a little beer and relax by the fireplace."

"Sounds great, you got a deal," replied Joey.

The two men shook hands, and the judge headed toward the door. He spun around, shaking his head. "I must be losing my mind," he said to Joey as he stood in front of the receptionist.

"Can you tell me what floor Christina Carlivatti is on and the room number?"

The receptionist went to her computer. "Fourth floor, room 411."

"Thank you, ma'am."

"See ya tomorrow, then," the judge said as he turned toward Joey.

"You got it."

The two men smiled at each other, and the judge hurriedly left the room.

When Joey arrived home, he went immediately to his office and sat down at his desk and picked up the telephone and dialed information. "Black Orchid Restaurant." The operator connected him to the number, and a man answered the call. "Black Orchid, how can I help you?" the voice asked.

"Is this Freddie?"

"Yes, this is Freddie."

"Freddie, this is Joey Cariola. I'm Judge Carlivatti's bailiff. He wants to see Sally tonight. What time will he be in for dinner?"

"It's hard to tell, Joey. He's all over the place. Hang on a minute, I'll look at the reservation book. We like to know when he's coming because sometimes we have to make something special for them. I'll be right back." Freddie returned in a few minutes.

"Joey, you still there?"

"Yes, I'm here."

"He's coming in at six. He leaves at about nine o'clock to go to Orlie's Joint to play poker, and that's the time the game starts."

"OK, Freddie, I'll tell the judge," Joey lied. "Thanks."

"No problem," Freddie replied.

Both men hung up the phone.

Joey got up from his desk and walked over to his bedroom closet, removing some shoes. He pulled away the carpet, revealing a floor safe that was embedded in the concrete. He opened the safe and pulled out his .38 caliber revolver. After placing everything back, he went over to his bed and set the alarm for seven o'clock. He had decided to take a nap; he stretched out on the bed fully clothed and closed his eyes. He jumped up at the sound of the alarm going off and glanced at the clock. The red digital numbers glowed seven o'clock. He picked up his gun from the dresser and loaded in nine rounds. Walking over to his bed, he took down the cross hanging over the headboard and placed it on the bed. He got down on his knees and prayed for several minutes, with the cross still in his hands, before walking to the garage and getting into his van.

On his way to the Black Orchid, he stopped at the minimarket to fill his thermos bottle with coffee. When he pulled up next to the restaurant, he spotted Sally's car parked one row back from the entrance of the restaurant. He pulled up directly behind Sally's white Lincoln Town Car and turned the heater in his van on high.

Joey glanced at the clock on his dashboard. It indicated it was eight o'clock; he had an hour to wait. He poured himself a cup of coffee and waited for Sally to exit the restaurant. Nine o'clock came and went. Joey was getting nervous and jittery. At twenty minutes after nine, Sally and five of his men emerged from the restaurant laughing and joking.

Joey shut off the engine and donned a face-covering knitted ski mask, leaving only his eyes exposed. He ran full speed toward the men, firing at Sally as he ran. He hit him five times in the chest, and Sally went down immediately on the wet pavement. The men, caught by surprise, now had their weapons in their hands and were firing close-range into Joey's body. Joey fell to the ground; he was dead instantly. Suddenly, to his men's amazement, Sally got up from the ground smiling.

"What the fuck!" uttered Jimmy the Brute.

Sally was laughing out loud at his men's astonishment. He opened his topcoat and then his suit jacket, revealing a bulletproof vest.

"Ya like it? I had it made—the best there is. So who is this dumb fuck who thought he could whack Sally Barratino? Take off that stupid fuckin' mask." One of the men leaned over and pulled off the mask.

"Anybody know him?" Sally asked.

"Ya, I do. His name is Joey Cariola. He's da judge's bailiff. The two guys are like brothers," said Vinnie Barratino.

"Gee, isn't that too bad," said Sally, laughing at his own sick humor.

Chapter 33

The telephone rang in Eddie D'Amico's apartment. Lorenzo LaRocca glanced at the clock as he walked over to pick up the phone. *Who the hell could be calling at six o'clock in the morning?* he wondered.

"Hello," he said into the mouthpiece.

The judge immediately recognized the voice. "Good morning, Lorenzo, this is Judge Carlivatti."

"Oh. Hi ya, Judge, how tings goin'?"

"Not good, Lorenzo. Not good at all."

"Gee, Judge, I'm sorry ta her dat."

"Where's Eddie?"

"He's in da shower. We're goin' fishin'. I'm makin' da lunch."

"Please have him call me as soon as he gets out. It's urgent."

"Ya got it, Judge."

The judge got off the barstool and walked over to the coffeepot and poured himself another cup of coffee and walked into the family room and slumped into his favorite chair to wait for Eddie to call. The portable phone in his hand rang; he glanced at the caller ID.

"Hi, Eddie."

"Morning, Carm, what's up?"

The judge got right to the point. "Sally had two goons kidnap Chrissy, and they raped her and left her for dead."

"That no-good cocksucker. When did it happen?"

"A couple of days ago. She's in the hospital. She's a fucking mess. I'd like to talk to you and run a few things by you . . ." The Judge paused. "What's your day like?"

"Shit, Carm, it doesn't matter. Just give me the time and place."

"Well, today's Saturday, and I was thinking of Jimmy's," the judge replied.

"I wasn't planning on going there today. Lorenzo and I were going fishing, and besides, the guys will all be there and we won't have any privacy. Why don't you just come over here?"

"Yes, you're right. I guess I just wasn't thinking straight. I'll be over in about an hour."

"OK, I'll have Lorenzo make some breakfast for us."

"In an hour, then." The judge hung up the telephone, deciding he would tell Eddie about the death of Joey Cariola in person.

Seeing Eddie had hung up the telephone, Lorenzo walked over and sat down across from Eddie.

"So what was dat all about?" Lorenzo asked.

"That fucking Sally had his daughter kidnapped by two of his fuckin' goons, and they raped her and left her out in the cold to die."

"Did she die?"

"Naw, thank God. She's in the hospital," responded Eddie.

"Ya know somethin', I've met a lot of bad motherfuckers in my time, but Sally beats dem all. He's da worst degenerate I've ever known. What da ya tink, should I wack 'im?"

"No, Lorenzo, you shouldn't wack 'im," Eddie laughed, smiling at his friend as he spoke.

"Well, da bastard deserves it. Be a plesur to see 'im croak," he responded as he walked out of the room.

The melodious chimes began to ring in Eddie's apartment, signaling someone was at the door. Eddie walked over to the door and swung it open.

"Morning, Carm."

"Hello, Eddie." The judge followed Eddie and sat down on the sofa.

"How about some coffee, or would you like a drink?"

"Coffee's fine, black."

Eddie called out toward the kitchen. "Hey, Lorenzo, bring out two cups of black coffee, will ya?"

Lorenzo appeared almost instantly and handed the first cup to the judge.

"Thanks, Lorenzo."

"No problem, Carm. I'm sorry to hear about your daughter."

The judge responded his acknowledgment with a nod of his head. Lorenzo laid his coffee mug on the table beside him.

"Lorenzo, don't bother making lunch. We're not going fishing today. We got bigger fish to fry today."

"OK, den, I'll be in my apartment. Just knock on da door when you're ready ta go."

Eddie waited for Lorenzo to leave the room.

"OK, Carm, start talking. Tell me how it all went down."

The judge began with his meeting at the Black Orchid, how Sally wanted him to fix the trial, his threats about killing his family one by one and then him. The sordid details of Chief Tacito's story of his daughter's kidnapping, the nervous breakdown of his wife, who would now require shock treatments to bring her around. He ended with the death of Joey Cariola. Eddie remained silent and spoke not a word as the judge choked up and cried on a couple occasions as he shared his story.

"I'm speechless, Carm. There's not enough for me to say how badly I feel for you. We've been friends for a very long time, and you know I love you like the brother I never had."

"I know, I know, Eddie," the judge said as he rose and walked over to where Eddie was seated. Eddie rose from his chair, and the two men embraced. The judge's body was convulsing as he gasped, trying to hold back his tears. It was Eddie who broke the silence.

"Come on, let's go in the kitchen. I have an idea on how we can fuck Sally right in his ass, and I'll make us some breakfast as I tell you."

"This I've got to hear," the judge replied, a strained smile on his face.

The judge walked over to the table, and Eddie poured him a cup of coffee as Eddie prepared breakfast. Eddie glanced at the clock on the kitchen wall. *Hmm . . .* , he thought to himself, *it took Carm over an hour to tell his terrible story.*

"How do you like your eggs?" Eddie called out as he stood in front of the stove.

"Over easy."

"Great, that's how I like mine. Hey, the toaster just popped, ya mind going over and buttering the toast?"

The judge finished his chore as Eddie put the bacon and eggs on the table and poured fresh coffee. They began eating their breakfast, and Eddie began to share his plan.

"Look, Carm, Sally's not stupid. He knows there's no way in hell anyone can fix a trial today—there's TV, cameras recording everything, news reporters in the courtroom. It just can't happen, but he is stupid enough to believe one thing. He believes money can buy anything, do you agree?" Eddie paused to wait for the judge to respond to his question.

"Well, it sounds plausible, but what are you driving at? I don't get the connection."

"You're going to call Sally and tell him you have a great idea how you can help him."

The judge broke in. "So what is this great idea?"

"You're going to convince him you can buy off the prosecutor for a hundred thousand dollars. He then will make mistakes like not provide the defense with all the evidence, pick dumb jurors who don't believe in capital punishment. In short, screw up the prosecution of the case so bad they will be found innocent and beat the rap."

"Come on, Eddie, that can't be done. Even if I found a prosecutor who would take the deal, we couldn't guarantee him he'd beat the rap."

"Carmen, have you gone brain dead on me? We're just going to make him think he can beat the rap and you are cooperating. This way, he'll lay off your family. All we care about is that the prick gets death or goes to jail for life."

The judge was now smiling broadly. "I like it, Eddie. You're a genius. I'll call him today."

"No, Carm, wait a couple of days. I have something I have to take care of first."

"OK, Eddie, but what am I going to do with the hundred thousand dollars?"

"You're not going to do anything. I want you out of this. You tell him you'll have me pick up the money and give it to the prosecutor. This way you're clean. He'll understand that."

"OK. Again, what are you going to do with the hundred grand?"

"What do you think I'd do? I'm going to set up a trust fund for Chrissy."

The judge chuckled at Eddie's answer. The two men rose from the table, and the judge was smiling, relieved at Eddie's solution to his problem. Eddie walked the judge to the door.

"Call me after you talk to Sally and make arrangements when I can pick up the cash."

"You got it," the judge replied, smiling from ear to ear as they shook hands.

Eddie walked over to the door that separated his apartment and Lorenzo's and knocked on the door.

"It's open," Lorenzo called out.

Eddie walked in. "You ready?"

"I was born ready," Lorenzo replied, smiling.

The two men were silent, deep in their own thoughts as they went down the elevator and out into the parking lot.

"Yer car or mine?" asked Lorenzo.

"Yours."

"OK, din, don't ya go sitin' in no backseat," said Lorenzo, smiling.

"I won't, I promise," Eddie laughed back.

They entered the white Cadillac Fleetwood Eddie had given Lorenzo as a gift. As the big white car exited the parking lot, Lorenzo asked, "Where to?"

"Sally's house."

Lorenzo turned to Eddie, a look of shock on his face. "Ya gata be kiden me."

"Drive," Eddie simply answered, smiling at his friend's astonishment. As they pulled into the driveway of Sally's house, it came to his mind. He spoke out loud, "Shit, I wonder if his kids are home."

"Naw, I herd der livin' wit his mother-in-law. Just him and his cousin Vinnie are livin' here now after he waxed his wife."

"Good!" Eddie exclaimed as he pushed the doorbell.

Sally answered the door dressed in a blue jogging suit.

"Well, well, if it isn't the Bobbsey twins. To what do I owe this momentous occasion?" said Sally sarcastically.

"Cut the shit, we need to talk," Eddie answered angrily as he pushed Sally out of the way and entered the house.

Sally was taken aback by Eddie's rudeness. "Follow me. We'll talk in the kitchen." The three men sat down at the kitchen table.

"So what's on your mind, Mr. D'Amico?" Sally asked sarcastically.

"I came to give you a fucking warning, you asshole. As of today, you're a dead man walking if you so much as touch any of Carmen's kids again. You're just going to be a dead man."

"Oh, is that all? Then you're in luck. I've already decided to leave his kids alone. I've decided to kill his wife instead. I figured, what's one more wife? I killed mine . . ." He paused and smiled. "And I guess today's as good as any to tell you that I killed yours. You really didn't think it was an accident?"

"I knew it, you rotten cocksucker," Eddie screamed out as he tipped over the table and pulled Sally from his chair and began to pummel him with powerful blows to the head and face. Sally fell to the ground, and Eddie began kicking him with all his might.

Hearing the commotion, Vinnie ran into the room with his pistol in his hand. LaRocca, anticipating someone would be coming, also had his weapon in his hand.

"Chill," LaRocca warned, "or you die."

Vinnie's eyes followed the red laser beam from LaRocca's weapon; it ended at his heart.

"Drop it," he ordered.

Vinnie's pistol fell to the floor, and Lorenzo walked over and picked it up.

"Ya satisfied now?" Lorenzo asked.

They looked down at Sally, who lay bleeding and unconscious on the floor.

"No, I'd rather have killed him," Eddie replied.

As they left the driveway, Lorenzo asked, "Where to?"

"Home. I want to walk across the street and talk to Carmella."

The two men remained silent as they drove. It was Lorenzo who spoke first.

"Ya know, Eddie, ya was right all along. Ya said ya tought Sally was behind dat accident dat killed Megan. I gotta say det prick had me fooled."

Eddie, shaking his head, slowly muttered, "He's gotta die."

When they arrived at the parking lot, Eddie spoke. "Stop here, I'm going across the street and see Carmella."

Eddie paused on the sidewalk a moment and stared at the large sign on top of the building with pride. It read, "Barratino Children's Home. He had made Carmella's dream come true, thanks to her father's money. He continued to walk across the street, entered the building, and pushed the call button on Carmella's penthouse suite.

"Good morning," the sweet-sounding voice of Carmella resonated through the speaker.

"Carm, it's me. I'm going up to your office floor. I don't want Nicoletta to hear the things I'm going to discuss with you."

"OK, Eddie, I'll be right down." The buzzer on the security lock unlatched. Eddie walked through the door and to the open door of the elevator and pushed number 3. Carmella was waiting for him as he exited the elevator. She gave him a warm hug and stepped back.

"Where did you get those marks on your face?"

"I just had a fight with Sally."

"Oh no, and Sally?"

"I left him unconscious on the floor."

"Well, I'm sure he deserved it. God knows he's possessed by Satan."

Eddie had followed her into her opulent large office and sat down on the plush white leather couch resting against the wall. Carmella sat down next to him and took his hand and cupped it in both of hers. With a soft tone in her voice, she asked, "So tell me, Eddie, what's troubling you?"

"That fucking Sally had Megan killed." The words gushed from his mouth, and tears began to immediately stream down his face.

"Oh God, no!" she exclaimed as she wrapped her arms around Eddie and began to weep with him. They remained locked in their embrace for a brief time, each deep within their own thoughts. Finally, Eddie rose and said, "There's more you should know." He then began to recount the despicable story of what Sally had done to Judge Carlivatti. He went into great detail about the kidnapping of his daughter, the breakdown of his wife, the death of Joey Cariola, and Sally's reasons.

She listened quietly as he related his sad tale. When he finished, he made a statement that caught Carmella off guard.

"Carmella, this can't go on. Sally has to die. Do you know how many people he has killed?"

"Eddie, I know much more than you think. I do," she replied.

Eddie walked back to the sofa and sat down next to her. Looking intently into her eyes, he asked, "Carm, would God forgive me if I killed Sally? He forgives us of everything if we ask forgiveness, doesn't he?"

She thought a moment and answered, "I think not, Eddie. You see, to be forgiven, you must have repentance in your heart and feel remorse for your deed, and you would have none of those feelings. In fact, I'm sure you would feel good and be happy you killed him. No, Eddie, don't let him drag you down to his level . . ." She paused a moment. "I do agree with you, though—he is evil to his very core and needs to die. The only question is, who's going to kill him?" she asked pensively.

Eddie looked at his watch. He didn't realize how long he had been talking to Carmella.

"I've got to get going!" he exclaimed.

She walked him to the elevator and gave him a long motherly hug.

"You be careful. God be with you."

"I love you, Carm," he called out as the elevator doors closed.

Chapter 34

S ally, Tony the Turk Scotto, Jimmy the Brute Testa, and Vinnie Barratino were seated around Sally's lawyer Tony Banducci's conference table. Sally had just finished discussing Judge Carlivatti's plan of bribing the prosecutor.

Sally was speaking. "Well, what do you think, Tony? Is it worth a shot? Could we maybe beat the rap?"

"Well, it can't hurt. I haven't asked for discovery yet, but from what I've heard through my sources, they got you by the balls. Did you get a call from Vinnie telling you they have been reconciling your accounts and there was over $135,000 missing?" Banducci paused.

"Ya, we had that conversation."

Banducci continued, "So, then, what was your reply?"

"I guess I told him Guido was a dead man."

"Is that right, Vinnie? Did he use those words exactly?"

"Ya, he said something like that. I don't remember the exact words he used,"

"OK, then, let's try another way. When you hung up the telephone, what was your impression on how Sally was going to fix the problem?"

"That he was going to kill Guido," Vinnie replied.

"Well, supposedly, the FBI has got that telephone conversation on tape, and if they do, it will be a hard rap to beat."

"So, then, let me ask you this, is it worth one hundred grand?"

"You guys will have to decide that. If you lose, you're facing death or life in prison. What are your lives worth? If this guy can fuck the case up enough and select soft jurors, you may be acquitted. On the other hand, if he purposely makes enough mistakes, we may get a mistrial, and that means we get another bite at the apple."

"Ya, I see what you're driving at. It's worth the dough to take a shot."

"Exactly. We need to pursue all options if we are going to have a shot at winning."

"OK, then, I thought you would think we should go ahead with this, so I came prepared."

Sally reached down on the floor and picked up a burlap sack and threw it across the table in front of Banducci.

"There's a hundred grand in there. Eddie D'Amico will be picking it up . . ." He paused a moment. "If I didn't have this thing hanging over my head right now, that fuckin' Eddie would be dead already."

"Come on, let's get the fuck out of here."

Judge Carlivatti was having dinner with his daughters. His wife was still in a sanitarium recovering from her nervous breakdown. The telephone rang, and Christina ran over to answer it. She returned carrying a portable telephone. She handed the telephone to her father.

"It's for you. Some guy named Sally."

The judge quickly walked over to the bathroom and closed the door.

"Hello, Sally."

"Well, I discussed our little matter with my lawyer, and he said I should take the deal. I left a little package with him. D'Amico knows him and where his office is. He can go there tomorrow and pick up the package."

"That's great, Sally. I'll do my very best for you."

"You better," Sally said and hung up the telephone.

The judge sat down on the commode and looked at his wristwatch; it was 7:00 p.m. *God, I hope Eddie's home*, he thought. He could hardly wait to tell Eddie the good news.

Eddie and Lorenzo were in the kitchen eating dinner when the telephone rang.

"Hello," Lorenzo answered.

"Hello, Lorenzo, it's Carmen, is Eddie there?"

"Ya, he's right here." The big man stretched out his long arm and handed the telephone to Eddie.

"It's the judge."

"Hi, Carm, what's going on?"

"Eddie, you're fucking brilliant! Sally just called me, and he bought the deal hook, line, and sinker. He said he left the money with his lawyer, and you can pick it up tomorrow. He indicated you knew his lawyer . . ." The Judge paused, waiting for Eddie to answer.

"Yes, I do. His name's Tony Banducci, and he's one hell of a lawyer."

"You know, Eddie, now my kids will be safe, and I was willing to kill myself to keep them safe, and you did it with just words. I owe you my life."

"Well, if you feel that strongly about it, you can quit the bench, and you can have Lorenzo's job," he chuckled, winking at Lorenzo as he spoke. "If you do, then Lorenzo can retire."

"I'm serious, Eddie—if there's anything at all I can do."

Eddie broke into his conversation. "I do have some parking tickets you can fix."

"You know, from the time we were kids, you always were a silly bastard. Go pick up the money," the judge chuckled into the phone and hung up, not waiting for Eddie to reply.

Eddie went over to his reclining chair and turned on the TV. After cleaning up the kitchen, Lorenzo walked into the living room and stood next to Eddie's chair.

"Ya wanna play some gin?" he asked.

"You know, Lorenzo, you're so good it takes a lot of thought and concentration for me to beat you. With all that's been going on, my brain is fried. I'm just going to crash here and watch TV."

"So why don't you just play me wit out your thought and concentration den so I can beat cha and take your dough?" Lorenzo was happy with his comeback; he took up a boxer's position and danced around Eddie's chair, jabbing him lightly on the shoulder twice.

"OK, ya wanna box, den?" Lorenzo asked, dancing around and throwing punches into an imaginary target.

"If I were going to box with you, I'd have a .44 magnum in my hand," Eddie quipped, laughing at his friend's actions.

"Den ya better have a full clip 'caus ya know me, I'd just keep boring in," Lorenzo replied laughingly.

"OK, den, I guess I'll go over ta Orlie's Joint and play poker." He turned and walked over to the door.

"Good luck, champ," Eddie called out, a broad smile on his face.

Eddie had dozed off in his chair. He was jolted awake by the sound of his door chimes. Rising to his feet, he glanced at the clock behind the bar. The digital numbers read eleven thirty. "Who the hell can this be at this hour?" he muttered to himself.

He opened the door and was surprised to see the beautiful Cat Ladd wearing a magnificent white mink coat. He stood silently for a moment, too stunned to speak.

"What about it, Eddie, are you going to ask me in?"

"Ya, sure, you just surprised me, that's all. You're more beautiful than ever," he said as he stepped back to let her enter.

"So what brings you here?"

"You," she replied simply.

"How long has it been since we saw each other?" she asked.

"Hell, I don't know, Cat. I think it's got to be well over a year."

She walked over to the bar and picked up a bottle of Crown Royal. Reaching into the refrigerator, she pulled out a handful of ice cubes and put them into the glass. Pouring an abundant amount of the liquor into the glass, she looked at Eddie and asked, "Mind if I make myself a drink?" she asked with a smile on her face.

"Why ask, you've already done it."

She took a long swallow from the glass and set it on top of the bar. She slowly walked toward Eddie, swaying her body from side to side as she approached him. He stood silently, transfixed by her captivating beauty.

"I can't tell you how many times I lay in bed at night wishing you were lying next to me. I can't tell you how many times I pleasured myself while I fantasized you were fucking me. I have always loved you, Eddie, and will to the day I die."

She now stood inches away from Eddie. He was aroused by her words and her beauty. They kissed passionately, her hot tongue deep into his mouth, her body grinding and bumping into his, her hand stroking the hardness between his legs. She owned him to do with him as she pleased; he had not been with a woman for months, not since Megan's death. He was ready for any and all the pleasures she was about to provide. She began licking his face and his eyes with her hot tongue. Finally, she suddenly stopped and smiled seductively at him.

"No fantasies for me tonight, Eddie. I want you, and I'll do all the tricks one could imagine. I want you to fuck me all night."

She opened the mink coat, revealing her beautiful naked body. Eddie stood speechless as she undressed him. She dropped to her knees and took his manhood deep into her mouth. He held her by the head and moaned in pleasure. She continued on until she could taste the sweetness of him in her mouth. She rose to her feet, kicking off her shoes as she walked over to a big overstuffed chair and sat down on the edge of the chair, spreading her legs wide and still smiling at Eddie. She stuck her fingers in her mouth and began to pleasure herself, watching Eddie and smiling. "Are you just going to stand there and watch?"

"Come on, baby. Now it's my turn," she taunted.

Eddie walked over to her and dropped to his knees and buried his head between her legs. She moaned in abysmal pleasure.

"Oh yes, baby, yes," she screamed out.

She lifted her legs and rested them on Eddie's shoulders, drawing his face closer into her body. The sweet taste of her was in his mouth, his darting tongue driving her to new heights of wanton pleasure.

"Oh yes, yes, Eddie, now, now . . ." His face was resting against her convulsing body as she reached her orgasm. Eddie rolled back and lay outstretched on the floor, watching her every move.

"Oh, baby, that was great," she said as she rose and went over to her purse and lit a cigarette. She grabbed an ashtray and went and sat down next to Eddie on the floor.

"You had enough?" he asked, smiling as he spoke.

"Are you kidding? I've been dreaming of this day for over a year, imagining it while I used my dildos and my hands pretending it was you. As soon as I finish this cigarette, I want you to take me into the bedroom and fuck me all night. I want to feel you deep inside of me and your lips on my breast." Her pornographic talk was turning him on again.

They walked to the bedroom holding hands each aroused by the thought of what was still to come. Eddie lay on his back, and she buried her head between his legs. When she had him aroused, she lay on her back with legs wide spread. "Fuck me, Eddie. Please hurry, I can't wait to feel you inside of me." He slowly penetrated her depths, playing and toying with her. "Please, Eddie, don't tease me. Harder, harder," she cried out. With a powerful thrust, he was deep inside of her, their bodies moving in unison. "Yes, yes, baby, harder, harder. Now, Eddie, now, together." Their bodies were now trembling in sublime pleasure. They embraced and kissed passionately.

"Man, I needed that," she whispered in his ear.

"Ya, me too. It's been many months since I've been with a woman."

"You've got to be kidding me?"

"No, it's true. I guess I've been too busy even to think about it."

"It's hard to believe that you could be too busy to get laid. Well, you just rest up. I'm going to put this horse through the paces a few more times tonight before this race is over," she said jokingly.

Cat was true to her words; it was early morning before they fell asleep in each others arms.

Eddie woke up and looked at Cat. *God, she's beautiful,* he thought. He picked up a blanket and stared at her naked body, her golden hair cascading down, partially covering her face. He gently covered her nakedness with the blanket and walked over to the closet. He reached in and brought out a bathrobe and slippers that had belonged to his wife. He laid the bathrobe on top of the bed and carefully placed the slippers on top of the robe. He glanced at the clock: 6:50 a.m. *Hmm, I think I'll take a steam today after that workout. Man, she's great sex. I didn't realize how much I've missed having a woman in my life,* he thought to himself.

Eddie had remained in the steam deep in thought of all the things happening in his life, but one thought kept reccurring. He was going to ask Cat to move in with him. He exited the steam room wrapped in a towel. He hurriedly dressed in a blue-and-white-trimmed jogging suit and running shoes to match. He quietly walked into the kitchen and saw that Cat was in front of the stove frying bacon. He quietly moved in behind her and kissed her gently on the back of the neck. She immediately turned and molded her body next to his and gently kissed his lips.

"I love you, Eddie," she whispered in his ear.

"Hey baby, the bacon's burning."

"Oh shit!" she exclaimed, returning to the smoking bacon.

They had finished breakfast. Cat had lit up a cigarette, and she watched with interest as Eddie lit up a large cigar.

"Eddie, I didn't know you smoked?"

"I don't do it very often, but I do smoke a good cigar once in a while."

"Really, so how do you tell a good cigar?"

"It's expensive," he joked.

"Listen, Cat, I've got something I'd like to talk to you about. After last night, you made me realize how much better a man's life can be if he has a woman to share it with . . ." He paused.

She looked deep into his eyes, wondering where he was going with this.

"And so, if I were to ask you to move in with me, what would the answer be?"

"Well . . ." She paused. "Why don't you ask me and see?" There was a dazzling smile on her face.

"Cat, will you move in with me?"

Tears began to slowly stream down her face. "Eddie, I'd go with you to the end of the world if you asked me to." She slowly rose out of her chair and went over and sat on his lap. She kissed him gently on the lips and laid her head on his shoulder. Her voice was with heavy emotion. "Eddie, I have loved you all my life, but you chose two others over me. I've lived with that hurt all these years. When Megan died, I thought for sure you would be coming back to me, but you never came. I waited over a year, and still you never came. Last night I decided I was not going to wait one more day. Would I move in with you? I'd go through the fires of hell if you asked me to."

They embraced, enjoying the warmth and presence of each other's company. It was Eddie who broke the silence.

"I've got a couple of stops to make. Go into Megan's closet and find some clothes to put on. She was about your size. Find a coat you like and leave the mink here. It's too ostentatious for day wear. As we're driving, we'll discuss the logistics of your move here."

"God, Eddie, you sound like we're building one of your projects."

"Life is full of expectations. We'll discuss what you can expect from me and what I'll expect from you."

After a half-hour wait, Cat walked into the living room.

"I'm ready."

"Wow, you look great, baby!" Eddie exclaimed with a smile on his face.

Cat began walking to the door that she came in.

"No, Cat, follow me." Eddie headed to the door between his and Lorenzo's apartment. He paused and knocked.

"Are you dressed?" Eddie called out.

"Ya, I'm dressed. Why, ain't ya ever seen me naked? Its open," the voice boomed out.

Cat had a puzzled look on her face as they entered the room and she saw the frightening figure of Lorenzo. She was astonished and moved a step back to get slightly behind Eddie.

"Lorenzo, this is Cat."

"Wow, she's beautiful. Is she real or a blowup doll?" Lorenzo joked. "Hi, Cat, I'm Lorenzo. Yur really somtin'. Ya might sa dat yur da cat's meow." Lorenzo burst out laughing at his own joke.

Cat moved forward with her hand outstretched. "Hello, Lorenzo. And you, you're one hunk of a man."

"Ya, dat's me, one hunk of a man. Ya know, I like her already. Ya outa keep her around, dat's what I say."

"I did. We just made the deal."

"Well, Cat, me and youse are gona be seein' alota each uder."

"That's great, Lorenzo." She walked up to him and stood on her toes and kissed him on both cheeks.

"Wow!" he uttered, putting his hand on his cheek. "I ain't ever gonna wash my face agin."

"Lorenzo, Cat and I have some running to do. Why don't you do whatever you do when you have nothing to do?" Eddie laughed at his play on words.

"What da hell ya talkin' about? Don't confuse me," Lorenzo joked back.

Eddie and Cat entered the hallway from Lorenzo's door and boarded the elevator.

"Wow, Eddie, I didn't know you had a trained gorilla."

On the ride down, Eddie gave Cat a brief rundown on Lorenzo's background. As they exited the elevator, Cat exclaimed, "You mean he actually killed people?"

"More than we can count," he replied as they entered the parking lot.

"Where's your car?"

"Right here," he answered and pointed to a sleek red Ferrari. Cat remained silent as Eddie maneuvered the Ferrari out of the parking lot.

"Eddie, are you rich?"

"Well, sorta," he replied. Little did she know the great wealth he possessed, thanks to Don Francisco and the sale of his construction business.

"Why, does it matter?"

"Hell no, baby, I'd be just as happy to be with you if we lived in a refrigerator box on a vacant lot."

"Damn, that's saying a lot. You certainly made your point," he laughed as he patted her on the leg.

"Would you mind telling me where we're going?"

"Well, I have a couple of stops to make, so I'm going to drop you off at the mall to do some shopping. Then I'll pick you up, and we'll go have lunch and discuss our future together."

"That all sounds great, Eddie, but I don't have that kind of money, and my credit cards are maxed out."

"Not to worry, I'm going to fix all that when I let you out of the car."

Cat was getting excited the more she found out about the handsome, fast-living man she had yearned to be with all these years. They reached the mall, and Eddie pulled into a fifteen-minute parking zone. He reached into his pocket and pulled out a large roll of one-hundred-dollar bills.

"Hold out your hands." He began to count as he placed the bills in her hand.

"Eddie, you're not on drugs or anything, are you? You just gave me five thousand dollars!"

"Honey, one thing I can do well is count money. Buy what you like and save the rest, and remember, there's plenty more where that came from."

"I'll call you when I'm done, and I'll meet you back here in the same spot."

She leaned over and kissed him on the cheek. She watched as he peeled away from the curb with tires screaming and smoke rising from them as he sped down the street.

Eddie walked out into the parking lot of the building where Tony Banducci had his office. He was carrying the burlap bag full of money. Arriving at the Ferrari, he popped open the trunk and threw the bag inside. He drove into a shopping center, which his attorney, Harley Jackson, owned and which housed his office. Finding a spot next to his suite, he parked the Ferrari and entered his office.

"Hi, Eddie," Helen, his longtime secretary, called out.

"Hi, Helen, is he in?"

"No, he's in court, but he should be in shortly. Is there anything I can do?"

"I'm sure there is. You do all the paperwork around here anyway."

"You got that right," she laughed back.

"All I need is a simple trust. Here's all the information." He handed her a paper he had retrieved from his pocket.

"This shouldn't take too long."

"All I want is the paperwork. You can do all the seals and book at your own convenience."

"Oh, in that case, give me about an hour and I'll have everything ready for you."

"Great. Thanks, Helen."

After leaving his lawyer's office, he drove to the bank. He walked in carrying the burlap bag full of Sally's money. Knowing where he was heading, he walked to the back office, knowing he would find the branch manager there. Eddie paused at the door a moment. Sensing Eddie's presence, the gray-haired man sitting at the desk looked up.

"Good morning, Eddie," the manager said as he rose from his chair with his hand outstretched.

"Morning, Clint," Eddie replied as they shook hands.

"What can I do for you today?" Clint asked as he eyed the burlap bag lying on his desk.

"I want to make a deposit."

"I see," Clint said as he peered into the bag. "So what did you do, rob a bank?" he joked.

"Naw, I've been saving one-hundred-dollar bills for years. I thought it was time I got them out of my apartment," Eddie lied. "I'm setting up a trust for Christina Carlivatti, which she can't withdraw until she's eighteen, so put it in an interest-bearing account. Oh, one other thing—put her father on the account also in case something happens to me. He can control the funds. Any questions?"

"No, oh well, yes, you don't have to tell me, but I'm curious. That's a lot of money to be giving a little girl."

Before he could answer, an attractive young woman entered the room.

"You rang?" she said with a smile on her pretty face.

"Yes, Margie, run this through the counter and log it in."

"Yes, sir," she replied, flirting with Eddie as she left the room.

Eddie was leaving Harley Jackson's office and dialed Cat's number on his car phone.

"Hello," her soft, sexy voice came through the earpiece.

"I'm on my way. Did you spend all the money?"

"Are you kidding? I just picked up a few little things that caught my eye, but I'm hungry."

"Great, we'll go to Rocky's. Do you like tripe?"

"Shit, no."

"Well, I love it. Rocky's got plenty of other things you can choose from. See ya soon."

"I'll be there. Look for an exhausted woman carrying two red shopping bags," she quipped.

"I'll keep my eyes open," he chuckled as he hung up the telephone.

Eddie and Cat were in the Ferrari heading back to the apartment.

"Wow, Eddie, that food was dynamite. I never had veal parmigiana before."

"You'll see, Cat, I'll make an Italian out of you before you know it," he said laughingly.

"That would be wonderful. I hope you plan on doing it by injection," she laughed.

"Hey, that's a great idea. I'll you give you a couple of injections when we get back to the apartment."

"I can hardly wait," she answered, placing her hand between his legs.

Chapter 35

Judge Carlivatti, Eddie, and Lorenzo were in the judge's chambers, seated at a conference table that overlooked the view of the city. The trial of Sally and his three cohorts had been in progress for seven weeks.

"So tell me, Carm, how do you think its going?" Eddie asked.

"Shit, I don't know. I'm not in the courtroom. All I get is bits and pieces from the court reporter and the security details. It doesn't mean much. It seems to me in the final analysis, it boils down to just one thing—is the jury going to believe the testimony of the FBI agent and the sheriff's captain? The case would have been much stronger if they had the voices of Vinnie and Sally on tape."

"So, Carm, do ya tink da gotta shot of beatin' dis rap?"

"Could be, Lorenzo. Remember, Sally claims he was in Chicago at the time of the hit. It'll be hard for them to prove he wasn't, and if they don't buy it, they could walk," Carmen finished, shaking his head in disgust.

"Damn it, Carm, there's got to be something we can do?" blurted out Eddie. "We can't let them bastards get away with this."

"We've done all we can, Eddie. The final decision is going to lie in the hands of twelve people. It is what it is. All we can do now is hope for the best, and that Tony Banducci is one hell of an attorney. He's driving the prosecution crazy."

Eddie suddenly rose to his feet.

"Come on, Lorenzo, let's get out of here. See ya, Carm. Oh, I forgot to give you these." Eddie reached to his inside pocket and pulled out some papers and handed them to the judge.

"What are they?" the judge asked, not bothering to read the documents.

"They are copies of Christina Carlivatti's trust and a deposit slip for one hundred thousand dollars," said Eddie, beaming with pride. "Oh, and I set it up so she can't touch the money until she's eighteen. Even then, all checks will require either your signature or mine, and in the event I should croak, you will become the administrator of the account."

"As usual, you thought of everything. I can't thank you enough for helping me out of this mess."

"Well, there's nothing to get cocky about. One thing's for sure—we're not out of this mess yet."

The two men shook hands, and Eddie and Lorenzo headed for the exit door.

Eddie and Lorenzo were in Lorenzo's car.

"Where to?" asked Lorenzo.

"Home. I've got some things I want to discuss with Cat."

"Ya, I bet ya do. Wit a gerges broad like dat, yu'll be doin' a whole buncha takin' with yur dick."

Eddie turned and smiled at his friend.

"Ya, partner, maybe some of that too," Eddie finished, giving Lorenzo a friendly jab on his side.

"So wad ar ya gonna talk about?"

"What if I said it's none of your fucking business?"

"Den I'd say ya broke da fuckin' rule. Best friends are supposed to tell each oder evry thin'."

"So, then, whose rule would I be breaking?" Eddie asked with a smile.

"Mine," replied Lorenzo.

"So when did you make this rule?" Eddie asked, enjoying the give-and-take of the conversation.

"Just now," was the response.

"Lorenzo, you are really a piece of work," Eddie joked.

"Ya, dat's me, all right. Lorenzo LaRocca, one real piece of work," he said proudly.

As they got off the elevator at the hotel, each man went to their apartment.

"Hi, Eddie," Cat called out as she entered the room when she heard the door close behind Eddie.

"Would you make me a martini? Then let's go in the living room. There's a couple of things I'd like to discuss with you, but I want to get out of these clothes and relax first."

Eddie returned in a lightweight gray jogging suit. Cat was seated on the couch; two drinks were waiting on the coffee table. He picked up his martini and flopped down into his favorite chair.

"So what's this meeting about? You're acting like it's serious."

"It is," Eddie replied.

Cat didn't like the way the conversation was going and became uneasy.

"Cat, who's taking care of your apartment complex since you moved in with me?"

"My sister. She's moved into my suite. She runs everything for me before when I went on vacations. The apartments will do just fine, but why do you ask?"

"Well, I want us to have something more permanent."

Cat broke into his conversation.

"I thought we had something permanent, Eddie. I didn't realize I was on trial," she finished sarcastically.

"I'm sorry, baby. Maybe I used the wrong choice of words when I said permanent. I mean, I don't want you to just be my beautiful trophy or my broad. What I want you to be is my wife."

Cat was dumbstruck, and tears began to stream down her face. She slowly rose and walked over to the footstool next to Eddie's chair.

"Eddie, I've loved you ever since we dated in high school. I was crushed when you got engaged to Megan. Then her father got involved, and she ended your relationship. You only came to see me when you wanted to get laid. But that was all right with me because I loved you so much. Then you married Danni, and I was crushed, and you screwed around with God knows how many women, including me, while you were married to her. Then Megan came back, and you divorced Danni and married Megan, and you never came to see me again in over a year. The only question I have now is if I wasn't good enough for you to marry those three times, what in the hell has changed that would make you want to marry me now? Aren't you satisfied just to have me just around to be your punching board to just fuck or get a blow job when you want one?" she finished angrily.

"Cat, everything you said is true, but people change. After Megan's death, I didn't even think of another woman. The other night with you was the first time I had sex since she died, and that was over a year ago. But that night, you woke something up that lay dormant inside me. I've got the same feelings inside of me that I had when we were so madly in love in high school. I want to marry you and give you the dignity of being my wife. I want to have kids and to be a father.

I want to have a family and do the things that normal people do. I'm ready to get out of this fast lane I been living in and enjoy life. I have enough money to live a hundred lifetimes, and I know now that deep in my heart, I've always loved you, so I'm going to ask you one more time, but it's only on one condition. I want to have children and be a father. If you want what I want, say yes. If you don't, then we can just keep on playing the same game we are playing now."

She rose from the footstool and sat on his lap, gently kissing and stroking his face. "I've loved you all my life. There is no reason I should stop loving you now. Of course I'll marry you and be the mother of your children. I love you enough to give my life for you. So come on, honey, let's go seal this deal in bed," she said, smiling as she grabbed his hand.

"What time is it?" Eddie asked as he rolled over to look at the clock.

"Eleven o'clock," she answered.

"Wow, that late. You weren't kidding when you said you wanted me to fuck your brains out, did I?"

"Not quite, do you want to go again?"

"I don't think so. I've got to save myself for our honeymoon. Speaking of that, when do you want to get married, and where are we going to do it?"

"Well, I thought Las Vegas—it's the Wedding Capital of the World. I was a witness for a friend of mine a few years ago. It was a nice place. I think the name of the place was the Heavenly Chapel. I believe it was on Third Street."

"You realize we will need witnesses. I heard horror stories. I don't want them to just pick some people off the street.

"Don't sweat it. I've got it figured out. I've got a friend named Ricardo Solitz. I bought some Cadillacs from him when he lived in town. Now he lives in Vegas and is the sales manager of one of the Cadillac dealers there. We've stayed in touch. I'm sure we can count on him. He's a good friend of mine. Let's see, there's another friend of mine. You'll like her—her name is Sheri Baines. She's tall and beautiful and has a terrific body. She's a waitress in one of the casinos, but her real love is her ranch. The last time we talked, she had eleven horses. Then I think it would be nice to have someone sing "Ave Maria." It's a beautiful song, and it will make the ceremony feel more like church."

"Let me guess, I suppose you have someone in mind for that too?"

"Yes, as a matter of fact, I do."

"And who might that be, pray tell," Cat asked, smiling at Eddie's excitement in planning for their wedding day.

"Well, her name's Sheri Askins, but her stage name is Sheri La Mour. She sings in the lounge rooms around Vegas, and she's got a great voice."

"Well, Mr. Smart Ass Wedding Planner, you forgot just one thing. Aren't we going to have pictures to look at when we are old and gray?"

"Oh shit, I did forget about that. Let me think. Oh, I got it. David told me once he was doing photography for a living. I always called him the Wizard. Man. He can do anything. He was a biker, a marine, an air traffic controller, but I don't have his number. But I know Sheri Askins can get him. They're good friends."

She snuggled up to him, impressed he could put things together in his mind so fast.

"So when do you think you want to do it?"

He paused a moment before answering. "How about day after tomorrow we leave. Tomorrow you go buy yourself a nice dress, do all your woman things—hair, et cetera, et cetera. Just bring what you need. You can buy all the clothes you want in Vegas. Does that sound OK?"

"Yes, Eddie, it's perfect. It all sounds wonderful. Now I want you to make love to me."

Eddie rolled over in bed and reached for Cat. She wasn't there; he glanced over to the clock on the nightstand. The digital numbers showed 6:30 a.m. *She's up already?* he thought to himself as he headed toward the kitchen. He found her at the table drinking a cup of coffee and smoking a cigarette.

"You're up early," he said as he poured himself a cup of coffee.

"Oh, Eddie, I couldn't sleep. I'm so excited about us getting married and going to Vegas. It's all like a dream come true. I called and made arrangements for our flight. We'll leave at 5:00 p.m. tomorrow. Now I have so much to do today I really need to get going."

"Well, you have three options—you can take the Ferrari, the Cadillac, or you can have Lorenzo drive you."

"Do you think Lorenzo would mind taking me? It would save me so much time not parking and all."

"I'm sure he won't mind. He likes you. He says you're hot. Just go knock on the door an ask him."

"Do you think he's up?"

"Ya, he's an early riser."

"OK, then." She walked out of the kitchen and headed to the door between the two apartments.

Eddie called information. "Tropicana Hotel, Las Vegas, Nevada." The operator connected Eddie to the number.

"Good morning, Tropicana," a sweet-sounding voice answered.

"Lisa Powers, please."

"I'll see if she's in."

Eddie was counting on the time difference. He knew it was later in Vegas.

"This is Lisa, how can I help you?"

"Hi, Lisa, this is Eddie D'Amico."

"Well, how are you? It's been a long time since we've talked."

"Yes, I know, over a year. I'm coming to Vegas to get married. Do you have a nice suite for me?"

"Of course, that's not a problem. When you coming in?"

"I don't know my arrival time, but I'll call you and let you know. Can you have the limo pick me up at the airport?"

"Sure, we can do that."

"Oh, by the way, is Johnny Johnson still driving for you?"

"Yep, he's still here, as ornery as ever."

"Great, I'll call you with the time."

The line went dead on both ends just as Cat returned to the kitchen.

"Well, you're all smiles, what did he say?"

"He said it would be his pleasure. He even said he'd take me to lunch, how's that for a deal?"

"Sounds pretty good to me. I told you he liked you. Now you'll have a good friend for life."

"That's reassuring. Now if anybody messes with me, I'll sic the D'Amico family gorilla on them." She laughed as she put her arms around Eddie and gave him a long, wet kiss.

"I've got to hurry and get dressed. What are you going to do today?"

"Chill out, just stay home, and do bum," he answered.

It was late in the evening when Lorenzo and Cat entered Eddie's apartment, each laden with shopping bags and boxes. Eddie looked at his wristwatch; it was 8:30 p.m.

"You guys have been gone all day."

It was Lorenzo who answered. "Shit, man, now I know what da broads are takin' about when da say der gonna shop till day drop."

"Well, are you going to show me anything?"

"Nope," Cat replied. "You'll see everything when I wear them."

Cat and Eddie spent the next day at home discussing their new life together, and both agreed they wanted to have a child as quickly as possible. Finally, it was departure time, and Lorenzo took them to the airport.

When they arrived at the airport, true to her word, Lisa Powers had the limo waiting for their arrival. Eddie spotted the limo driver, Johnny Johnson, in the crowd, and they walked over to where he was standing. The two men fondly embraced.

"Hi, Eddie, you look great. It's been a long time."

"Ya, Johnny, over a year."

"Lisa told me you're here to get married, and of course, this beautiful woman here is the Mrs. D'Amico-to-be. Hello, m'am," he said with his hand outstretched. "I'm Johnny."

"Hello, Johnny, I'm Cat."

"I've got to tell you, Cat, you are absolutely drop-dead gorgeous," he said with a wistful sigh.

She blushed at his statement and replied, "Thank you, Johnny. You're very kind."

"It's the truth, Cat. Nothing but the truth."

Eddie stood by, proudly smiling as the exchange of words took place. Cat walked up to Johnny and placed a kiss on each cheek.

"Wow!" he exclaimed. "You're a sweetheart."

The pleasantries over, they went to the baggage claim, picked up their luggage, and went to the waiting limo. When they arrived at the room, Cat was taken aback by its splendor.

"Look, Eddie, a spa tub right here in the bedroom. It's got mirrors all around it, and even mirrors on the ceiling over the top of it. Why do they do that?"

"Can't you guess?" he replied.

"No, why? Tell me."

"Well, some people like to make love in the tub, and with the mirrors, they can watch themselves in action."

"Oh man, what a turn-on that must be. Can we try it tonight?"

"Of course." He smiled.

After a dinner of steak and lobster, they went to the ballroom and danced. The orchestra was playing soft, soothing dance music. Cat was a bit tipsy from all the champagne she had consumed. They were slow-dancing, their bodies hard-pressed against one another, Cat grinding her body seductively against his.

"Eddie, I'm getting so horny I can't stand it. Take me upstairs and fuck me in front of all those mirrors. I've been thinking about it all night."

Arriving at the room, she immediately stripped naked and walked over to the spa and turned on the motor. The motor purred quietly as bubbles began to dance merrily around the surface of the tub. She went into her luggage and pulled out a bottle of lotion. Returning to the tub, she sat down on the large deck encircling the tub and placed her legs into the water. Eddie was getting undressed and sat down on the bed and wondered what she was going to do next. He didn't have to wait long. She poured a generous supply of the lotion on her hand and began to pleasure herself; she began to moan and shiver. She was turning him on with her singular self-gratification. He quickly finished undressing and walked to the edge of the tub.

"Watch me, baby, watch me," she called out softly, a husky sexual tone in her voice as she quivered in delight.

Eddie watched as she drove her fingers deep inside of her, moaning in delight with the abysmal pleasure she was providing herself. Her self-indulgence completed, she pushed herself back on the carpeted deck, pulling her feet out of the water.

"Come on, baby," she whispered seductively with her eyes closed. "Come on and fuck me. I want to watch as you and I become one."

Eddie jumped up onto the deck and covered her body with his and slowly penetrated the depths of her. She moaned in ecstasy as she turned her head to the right to watch.

"Go slow, Eddie. I want to enjoy every minute of this."

She arched her back to draw him closer and deeper inside of her.

"Now, baby, now. Harder, harder, together, together," she called out softly.

She felt his ejaculation beginning to pour inside the depths of her; she wrapped her legs around his body and pulled him in tight against her.

"Now we are one!" she delightfully exclaimed. "Wow, what a turn-on."

Eddie withdrew and stepped back to the middle of the bubbling tub. She got into the tub and knelt down on her knees beside him. She took his manhood into her hand and looked up at Eddie.

"We can't waste any of this if we're going to have a baby," she joked.

With that, she took him deep into her mouth as he held her head and moaned in pleasure.

Eddie and Cat woke up early and showered together. Today was their wedding day, and they were excited. They ordered room service and enjoyed a wonderful breakfast. Both of them began to get dressed, each in their own thought. Finished, they stood in front of the large full-length mirror. Cat looked magnificent. She had purchased a simple white lace dress that was skin tight and accented her beautiful trim body; the dress was short and revealed her shapely long legs. Eddie had on his white Oleg Cassini jacket with gold buttons and black silk pants. He had on a black tie and a black handkerchief in his jacket pocket. Together they made a handsome couple.

"Not bad, huh!" Eddie exclaimed, a broad smile on his face.

"Not bad at all, Mr. D'Amico." She smiled back.

"Cat, do you think we made a baby last night?"

"How the hell would I know? Only God knows the answer to that question." She laughed at his foolishness.

The white Tropicana limo cruised slowly down Third Street and stopped in front of the Heavenly Chapel. The front yard was beautifully landscaped, and Eddie's friends waved and smiled as they arrived.

Johnny said, "I'll wait out here."

"Come on in."

"No, Eddie, I might get a ticket, and if I do, they'll make me pay."

"Johnny, if you do, I'll pay."

"In that case, no problem," Johnny said as he fell behind Eddie and Cat as they opened the small gate in front of the chapel to greet Eddie's waiting friends.

Eddie introduced the women first: "Sheri Baines, this is Cat, soon to be Mrs. D'Amico."

Cat had an infectious and warm personality. "So you're the one he calls Cowgirl. He described you perfectly. You are beautiful." Sheri gave her a big hug.

"And this is Sheri Askins, better known as Sheri La Mour."

"Eddie told me how beautiful you sing, but he didn't tell me how pretty you were. Now I have two new friends, both named Sheri." The two women hugged; words were unnecessary.

"And this is Rick Solitz."

"You're the car guy. If I need a new Caddy, you're the one I come to see?"

"Of course," he replied, a broad smile on his face.

She reached out and grabbed his hand and planted a kiss on his cheek. "Pleased to meet you, Rick."

"And me to you," he replied, still smiling.

"And this is David," Eddie said.

"No, I thought you told me his is the Wizard. Do you mind if I call you Wizard?"

"Not at all, Cat, not at all."

"Then Wizard it is. Hello, Wizard." She smiled widely, revealing her sparkling white teeth.

"Let's go in and get it done," Eddie said, grabbing Cat by the hand, and together they walked into the chapel, followed by the others.

"I now pronounce you man and wife. You may kiss the bride."

They kissed gently on the lips.

"I love you more than words can express," she whispered into his ear.

"I love you too, Mrs. D'Amico."

They all filed out of the chapel and entered the waiting limo for the trip back to the Tropicana. They had a special dinner that was prepared by the maitre d', Pietro; champagne flowed like water, and a good time was had by all. It was after midnight when Eddie and Cat arrived at their room. Exhausted, they disrobed and crashed out on the bed. Tomorrow they would start a new day as man and wife.

The next morning, they decided to stay in Vegas and enjoy all the wonderful things the city provided. They visited the Boulder Dam, attended shows with world-class entertainers, and enjoyed all the fine dining in the different casinos. They had a great time bonding and finding out how much they had in common. It was on the eleventh day that they got the good news Eddie had been waiting for. It was early morning when the telephone in the room rang. Eddie had just gotten out of the shower; he wrapped a towel around himself and picked up the telephone. Cat lay sleeping on the bed, oblivious to the telephone ringing in her ear.

"Good morning," Eddie answered.

"Eddie, it's Carm. We won, the dirty pricks are going to jail for life."

Eddie was elated with the news. "So tell, what broke the case?"

"They proved Sally was not in Chicago on the night of Guido and his wife's murder."

"So how the hell did they do that?"

"The FBI brought in no less than five handwriting experts. They unanimously agreed the signature on the check-in registration book was not Sally's but just a good forgery. It had something to do with the *s* and the *b* and the slant of the writing."

"Wow, this is really great news. We'll come right back home and celebrate."

"On one condition, Eddie. I owe you my life. It's my treat."

"Carm, you don't owe me shit."

"It's my treat, Eddie, capisce? Oh, by the way, my congratulations to you and Cat."

"I love her, Carm. I really do."

"Great, that's the way it's supposed to be. I wish you both a happy life together."

"Thanks, Carm."

The lines went dead.

Eddie shook Cat gently. She woke up and rubbed her eyes.

"What time is it?" she asked softly.

"I don't know, but we're going home today. We got some celebrating to do. I'll tell you all about it later."

"OK, Eddie, if you say so."

She got out of bed and headed toward the bathroom.

The Story behind the Story

Well, dear reader, together you and I traveled down thirty-five chapters of a story that I noted was inspired by true events. To give you an insight of where truth ended and embellishment took over, I have decided to share the story behind the story with you.

In general, it was a life I lived many years ago filled with many of the characters whom I was raised with and grew up to know as friends. Growing up in the neighborhoods, we had one of two choices to make—to choose a puritanical line of honesty, hard work and obeying the laws of the land, or to choose gambling, prostitution, drugs, and believing the law was made for others and not for people like us. With God's blessing, I somehow made the right choices; but throughout my life, I would never be able to shake or forget the friendships of those whom I grew up with that had made the other choices.

As I reflected back on the memories of my life, I realized that I had an amazing and interesting story inside of me that was just begging to be released from my brain and shared with others. So I began to write my story. No sooner had I begun to put pen to paper than I received an anonymous note from behind prison walls. The note simply stated, "Be careful."

I fully understood the ominous meaning of those two words. To write my book would have death knocking at my door. So I waited. Now thirty years have passed; time, old age, and death have now allowed me to unlock the memories of days long past and share my story with you. I have decided at this point in my story to enlighten you and share with you some of the stories behind my story.

Let me first begin with Eddie D'Amico, who is for the most part me. My name is Eddie, and I borrowed the name *D'Amico* from a friend of mine. Much of my story can be found in the archives of the library in which my story took place, as many of the things that I had shared with you were well published in the newspapers.

I will start with Don Francisco Barratino. He was a real person and as powerful and as handsome as I described in my story. His name was changed for obvious reasons. He was a good friend of mine.

Jimmy's Restaurant was a real place in the public market. Each weekend, the farmers would bring in their wares, and tens of thousands would come to shop. Many of the characters you met in my story, including myself, would go there each Saturday and hang out with their friends and get the best breakfast in the world. For many, it was a ritual that lasted for many years and remains the same to this very day.

Many of the characters described in my story all hung out at Jimmy's for years and were all good friends of mine, as noted in my storyline, and were all real people. For the most part, many of the names I chose were borrowed from my relatives and friends.

Now, about some of the characters: Cat Ladd was a girl I went with in high school, and we remained friends for many years. Her name was Jackie, and she truly was drop-dead gorgeous. Bee Stinger is my cousin Bee, who was a detective until he retired. We still talk by phone every day. Allan D'Amico is also my cousin, and we are still very close. Allan has also enjoyed reading this novel as I wrote it and mailed him copies of the finished chapters. One-Eyed Jack Shepard was a good friend of mine. He did not have one eye, and his name was not Jack.

Danni was my first wife, and the story of the vibrator actually took place. The story of the stripper crashing her car through the house was also a true story. The story of the sheriff's captain's confession, where he lied in court and had the criminals released from jail, is also true. I led you to believe that the sheriff's captain went to prison after his confession, but in real life, he committed suicide. The whole story is chronicled in the newspapers of the public library.

Rocky Marciano was also a good friend of mine. I loved traveling around with him and enjoyed meeting the legions of people who would congregate around him for autographs, even after he retired. I attended his funeral in 1969 at his mother's home in Brockton, Massachusetts, in which he had a closed coffin. It was truly one of the saddest days of my life.

Well, dear reader, I could go on and on, and more than likely write a book about the book. So, then, let us get back to our story.

I want to confess to you that as we have traveled in time together through the pages of my story with the power of my pen, I have done my very best to try and fool you and to mislead you by sending you false signals that would draw you offtrack, to force you to form your own conclusions, to second-guess me and believe you had the answers for what would happen next. Only to find out I had fooled you time and again.

So now, dear reader, we are only three chapters away from the end of my story. I have saved the very best for last. Though the chapters are short, I will not let you down. There are surprises in each one of the chapters left for you to enjoy.

Read on!

Ed Frederico

Chapter 36

Following Eddie and Cat's wedding, they flew to Italy to spend some time visiting Frederico Fellini. Cat so enjoyed Frederico's charm and hospitality that they remained in Italy for three months. It was in Italy that Cat found out she was three months pregnant, and she wanted to return home and make arrangements for the baby to arrive.

During their trip to Italy, Lorenzo looked after Carmella and her mother. Carmella had asked her unmarried sister, Margaret, to move into the home with her to assist in taking care of Nicoletta, whose health was failing.

Nine months had passed, and Cat was due to have the baby any day now. Both Cat and Eddie were excitedly waiting for the baby boy to arrive, but they were at odds as to what to name the baby.

*   *   *

Our story begins in the home of Danny Stoianovich, the sheriff's captain who perjured himself at the request of the FBI, which eventually sent Sally and his men to jail for life in the killing of Guido Luciano. Sofia, his wife, was making breakfast as he prepared to go to work.

"Danny, your breakfast is ready," she called out.

She placed the breakfast in front of him.

"What's the matter, honey? You've been acting strange lately. What's wrong?"

He pushed the plate away untouched. "Sofia, I told a lie in court that put four men in jail for life."

"Oh my god, Danny, how could you do such a thing?"

"Sit down, I'll tell you."

"The FBI said that when Vinnie Barratino told him Luciano was stealing money, his cousin Sally said he was going to kill him, which he eventually did."

"Oh my god, Danny, how could you do such a thing?"

"Well, the FBI knew he killed him but couldn't prove it in court. They said Sally was evil and killed other people and needed to be in jail. Do you remember the massacre in the park when those black guys got gunned down?"

"Yes, I remember that," she answered.

"Well, they said Sally ordered those killings. It just seemed like the right thing to do, get those murdering bums off the street, but now I can't live with myself anymore."

She reached out across the table and placed her hand on his. "You know why you can't live with yourself Danny—because you made a decision that was God's to make, not yours. You played God, Danny!"

"So now what am I supposed to do? If I tell the truth, they'll all get out of jail, and maybe I will go to prison."

"Don't go to work today. Go see Father Azzi. Tell him your story and see what he says."

"You're right, Sofia, but what about you? What happens if I go to jail?"

"God will provide, he always does. Go now. Go see Father Azzi."

Danny and Father Azzi were sitting in the rectory behind the church that housed the priest's office.

"So, Danny, tell me what's so important that you had to see me right away?"

Danny lowered his head in shame and began to slowly tell his story. Father Azzi listened without interruption. When Danny had concluded his story, the priest spoke.

"Well, my friend, and what did you come to see me for, Danny?"

"Tell me, Father, what should I do?"

"You will have to decide that for yourself, but I will ask you one question that might give you the answer. What would Jesus do?"

"You're right, Father. There is only one answer," Danny replied. "Tomorrow I will call a news conference and confess my sins for the whole world to hear."

The two men arose from their chairs, and the priest walked around his desk, and the two men embraced.

"God be with you, Danny."

"Thank you, Father," Danny responded as he walked out the door.

*   *   *

It was ten o'clock the next morning when the telephone in Eddie's apartment rang.

"Good morning," Cat answered.

"Oh, hi, Carm. Channel 11. OK, I'll tell him right away."

She hung up the telephone and raced toward the living room.

"Honey, hurry, put on Channel 11. Carmen just called." She finished as she entered the room.

When the news bulletin was over, Eddie muttered, "Holy shit."

"So what does 'holy shit' mean, Eddie?"

"'Holy shit' means we got big fucking trouble coming."

"I've got to go see Lorenzo," he said as he walked toward the adjoining doors. Without knocking, he entered the apartment. Lorenzo was startled and looked up from the racing sheet he was studying.

"Hey man, what's up?"

Eddie told him the story of the sheriff's captain's confession, and that he believed the minute Sally got out of prison, he'd put a contract out on him and the judge for setting him up.

"Oh shit, man, dat ain't no problem at all. Da minute he's out, I snuff him, and da problems all solved. Not to worry, Eddie. Just leave it all to Lorenzo."

Eddie left the room feeling better after his conversation with LaRocca.

Cat was waiting for Eddie to return so they could finish the discussion they were having—to choose the name for the boy that would be arriving any day now.

"Well, did you fix your big trouble?" she asked as Eddie entered the bedroom.

"I hope so," he replied. "I hope so."

He sat down on the edge of the bed and watched as she brushed her long blonde hair; he looked at her reflection in the mirror. *Man, she's beautiful,* he thought to himself.

"Well, Mr. Genius, how are we going to resolve this Mexican standoff with the baby's name?" she asked.

"I just don't like the name *Darrell.*"

"Why not? It sounds so professional, and besides, I like the *D. D.* connotation. Darrell D'Amico—to me it sounds great, not like Rocky. Hell, that sounds like a prizefighter."

"Well, it should, baby. You never heard of Rocky Marciano. He retired undefeated, heavyweight champion of the world. He was my friend. I chummed around with him when he was in town," he said proudly.

"OK, Eddie, then let's make a wager," she said, rising from her seat and walking over to the bed.

"I'm going to flip this quarter. Heads it's the champ, and tails it's Darrell. Agreed, and no more discussion."

"Agreed, it's a great idea," he answered.

She flipped the coin high into the air, and it landed on the unmade bed.

"Oh shit!" she exclaimed, laughing. "We're going to have a Rocky in the house."

Eddie took Cat into his arms and began to kiss her passionately.

"I love you, Cat," he whispered in her ear.

"I love you too, Eddie," she replied, "but I got a Rocky down there who's going to jump out any day now," she laughed.

"Ya, I guess you're right. No sex for Eddie until Rocky arrives," he said wistfully.

They remained locked in their embrace, enjoying the feeling of love and devotion that coursed through their bodies like some mystical spirit.

Two weeks had now passed since Danny had made his startling confession. Sally and his men had already been released, and a party was being held at the Black Orchid celebrating the boys' release from prison. In Freddie's office, Sally was sitting behind the desk, and two men wearing topcoats and their hats still on their head were listening to Sally speak.

"I brought you guys in from out of town because I don't want any of my people being involved with this hit. This here picture is Eddie D'Amico—you whack him first. He lives at the 111 East Avenue Hotel. When he leaves the hotel, don't follow him. Just wait until he returns. This big guy is Lorenzo LaRocca. Don't fuck with him. If he's with Eddie, then don't make the hit. Get him when he's alone. LaRocca's a dead shot. If you try to hit him when he's around, I'll guarantee you, one of you, or both of you, will die. You won't have enough bullets to stop him. Capisce?"

"Capisce," the man replied. "And this guy, who is he?"

"He's a judge named Carmen Carlivatti. His street address is on the back of his picture. He has a limo pick him up in the morning and drop him off at night. The best time to do him is at night. The minute the limo pulls away, you have a clean shot at him as he walks up the sidewalk to his house. Capisce?"

"Ya, we get it, but there's just one thing. You never said there was a judge involved in the deal. Wit da judge, the price goes up."

"How much?"

"Five grand."

"Done."

Sally began counting out the money. "Here is half. When the job is done, I'll give you the rest."

"Fair enough," the man replied.

The two killers rose and left the room.

Sally sat back and smiled. *I been waiting a long time to get even with that fucking Eddie*, he thought.

* * *

It was the morning after Sally had put out the contract on Eddie and the judge. Eddie and Lorenzo were having breakfast, waiting for Cat to call and set up a time to pick her and the baby up from the hospital. The telephone rang.

"I'll get it."

"Hi, honey," he answered.

"Hi, honey, how did you know it was me?"

"Well, you see, when it's you, the phone takes on this sweet little tinkling sound," he laughed.

"You are a real piece of work, Mr. D'Amico," she laughed back.

"So what time shall it be?"

"Well, I'm going to take a shower and do my hair a little. It looks like a scarecrow from lying in this bed. Let's say about noonish."

"OK, baby, then noonish it is."

"Oh wait, Eddie, don't hang up. Remember to bring the car seat I bought so that I can strap him in the backseat."

"Got it. Anything else?"

"No, that's all."

"Ten-four, good buddy," he replied and hung up the telephone.

Lorenzo had taken in the whole conversation.

"Ya want I should go wit cha?" he asked.

"Hell no, man. Those babies get one look at you, and you'll scare the shit out of them," Eddie laughed.

"Ya, dat's right, like Franken-rocca," he said, raising his arms and making a frightening sound with his voice.

"Listen, Dr. Franken-rocca, do you mind if I borrow your car? My Caddy's being serviced, and I don't want to take the Ferrari."

He threw the keys over to Eddie—"No problem"—and headed to his apartment.

Outside, a black van was stationed watching the exit door. The two hit men were watching a baseball game on a portable television set.

"Look, he's coming out and getting into that white Caddy."

"Well, let's see how long it takes him to get back."

The two men continued to watch their ballgame as Eddie drove away. Arriving at the hospital, Eddie had parked the car in front of the door as a nurse wheeled Cat out in a wheelchair. Eddie was carrying Cat's suitcase in one hand and baby Rocky in his arms. He popped open the trunk and threw in the luggage; then he proceeded to strap Rocky into the car seat in the rear. Cat gave Eddie a long, passionate kiss.

"I love you, Eddie. So now we are a family. You know, honey, isn't life strange? When we were going to high school and so much in love, who would ever thought we'd wind up getting married, and with a baby to boot—and of course, you being rich also helps too."

"Well, the only answer I can think of, it was all meant to be—a perfect life for the three of us. Oh, by the way, did they tell you how long we have to wait before we can have sex?"

"That will be my surprise. I'll tell you when we're in bed tonight."

"Hmm . . . sounds like a deal to me."

They drove home in silence, each wrapped up in their own thoughts. Eddie pulled into the parking lot and parked the car into the reserved space. Eddie popped the trunk and walked to the back of the car to get the luggage. Cat exited the passenger side and was going to open the rear door to get Rocky when she spotted a black van coming toward them at breakneck speed with a rifle barrel protruding from the passenger window.

Oh my god, Eddie, she thought and raced to the rear of the vehicle, pushing Eddie in and covering his body with hers. *Rat tat tat.* A continuing staccato blast kept emanating from the deadly weapon, punishing Cat's body with bullets as each one struck her. The force of Cat's shove and her body lying on top of his made it difficult for Eddie to pull himself from the trunk. Finally, he succeeded and rolled up his jacket and placed it under her head as he gently laid her down on the pavement.

"Cat, Cat, oh no." Tears were now streaming down Eddie's face. Cat's eyes slowly opened; a small stream of blood was dripping from her mouth.

"Damn, Eddie, I told you once I would die for you," she choked. "I never thought it would be this soon," she gasped. "Please promise to tell Rocky about me."

"I will, I promise."

"Cat, don't leave me. Oh no, not again."

Cat's eyes flickered.

"One last kiss before I go, Eddie."

Eddie bent over and placed a gentle kiss on her bleeding mouth as her last breath of life ebbed away and death took over Cat's beautiful body. It was several hours before all the necessary details with the police department and arrangements with Giovanni Garbelli to pick up the body were made.

Carmella, Eddie, and LaRocca were in the living room of Eddie's apartment. It was agreed that for the short term, Carmella would take Rocky home.

"Holy shit!" Eddie exclaimed as he jumped out of his chair. "Carm's next."

He swiftly ran to the telephone and dialed the judge's number.

"Hello," the voice answered.

"Hi, Rose, it's Eddie. Can I talk to Carm please?"

"He's sleeping, Eddie, can it wait?"

"No, Rose, it's super important."

"What's up, Eddie?" the judge asked.

Eddie told him the whole story of what transpired that day.

"Holy shit, I'm sorry about Cat. My god, Eddie, she gave her life for you."

"I know, I know. I wished it would have been me instead of Cat. But, Carm, now it's you. You've got to get out of town tonight. Go see a relative, get the fuck out of town, and don't come home until I call you personally."

"But . . . but—"

"No fucking *buts*, Carm, or you're going to be next."

"OK, OK, I got it. I'll call you when I get somewhere. Thanks, Eddie." The line went dead.

"So tell me, Eddie, what da ya plan to do wit Sally," Lorenzo asked.

"Kill him," he replied.

Carmella jumped out of her chair. "Have you lost your mind? That's premeditated murder. That's a death sentence or life in prison. Any chance you've had for heaven is gone because you will have no sorrow, no regret, and without that, there can be no forgiveness."

"I don't care anymore, Carm. This is personal. And, Lorenzo, I don't even want you to think of doing me any favors. This is between me and Sally."

Don Francisco had given Eddie a family plot in the Barratino area of the cemetery, and that was where he had buried Megan, and now he had had buried Cat beside her. The funeral was now over. Lorenzo was driving home from the cemetery; Carmella and Eddie were in the back talking.

"Tell me, Eddie, what did you mean when you said you had a couple of days of Barratino family business to clear up and then you were going to kill Sally?"

"Well, the business is simple. There will be a trust fund, but only the interest in the trust can be used each year. This means the trust will be around forever for all future generations of family members to draw from. And believe me, Carm, the trust is huge. There's enough for ten families to draw from forever."

"I got it, Eddie. That sounds believable. Would you come over sometime and explain all this trust information to my sisters?"

"Of course I would."

"I love you, Eddie. I just wish you would have been my brother instead of Sally."

"It is what it is, Carm," he replied.

Lorenzo dropped Carmella at the home. She went into her office and immediately dialed Sally's number.

"Hello," the voice said.

"Sally, that you?"

"Ya, it's me. What da ya want, Carmella?"

"Listen, Eddie told me something about Dad's fortune today. Sally, there are millions involved. Can you come over tomorrow, and I'll tell you all about it?"

"Ya, sure, what time?"

"Let's say seven o'clock. My chores will be done, and we can talk. I'll even have time to make you some of that apple pie you like so much."

"OK, then, see you at seven," Sally replied, and then he hung up the telephone in her ear.

Chapter 37

Carmella was in her office reviewing her secret book of notes that she was paying cousin Vinnie Barratino to provide her secretly. She was deep in thought when the buzzer on the stove went off, startling her. She rose from her chair and briskly walked into the kitchen to take the apple pie she had promised to make for Sally out of the oven. She picked up two hot pads and carefully removed the pie and set it on top of the stove to cool. She glanced at the clock on the stove; it read 7:20 p.m. *He's late*, she thought to herself. She arranged a coffee tray and carried it back to her office, setting it on a table beside her desk. She had made up her mind to have her discussion with Sally in her office. Before sitting down at her desk, she walked over to the small bar in the corner and poured herself a small glass of port wine. Walking back to her desk, she sat down and took a sip of wine and took out her rosary and began to pray with her eyes closed. Deep in prayer, she was startled when the intercom went off.

"Is that you, Sally?"

"Ya, it's me."

"I'm on the fourth floor. The elevator will open in my office."

Rising from her chair, she walked over to the elevator to meet Sally.

"You don't look like a nun," said Sally sarcastically.

"Well, these are just my comfortable evening clothes. We don't need to wear our habit at night."

Sally walked around the apartment and returned to the office after taking everything in.

"Hell of a joint ya got here. Did D'Amico do all this?"

"Of course, who else," she replied.

"Ya, he paid for it with all the fucking money he stole from me, the no-good bastard."

Carmella ignored his outburst. "Well, I asked you here to tell you about Dad's fortune, but first, let's have a cup of coffee. And I made you the apple pie you like so much. Did you eat dinner yet?"

"Nah, I had a sandwich at the Black Orchid for lunch, and I am a little hungry."

"Great, I'll make sure I cut you a nice big piece of pie."

Carmella returned with a large piece of pie and set it on the table in front of him. He silently began devouring it the minute she set it down. Now pouring him a large mug of hot coffee, she asked, "Sally, do you still like a lot of sugar in your coffee?"

"Ya, three spoons."

"Three spoons it is," she replied.

She returned to her desk and watched Sally consume the pie as she took a few more sips of wine.

"Well, are you ready to hear about the money now?"

"Ya, but I'm gonna get me another piece of pie. You still got that magic when it comes to making pies."

Carmella kept watching the clock on her desk as if she was timing something.

She began to recount the story of the trust fund and the millions of dollars available for life.

"Sally, are you all right? Your face looks like you're getting flushed."

"Ya, I am feeling a little woozy."

Looking at the clock, she knew it was time to tell Sally the real story why she invited him to her home.

"Well, Sally maybe it's time to stop talking about money because you're not going to be around to enjoy any of it anyway. Let's talk about the people you killed instead." She took out the book with all the information that Vinnie provided.

"What da fuck ya talkin' about? How da ya know who I killed?" he said, slurring his words badly.

"Oh, you will see, Sally. Jesus had Judas who sold him out for thirty pieces of silver. Your Judas was our cousin Vinnie, but he cost me much more than thirty pieces of silver, but the money I spent was well worth it." She smiled, taunting him.

"Fuck you, you don't know anythin'."

Sally's face was turning red, his eyes blinking uncontrollably, and he was struggling to sit upright in his chair.

"Let me show you how much I know about you. Let's go down the list of the people you killed. Let's begin with the Lacavoli brothers; the massacre at the park; your own wife, Connie; Guido Luciano; Eddie's wife, Megan, and their baby; Duke Donnelly; Cappy; Billy B; Billy the Bomber; Christina Carlivatti; Joey Cariola; and now Eddie's wife, Cat. Count them, Sally. Fifteen people that we know of."

"Naw, you're wrong," he slurred, fumbling for his gun. "Make it sixteen. I'm going to kill you too."

He tried desperately to focus his eyes on Carmella, and when he did, he saw she held a small revolver in her hand.

"So what do you think you're going to do wit dat gun, kill me?"

"I got news for you, you evil monster, I already killed you. You know that apple pie you liked so much, it has enough arsenic in it to kill an elephant, and that mug of coffee you drank was laced with antifreeze—you know, ethanol. You never even tasted it with all the sugar you put in it. You've only got a few moments left."

"I'll kill you, you rotting cunt," he muttered.

Sally fumbled, trying to reach for his gun. Death was coming upon him quickly, and he could no longer control his body and began to slowly slip to the floor.

Carmella was smiling evilly. "The world would be rid of you, and just think, Sally, the fires of hell are waiting for you. You will roast there for all eternity. Your master will be Satan. You will know only pain and suffering for all of the evil you have done here on this earth."

White foam and bile was coming from his mouth, and his body began to shake and convulse as death inched closer by the minute.

He choked and said his last words: "Fuck you cu—"

Carmella pulled his dead body away from his chair and took off his shoes and socks, expecting to find the cloven hooves of Satan, but he had none.

Carmella walked over to her desk and poured another glass of wine. She raised her glass in a toast. "To Sally, may you rot in hell forever. And to all the good, innocent people you killed—may they be in heaven and enjoy eternal life." She emptied the glass with one gulp, and threw the glass against the wall, shattering it. Sitting down at her desk, she picked up the telephone and dialed a number.

A woman's voice answered, "Police Department."

"Yes, ma'am, I want to report a murder," she stated softly. "I just killed my brother."

"Where are you located?" the woman asked.

"At the Barratino Children's Home. Come up to the fourth floor."

She hung up the telephone and dialed Eddie's number.

"Hello," answered Lorenzo.

"Is Eddie there?"

"Ya, we're playing gin rummy. It's Carmella," he said, handing the phone to Eddie.

"Hello, Carm, what can I do for you?"

"Call Tony Banducci. I just killed Sally."

"What!" he exclaimed. "Where are you?"

"Across the street at the home."

"Where's Sally?"

"On the floor in my office."

"Oh my god, don't move. Lorenzo and I will be right over."

Chapter 38

T hree weeks had passed since Carmella had poisoned Sally. Eddie stepped out onto the balcony of his apartment and watched the sun slowly signal the beginning of a new day painting bright red colors of orange and red over the horizon. His thoughts were of his two wives: Megan and Cat. Sally had killed them both, and now Carmella had killed Sally. The autopsy on Sally's body had been completed, and now Sally was scheduled to be buried today.

Last week, when he had buried Cat, Nicoletta had asked him to attend Sally's burial. Nicoletta and Carmella, who was out on bail, had refused to have a priest give last rites at the grave site. Carmella had told Eddie where Sally was going; there would be no salvation for him.

Ah, what the hell, he thought. *I'm not doing it for that no-good bastard. I'm doing it for the family.* Having made up his mind, he jumped in the shower to get ready to go. Just as he got out of the shower, the telephone began to ring. He raced over and caught it in the nick of time.

"Hello," he said.

"Buon giorno, Edwardo, come stai?" It was the unmistakable voice of Marisa Danielli.

"Ah, Signora, how are you? It's been a long time since we talked. You are still getting your envelope each month on time, I hope?"

"Oh yes, Edwardo, you hava been very kind."

"Well, Signora, it's not really me. Those were the instructions Don Francisco left for me to follow."

"Yesa, I know, but you hava been very kind and generous on whata you giva me ina mya envelope now."

Eddie laughed. "There's a lot more where that came from, it's no problem. So how can I help you today?" he asked politely.

"Well, I'ma wanta tella you how sorry I am to heara about your wife. Sally, he's evil, and hesa owned by the devil, so now he will burna in hell forever."

"I'm sure you're right," he answered.

"Well, anyway, I calleda to aska you a question—are you going to the cemetery today?"

"Well, to tell you the truth, I wasn't going to go, but I changed my mind. I am going, but why do you ask, Signora?"

"That'sa good you go. Whena it's all over, me and you have a little talk, OK?"

"Of course, then I'll see you later."

"Buon giorno, Edwardo." The line went dead.

The grave site was ready for Sally's burial. Nicoletta was in her wheelchair surrounded by her five daughters: Carmella, Mickey, Margaret, Angie, and Flora. Eddie was standing next to Nicoletta, holding her hand. Two cemetery workers were standing by a nearby tree with shovels in their hands, waiting for the ritual to be over. The undertaker dressed all in black walked over to Carmella.

"Do any of you want to say anything since you have no priest here?" he asked.

Carmella gave Giovanni Garbelli a sheet of typewritten paper. He glanced down and read the paper, a shocked look on his face. He looked up at Carmella.

"Are you sure you want me to read this?"

"Yes," she simply replied.

Giovanni walked over to the head of the casket and began to read just as Signora Danielli appeared from behind a nearby tree and stood behind Eddie.

"Here lies Salvatore Barratino, whose time on this earth has passed. He was an evil man without a heart and without a soul. He brought pain and suffering to the many people he had killed to serve his own evil purposes. The Barratino family wishes to send him into the ground with this curse upon his head. May the gods of the heavens and the universe commit him to burn in the fires of hell for all eternity."

Giovanni finished reading the document, shaking his head as he called for the limo to take the family home.

Eddie walked over to Megan's and Cat's grave sites and placed a small bunch of flowers on each grave. Then he knelt down between them and prayed. Signora Danielli walked over to a bench that was sitting against the trunk of a large weeping willow tree. Eddie rose from his knees and began walking toward the bench to meet with Signora

Danielli, who stood up to greet him as he arrived. She embraced Eddie and dried the tears streaming down his face with the lace handkerchief she was holding in her hand. They continued to silently embrace each other and sat down on the bench. Eddie was curious, wondering what Signora Danielli could possibly have to tell him.

"Well, Edwardo, it'sa time I tella you a story only I in the whola wide world know. Did you ever wonder all these years why Don Francisco loveda you so much?"

"No, not really. I never even gave it a thought. Why in the world should I even question something like that?"

"Then I tella you something thata only three people in the world know about. Those three people were your mother, Don Francisco, ana me. Now, your mother and Don Francisco a morta, so now it's justa me, the only person who knows the story I'm going to tell you now. When your father went to jaila for five years, Don Francisco, he gets your mother pregnant. Youra father, he thinksa he maka your mother pregnant before hesa go to jail. I'm the midwife, and only your mother anda I know that Dominic is not your father, but it is Don Francisco who is your father."

"So, Signora Danielli, are you telling me all these years that it was Don Francisco who was really my father and not Dominic?" he asked with a shocked tone in his voice.

"Yes, Edwardo, but there isa more. Three yearsa later, Dominic isa still ina prison, anda Don Francisco makes your mother go pregnant again, buta now they knowa ita can't be Dominic whoa maka your mothera go pregnant this time, so Don Francisco sends me and your mother to New York to hisa cousin Fico till the bambino isa born . . . ." She paused, letting her story sink in.

"Well then, how did all this adoption crap come about?" he asked, shaking his head in disbelief.

"Well, after Salvatore is a born, Don Francisco tells everyonea it's Fico's baby, but his wife, she's a died having the baby. So Don Francisco adopts baby Salvatore, anda nobody knows Don Francisco makea your mother go pregnant for the second time and he is really Sally's father."

"My god, so what you're saying is all this time, Don Francisco was my real father, not Dominic, and Sally was my real brother. Signora Danielli, this is so hard to believe."

"You believe it, Edwardo. It'sa all true. I was the midwife and delivered you and Salvatore. I woulda tell you sooner, butta I promised

Don Francisco I woulda taka our secret to my grave, but nowa there is no reason to hide the truth."

They rose to their feet and shared a long embrace.

"Thank you, Signora. Thank you for telling me who I really am."

Eddie started walking toward the road. Lorenzo spotted him and came to pick him up. Eddie jumped in the car.

"Lorenzo, you are not going to believe the story I'm going to tell you," Eddie said as he slammed the car door shut.

*   *   *

Sequel: *And the Family Marches On!*

Another Mob Figure Slain

Exit 45

Gunned at Victor Motel

Map locates Exit 45 Motel.

Mob insiders squeal; Federal jury indicts 10

Cops against cops

D. & C. APR 15 1979

and the mob went free

DEFENDANTS IN RACKETEERING AND CONSPIRACY TRIAL

████████ J. "RED" ████████ 72, was accused of being the "boss" of the organization. He was convicted of both charges.

████████ ████████, 60, was accused of being second in command. He was convicted of both charges.

████████, 45, described as the "underboss," was considered to hold the third-highest position in the organization. He was convicted of both charges.

████████ M. ████████, 41, was a member of the organization, according to prosecutors. He was convicted of both charges.

████████ ████████, 42, was a "captain" in the organization, prosecutors said. He was convicted of both charges.

Seven found guilty in racketeering trial

From page ████████ OCT 3 1 1984

As the seven men were escorted out of the courtroom, ████████'s wife, Rita, threw her husband a kiss. ████████ waved and smiled to his wife and daughter, Andrea.

The indictment had accused all 10 men of participating in an organization responsible for such racketeering crimes as murder, attempted murder and extortion.

Many of the crimes occurred during a 1978 struggle for control of organized crime in ████████ The struggle, marked by a series of bombings and shootings, included the July 1978 murder of Thomas ████████ and attempts on the lives of Rosario ████████ and Dominic "Sonny" ████████

In order to find the defendants guilty of violating the federal RICO statute (Racketeer Influenced and Corrupt Organizations act), the jury had to find that they had been involved in at least two of the 10 racketeering crimes charged. ████████ did not ask the jurors to specify the racketeering crimes in rendering their verdict.

Federal prosecutor Douglas ████████ declined to say what aspects of the prosecution case he believed were key factors.

He noted that state, local and federal law enforcement agencies were involved in the four-year investigation that resulted in the November 1982 indictment. "I am very pleased at the joint effort by the law enforcement agencies," he said. "It was an effort to put an end to the war."

Defense attorneys for the convicted men expressed disappointment.

"I thought the five witnesses were the most abominable witnesses I've ever seen," said ████████ attorney, Harold ████████, referring to the five government informants. "When you have to rely on murderers and perjurers, then there's something wrong with the system."

Although he said he planned to appeal, Robert M. ████████'s attorney, also complimented his adversaries. "I think the prosecution after two and a half years of preparation were very tough . . . but very fair and honest and I commend them."

"It seems to me when a jury needs seven days to reach a verdict, that in and of itself is reasonable doubt," said ████████ attorney, John ████████

Yet one juror said: "We spent a great deal of our time ████████ sure. We all took our roles very seriously. We wanted ████████ a reasonable doubt."

Wednesday, October 31, 1984

Detective admits
he lied

Mob War Here ✓

It's three down and four to go if the pattern of violence continues against the "social clubs" that police say are the top mob-controlled gambling parlors in the city.

The three spots hit by bombings in the last few months are the 1455 Club at 1455 ▮▮▮▮▮ Ave. (yesterday); the Social Club of Monroe, 1266 ▮▮▮▮ ▮▮▮▮▮ (Friday), and the Yahambas Social Club, 221 ▮▮▮▮▮ St. (January).

The four parlors which so far have gone untouched by violence, police say, are the Northway Social Club, 234 ▮▮▮▮▮▮▮▮; the Caserta Social and Political Club (▮▮▮▮▮▮) at 44 Lake Ave., and parlors at 138 ▮▮▮▮▮ and 253 ▮▮▮▮▮▮.

The mob hauls in an estimated $2 million profit from gambling at the seven places in a year, police and street sources say.

The underworld gets a "vig," or commission of 15 percent from the clubs' share of the gambling money, which accounts for the estimated $2 million.

It's that money skimmed off the top — easy money — which two local mob factions are struggling to control, police say.

"And it is not just control of the gambling they want. This is for all the vices (including drugs and prostitution)," said a high-ranking police official.

YOU HAVE TO "know somebody to get into any one of the big seven gambling parlors, police say.

"You've almost got to be born to it," said a police official. "They don't take kindly to strangers. You've got to have a trusted man, who is willing to vouch for you with his life if necessary, to get in," he said.

Once inside, a stranger would find the clubs lacking in luxury, sparsely furnished, and — although big on betting — willing to take $2 bets, the minimum.

Pinochle predominate during the day there, with most of the heavy betting on blackjack and rough-and-tumble blackjack at night. The club operates practically around-the-clock. The "rake" or cut for the house is estimated at between $150 and $400 per hour. The dealer takes in the rake.

The doorman provides security, flicking a light switch when police approach.

44 Club Unlikely Target

If there is another bombing, police believe the most unlikely target would be the 44 Club because of the heavy security around it, and the traffic outside.

A gambling parlor that apparently has increased its business during the last few years is the Yahambas where, after getting past the doorman, you'd pass a counter into a large gambling room, police said. Poker and blackjack are the steadiest games there.

Jimmy ▮▮▮▮▮▮, father of slain Mafia underboss Salvatore "▮▮▮▮▮▮▮▮▮, was frequently seen in the club after the Young Men's Club at 138 Lyell Ave. closed down about three years ago.

The Yahambas is open most of the day and night. A man delivering doughnuts for the early-morning trade has been seen there, police said.

One of the biggest bookmaking joints in the city is the Social Club of Monroe, where playing cards is secondary to playing the horses and betting on sports, sources said.

The club is mainly a daytime operation and often closes about 8:30 p.m., police said. Bookmaking accounts for about 75 percent of the club's handle — up to $8,000 a day — while the rake from card games averages about $80 an hour.

The club used to be run by Joey ▮▮▮▮▮▮▮, stepson of alleged mob boss Salvatore ▮▮▮▮▮▮▮▮▮▮▮. Tira-

Montage shows Salvatore ▮▮▮▮▮▮▮▮▮▮▮ and wreckage of his car after bomb killed him last April 23.

My Friend Rocky Marciano | Me in my HEAVIER Days

A Man of many Talents

Founder and President of Genesee Valley Kidney Foundation

Founder and President Boy and Girl Club, Lake Havasu City AZ

Member of Lake Havasu City Council for four years

Member of Lake Havasu City Planning Commission for six years

Talk Show Host, Radio and Television on Christian Network for three years

Talk Show Host , Radio Rochester NY for three years

Master of Ceremonies Lake Havasu Chili Cook Off for ten years

Officer and Member of Elks Lodge 2399 Lake Havasu City for 28 years

Site Development Contractor

State Approved Paving Contractor—New York and Arizona

Political and Campaign Manager for individuals in New York and Arizona

General Contractor and Home Builder

Designer of Homes and Commercial Buildings

Plane owner and Pilot, 6200 Hours Logged

And NOW AUTHOR!

Acknowledgments

To my wife, Nancy, for the great work she did on the first twenty-four chapters of my book.

To Judith Johnson, without her help and endless encouragement, this book would have never been completed.

To my cousin, the "Big Boper", Lou Tacito, who researched and provided me with all historical facts in the book.

My cousin, Geraldine Tacito, who critiqued my chapters as I wrote them.

Sherri Haines, who critiqued my chapters as I read them.

A special thanks to my typist, Francine Justeau, who interpreted my handwritten pages and corrected my spelling and punctuation.

To my good friend, who I will call "Handsome Harry", John Eisele, for his good looking face on the cover.

Eric Jamison of Studio J, Inc., for the great work he did on photographing.

To Captain Lynde Johnston, head of the physical crime unit, and Glen Weather, for their help in researching the dates and other information of the murders that took place. Their help was invaluable, as it gave my cousin, Bee, the information he needed to research public records which are now part of the book.

Also to Michelle Sabana, my terrific Publishing Consultant.

To Kay Cortes, my Submissions Representative, whose help and guidance was invaluable—taking a novice like me through the process.

Lastly, to Duane Lehman, my good friend who did such a terrific graphics and design job on the cover. Vegas Quality Printing.